THE
BOTANIST

M.W.
CRAVEN

Also by M.W. Craven

Washington Poe series
The Puppet Show
Black Summer
The Curator
Dead Ground
The Cutting Season
Cut Short (short story collection)

Avison Fluke series
Born in a Burial Gown
Body Breaker

For Bracken

What is there that is not poison? All things are poison and nothing is without poison. Solely the dose determines that a thing is poison.

Paracelsus (1493–1541)

Chapter 1

Iriomote Island, Japan

There were bastard trees and there were wait-awhile trees and there was a building that didn't exist.

The bastard trees had masses of six-inch thorns protecting their trunks. Touch one of those and you'd learn a sharp lesson. The wait-awhile trees were less stabby, but equally annoying. Their thin, hook-tipped vines dangled from branches, catching, entangling and immobilising the unwary.

But it was the building, not the flesh-piercing thorns, that held everyone's attention. It was squat and grey and had been reclaimed by nature. Thick roots had prised apart stonework and collapsed one of the walls. Guano from the fruit bats roosting in the tree canopy had painted the roof white.

The group stared in astonishment.

'What is it?' Dora, a woman in her early twenties, asked. She was halfway through her gap year. In six months she would do what her father wanted and take a job in the City, then marry her portfolio manager fiancé and knock out a brood of zestless children.

'I'm not sure,' their guide replied. He was called Andrew Trescothic and he had trained in the black art of jungle navigation with the British Army in Belize. 'Probably left over from the war. There are supposed to be some Operation Ketsu-Go buildings on the island somewhere.'

'Ketsu-Go?'

'The suicidal defensive strategy designed after the Emperor realised he could no longer win. Called for the entire Japanese population to resist an invasion under the banner "The Glorious Death of One Hundred Million". He thought if the Americans were facing catastrophic casualties it might undermine their will to fight for an unconditional surrender. Maybe opt for an armistice instead, one that didn't involve occupation of the Japanese mainland. Part of the strategy was to build inland fortifications to store fuel and ammunition. This building's not accessible for fuel, so I suspect it was used as an ammo dump. The allies emptied them after Japan's surrender, but most of the buildings were left intact.'

'Wow,' Dora said. 'So nobody's seen this since the war?'

'It's possible.'

It wasn't. Trescothic was a no-frills kind of guide and he had been leading groups across the jungle island for five years now. He knew where all the Operation Ketsu-Go fortifications were, and he made sure each group 'discovered' one on every trip. After they had taken their photographs and had a poke around, he would leave it a year or so. In an environment as harsh as this it wasn't long before the building looked as though it hadn't been touched in decades. He figured it was a harmless deception and it certainly increased the size of his tips when they got back to base camp.

'Can we go in?' Dora asked.

Trescothic shrugged.

'Don't see why not,' he said.

'Cool!'

'But watch for snakes.'

All that remained of the wooden door were rusty hinges. Dora and most of the others entered cautiously.

The last one, a man wearing an unacceptable hat, turned and said, 'Aren't you coming, Andrew?'

He shook his head.

'Maybe later.' Andrew knew what was in there. A boxy room and a large underground storage area. Japanese signs on the walls and animal scat on the floor. Same as all the others. He reckoned they'd be inside for fifteen minutes or so. Five upstairs, five in the underground storage room and five more for happy snaps. Plenty of time to get a brew on.

He hadn't even had time to pop in a teabag when he heard Dora scream. He sighed. They'd probably stumbled across a dead animal.

2

It had happened in a different building a couple of years earlier. A group discovered the decomposed body of an Iriomote cat, a sub-species of leopard only found on the island. It had fallen through a hole in the roof and trapped itself. Poor thing had starved to death.

Trescothic got to his feet and entered the old fortification. He could hear the group. They were in the underground storage area. He jogged down the stairs but was met by Dora running back up.

'I think I'm going to be sick,' she said.

He sighed again. These city slickers really needed to toughen up. The same thought crossed his mind at least once a trip. These modern-day explorers weren't as robust as the squaddies he had trained with all those years ago. The slightest thing upset them. A dead animal, a mean comment on Twitter, a dodgy statue . . .

He fixed his face into the stern, no-nonsense ex-soldier the group expected him to be, and entered the storage area.

Thirty seconds later he was back outside, panting heavily, scrambling for the satellite phone in his rucksack.

It wasn't a dead animal that had caused Dora to scream.

This was something else entirely.

Something monstrous.

At the same time as Trescothic was on his satellite phone, a non-descript man wearing unremarkable clothes stepped out of a plain white van in a car park on an industrial estate on the outskirts of Glasgow. He walked into Banner Chemical Supplies and approached the counter.

'I'd like two hundred litres of acetone, please,' he said to the man wearing a polo shirt bearing the company insignia – a stylised B, underscored with a test tube.

'You got photo ID?' the man said. 'Acetone is a category three precursor chemical as it can be used to make explosives. Company policy is we take IDs.'

The nondescript man produced a driver's licence bearing an instantly forgettable name. The man behind the counter entered the details into his computer. After the acetone had been paid for, he said, 'You parked outside?'

'I am.'

'The guys will bring it out for you. Help you load it.'

'Thank you.'

'Oh, one last thing. I need to put down something in the "reason for purchase" field on the computer.'

'I have a vermin problem,' the nondescript man said.

Chapter 2

*Eighteen months later. The Morgan Soames Hour
television studio, London*

The lights were set to run hot, the interview was running hotter.

Too hot.

Far hotter than had been anticipated.

'It's too controversial,' the studio owner had said all those weeks ago.

'I prefer "provocative",' the director, a woman called Justine Webb, had replied.

'We'll get hundreds, maybe thousands of complaints.'

'It'll be a ratings smash.'

'I'm not sure.'

'And I have the final say on editorial content. We're doing this.'

There'd been meetings and committees long before the director and the owner had had their dance, of course. Where Kane Hunt was involved, this was to be expected. Controversy – all of it carefully curated – followed Hunt wherever he went. Live TV appearances were increasingly rare.

But *The Morgan Soames Hour* had never shied from controversy.

In the end it came down to two things: their commitment to balanced news and whether or not their presenter, Morgan Soames, would be able to handle him.

The argument for balance went like this: Saffron Phipps was due on the week before the proposed Hunt interview, and her views, albeit from the opposite end of the spectrum, were equally as extreme. Phipps argued that Valerie Solanas, the author of the 1967 *SCUM Manifesto*, had been on to something. Phipps wasn't suggesting, as Solanas had, that men should be eliminated. But she *was* arguing that Solanas had been correct when she wrote that, because men only had one X chromosome, they were genetically deficient, incomplete females. This deficiency explained why males were emotionally limited, egocentric, lacking in empathy and unable to relate to anything other than their own physical sensations. Kane Hunt was the anti-Phipps, the counterpoint to the *SCUM Manifesto*. He would provide the balance *The Morgan Soames Hour* prided itself on.

For those *against*, the argument was far less nuanced – Kane Hunt was a misogynist who spouted his vile philosophy, not because he genuinely believed that men had a fundamental right to sex, but because it sold books. Having him on the show would give his new book a major marketing boost.

On the second point, whether Morgan Soames would be able to handle him, there had been no disagreement. She had the biggest pair of balls in any room she was in.

It was settled with a vote – the first one the production team had ever had over a guest. Justine, the director, voted no. She was responsible for the way the show was shot and it would be her dealing with the inevitable fallout. The head writer said no, too. He didn't want to put his staff in the lion's mouth if Morgan ended up looking foolish.

The social media manager couldn't say yes fast enough, of course. She knew an upcoming Twitter storm when she saw one. The television channel said yes, too. Ratings would rocket and they would cash in.

The rest of the production team was evenly split. Allan, the show's producer, had had the casting vote. In his heart he'd wanted to say yes. Whatever that little twerp Kane Hunt's views were on women, Morgan was an apex predator. She would eat Hunt alive and 99.9 per cent of the country would rejoice when she did. And it *would* be relevant – for too long Hunt had been getting a free ride. His claim of media censorship was a calculated strategy. If he were outrageous enough, he could never appear on television, and if he were never on television his views couldn't be challenged. Censorship was the shield he cowered behind. He coveted it because he relied on it.

But Morgan had been taunting him for months. Every opening monologue of her show began with a dig at him. Every closing piece ended with him being the butt of a joke.

She had been daring him to appear.

To the surprise of everyone, Hunt had said yes. Publicly. He would appear on her show as long as it was one-to-one and he was given the questions beforehand. Morgan didn't play that way, though. She would give him time to answer, but he didn't get to dictate the direction. Hunt had reluctantly agreed. If he backtracked now, he knew Morgan would laugh about it for years.

So Allan had wanted Kane Hunt on the show.

But he had voted no. Allan's surname was Webb, the same as Justine's, and that was because they were married. They had worked together for twenty years and had been husband and wife for ten. They were a team both on and off the pitch. Professionally and personally, his job was to have her back.

It fell to Justine to let Morgan know. She had decided to tell her shortly before that night's show, hoping it might limit the amount of time for abuse. Morgan had interviewed impeached presidents and disgraced prime ministers. She'd trapped royals in lies and reduced war criminals to tears. She wasn't a woman to mess with.

Justine had knocked on her dressing-room door and entered. Morgan had been in makeup, her stylist, and long-time sounding board, fussing around her hair with a tiny brush and a small bottle of spray. Tissue wedged between her neck and the collar protected her two-thousand-pound navy blue Oscar de la Renta bell-sleeve blazer from the harsh studio makeup she had to wear. Off camera she looked like a supervillain, *on* camera she would look perfect.

Morgan had turned, fixed Justine with those steely grey eyes and gave her a reverse head nod. Her auburn hair, rich and glowing, didn't move.

'Quick word, Morgs?' Justine had said.

'Shoot,' she'd said. 'Just rehearsing tonight's monologue. Want to get in one more joke about the PM standing in dog shit yesterday.'

'I don't know why she's bothering – it's pretty funny already,' her makeup artist had said.

'It's about Kane Hunt,' Justine had said. 'We can't make it work.'

'Oh?' Morgan had said, her voice edged like a razor.

'Production are in agreement. There's just too much risk. If it's any consolation, the vote was very close.'

Morgan had turned back to her makeup. Started touching up her hair. She eyed Justine in the mirror.

'Fuck your vote,' she'd said.

And that was that. Justine had slunk out to find the studio owner.

'He looks hot,' Justine said.

'Hot?' Allan replied.

'Not "sexy" hot, I mean he's sweating.'

'I'm not surprised, he's only five feet away from the quartz lamp.'

'Quartz? I didn't know we had any left. Why aren't we using LEDs?'

Quartz lamps had been an industry staple for years, but they gave off a lot of heat and used a lot of juice. They'd been superseded by LED lights, which essentially did the same job but without the excessive heat or drain on the electricity budget.

'Morgan wanted them,' Allan said. 'Only on Hunt's side, though. She wanted him pale and sweaty.'

Justine considered that for a moment. 'Damn, she's good,' she said.

They were in the gallery, the room where the composition of *The Morgan Soames Hour* took place. The 'glass cockpit' – the virtual monitor wall displaying multiple sources of information – dominated the room. Justine and Allan preferred being on the studio floor, leaving one of the assistant directors to oversee the gallery, but tonight they wanted to be near the vision mixer. He was called Yosef and he was seated in front of his control panel, selecting which camera to use. Justine and Allan usually let him work with minimal oversight. Morgan trusted Yosef to get the right mix of her and her guest, to know when she wanted to be on screen when she asked a question, or whether it was the guest's reaction that was more important.

Tonight was different. Justine, as the only person with the authority to shut down a live show mid-broadcast, had to be there to give Yosef the instruction, and Allan wanted to be with her in case she needed to talk it through. Shutting down a live show was the biggest decision a director could make.

They were half an hour in, and it had been so far so good. Morgan had kept it tight and Kane Hunt had been fairly uncontroversial.

They watched as Morgan reached behind her desk and brought out the only prop she was scheduled to use. It was a book. Independently published, but with high production values.

'He doesn't look well, does he?' Justine said.

Hunt was over-gelled and under-dressed. He wore a pilot's jacket and ripped jeans, like he was auditioning for an amateur production of *Rebel Without a Cause* rather than appearing on the most prestigious chat show on television.

'He doesn't, actually,' Allan agreed. 'He's drinking a lot of water and he can't stop rubbing his eyes.'

'As long as he doesn't die during the next thirty minutes,' Justine said.

'Tell me about your new book, Kane,' Morgan said. 'It's called *The Chad Manifesto*. I understand "Chad" refers to attractive, popular men who are sexually successful with women?'

'That's right,' Hunt said. 'Chads are the sheer dumb-luck winners of the genetic lottery and a recent study suggests that although they make up just twenty per cent of men, they're having eighty per cent of all sex. That's a mathematical problem for the rest of us – there simply aren't enough women left. *The Chad Manifesto* aims to redress this rigged game.'

'I see,' Morgan said. 'And this theory forms part of the incel movement?'

'Yes. Involuntarily celibate.'

'The ideology that women's bodies are natural resources?'

'Exactly.' Hunt leaned forward, looked engaged. 'At the minute, men, through no fault of their own, are finding themselves locked out of what is now a deregulated sexual marketplace. *The Chad Manifesto* advocates a fairer distribution system. No man in the twenty-first century should be deprived of sex.'

'Deprived of sex?' Morgan deadpanned.

'You don't seem convinced.'

'I'm not. To me, your position that women are little more than

9

inconveniently sentient bodies is plainly ridiculous.'

'Is it though?' Hunt countered. 'You have to remember, for ninety-nine per cent of human history women didn't get to choose their sexual partners. There was no such thing as dating. Women were given to men in arranged marriages or seized as spoils of war. This relatively recent cultural shift has left some men disenfranchised.'

Morgan picked up the book and flicked through it.

'I understand you have a solution?' she said.

Back in the gallery, Justine said, 'She's giving him an easier ride than I thought she would.'

'She is,' her husband replied. 'That's what's worrying me.'

'Me too.'

'And she wouldn't tell you what she has planned?'

Justine shook her head.

Allan stepped closer to the button that stopped the live transmission.

'Our solution is simple,' Hunt said. 'We propose a complete over-haul of the Sexual Offences Act, specifically the sections relating to prostitution.'

'That's it?' Morgan said. 'You want to legalise brothels?'

'No, but changing this draconian law is necessary for what's to come. For our proposal to work we would need the sections relating to paying for sexual services, soliciting, advertising and controlling prostitution for gain, scrapped completely.'

'So you *do* want to legalise brothels?'

'Not at all,' Hunt said. 'But we do want to revolutionise the sex market.'

'I think you'd better explain.'

'Monetising the sexual marketplace makes complete sense in this day and age. Everything else is for sale, why not sex? And given how much money is spent courting women, there would also be a steady and sizeable revenue stream for the government.'

'You're suggesting state-run prostitution?'

'I most certainly am not. The government bungles even the

simplest of tasks. What we need is the invisible hand of the free market. This country's strength has always been its entrepreneurs and we want them running the sexual marketplace.'

'How would it work, Kane?' Morgan asked. 'Mega brothels? Legalised kerb crawling?'

'A subscription sex service,' Hunt replied. 'Similar to Netflix or Amazon Prime. Men would pay a monthly fee and the women would get a stipend. The same way you might select a movie or a TV show now, depending on the package you've subscribed to, you would simply select the woman you want. They would be rated from one to five and the higher-rated ones would use up more of your credit. For example, a basic package might get a subscriber three hours of sex a month with a two-star woman, or five hours with a one-star. Not in a brothel, but in their homes. The premium packages would obviously attract longer hours with women of a higher rating.'

'And who would rate the women? People like you?'

'The market,' Hunt explained. 'And the subscribers would be rated too. The same way Uber drivers and customers rate each other. The lower your rating, the more you pay. Lower-rated women would obviously earn less than higher-rated ones, so it's in everyone's financial interests to make each session as satisfying as possible.' Hunt picked up his glass and drank half the water. 'And once the private sector gets involved, with their expertise in marketing, it will quickly become progressive and mainstream,' he continued. 'And although initially conceived as a service for incels, we would expect to see subscription sex services for the whole LGBTXYZ alphabet within two years.'

'How commendable.'

'You're sceptical, but remember this: people said the same thing about internet dating. Now the market's worth billions. And not only will this bring the government millions of pounds in tax revenue, it's also a public health issue.'

'How so?'

'Women have to understand, if they keep kicking good dogs, eventually they'll turn into bad dogs. We believe men being disenfranchised in the sexual marketplace is the leading cause of rape in the UK, and in the US it's been linked to mass shootings. The policies contained within the manifesto address all this.'

'You want to go to a break?' Allan asked Justine. 'Let Morgan regroup. Hunt kinda won that exchange. Internet dating *is* mainstream now. Who's to say this wouldn't work?'

'I say it,' Justine replied. 'All women say it. Anyone with a shred of decency should say it.'

'Absolutely right,' Allan said, recognising a minefield when he'd stepped into one. 'It's a vile idea.'

His wife smiled. 'Don't worry,' she said. 'Morgan's got this.'

'I'd like to move on to you personally, if I can, Kane?' Morgan said.

'Shoot.'

'Are you lactose intolerant?'

'Excuse me?'

'It's a simple question. Are you able to digest dairy products?'

Hunt frowned. 'I'm not sure where you're going with this, Morgan,' he said.

'You're not the only one,' Justine said to her husband.

He shrugged.

'What the hell is she up to?' she added.

'No, I'm not lactose intolerant,' Hunt said. 'Why would you think I am?'

'Because you get a lot of milkshakes thrown over you and I was wondering if that's why you felt you needed a bodyguard tonight.'

'I have a high profile. I get death threats.'

'I wasn't aware of this. Have you reported any of them to the police?'

'Half the police force are women,' Hunt sneered. 'How seriously do you think they're going to take a threat against me?'

'About as seriously as the rest of us, I'd imagine.'

Hunt reached into his inside pocket and withdrew a folded piece of paper. 'Here, have a look,' he said. 'This is the latest one – it came a few days ago.'

He passed it across. Morgan opened it. Something fell on her lap. She picked it up.

'Close up on that,' Justine said.

Yosef did his thing and the master screen was filled with Morgan's hand.

'What the hell . . .?' Allan said.

It was a pressed flower. Delicate lilac. Star-shaped with five pointed petals. Pretty. Non-threatening.

'It's a flower,' Morgan said. 'So what?'

'Read the note,' Hunt replied.

Morgan was too much of a pro to read out loud something she'd only just been handed. She scanned it for anything tricky, but there was nothing. It was a poem.

'It's an octave,' she said. 'An eight-line stanza, if I'm not mistaken.'

She tilted it so camera three could pick it up, then read it out.

> Under the hanged man's hood,
> Beneath his dripping blood,
> Below the yellow fruit,
> Lies the screaming root.
> Close your ears, tear it from the ground,
> Dry it out and start to pound,
> And when you start your endless sleep,
> Beside your casket, none will weep.

'I don't understand,' Morgan said after she'd finished. 'Why do you think this is a death threat?'

'Are you saying it isn't? It mentions a casket.'

'It's a pretty flower tucked inside some bad poetry. I don't think we need to bother the SAS just yet.'

Hunt said nothing. The sweat on his brow was rolling down his face now. Morgan hoped Yosef was picking it up. She was sched-uled to go to a commercial break, but she decided to press ahead. 'Although, I'm not surprised you feel you need protection,' she continued.

'I'm not sure I follow.'

'Does the name Anita Fowles mean anything to you?'

'I don't recollect—'

'She's the law student who unsuccessfully sued you after a picture of her naked found its way on to your website.'

Hunt shrugged. Smirked a little. 'The courts have already ruled on that matter.'

'Yes, they have,' Morgan confirmed. She paused a beat then added, 'Are you scared of women, Kane?'

Hunt laughed. A bead of sweat dropped off his nose and he hacked out a cough. 'Of course not. What's there to be scared of?'

'You tell me?'

'Women aren't scary, Morgan. Not even you. But not everyone's in as fortunate a position as me; some men *do* feel intimidated. It's why I wrote *The Chad Manifesto*.'

'But my understanding is whenever you think of women your little thing shrivels in on itself. It doesn't matter that you're popping Viagra like they're chocolate-coated peanuts, your soldier no longer stands to attention.'

'Oh my giddy aunt,' Justine said. 'Camera one on Hunt's face. Now, Yosef!'

'On it.'

Even the glare of the quartz lamps couldn't hide the flush that started at Hunt's neck then quickly ran up his face. He clenched his jaw. A vein on his forehead began ticking.

'Beautiful,' Justine said.

'What the hell are you talking about?' Hunt cried. 'I've never used Viagra! Every woman I hook up with, and there have been hun-dreds, has an evening they never forget. And it's one hundred per cent natural.'

'I think that's the first truthful thing you've said all night,' Morgan said, her voice dangerously sweet. 'The women you take home *do* have an evening they can never forget. Even after professional therapy.'

'I really don't know where you got that from, but if I were you I'd sack your researchers. You might find yourself in serious legal . . .'

He trailed off when Morgan revealed the prop she'd been holding back from everyone, even Justine. She upended a tote bag and something fell on the glass table.

It was penis-shaped, made of black silicone and attached to a harness. It looked both sleazy and pitiful in equal measure.

'What the hell is that?' Allan asked, his eyes glued to the monitor.

'Oh my God, it's a penile sleeve!' Justine replied. 'It fits over an impotent guy's dick and it's secured with those straps. Means they can have penetrative sex. Sort of. What's she doing with it on live television?'

'How would you know—?'

'I did that documentary on erectile dysfunction a few years back, remember?'

Allan did. It hadn't been cutting-edge television, but it hadn't been a bad programme.

'Should we cut to a break?' he said, his fingers hovering over the red button.

'Seriously? You want to cut Morgan off now? She'll skin us and wear us as hats.'

'Fair enough.'

'But get ready,' Justine said. 'Hunt looks like he's about to have a heart attack.'

Justine wasn't exaggerating. Hunt didn't look well. Morgan pushed the penile sleeve across the table. She used a paper tissue.

'You left this at Anita Fowles's flat,' she said. 'She asked if I could return it to you.'

'Th-th-that's not mine!'

'It isn't?'

'Of course not!'

'But it *looks* like yours.'

'It looks like . . . What the hell do you mean it *looks* like mine?'

'Oh sorry, didn't I say? Unbeknown to you, Anita filmed you stuffing your flaccid little thing into this contraption. When she asked why you were wearing a strap-on, you burst into tears.'

'She signed a non-disclosure agreement,' Hunt said. 'Even if there were a video, which of course there isn't, she couldn't show it to anyone.'

'You're right, of course, Anita did sign an NDA,' Morgan agreed. 'They *all* signed NDAs. It's why to date nothing's surfaced on the internet. Unfortunately for you, Anita's a law student, and the video she took also has you performing your party trick: lighting a cigarette with an electronic stun gun. Does that ring a bell, Kane?'

Hunt said nothing. He began to hyperventilate.

'Now, you may not know this, but like all contracts, NDAs cannot be used to protect illegal activities. We've taken legal advice and your possession and use of an illegal weapon appears to have rendered the NDA null and void.'

'I don't feel well,' Hunt said.

'No?' Morgan said. 'Well, I don't think this will make you feel any better. Because you'd already shared a picture of Anita online, she felt it only fair to reciprocate. The moment we went on air, Anita sent her video to a bunch of websites and newspaper editors and—'

'No, really, I don't feel . . .'

Hunt slumped in his seat. He stayed there a moment then collapsed on to the polished studio floor. Unconscious, he vomited.

Justine stared in horror at the monitor. Yosef had switched the live feed to Morgan's stricken face, but camera three was still on Hunt's. It was beetroot red. Vomit dribbled from the corner of his mouth.

'Go to a break!' Justine screamed.

Allan punched the cut button and the live feed went dead.

And on the studio floor, Kane Hunt got on with the business of dying . . .

Chapter 3

'Poe, why would someone want to buy my toenails?'

Most of Detective Sergeant Washington Poe's tea squirted out of his nose. The rest he spat over his chin and T-shirt. Beside him, her eyes glued to high-tech binoculars, Detective Inspector Stephanie Flynn sniggered.

It wasn't the strangest thing Matilda 'Tilly' Bradshaw had said to him. It didn't even make the top five, but without warning or context, it probably crept into his top ten. Maybe number nine. Weirder than when she'd asked him to rank his favourite cloud formations, but definitely not as bad as the time she asked him to check the mole on her bottom.

'You taking this one, boss?' Poe sighed, glancing down at his T-shirt. He was down to his last clean one.

Flynn shook her head but kept her eyes trained through the binoculars. Her blonde hair was tied back and it swung like a horse's tail.

'Not a chance,' she said. 'She asked you, and I've just sat through an hour of why I should still be breastfeeding.'

'You *should* still be breastfeeding, DI Flynn,' Bradshaw said. 'The World Health Organization is very clear on this: breastfeeding for eighteen months gives babies additional nutrition and illness protection. It helps fight disease all the way through the second year.'

'Yeah? Well, they aren't your nipples he's chewing on.'

'Are they cracked? Have you tried using breast milk as a moisturiser?'

This time it was Poe's turn to snigger. Bradshaw had yet to encounter a social situation she couldn't make more awkward.

'No, thank you, Tilly,' Flynn replied. 'And I've spoken to my doctor. He's quite happy for me to start weaning.'

Bradshaw frowned. Doctors were only one step above dentists, as far as she was concerned. Barely functioning morons.

'Anyway,' Flynn continued, 'weren't you trying to sell Poe your toenails . . .?'

Chapter 4

It was the strangest stakeout Poe had ever been on.

Three days in the box room belonging to Mr and Mrs Emsley, the octogenarian couple who lived opposite their target.

Three days of nothing.

No sightings, no hint that anyone even lived in the house they were watching. Just three days of rain, wind and sleet and the occasional visit from Colin, the Emsley's arthritic and flatulent Miniature Schnauzer.

Christmas had been and gone, the January wind was raw and the drab clouds were low enough to touch. The temperature hovered just above freezing. Cold enough to ache the bones; not cold enough to let snow settle. It didn't matter how careful Poe was, every time he stepped outside, the bottom six inches of his jeans ended up spattered with dirty water.

Even the Emsleys – initially excited to be hosting the Serious Crime Analysis Section, the National Crime Agency unit tasked with hunting serial killers and serial rapists – had had enough. Mrs Emsley had been dropping hints all morning about a cheap Saga cruise she and her husband had been offered.

Flynn had told her that it wouldn't be too much longer. She wasn't lying. There were almost thirty cops dotted around the target's house and she didn't have a bottomless budget.

At least they were inside, Poe thought. The Emsleys' box room was the command centre for the surveillance operation. Flynn needed somewhere with a decent signal and an unrestricted view of the target's house. She also needed somewhere dry and private so she could express her milk. Bradshaw had told Poe that if Flynn didn't do it regularly, her breasts ached. He didn't ask how she knew this.

Poe had been on stakeouts before. Hundreds of them. He had been a cop for a long time and they were second nature. Flynn had been on almost as many.

But neither of them had been on one like this.

One of the reasons was their target. The media had dubbed him Spring-heeled Jack, and for three weeks he'd been terrifying the women of Watford. A vicious rapist hiding behind a Guy Fawkes mask, he'd committed a series of brutal sex attacks in broad daylight. During six of his eight offences, members of the public had tried to apprehend him. And on one occasion a police dog unit with two Alsatians had been in the area.

He'd escaped.

Easily.

Because Spring-heeled Jack was a *traceur*. A practitioner of parkour, the combined discipline of, among others, freerunning, jumping, swinging and climbing. Each time he had been chased – and Poe was convinced being chased was the real thrill for Spring-heeled Jack – he had been caught on CCTV and mobile-phone footage. The way he climbed buildings, leaped huge distances and vaulted over his pursuers when he was cornered almost defied belief.

It was why so many cops on this operation were young and athletic. One of the women had represented Great Britain at the Olympics. It was also why, despite the lack of action and the miserable weather, each time Poe did a welfare check, he didn't hear a single gripe. They wanted Spring-heeled Jack off the streets and they wanted him to know he wasn't the only one with fancy tricks.

The other reason the stakeout was strange was because Bradshaw was there. She was an analyst, and analysts didn't go on surveillance operations. Poe had never been on a stakeout with a civilian before. It wasn't professional snobbery; they were allowed to join a union, the police weren't.

On this occasion, Bradshaw had insisted.

She and her team, affectionately known as the Mole People because they tended to squint when they stepped outside, had written the computer program that analysed and put values on the moves Spring-heeled Jack had used on the captured CCTV and mobile-phone footage. They compared them against thousands of hours of freerunners' and *traceurs*' videos on YouTube and other websites. Their not unreasonable view was that someone with Spring-heeled Jack's parkour skills was unlikely to hide them. If he was a showman when he committed rape, he would also be a showman when he wasn't committing rape.

And it worked.

They had compiled a list of six people within their margin of error. Good police work narrowed that list down to one suspect: Patrick 'the trick' Barnetson.

Flynn made the decision to take him at his home. A covert entry team established he wasn't in, but DNA samples taken from his toothbrush confirmed Barnetson was indeed Spring-heeled Jack. Rather than go public, Flynn decided to wait. There was a risk of further victims, but exposure might force him to flee. And because of his parkour contacts in non-extradition countries, it was possible he could disappear forever.

Bradshaw had mapped out the area around Barnetson's address and rendered it into a 3D computer model. She had carried out a series of simulations that predicted where he might run, and the moves he would make, if he managed to evade the cops attempting to arrest him at home. She claimed she had to be on the stakeout so she could direct the chasing cops.

The *real* reason became apparent when they had settled in for the long haul. Appalled at Poe's stories about the food on stakeouts, Bradshaw had taken it upon herself to make sure the breastfeeding Flynn still had a nutritionally balanced diet. And because she didn't think it would be fair for Poe to eat pies, chips, kebabs and Chinese takeaways while Flynn ate fruit, vegetables, seeds and oily fish, she'd taken matters into her own hands. She had told Poe that Flynn was arranging the food, and had told Flynn that Poe was doing it. And because Bradshaw had never deliberately deceived anyone in her entire life, neither had thought to check with the other.

The first indication that something was wrong, was when Poe stepped into the box room – it didn't smell like a kebab shop.

Flynn looked at his empty hands and said, 'Where's the fucking curry, Poe?'

Instead of the baked, fried and sugary snacks they'd been looking forward to, Bradshaw had brought date and goji berry bars, fresh fruit, hummus with carrot batons, unsalted nuts and peculiar-smelling bread. She had also brought a mini-fridge so they wouldn't need to use the Emsleys'.

'It's got yoghurt in it, boss,' Poe had whined. 'You can't have yoghurt on a stakeout.'

'But it contains active bacteria, Poe,' Bradshaw had said.

'Why don't you stick your bacteria up—'

'That's enough, Poe,' Flynn cut in. 'And, Tilly, stop winding him up.'

'Where are the crisps?' Poe had said, the moment Bradshaw left the room. 'The cheap sausage rolls, the fizzy sweets, the meat with the weird little tubes inside?'

'We'll go to the shop when she's asleep,' Flynn said.

'She doesn't sleep and we're in the middle of a bloody housing estate. The only shop within walking distance is a newsagent and we can't leave a strange car nearby in case it spooks Barnetson.'

Flynn had sighed.

'We'll manage, Poe.'

Bradshaw had returned with a brown paper bag. Poe glared at it – it didn't even have the decency to be grease-stained.

'Would you like a wasabi-coated mung bean, Poe?' she said. 'They're organic.'

As Poe went off into yet another rant, Flynn muttered to herself, 'There has to be an easier way to earn a living.'

Chapter 5

Tilly Bradshaw was a human outlier. A maths genius in a field that didn't like to use the word. And although maths was her first love, she was a true polymath – a person able to draw on complex bodies of knowledge to solve multifaceted problems. Had done since she was plucked from school at the age of thirteen and given a fully funded place at Oxford, where her once-in-a-generation mind could flourish and realise its true potential.

Academically she'd exceeded everyone's wildest expectations. When her studies had finished, she stayed on to do research. Companies around the world threw money at her. Her relieved parents believed their intellectually odd-shaped daughter had found one of the few odd-shaped holes available to her.

And for years that was enough.

Until it wasn't.

Without telling anyone, she successfully applied for a profiler's job with the Serious Crime Analysis Section. After correcting three of the questions on the entrance exam, she handed in what would turn out to be the highest ever score, a score that could be equalled but never beaten. On an exam where the average mark was 63, she scored a perfect 100 per cent.

She started working for SCAS.

And to everyone's surprise she struggled.

She was brilliant, able to do the things others couldn't. Things no one else could even *think* of. She could devise bespoke solutions and she could spot patterns in data faster than any computer. She became the leading expert in almost every crime science there was. Forensic accounting, digital and multimedia, fingerprint analysis, bloodstain patterns, firearm and toolmark examination, geographic profiling, gait analysis. She even studied forensic astronomy so she could determine the appearance of the sky at a specific point in the past.

She should have been the most valuable asset in UK law enforcement.

But what the professors and visiting academics, even her parents, had failed to understand was, putting Bradshaw into adult education at such a young age had consequences.

They had stolen her childhood.

More importantly, they had robbed her of the chance to interact with people who weren't like her. She developed no social skills, believed everything she was told and was unable to recognise irony or sarcasm. And, because what was in her head didn't readily translate into words people could understand, her guileless honesty was mistaken for rudeness.

She wasn't easy to get on with.

She was different.

And it doesn't matter where you are, different people get bullied.

Some SCAS employees, jealous of her abilities, stole her personal items. They dared each other to get her to do more and more outrageous stuff. They called her names.

She withdrew into herself. She was miserable.

And then Poe had entered her life. He was returning to work after an eighteen-month suspension and needed SCAS's best profiler in the field with him. Flynn, now promoted to Poe's old detective inspector role, had mentioned Bradshaw. Poe had spoken to her and realised two things. The first was that underneath all the awkwardness and unintentional rudeness was an extremely kind and brilliant young woman.

The second thing was she was being bullied.

And Poe *hated* bullies.

Always had, always would.

They elicited a primeval response: a staggering overreaction.

SCAS soon learned that if they bullied Bradshaw they might as well have bullied Poe. In fact, they would be better off doing so. The consequences wouldn't be as severe.

In life experiences they were poles apart – he'd had some, she hadn't – and intellectually they could barely understand each other. They shouldn't have got on.

But they did.

Because underneath all the childlike gawkiness, the tactless comments, the lack of humility, Bradshaw was the nicest person he had ever met. Loyal to the point of stubborn – a trait they shared – generous to a fault and, in defence of Poe, as fierce as a honey badger. She had saved his life twice, stopped him from being charged with murder once and had helped him catch countless bad guys. She also helped him manage his demons. Showed him that the dark, self-destructive path he was heading down wasn't the only way. There was a lighter side of the street to walk on.

And in return, he helped her navigate the complicated and nuanced world she was still coming to terms with. He showed her how to communicate with her colleagues without upsetting them. She got better at understanding body language and sarcasm and irony.

But, she was still Bradshaw. The wonderfully innocent social hand grenade, the same person who had told the Bishop of Carlisle she didn't drink liquorice tea because it gave her diarrhoea. She only ever wore T-shirts and cargo trousers, and, despite being able to afford a more modern pair, still preferred her Harry Potter-style glasses, her grey eyes magnified behind the thick lenses.

So when she said someone wanted to buy her toenail clippings, it wasn't the opening line of a joke.

Someone really did want to buy them.

Chapter 6

'Tell me exactly what happened,' Poe said.

'I was playing *Dragonlore* last night and Nedski42 offered to buy them,' Bradshaw explained. 'More money if I send one from each toe.'

'And he's one of the other players?'

'He is. He's not very good.'

'You haven't met him?'

'Of course not.'

'And your identity's hidden, I take it?'

She snorted. Bradshaw took her online security seriously.

'So who is he?' Poe said.

'I don't know, Poe. Am I to find out? I thought I'd check it wasn't weird first.'

'It's definitely weird, Tilly. Maybe not dangerous-weird, though. Get me his ID and I'll make some enquiries.'

'What does he want them for, though? It's just hardened protein.'

Poe didn't want to speculate. 'Nothing nice,' he said. 'Just out of curiosity, how much did he offer you?'

'One hundred pounds, Poe.'

'Bloody hell. Tell him he can have mine for fifty quid. I'll post them tonight.'

Flynn jumped to her feet. 'Right, there's only so much of this shite I can take,' she said. 'Sit on the scope, Poe, I need to stretch my legs. I'll walk down to the newsagent. We're out of milk.'

'There's some of Tilly's almond milk in the mini-fridge,' he said. 'It's quite sweet, but it's fine in a brew.'

'I used the last of that on my muesli this morning, Poe,' Bradshaw said.

He looked at his mug. 'So, what's this in my tea?'

Bradshaw shrugged. 'I don't know.'

Flynn stared at him, her eyes widening. 'Oh, you've got to be kidding me,' she said.

Realisation dawned on Poe. 'I haven't . . .'

'You bloody well have!' Flynn snapped. 'Forty minutes it took me to squeeze that out!'

'What?' Bradshaw asked. 'What's Poe done, DI Flynn?'

'He's been putting my breast milk in his tea, Tilly.'

'Why would he do that?'

Flynn threw up her arms. 'Why does Poe do anything?' she replied. She stomped out of the room, muttering obscenities down the stairs.

'Don't worry, Poe,' Bradshaw said. 'If it's good enough for DI Flynn's baby, it's good enough for you, right?'

Poe scowled. 'No, *not* right,' he said, getting to his feet. 'Look through these binoculars for five minutes, will you?'

'Where are you going? DI Flynn said you had to look through them.'

He threw his mug in the bin. 'I'm going to brush my teeth fifteen times.'

Poe returned ten minutes later, his face ashen. Flynn was back on the binoculars.

'Stop being such a drama queen, Poe,' she said. 'There's a shop in Covent Garden that sells breast-milk ice cream.'

'Yuk,' Bradshaw said. 'Even if I wasn't vegan, I wouldn't try that.'

Poe didn't respond.

'What's the matter, Poe?' Bradshaw said, more attuned to his moods these days.

'I need to go,' he said.

'Now?' Flynn said.

'Now.'

'You can't. I need to take breaks and Tilly can't command the guys on the ground.'

'I've got to go *now*, boss.'

'Why, for God's sake?'

'I've just taken a call from Northumbria Police.'

'If they're making a referral, it'll have to wait.'

'It's not a referral.'

'What did they want then?'

'It's Estelle Doyle,' Poe said.

'What about her?'

'She's been arrested for murder.'

Flynn paused for less than a second.

'Go,' she said.

At about the same time Poe was racing north to find out exactly what had happened to his friend, the Right Honourable Member for Sheffield East was receiving a pressed flower in the post . . .

Chapter 7

Poe could count on one hand the number of friends he had. And he'd still have his thumb left.

There was Bradshaw, of course.

And he'd known Flynn for years.

His full-time neighbour/part-time dog sitter, Victoria Hume, he considered a friend, too.

And then there was Estelle Doyle.

Like Bradshaw, she was brilliant. Unlike Bradshaw, who always walked down the sunny side of the street, Doyle's personality lurked in the shadows, in the half-light. She was considered the foremost forensic pathologist in Europe and was Poe's go-to person any time he had questions about something wet and organic.

Ordinarily, she treated police officers with disdain. Her legendary barbed tongue meant some detectives refused to use her. But for some reason she tolerated Poe. Would take the time to ensure he understood something. She worked long hours when he needed her to. Even attended his crime scenes, and she *never* did that. She had once described him as a perennial underdog with Capraesque qualities. Poe had been too scared to ask what she had meant.

And she shamelessly flirted with him. She said things that made him blush. Wore figure-hugging clothes that had him squirming. Her heels and cheekbones were high, her lipstick scarlet. Her eyebrows could have been carved with a scalpel.

Poe was terrified and bewitched in equal measure.

But he liked her. Considered her a friend. Knew in his gut that she would be there for him, *really* be there, when it mattered.

The detective inspector he'd spoken to wouldn't give any details. Just said that Doyle had been arrested for murder and since being taken into custody had only said three words: tell Washington Poe.

'Please consider yourself told,' the DI had said.

'I'll be there in five hours.'

'This was a courtesy call, Sergeant Poe. It's a Northumbria case – stay out of it.'

'I'll be there in five hours,' he'd repeated.

Poe glanced at the dashboard clock and decided he wanted to be there in four. He pressed down on the accelerator.

Chapter 8

Bradshaw rang as he was passing the *Angel of the North*, the twenty-metre high steel sculpture that overlooked the A1 near Gateshead.

'Are you there yet, Poe?'

'Not yet, Tilly. What's up?'

'Spring-heeled Jack's been arrested.'

'You got him?' he said, surprised.

'Yes. DI Flynn noticed him climbing over his garden fence. She thinks he'd seen some of the police watching the house but he needed his passport. It was in his pocket when he was arrested.'

'Did they grab him inside?'

'Gosh, no!' Bradshaw said. 'He jumped out of a top-floor window then took off down the seventeenth simulation route I'd mapped out.'

'Remind me which one that was.'

'It was where he broke into the house three doors down, ran up their stairs then jumped out of a back window on to an apple tree. He could then leap on to the roof of the shop next to the railway line.'

'So who got him?'

'DI Flynn was the one who arrested him,' Bradshaw said. 'I followed her in case he ran, of course. I watched her catch him.'

'Did he resist arrest?' He hoped so. Flynn was a black belt in Krav Maga, and was more than a match for someone who was good at jumping.

'He did.'

'Is the boss OK?'

'She has a limp.'

'Did she fall?'

'No, Poe. She kicked Spring-heeled Jack so hard in the testicles she bruised her foot.'

'Ouch.'

'And then she said, "Try jumping now, you F-word C-word."'

Poe laughed. At least something good had happened today.

'Do you know anything more about what's happened to Estelle Doyle?'

'Northumbria aren't saying anything. I may need your help at some point.'

'I'll leave now.'

'No, get the boss's permission firs—'

'I'll leave now, Poe. We have to help Estelle Doyle. She would help us.'

'That's true.'

'And she's very fond of you.'

'She's fond of all of us, Tilly. I don't know why, all we ever do is cause her trouble.'

'No, Poe,' Bradshaw said. 'She likes us, but she *really* likes you.'

'What makes you say that?'

'Because she told me.'

As soon as Bradshaw had hung up, Poe rang Flynn. 'Boss, I've messed up,' he said. 'I asked Tilly for help.'

'And let me guess, she's already on her way.'

'Sorry.'

Flynn sighed. 'I'll put you both down as being on leave until we know more,' she said.

Chapter 9

Estelle Doyle was being held at Newcastle City Centre Police Station. It was at Forth Banks, near the Centre for Life, the science village in Times Square. Poe drove past it to the multistorey car park in the nearby Copthorne Hotel. There were closer places but there was more chance of him finding a one-ended stick than working out how to use his mobile phone to pay for on-street parking. He pulled his ticket from the electronic barrier machine, parked, and walked back up the hill.

'I'm here to see Estelle Doyle,' he said to the woman behind the desk. 'I believe she's being held here.'

'Can I see some identification, sir?'

Poe slid his NCA ID card though the slot in the screen. Although he was triple-warranted, meaning he had the combined powers of the police, customs and immigration, he knew that didn't mean anything up here. He was skulking around someone else's backyard and they weren't about to throw him a welcome parade.

The woman entered his details into her computer, then picked up the receiver on her desk phone. She whispered into it, stealing glances at Poe as she did. Before long, a beefy-faced sergeant appeared. He had a rugby player's ears, a beer drinker's nose and a mole on his chin that looked like a sultana. He also wanted to see Poe's ID.

'I thought you were told not to bother coming?'

'Yet here I am,' Poe said.

'I'd better tell someone who might give a shit then,' he said. He took him through to the custody suite and pointed towards some moulded plastic seats bolted to the floor. 'Wait there. This may take some time.'

Poe took in his surroundings. The custody suite looked like a state-of-the-art airport check-in area, easily the most modern he'd seen. The cells were in blocks of ten. The sign above him suggested Poe was seated near cells forty-one to fifty. He wondered how high the numbers went.

It was as busy as an ants' nest and just as organised. Cops, some in uniform, some in plainclothes, marched around purposefully. Nobody paid him any attention. He checked his emails, expecting to see one from Flynn telling him how she'd managed to kick yet another suspect in the balls. It was becoming a habit with her. To his surprise there wasn't one. Wasn't one from Bradshaw either. He was about to send Bradshaw a text asking her where she was, when a beleaguered-looking Asian woman approached him.

She was wearing the type of suit he'd worn when he was with Cumbria CID. Smart, but machine washable. Her hair was clipped short – wouldn't take long to sort out if there was a middle of the night call. Probably a detective inspector, maybe higher. She certainly looked tired enough.

'Sergeant Poe?' she said, taking the seat beside him.

'That's right.'

'I'm Detective Chief Inspector Tai-young Lee. I understand you've asked to see Professor Doyle?'

'I have.'

'Are you her legal representative?'

'I think you know I'm not.'

'That's right, you're not. You're National Crime Agency.'

Poe nodded. 'I'm the DS in the Serious Crime Analysis Section.'

'The serial killer unit?'

'Close enough.'

'Can I ask what the NCA's interest is?'

'I don't know.'

'Excuse me?'

'I haven't spoken to her yet. Professor Doyle asked for me personally.'

'Not true,' Tai-young Lee said. 'She actually said, "*Tell Washington Poe.*" So I'll ask again, what's the NCA's interest?'

Poe decided honesty was the best policy. He held up his hands

34

and said, 'The NCA isn't interested in this case, ma'am, *I'm* interested in it.'

'And why would that be? I understand when my DI informed you of Professor Doyle's arrest, you left the Spring-heeled Jack operation in Watford and rushed up here.'

'You're well informed.'

'It's my job to be well informed. Congratulations on the arrest, by the way. I hope no one was hurt?'

'Just him.'

'Resisting arrest?'

'I'm sure that's what the paperwork will say.'

Lee said nothing.

Poe filled the silence. 'Look, ma'am, I have no idea what's happened and I have no idea why Estelle asked for me. All I know is that she's my friend and I'd like to see her.'

'I'm afraid that won't be possible.'

'Why not?'

'Two things: one, this is an active investigation and you're not part of it.'

'And the other?'

'I don't know anything about you, Sergeant Poe.'

Poe paused. Wondered why he was always getting himself into situations like this. Decided analysing his world of permanent conflict could wait.

'Well, ma'am, we have a problem,' he said.

Chapter 10

'I can see how you might have a problem, Sergeant Poe,' Tai-young Lee said. 'I fail to see how I have one.'

'You have a problem, ma'am, because the woman you've arrested is an NCA asset. She has been for some time now.'

Lee frowned. 'I wasn't aware of this,' she said.

'I'm making you aware. SCAS pay Professor Doyle an annual retainer. Technically she's an employee, although I wouldn't mention that to her if I were you.'

'She's been arrested for murder and, without appearing prejudicial, the evidence is overwhelming. Unless you're about to tell me she has diplomatic immunity, she's not walking away from—'

'Are you ambitious, ma'am?' Poe cut in.

Lee shrugged. 'As any Korean whose parents wanted their only child to be a doctor.'

'Then let me see her.'

'Are you threatening me, Sergeant Poe?'

'Of course not, ma'am. But maybe you should take five minutes to check me out. Decide how much of me you want in your life because I'm certainly not leaving this alone.'

She stood up, muttered, 'I could really do without this right now,' then stormed off.

Poe went back to his emails. Still nothing from Flynn or Bradshaw.

Tai-young Lee returned fifteen minutes later. She didn't look happy.

This time she didn't sit. Poe didn't stand. If she needed to tower over him in a management powerplay, that was fine. He was there for Doyle, not his ego.

'It seems my chief super knows of you, Sergeant Poe,' she said. 'He said you went toe-to-toe with the security services last year and came out on top.'

'That's been exaggerated,' Poe said.

'He seemed impressed.'

'He really shouldn't be.'

'Good, because I'm not. All I see is someone trying to interfere in an active investigation.'

'I promise you I'm not—'

'But,' she said, clipping his half-arsed protest, 'as a courtesy to the NCA we *will* allow you to see Professor Doyle. As it's not a legally privileged meeting, the recording equipment will be switched on and I'll be listening. If I think you're about to disclose things we aren't ready to disclose, I'll stop the interview and arrest you for interfering in a police investigation. These terms aren't negotiable.'

There was nothing to consider. 'Fine,' he said.

She sighed. 'What's this really about, Sergeant Poe? Why did she want you informed?'

'No idea,' he said. 'But I think you'd better tell me what happened.'

Chapter 11

'The shout came in yesterday evening,' Tai-young Lee said. 'The location's a bit rural so it was twenty minutes before uniform got there. They secured the scene then called it in. I was duty DCI and was there within the hour. Uniform had held the paramedics at the outer cordon as it was obvious the victim had wounds incompatible with life.'

'Who was the victim?'

'Professor Doyle's father, Elcid.'

'Manner of death?'

'Nothing official yet, obviously, but I can tell you there was a bullet hole in his head and two more in his chest. He was still in his chair.'

'Witnesses?'

'None.'

'Who called 999?'

'She did.'

'Who, Estelle?'

Lee nodded.

'She was there?' Poe said.

'She says she found him.'

'Go on.'

'Nothing more really,' she said. 'We conducted some enquiries then arrested Professor Doyle for the murder of her father.'

Poe shook his head. 'You haven't arrested the most gifted forensic pathologist in Europe just because she discovered her father's murder,' he said. 'You have more. What aren't you telling me?'

Lee eyed him shrewdly. 'We're getting into disclosure territory here, Sergeant Poe,' she said. 'Some of this hasn't been shared with the suspect yet.'

'I'm a cop front and centre, ma'am. If you have evidence then tell me. I won't share it unless you tell me I can.'

She hesitated, and for a moment Poe thought she was going to refuse. Instead she said, 'The early line of enquiry was that Elcid Doyle had interrupted a burglary. He's a wealthy man and the family home is full of antiques and valuables. Early evidence supported this.'

'Such as?'

'Manner of entry was a broken window.'

'But . . .?'

'If he'd interrupted a burglary, why was he sitting down?'

'I can think of thirty reasons right off the top of my head,' Poe said. 'The killer could have forced him. He might not have interrupted him at all, he could have been expecting the house to be empty and walked into the room while he was having a nap.'

'What do you know about glass analysis?'

'Not much.'

'But you know that direction of impact is determined by the angle of the fractures, right?'

Poe nodded. He didn't understand the physics, but he knew when determining if a window had been broken from the inside or the outside, CSI technicians looked for conchoidal fractures, the ridges found on the edges of broken glass. They govern the side that the force was applied.

'The glass was broken from the inside?' he asked.

'The fracture's conclusive,' Lee replied. 'We also have a time discrepancy. Professor Doyle left the post-mortem suite at half past four and called 999 an hour and a half later. Her father lived just outside Corbridge. That journey takes less than an hour, even in rush hour.'

'Have you asked her about that?'

'Not yet.'

'OK,' he said. 'You have a crime scene with inconsistent broken glass and you have an easily explained time discrepancy. Neither of these things make Estelle the killer. But you arrested her anyway. You seem like a bright cop – what aren't you telling me?'

'Do you know what an FDR test is, Sergeant Poe?'

Poe did.

'Shit,' he said.

Chapter 12

The Firearms Discharge Residue test, shortened to FDR, is a simple swab that shows whether fused particles of barium, antimony and lead, invisible to the naked eye, are present. A positive test indicates a gun has been fired.

Poe knew FDR was a limited form of evidence. It wasn't infallible, it wasn't a literal smoking gun. There were numerous ways to get a false positive. Residue from brake pads, fireworks, arc welding and even key cutting had all been incorrectly identified as FDR.

But it didn't look good.

'Where?' he asked.

'On her hands,' Lee replied. 'The responding cops put them in forensic paper bags and secured them at the wrist as a precaution. I had CSI swab her when I started questioning the evidence. Further analysis revealed it was an exact chemical match with the residue we took from the victim.'

'You used gel swabs on her eyelids? Took hair combings?'

'We did.'

'And?'

'Negative.'

'None on her clothes either, I take it?' Poe said. 'You'd have mentioned it if there was.'

'There wasn't. But it looks like a small-calibre weapon was used. There wouldn't have been much blowback.'

Poe paused. 'You haven't got the gun yet, have you?'

'Not yet.'

Poe made a mental note of this. Juries didn't like it when the prosecution couldn't provide the murder weapon.

'Anything else?' he asked.

'I'm afraid so. And it's the big one. Nothing that can be easily explained.'

'Go on.'

'It snowed for an hour yesterday afternoon. Started at three, an hour and a half before Professor Doyle left work. Didn't thaw until today.'

'So?'

'Professor Doyle arrived at her father's at six p.m.'

Poe waited.

'Rigor hadn't yet set into the victim's face or hands when the FME arrived.'

'And?'

'And there was only one set of footprints going into the house. Hers. They went from her car to the front door. There were no other footprints in the snow anywhere around the house. No one climbed out of a window and no one walked out of the back door.'

Poe sighed. This was bad.

Rigor mortis, or post-mortem lividity, was the stiffening of the corpse caused by chemical changes in the muscles. It started in the face and hands within two hours after death and was usually complete within six. Elcid Doyle had been dead for less than two hours when he was discovered, which meant he'd been killed *after* it had snowed, not before. This was a big problem if the only footprints outside the house were Doyle's.

'The snow hadn't covered any other prints?' he asked.

Lee shook her head.

'It only snowed for an hour and it wasn't heavy enough. Barely a centimetre.'

Poe said nothing.

'So you can see why she's a person of interest.'

'You have a view on motivation?' Poe said, refusing to be drawn.

'We've only had a day.'

Poe waited. Someone as good as Tai-young Lee didn't leave her engine in neutral for long. She had physical evidence in the FDR residue, circumstantial evidence in the broken glass and compelling evidence with the lack of footprints. She would already be hammering the big one – motivation. If the prosecution failed to answer the 'why?' question, juries were far less likely to convict.

'Fine,' Lee said. 'You know she didn't get on with her father?'

'You misunderstand the nature of my relationship with Professor Doyle, ma'am. It's purely professional. I've never seen her outside of work and I've never had a discussion about her private life.'

Except that wasn't entirely true, he thought. The last couple of times he had seen her, he'd got the distinct impression she was on the verge of asking him something. Something personal. And Bradshaw had been hinting at it for months. He hadn't pursued it for one simple reason – he was scared. Not scared of Doyle, as terrifying as she was, albeit in an attractive way. No, he was scared of opening up to someone. Allowing vulnerability into his life.

'He'd wanted her to be a stay-at-home daughter, apparently,' Lee explained. 'They had a big falling out when she chose to study medicine. Cut her out of his will. He had planned to leave her nothing.'

'They'd reconnected?'

'Quite recently. We've seen his last will and he had added a valuable house to what she was due to inherit. Dated and witnessed just a year ago. Professor Doyle was in the solicitor's office when it was signed, so we know she's seen it.'

'You think she killed him in case he changed his mind?'

'It's a theory.'

'Not a great one.'

'I'm sorry, Sergeant Poe, but unless someone levitated in and out of the house, she was the only one with the means, motive and opportunity. And while the investigation *is* at an early stage, I do not believe there are any outstanding suspects.'

Poe had heard enough. 'I'd like to see her now,' he said.

Lee took the seat beside him and tapped something into the gadget she was holding. It was slightly bigger than the over-sized iPhone Bradshaw used.

'I'll have her brought to Interview Room Four,' she said.

Interview Room 4 was in the custody suite. C116 was written underneath. Poe assumed that was for the benefit of the facilities management company.

He opened the door and stepped inside.

Doyle was already seated, her eyes staring at her lap. Poe knew she would hate him seeing her like this. He took the seat opposite and put his hands on the table.

'Estelle,' he said. Nothing. She didn't move a muscle. 'Look at me, Estelle.'

She raised her head. Slowly. Held his gaze. Her eyes were swollen and Poe saw nothing but grief. Her makeup had run. She was in a shapeless paper evidence suit. She looked small and afraid, a far remove from the cold logic and feigned detachment he had grown used to. But he saw defiance, too. Doyle was still in there somewhere. She wasn't defeated yet.

He reached across the table and grabbed her hands. 'It's going to be all right,' he said.

Chapter 13

'Tell me what happened, Estelle,' Poe said. 'Don't try to second-guess what I want to hear – I need it all.'

'What do you know?' Doyle said.

'I can't tell you. If I do I'll be dragged out and arrested.'

'Well, we can't have that.' Stroppy. Feeling sorry for herself.

'We can't!' Poe snapped. 'Because I won't be able to do what you need me to do if I'm in the next cell.'

She stared at him, surprised. He'd never raised his voice to her before.

'I'm sorry,' she said.

'You have nothing to apologise for, but we are up against it. Detective Chief Inspector Tai-young Lee is not an idiot and she has a solid case. I need a thread to tug on.'

'Do they really think I killed my father?'

Poe considered the question. Decided he was OK telling her. She'd been arrested for his murder after all. 'This isn't a holding arrest, it's the real thing,' he said. 'They've talked me through the evidence and it's compelling. They aren't looking for anyone else.'

She held his eyes. 'Ask me then,' she said.

'Ask you what?'

'You *know* what.'

'I honestly don't.'

'Ask me if I did it.'

'Why would I do that?' Poe said. 'I *know* you didn't do it.'

'How can you be so sure? You barely know me.'

She stared at him so intensely that he started reddening. He held her gaze nonetheless, knew she needed to know why. 'Because you asked for me,' he said.

Her expression softened. 'Thank you, Poe,' she said.

'Tell me what happened, Estelle.' He removed his notebook and looked at her expectantly.

'It's a short story, not even a novella,' she said. 'I received a text from Dad at lunchtime asking if I wanted to join him for dinner. I sent one back saying I was finishing work early and would be with him as soon as I could.'

'Did he often invite you to dinner?'

'More recently, yes.'

'Why?'

'Because of you.'

Poe waited for her to elaborate. Even arrested for murder, she couldn't help but play with him.

'Not biting, Poe?' she smiled.

'Not today.'

'It's because of my involvement in your last few cases. My name's been in national rags a few times and it's made him quite the celebrity with his grouse-shooting cronies. I think he'd finally realised I hadn't let him down.'

'And until then, that's what he thought?'

She shrugged. 'He had wanted a son,' she said. 'Made no bones about it. And just as he was getting used to having a daughter for an heir, I went and disappointed him again.'

'By going into medicine?' Poe said. 'By becoming a doctor and training as a pathologist? By becoming a leader in your field?'

'He's from a different era, Poe. You can't judge him by modern standards. I tried for years and it only drove us further apart.'

'But he was coming round to having a successful daughter?'

'Slowly. He's a proud man and I can be . . . wilful. But, yes, we'd worked things out. He'd attended some of my lectures, which was nice. We would have dinner in Newcastle sometimes. Take in a show at the Theatre Royal. He loved that the Royal Shakespeare Company's northern home was up here. We went to see *The Taming of the Shrew* last year and had tickets to see *Measure for Measure* in March.'

Poe wrote down Shakespeare then crossed it out. He didn't think the Bard was involved. 'Did he say why he wanted to meet you?' he said.

'No, but that's not unusual. He's old-fashioned and doesn't like using his mobile.'

'OK. What happened next?'

'It's all in the statement I made.'

'I haven't seen it yet.'

'I drove to my father's. The roads had already had a bit of traffic on them by then, so the snow was mostly slush.'

Poe wanted to ask if she had stopped for petrol, or nipped into a shop to buy her dad a bottle of whisky – anything that might explain the missing thirty minutes. The moment he did though, Tai-young Lee would throw him out for disclosing evidence and leading Doyle to a possible explanation. He could ask about facts, he couldn't suggest things.

'What then?' he asked.

'I parked in front of the house, then used my key to open the door.'

'In front of the house? Does that mean in a driveway or was it on-street parking?'

Doyle smiled sadly. 'On the drive, Poe.'

'And you walked from your car to the front door?'

'I did.'

'You didn't look through a window first?'

'Why would I have done that?'

'Fair point. Did you knock or ring the bell?'

'I have a key.'

'Was the door locked?'

'It was.'

'What did you do after you entered?'

'I hung up my coat and went to join my father in his study.'

'How did you know he'd be in there?'

'He's always in his study. It's where his books and paintings are.'

'Go on.'

'I opened the door and said hello.'

'You couldn't see him?'

'His desk chair was facing the window. He had his back to me.'

'What did you think when he didn't answer?'

'I assumed he'd fallen asleep. The fire was on and the room was warm.'

'What type of fire?'

'Log.'

'Was it flaming or smouldering?'

She paused, then said, 'The wood was glowing but there weren't any flames.'

Poe made a note. He underlined it three times then wondered if he'd done the right thing. Lee hadn't mentioned the fire. Had he just given her more circumstantial evidence? Wood fires went out if they weren't tended.

'Continue,' he said.

'He was slumped in his seat. At first I thought he'd collapsed or had a stroke, but then I saw the threads of blood hanging from his chin. I bent down so I could see his face. Saw the bullet hole in his forehead. I knew he was dead, but I checked his pulse anyway.'

'Why?'

'He was my father.'

'Which artery did you check?'

'The carotid.'

'The neck?'

'Yes.'

'Which hand did you use?' Poe said.

'Excuse me?'

'Which hand did you use to check his pulse?'

If she'd used both hands he could explain how the gunshot residue had been transferred. Knocking down the wall of evidence would have to be done one brick at a time.

'My left,' she said.

'Just your left?'

'Yes. I've attended enough crime scenes to know not to touch anything. I confirmed life was extinct then called 999 on my mobile. I stayed with his body until the first police officers arrived.'

'How long between finding your dad and calling 999?'

'No more than a minute.'

'You're sure?'

'I checked his pulse then rang the police, Poe.'

'And you didn't leave the room?'

'No.'

'And you hadn't been in any other rooms before you went into the study?'

'You've already asked me that. No.'

'What happened when the police arrived?'

'I shouted that the door was unlocked and they should come straight in. As soon as they were in the room I told them my father was dead, that it was a murder and that they needed to secure the scene.'

'Which they did?'

'They knew what they were doing.'

'When were your hands bagged up?'

'An hour or so later.'

'And other than touching your father's neck with your left hand when you checked his pulse, you hadn't touched anything?'

'I knew not to,' she said. She then mumbled something he didn't catch.

'Say that again, Estelle.'

'I said I didn't touch anything as I didn't want to disappoint you. I'm not stupid, I knew what it looked like. And I knew at some point it was likely you'd be asking to see what had happened. I didn't want you thinking I'd panicked. I didn't want you thinking less of me.'

Poe was lost for words. 'Why would I think less of you?' he said eventually. 'You'd just found your father's corpse. There was a bullet hole in his head. If you can't panic then, when can you?'

Doyle said nothing. Poe noticed the nape of her neck had flushed red. He decided to move on. 'We'll circle back to that,' he said. 'When were you arrested?'

'Around eight p.m. That chief inspector you mentioned read me my rights. Uniform handcuffed me and I was brought here in a van.'

'Were you in the house the whole time?'

'No, I was waiting in a marked police car.'

'They brought you back here and swabbed you? Took your clothes?'

Doyle nodded.

'And when they asked who you wanted informed of your arrest, you didn't say a solicitor, you said me?'

She nodded.

'Why?' he asked.

'I'm in trouble, Poe. And the fact you've been asking questions about where my car was parked, about the state of the fire, means it's even worse than I imagined. I called you because you're the only person I trust.'

'You don't trust Northumbria Police?'

'I don't trust them not to accept the first explanation that presents itself.'

Poe put his notebook in his pocket and stood up. 'I'll speak to DCI Tai-young Lee,' he said. 'See if I can get her to consider bail. I'll start working on what they have.' He checked his phone. Still nothing from Bradshaw or Flynn. 'Tilly is coming up to help. I'll be back to see you as soon as the evidence has been laid before you. We can go through each bit then. Is there anyone you want me to contact?'

'No, thank you, Poe.'

She stood up, too. Didn't seem to know what she should do next. Poe knew he shouldn't hug her, that Tai-young Lee would be furious, but he knew Doyle needed it. Needed the human contact.

Plus, he wanted to level the playing field a bit.

He walked round to her side of the table and embraced her. They were being recorded so he put his face close to hers and held the back of her head.

'No comment on the fire,' he whispered into her ear. 'No comment on where you walked, what you touched and what rooms you went in. If they ask about your journey from the hospital to your dad's, what do you say?'

'No comment,' she whispered back.

'I'm going to get into trouble now,' he said, pulling back so she could see his face.

He winked and waited for the interview room door to burst open.

'What was that whole "because you asked for me" thing?' Tai-young Lee said after she'd hauled him over the coals.

'It means she doesn't trust Northumbria to get to the bottom of this,' Poe replied. 'She wants someone who won't take the path of least resistance.'

'No offence taken.'

'I don't care. You've already made up your mind.'

'You're going to be the spectre at my feast, aren't you?' she said.

'I'll try not to be, although it usually ends up that way. I *do* know you've got the wrong person.'

'I've heard you're a stubborn bastard, Sergeant Poe, but you seem surer than you have any right to be. Why is that? What are you seeing that I'm not?'

'The evidence, it's compelling.'

'What's your point?' She frowned. 'Compelling evidence is a good thing, surely—'

'*That's* my point!' he snapped. 'The compelling evidence is my point. Estelle Doyle is one of the most intelligent people I know, and if she wanted to get away with murder there's not a thing you or I could do to stop her. In fact, I'd . . .' His mobile began chirping. 'Sorry,' he said. 'I usually have it on silent but I'm expecting someone and they're late.' He checked the screen. It was Flynn. He answered it. 'Boss, where the hell have you been? I've not heard a peep since I left Watford.'

'I'll explain—'

'And where's Tilly? I was expecting her an hour or so ago – I'm starting to worry.'

'Tilly's with me,' she said.

'I don't understand. I thought she was coming up—'

'Poe, we have a problem.'

Chapter 14

'I need you here, Poe,' Flynn said.

'I can't leave Northumberland now. Estelle's in trouble and these idiots have fixated on the first solution that's presented itself.'

'I'm standing right next to you,' Tai-young Lee said.

'Sorry,' Poe mouthed.

'I've been briefed,' Flynn said. 'The murder scene won't be released for at least two days and Estelle's going to be remanded into custody later. You're not her legal rep so you won't be able to visit until she's been through induction. That won't be until the day after tomorrow in all likelihood. There's nothing you can do right now and if you hang around you're only going to get into trouble.'

Poe didn't respond. Flynn was wrong. There *were* things he could do now. He could check the route Doyle had taken. He could find out who else knew Elcid Doyle had put his daughter back in his will. See if her gain was someone else's loss.

'Anyway,' Flynn continued, 'this isn't me asking, it's a direct instruction from Director of Intelligence Van Zyl.'

'Van Zyl? He doesn't get involved in operational decisions. What's going on?'

'I'll tell you when you get here.'

'And where's "here"?'

'South Yorkshire,' Flynn said. 'The constituency home of the Right Honourable Member for Sheffield East.'

Newcastle to Sheffield was a two-hour drive. Poe tried calling Bradshaw as soon as he was on the A1 but she wasn't answering. He tried calling Flynn next but she was ignoring him, too.

It was all a bit odd. He decided not to worry about it.

He opened his satnav, punched in the postcode Flynn had given him and thought about Doyle instead. The missing thirty minutes would turn out to be nothing, something easily explained that no one had thought to check. It was where he'd start, though. Like any case with seemingly solid evidence, the moment you pulled the first brick from the wall, the rest began looking shaky. The firearm discharge residue on her hands would have to be explained but he wasn't concerned about it. Prosecutions were rarely built around FDR these days. All Poe had to do was find whatever it was she had touched that had caused the false positive.

The window being broken from the inside rather than the outside wasn't bothering him either. It was a fact a murder had been committed, and Tai-young Lee was right – whoever had killed Elcid Doyle had tried to make it look like a botched burglary. That was where Doyle's defence would begin and end.

The only thing he couldn't explain – and the bit that worried him the most – was the unblemished snow. Lee said there was only one set of footprints. They went from Doyle's car to the front door. There were no others around the house. Poe couldn't explain that.

If it got to court, Doyle's barrister would ask the jury where the murder weapon was, if she hadn't left the house. Poe was sure Lee and the CPS were already thinking about how to respond. Poe reckoned their argument would be that she'd hidden it too well. It was certainly more plausible than an unidentified killer levitating out of the house.

As things stood now, a jury wouldn't need more than thirty minutes to bring back a guilty verdict. His job was to make sure it never got that far.

Not once did he doubt Doyle's innocence.

Poe headed into Halfway, a ward in the eastern part of Sheffield. He got stuck in a confusing one-way system for a few minutes but eventually pulled up at the end of a line of police cars in Beaumont Street.

As soon as he stepped out of his car, a uniformed police officer approached him. 'Can I help you, sir?'

53

'Doubt it,' Poe said, showing him his ID.

He nodded then said, 'The NCA contingent is down there. I'll escort you.'

Flynn was in the back of a police incident control trailer.

'Ah, he's here,' she said to the man standing next to her. 'Poe, this is Chief Superintendent Stewart. He's South Yorkshire Constabulary's district commander for Sheffield.'

'You're late, Sergeant Poe,' Stewart said. 'You should have been here an hour ago.'

'Why, what happened?'

'Excuse me?'

Poe turned to Flynn. 'Where's Tilly?'

'Busy.'

'OK, what was so urgent you made me leave an active murder investigation?'

'An investigation you have no official role in?'

Poe remained silent.

'Did you happen to catch *The Morgan Soames Hour* this week?' Flynn continued.

'What's that?'

'A weekly chat show.'

'I don't have a TV.'

'I do wish you'd take the occasional interest in popular culture, Poe.'

'Popular culture sucks.'

'Did you watch *Parkinson* when it was on?'

'I did.'

'Well, it's a bit like *Parkinson*. Only Rod Hull wouldn't have dared attack Morgan Soames with an emu.'

Poe nodded. The belly laughs coming from the Parkinson household must have been deafening the day Rod Hull fell off his own roof and died. 'What about it?' he said.

'Have you heard of Kane Hunt?'

'The red-pill pudding head?'

'That's him. Three days ago he was a guest on *The Morgan Soames Hour*. During the interview he showed Morgan a death threat he claimed to have received.'

'What type of threat?'

'A pressed flower and some bad poetry.'

'And?'

'And he collapsed on air,' Flynn said. 'Doctors turned off his life support machine this morning. He never regained consciousness.'

'And this is the party, is it? You should have said, I'd have brought some balloons.'

'Is he always like this?' Chief Superintendent Stewart asked Flynn.

'Always,' she replied. 'Anyway, the toxicology report showed he'd been given a lethal dose of hyoscine.'

'Which is?'

'It's a medicine used to treat motion sickness and postoperative nausea. Accidental poisonings are very rare but this seems to have been an unusually concentrated dose. We're still waiting for a Yank specialist from the Centre for Disease Control to get back to us.'

'How was it administered?'

'We don't know.'

'*When* was it administered?'

'We don't know.'

'Was the flower petal relevant?'

Flynn said nothing.

'Let me guess, you don't know,' he said.

'We've only just been given this, Poe,' she said. 'Local police were in charge up until a few hours ago.'

'What's changed?'

'I don't understand.'

'Yes, you do. Why are we involved? Women must have been queuing up to murder that gormless twit. Something must have changed for Director Van Zyl to order our involvement. What is it?'

'I need you briefed on Kane Hunt first.'

'Fine,' Poe said. 'Do you have a copy of the poem?'

She handed him a sheet of A4 paper from her file.

Poe read it out loud, 'Under the hanged man's hood . . .'

'Not exactly Keats, is it?' Flynn said when he'd finished.

'Has the language been analysed?'

'That's what Tilly's doing now,' Flynn said. 'She's having the flower petal identified as well. I'm expecting her back any time.'

'You tried opening a bag of salty snacks? That usually brings her running.'

'Oh ha-de-ha-ha, Poe,' a voice said from behind him. 'And I'm only looking after your heart.'

He turned. Bradshaw had arrived.

Chapter 15

'Hi, Poe,' Bradshaw said. 'How's Estelle Doyle?'

'Where've you been, Tilly? I thought you were coming up to Newcastle?'

'Director of Intelligence Edward van Zyl said I wasn't allowed.'

Poe grunted in annoyance. He respected Flynn and he respected Van Zyl, but he much preferred it when they let him do what he wanted.

'How's Estelle Doyle?' Bradshaw said again.

'Not great, Tilly. I know she's being set up, but I can't see how. There's a problem with footprints in the snow that unless—'

'I'm sorry, Poe,' Flynn cut in, 'but this will have to wait. We have a time-sensitive situation here.'

He frowned. Kane Hunt couldn't get any deader. What hadn't he been told?

'Tilly,' Flynn continued, 'tell me what you have.'

'Oh, yes,' Bradshaw said. 'I've logged into my British Library account and, now hyoscine has been identified as the murder weapon, the poem makes a lot more sense. We've also identified the petal.'

'And?'

'It's from the plant genus *Mandragora*. Its common name is the mandrake and, outside of Agatha Christie's *Black Coffee*, the last person to have used hyoscine as a murder weapon was Doctor Crippen.'

'Tell me about the poem,' Poe said.

'You'll remember the mandrake plant from *Harry Potter and the Chamber of Secrets*, Poe?'

'I don't have a television. Why do I need to keep saying this?'

'We watched it when you came to my house for Christmas. Even you should be able to remember that, it was less than a month ago.'

Poe winced. Christmas at Bradshaw's had been . . . different. Her unbridled enthusiasm juxtaposed with his misanthropic approach to the festive season had definitely proved what happens when an unstoppable force meets an immovable object. The immovable object is forced to wear a paper hat and sing Christmas carols.

'Was that the one about the boarding school for wizards?'

'Yes!'

'It's possible some of the salient details escaped me.'

'When you were asleep, you mean,' Bradshaw said.

'I didn't fall asleep – that would have been rude, Tilly.'

'Oh pur-lease. You had four bottles of beer with my dad at lunch-time. You were asleep.'

Chief Superintendent Stewart cleared his throat. 'DI Flynn?' he said.

'Yeah, pack it in, you two,' she said. 'Can we at least *pretend* we're normal?'

'Sorry, DI Flynn,' Bradshaw said. 'As I was saying, the poem makes more sense now. "Under the hanged man's hood, Beneath his dripping blood" references the superstition that the mandrake plant would only grow where the blood of a hanged man had soaked into the earth. "Below the yellow fruit" is easy, the Mediterranean man-drake has a yellow plum-like fruit. The bit about closing your ears and tearing it from the ground refers to the legend that when the root is dug up, its scream will kill anyone who hears it. It wasn't just J. K. Rowling who wrote about this; Shakespeare also mentioned it in *Romeo and Juliet*.'

'OK,' Poe said. 'We have someone who has access to dangerous medicine and a sardonic grasp of folklore.' He turned to Flynn. 'But we're not here for that, are we?'

Flynn looked at Chief Superintendent Stewart. He nodded.

'No, Poe,' she said, 'we're not here for Kane Hunt; we're here for something else.'

Chapter 16

'Does the name Harrison Cummings mean anything to you, Sergeant Poe?' Chief Superintendent Stewart asked.

Poe frowned. The name seemed familiar but he couldn't recollect why.

'No?' Stewart continued. 'He's the Tory Member of Parliament for Sheffield East.'

Now he remembered. The Right Honourable Harrison Cummings had been a junior minister in the Department for International Trade who had been caught taking taxpayer-funded junkets all over the world. He'd declared them as fact-finding missions, laying the groundwork for future trade deals. In fact, he'd been on corporate-sponsored big-game trophy hunts.

The matter had come to light when his daughter had stumbled across some photographs in a hidden cloud folder. Cummings had posed with animals he'd shot from a concealed hide – lions, giraffes, elephants, even the incredibly endangered Sumatran rhino. Disgusted with her father, she shared them with a journalist.

Instead of immediately splashing them all over the front pages, the reporter assigned to the case held off. She sensed there was more to the story than just another MP getting caught with his snout in the trough. So she dug in, did some old-fashioned investigative journalism.

And uncovered the biggest parliamentary scandal of the year.

Harrison Cummings hadn't just been spending public funds on expensive and morally repugnant trophy hunts, he had been accepting junkets from lobbyists all over the world. They would take him on expensive trips and in return he'd petition his own government to introduce legislation. The investigative reporter uncovered a paper trail that showed Cummings had lobbied for British police to routinely carry firearms, a policy that American arms manufacturers believed would expose the UK to less punitive gun laws. He'd been gifted a rose gold Breitling Chronomat, a watch worth fifty-thousand pounds, for his troubles. After he'd been bought by big tobacco, he had pushed hard for the plain packaging law on cigarettes to be overturned. Courtside seats for the New York Knicks and the Chicago Bulls at Madison Square Garden, courtesy of big pharma, persuaded him it was time to re-examine the price the NHS paid for American drugs.

In a sting operation, the mic'd up reporter, who'd been posing as a representative from a fracking company, had asked what his constituents would say when they found out carcinogenic chemicals would leach into the groundwater. He'd responded by saying, 'Fuck those northern bastards.'

When the newspaper printed its story the country went berserk. Cummings had the whip withdrawn. He was stripped of his position in the Department for International Trade. Unbelievably, he refused to stand down as an MP. And, because he hadn't broken any laws, a special election couldn't be triggered.

Poe didn't need a calculator to do this sum.

'There's been another death threat, hasn't there?'

Chapter 17

Flynn handed Poe a tablet.

'This was delivered to Harrison Cummings's constituency office yesterday,' she said. 'One of his staff opened it. We believe it's from the same person who murdered Kane Hunt.'

On the tablet was a photograph of a typed poem. Poe read it out loud.

> You strange, astonished-looking, angle-faced,
> Dreary-mouthed, gaping wretch.
> What is it you do?
> How do you vary your vile days and nights?

'It's a fragment from a poem called "To a Fish",' Flynn said. 'It was written by Leigh Hunt back in the 1800s.'

Poe read it again. 'What's that underneath? Looks like it's been initialled.'

'It's not an initial,' Flynn said. 'If you swipe right you'll see a blown-up photograph.'

Poe did. Flynn was right – it wasn't someone's initials; it was a hand-drawn symbol.

二

'Is there a cryptographer we can run it by?' he said.

'No need. It's the Japanese number two,' Flynn said. 'Tilly recognised it immediately – she knows how to code in Japanese.'

'Of course she does,' Poe said, winking at Bradshaw. 'Anything else?'

'Just like Kane Hunt, the poem was accompanied by a pressed flower.'

'Same type?'

'No,' she said. 'This one was from a plant called,' she checked her notebook, '*Houttuynia cordata*. Its common name is fish wort. It's native to South-east Asia.'

'Do we have a theory?'

'Tilly thinks he's planning to use the toxins in the fugu fish to poison Mr Cummings.'

'Obviously we don't want this to happen,' Chief Superintendent Stewart said.

'The fugu?' Poe said. 'The pufferfish the Japanese consider a delicacy?'

'That's right, Poe,' Bradshaw replied. 'I'm surprised you know about it.'

'It was on an episode of *The Simpsons*. Homer ate some. I watched it when I was in the army.'

Bradshaw rolled her eyes. 'Yes, well, tetrodotoxins found in the intestines, ovaries and liver of certain species of fugu fish can have a median lethal dose of up to 906 micrograms per kilogramme.'

'That's bad, is it?'

'A microgram is a *millionth* of a gram, Poe. Put it another way, poison from certain species of fugu fish is potentially twelve hundred times deadlier than cyanide. The amount needed to kill an adult male would be so small you wouldn't be able to see it unaided. And it works quickly, usually within fifteen minutes.'

'Something this poisonous must be highly regulated?' Poe said. 'I assume you can't just waltz into an Asian supermarket and buy a fugu?'

'The Japanese eat ten thousand tonnes a year, but it's banned in the UK and the EU,' Bradshaw confirmed. 'I've undertaken some quick research and it seems there's a private supper club in London that serves it.'

'So the poison would be tough, but not impossible, to get hold of. Could this be a copycat? You said the poem and the pressed flower were revealed on live television. Could we simply be dealing with a crank?'

'We *have* been dealing with cranks, Sergeant Poe,' Chief Superintendent Stewart said. 'Every police force has.'

'But we're here, anyway,' Flynn said. 'What does that tell you?'

'There's something else,' Poe said. 'Something that wasn't on television. Something that's been kept back from the media.'

'The envelope the poem and flower came in. We've been through the TV show frame by frame and at no point was the back of it shown.'

Flynn scrolled through some photographs on the tablet, stopped on the one she wanted, and handed it to Poe.

The photograph was a hand-drawn picture of a flower. It was in black ink and incredibly detailed.

'Tilly says it's a scientific illustration, the type you'd be taught to do at university.'

'I've compared it to a photograph of the genus of mandrake plant that killed Kane Hunt and it's accurate and to scale,' Bradshaw said. 'This is a highly skilled drawing, Poe.'

'And there was a drawing on the back of Harrison Cummings's envelope as well, I take it?'

'Of the fish wort plant,' Flynn confirmed.

'OK, I'm sold,' Poe said. 'I take it South Yorkshire have Harrison Cummings safe?'

'He was never here,' Chief Superintendent Stewart replied. 'He's a Londoner, parachuted into a safe Tory seat. Spends the least amount of time here he can. Officially leads the table in most cancelled constituent surgeries.'

'Where is he now?'

'London,' Flynn said. 'Parliamentary and Diplomatic Protection have him.'

'So he's safe?'

'He is.'

'We'd better get started then. We got somewhere to work?'

'Chief Superintendent Stewart has very kindly put a room aside at their operations complex. We'll go there now. See if we can come up with some lines of enquiry.'

'You lead, I'll follow.'

Her phone rang. Instead of answering him she gave a thumbs-up and wandered off.

'You'd better give me the postcode, sir,' he said. 'She could be a while. Tilly and I can make a start.'

Chief Superintendent Stewart told him what it was.

Poe keyed it in and the address appeared on the centre console. 'Is this a joke?' he asked.

'I'm afraid it isn't.'

'Letsby Avenue. As in "let's be 'aving you"?'

Stewart nodded, embarrassed.

'The town planner turned a blind eye to what the property developer had named it,' he said miserably. 'And by the time any of us realised, the damage was done. Retrospectively objecting would have made us appear curmudgeonly. Now I have to have this conversation every few weeks.'

Flynn walked over.

'You know about this, boss?' Poe said. 'South Yorkshire's operation complex is on Letsby . . . What's up?'

Her face was ashen.

'It's Harrison Cummings,' she said. 'He isn't safe. He's dead.'

Chapter 18

'This is a whole new thing now,' Poe said.

Chief Superintendent Stewart grunted.

Poe could tell he was relieved that Cummings had died under the protection of Parliamentary and Diplomatic Protection, rather than under the protection of South Yorkshire Constabulary. Poe didn't blame him. People would lose their jobs over this. Cummings was universally despised but, in these polarised times, being despised by the population was an occupational hazard for politicians. They would all be feeling a little less safe right now.

They were in a small incident room in South Yorkshire's Operations Complex. Bradshaw hadn't bothered setting it up as it wasn't clear if they'd be staying. There was a conference table, chairs, a flask of coffee, and a monitor on one of the walls.

Flynn opened the door and walked in.

'Anything, boss?' Poe said, getting up and filling her a mug.

'Toxicology will have the blood tests back soon, but that's just semantics,' she said. 'He was under twenty-four-hour protection and someone got in nonetheless. The A&E consultant admitted it could have been a neurotoxin that killed him.'

'So it *was* fugu poison?'

'Looks that way.'

'What happened?'

'We don't know much,' Flynn said. 'Only that he'd thrown a tantrum when he wasn't allowed to go to his club for lunch. Decided to have a bath instead. After an hour's silence one of Protection Command thought he'd better check on him. Found him dead.'

'Who else was in his house—'

'The walk-through video's just arrived,' Bradshaw cut in. 'I'm sending it to the big monitor.'

The screen on the wall flickered into life. The crime scene manager introduced himself then walked and talked his way through Cummings's flat. He started at the front door then methodically went through every room. He described what he was seeing in a clear, measured voice but offered no opinions. It wasn't his job – a video walk-through was about facts.

The flat was large and lavish, the furniture over the top and ostentatious. Oil paintings hung from the wall and intricately weaved rugs covered the floor. No one needed to ask what Cummings had been spending his money on. This was a man who had liked the finer things in life.

The crime scene manager eventually made his way into the bathroom. It was wall-to-wall marble and enormous. There was a toilet, a bidet and an overhead rainfall showerhead with six body-massaging jets. The bath was deep and sunken with ornate gold taps.

The crime scene manager focused on the corpse of Harrison Cummings. He was on his back in the cold water, his pubic hair floating like a patch of seaweed. Dry vomit covered his chin and upper torso. It stopped at the waterline. His face was in rictus – he had died in agony.

The bathwater had a brownish tinge.

'The accompanying report says that the faeces in the water doesn't appear to be the usual post-mortem relaxation of the sphincter muscle,' Bradshaw said. 'Mr Cummings lost control of his bowels while he was alive.'

'Whatever it was, it came on quick then,' Poe said. 'He didn't even have time to get to the toilet before he spewed and had diarrhoea. Does that fit with what we know of fugu poison?'

'If it was a massive dose I'd say it's exactly what I'd expect,' Bradshaw replied. 'There'd be paralysis and extreme abdominal pain. Even if he'd been able to cry out for help – which I doubt – he'd have been dead before the paramedics arrived.'

'Poor sod.' Poe's eyes remained fixed to the monitor. The video moved away from the corpse. 'What's that?'

Bradshaw pressed pause. 'It's an empty wine glass, Poe,' she said.

'And there's the bottle,' he agreed. 'Are you thinking what I'm thinking?'

'I think we are. Because hot baths open blood vessels and increase body temperature, and because alcohol does the same, combining the two doubles the risk of heat exhaustion, strokes, even heart attacks. Only an idiot would drink wine in the bath.'

'Yes, that. And also because fugu poison works so quickly, the poison could have been in the wine.'

'I'll make sure it's seized,' Flynn said, getting out her phone.

'Done,' Flynn said. 'They've secured the wine, the glass and everything else in the bathroom. Samples are on their way to the lab. Protection Command have handed the investigation over to the Met and they're waiting for us in Cummings's flat.'

Poe's own phone rang. It was a withheld number. He pressed the green icon and said, 'Poe.' He listened for a few seconds then said, 'I'm on my way.'

'What is it, Poe?' Bradshaw said.

'It's Estelle – they've charged her with murder.'

'Go on then,' Flynn said. 'Catch up with us later.'

Chapter 19

Poe was soon touching ninety on the A1. His mind was a jumble, the two cases bleeding into each other.

'Cases,' he muttered. 'I wonder . . .'

He called Flynn through the car's Bluetooth connection.

'Poe, what's up? You can't be there already?'

'I've been thinking, boss. You've seen the inside of Cummings's flat, the type of things he likes. What was your impression of him?'

'Awful. Textbook case of money not buying class. Everything was expensive, but there was no sense of personal taste, no theme. It was as if he were collecting things just because he had the money.'

'I agree. He was a status-symbol magpie.'

'What are you thinking?'

'I'm thinking people so far up their own arses don't go to Oddbins to buy their wine. I doubt he even went to Waitrose. Cummings will have been a collector, which means he was either part of some swanky wine club or—'

'Or he had a wine merchant,' Flynn finished for him.

'Exactly. It's probably nothing, but it might be worth bringing them in. Someone might have slipped a snide bottle into his delivery.'

'Or it could have been sent as a gift?'

Poe considered this. 'Possible,' he said. 'As long as he believed it came from someone he knew. People like Cummings don't drink from bottles they've been gifted by strangers in case it's piss.'

'A gift from someone he knew, or the wine merchant then.'

Poe was silent a moment.

'It's a line of enquiry,' he said. 'May not come to anything, but at least we're ruling things out.'

***

DCI Tai-young Lee had called Poe as soon as the custody ser-geant had charged Doyle with her father's murder. She told him she believed they'd passed the threshold test, the evidential stand-ard that must be met before the case can be referred to the Crown Prosecution Service for a charging decision. The CPS had reviewed the evidence for less than thirty minutes before authorising a murder charge.

'Face it, Poe,' Lee had said, 'we have more than enough.'

'You don't have a murder weapon,' Poe had replied.

'She *has* hidden it well, but she didn't leave the house so it's either in there somewhere or within throwing distance of a window. I have dogs there now. It's just a matter of time.'

'I want to see her.'

'Fine,' she had sighed.

Tai-young Lee met Poe at the front desk and took him straight through to the custody suite. She told him he could see Estelle in her cell. He got the impression that now she'd been charged, Lee wasn't bothered about secret conversations. Poe was the CPS's problem now.

'I'll get you both a brew,' she said. 'Her cell's unlocked.'

Poe knocked on the cell door then opened the Judas hatch, the vision panel that allowed custody officers to check they weren't walking into an ambush. Doyle was lying on the thin mattress, her back to the door. Given what was happening, he doubted she was asleep. He opened the door and stepped inside.

'Estelle?'

Doyle turned. Her eyes were red raw and sunken. 'Poe,' she said, her voice cracking. 'You didn't have to . . . you shouldn't be . . .'

'What? I shouldn't be here supporting my friend? I hope that's not what you were going to say, Estelle.' He perched on the mat-tress and she sat up to make room. 'Nice place you have,' he said. 'Minimalist.'

She forced a smile. 'I'm a simple gal.'

'What do you know?'

'Only what you and my solicitor told me,' she replied. 'You said not to say anything and she said the same.'

'And you haven't?'

She shook her head. A teardrop fell free and landed on Poe's arm. He touched it. The moment felt intimate.

'Have you seen the evidence?' he asked.

'I have.'

'And your solicitor?'

'They've disclosed everything, I'm told.'

'What does she think?'

'The lack of a murder weapon isn't enough for a not-guilty verdict.'

'I agree,' Poe said. 'I'll need you to call her and get me assigned as a criminal defence investigator. Tell her I'll do it for free.'

'Don't you have other cases?'

'Nothing this important.'

Tai-young Lee knocked, then opened the door. She handed them cups of tea.

'Thank you, ma'am.'

'I'll leave you to it, Poe,' she said. 'Take as long as you need. Nothing's happening until tomorrow.'

Poe waited until the door had shut before saying, 'Has tomorrow been explained to you?'

'It has,' Doyle said. 'I'm not sure it's actually sunk in though.'

'You'll be transported to Newcastle Magistrates' Court in a prison van. You'll stay in the court cells and you'll see your solicitor. When your case is called you'll be handcuffed to a dull-eyed security guard and taken upstairs. You'll be presented to the court behind security glass. This will be public and there'll be press there.'

'They know already?'

'Not unless it's been leaked,' Poe said. 'But the press are always at court.'

He didn't add that the deaths of Kane Hunt and Harrison Cummings would be dominating the news this week. She'd caught a small break, but there was no point saying this. The press would make time for her eventually.

'The CPS solicitor will read out the charges and you'll be asked to confirm your name and address,' he continued. 'You don't have to answer but there's no reason not to.'

'And then do I plead not guilty?'

'No. Magistrates can't hear murder cases so they'll commit it to Crown Court. It's there you'll enter your plea.'

'Will I come back here afterwards?'

'No. You'll be remanded in custody and that means you'll go to HMP Low Newton. It's a women's prison near Durham.'

'How long will I be there for?'

'Until I convince a judge to bail you. And I'm starting on that right now.'

'Starting what?'

Poe fixed his eyes on hers. 'Pulling their case to bits,' he said.

Chapter 20

With a meeting arranged with Doyle's family solicitor for the following day, Poe decided to go home. He collected Edgar, his springer spaniel, from his neighbour, Victoria, and bought a fish supper from the Shap Chippy. He pulled up at the Shap Wells Hotel and Spa, where he had a longstanding arrangement to use their car park. Herdwick Croft was two miles from the nearest road and could only be accessed on foot or by the quad bike he kept at the hotel. Poe usually walked – it gave him space to think and Edgar got a decent run – but it would be pitch black soon and Shap Fell had teeth.

Poe hadn't been home for a week and when he crested the last hill and saw his dilapidated shepherd's croft, like a massage for the mind, tension he'd been unaware of eased slightly.

Herdwick Croft stuck to Shap Fell like a particularly stubborn wart. It was two hundred years old, but looked as though it had been there forever. The walls had been constructed from pink granite, formed 400 million years ago before being cut from the nearby quarry and sent all over the world. Shap pink granite could be seen in some of Britain's grandest buildings – from Saint Mary's Cathedral in Edinburgh to Saint Paul's in London. The granite at Herdwick Croft had been exposed to the elements for so long the pink crystals were no longer visible. A crust of lime-green lichen, thicker than a coat of paint, had flourished and spread and his home was now the same colour as Shap Fell. It was as much a part of the landscape as the trees and the sheep. It had faced down the Beast from the East, the Pest from the West, and a thousand other storms with little more than a shrug and a 'Is that the best you can do?' attitude. In all the time Poe had lived there, not even a slate tile had come loose.

It wasn't so much Poe's happy place as his refuge. The place where he felt safe. Bradshaw had once described Herdwick Croft as his Fortress of Solitude and he'd made the mistake of asking what that meant. He had then been forced to sit through a tedious film where a man wearing a blue onesie and red underpants made time go backwards by flying around the Earth really fast. Bradshaw had explained the pseudoscience behind it – something to do with him flying faster than the speed of light – but then spent an hour debunking it. She'd said that the only way time could go backwards was if there was a break in the spacetime fabric, and that would take infinite force, something that couldn't exist in a finite universe. Poe had asked her what the hell she was yabbering on about.

By the time he had lit his wood-burning stove and fired up his generator, his chips were at that perfect temperature. Not too hot, not too cold. Warm and mushy, dowsed with sharp vinegar and liberally covered with sea salt, they were as comforting as comfort food got.

Edgar stared at him, a thin thread of drool hanging from his bottom lip. He gently whined.

'Stare as much as you want, mate – you're not getting any,' Poe said, his mouth full of battered cod, passing him a chunk of fish even as he said it.

The spaniel threw back his head, wolfed it down like a gannet and went straight back to begging.

'Greedy bastard.'

After he'd finished eating, Poe fixed himself a mug of strong tea and sat beside his now sleeping spaniel.

'What's going on, Edgar?' he said. 'How can someone kill Estelle's dad then disappear without leaving a mark in the snow?' The spaniel snored. 'And how did she end up with gunshot residue on her hands but not her sleeves?'

Poe opened a fresh notebook and jotted down what he thought would be the CPS's lines of attack. He rated the strength of each out of five.

1. Firearms discharge residue on her hands. 4/5
2. A window was broken from the inside, not the outside. Appears to be staged. 3/5
3. Her journey home took 30–40 minutes longer than it should have. 1/5
4. Motivation: Estelle's just been written back into her father's will. Slim but juries like to know 'why' something happened. 3/5
5. Unblemished snow proved no one else was in the house when Elcid Doyle was killed. 5/5

When he'd finished he flipped the page and started a new list, rating possible counter defences. He would show it to Estelle's solicitor tomorrow.

1. FDR tests give false positives (Tilly to help). Should be a stronger defence but juries like forensic evidence. They trust it. 2/5
2. Elcid Doyle has clearly been murdered and if Estelle didn't do it, someone else did. Said person also staged the burglary. Getting the jury to go along with the 'someone else did it' defence will be difficult. Check Estelle's barrister is already rehearsing it. 3/5
3. Estelle's journey taking longer. Irrelevant. Any half-decent barrister will explain this away. I can come up with ten reasons and I'm tired and full of chips. 4/5
4. The rebuttal of the CPS's claim there

was motivation will have to wait until I've spoken to the solicitor. Will give it a provisional score of 3/5, the same as the CPS's.

5. *The snow is the load-bearing evidence in this case. They'll play DCI Tai-young Lee's video evidence and show the snow around house was pristine and footprint free. Unless we can explain this, the 'someone else did it' defence can't be used. 0/5*

When Poe had finished, he totted up the scores. The CPS led by five points and Poe thought he was being harsh on them. He reckoned they were in a far stronger position than that. He sighed and reached for his phone. It was late, but he knew Flynn would still be awake.

'Got two minutes, boss?'

'Of course,' she said.

He laid out the CPS's case and how Doyle's barrister might be able to respond.

'You've got nothing,' Flynn said when he'd finished. 'Worse than nothing, actually.'

'Worse than nothing? I don't understand. We both know FDR is shit evidence and I can throw enough confusion at their timeline to make them drop it. And motivation always comes down to which side has the best barrister.'

'You're not getting it, Poe. Even if you do your thing and scrape through a not guilty, anyone who counts will think Estelle got away with murder. How do you think she'll cope with that?'

'Not well,' he admitted.

She took a moment then said, 'And despite the overwhelming evidence, you're convinced she didn't kill her father?'

'I am.'

'Why?'

'Because she asked for me.'

'Not good enough, Poe,' Flynn said. 'You two have a lot of time in the bank. She'll have known you'd drop everything and come running. She could simply be allaying your suspicions by asking you to do what she knew you would do anyway.'

He hadn't considered that. Then he felt bad he'd doubted Doyle, even for a second.

'She didn't do it,' he said. 'She made no attempt to explain anything away and she's far too intelligent to leave as much evidence as she allegedly did. She's being set up by someone who doesn't understand that sometimes less is more.'

'OK,' Flynn sighed. 'If it helps, I don't think she did it either. But you say she's been crudely set up, I say she's been *effectively* set up. The evidence against her isn't open to interpretation. A first-year CPS barrister could take the jury on a logical journey that ends with Estelle Doyle shooting her father.'

'I have my work cut out,' Poe agreed. 'What's happening in London?'

'We're waiting for confirmation the neurotoxin was in the wine. CSI have almost finished with Cummings's flat so we'll be allowed in tomorrow afternoon. I'll need you back by then.'

'I need to stay here.'

'We're not having this discussion, Poe. Right now there's nothing you can do. Speak to the solicitor tomorrow then get down here.'

Poe said nothing.

'Look, I'm not stupid,' Flynn said. 'I know you're going to work this, but I need you doing your job as well. If you manage your time, there's absolutely no reason why you can't do both.'

'Can I borrow Tilly?'

'Sorry, Poe, I can't take resources away from a legitimate investigation to help in a personal matter. I just can't. People could die.'

He sighed. She was right, of course.

'But . . . you know as well as I do,' Flynn continued, 'I can't tell Tilly what to do in her spare time.'

'And if you tried she'd ignore you.'

'I swear you two are why I keep finding grey pubes.'

The line went dead.

Chapter 21

Estelle Doyle's solicitor worked out of an office on Grey Street in Newcastle. It was an elegant part of the city, with tall sandstone buildings topped with domes, turrets and spikes. It had bars and restaurants, even a theatre, and was considered one of England's finest streets. The ground floors catered to high-end shoppers and the night-time economy, while the upper floors housed professionals such as solicitors, accountants, architects and chartered surveyors.

Poe located a parking space and, not knowing how long he would be, fed a load of pound coins into the meter. He found the building number he'd been given. A discreet brass plaque said floors two to four were the offices of Howey, Sellars & Watson.

The receptionist asked him to wait but he had barely sat down when his name was called. A woman in a dark business suit approached him and held out her hand.

'I'm Ania Kierczynska,' she said. She was tall, dark-haired and had a no-nonsense look. 'I'm a junior partner here. Mr Howey has asked me to see you this morning.'

'No offence, why can't I see him?'

She smiled, as if she'd expected the question. 'Sergeant Poe, Mr Howey is in his eighties – just how involved do you think he is in the day-to-day running of his accounts?'

'Not much?' he ventured.

'I run everything past him, of course, but in all but name *I'm* the Doyle family's solicitor.'

'I owe you an apology then,' Poe said. 'Can we start again?'
'Of course.'

'Good morning, Ania. My name's Washington Poe and I'm a detective with the National Crime Agency.'

'I know. Shall we go to my office?'

Poe followed her up two flights of stairs before being ushered into a grand, but cold, room. He reckoned this type of building was rarely warm, but the prestigious address made up for the lack of modern heating. Ania took a seat at the small conference table and invited him to do the same. Without asking, she poured two cups of coffee, putting milk in one.

'I'm told you take it black?'

Poe nodded. 'What else have you been told?' he asked.

'That I am to give you full access to the evidential disclosures the police and CPS have sent,' she said. 'That I should officially hire you as an investigator. And then I should get out of your way.'

'Estelle can be very direct sometimes.'

'Her instructions were very clear,' Ania agreed.

'And will you?'

Instead of answering she opened a file. Poe's face was on the top page.

'You've done your due diligence then?' he said.

'Of course.'

'And?'

'All available information suggests you are dangerous, Sergeant Poe. That we would be foolish to have anything to do with you. You're anti-authoritarian and you have a discipline problem. In short, you can't be controlled.'

'You found out all that in one night?'

'We have our sources. Putting this dossier together was not difficult. It seems people are happy to talk about you.'

'Not sure how I feel about that.'

Ania responded by blowing on her coffee. She took a sip then eyed him over the rim of the cup.

'I'm not getting access, am I?' Poe said.

'Elcid Doyle has used this firm all his life, and his father before him. I have only met Estelle once but that was enough.'

'Enough for what?'

'To know that she was cut from the same block. That she's a good person.'

'She's more than that,' Poe said. 'She's my friend. And trust me when I say this, I don't have many.'

'Yet this firm is now tasked with explaining the seemingly unexplainable. The senior partners met last night to discuss how this matter should be handled.'

'Let me guess, you don't want me interfering? You can't have someone "dangerous" damaging your reputation.'

She put her coffee down with a thump. 'You misunderstand me, Sergeant Poe,' she said. 'Dangerous is the only thing that can save Miss Doyle right now. Tell me what you need.'

Chapter 22

'Tell me about this will,' Poe said.

'Why?'

'The police think it's motivation.'

'Really?'

'Heard it straight from the senior investigating officer's mouth.'

'They've got it wrong,' Ania said. 'Elcid *had* updated his will recently, and it *was* in Estelle's favour.'

'I sense a "but" coming.'

'It's only in her favour if you consider it in the binary. If I were forced to answer yes or no, I would say yes, the new will *is* better for Estelle.'

'But if you were allowed to give a fuller answer?'

'I would say the new will only increases Miss Doyle's inheritance by around five per cent.'

'I thought she'd been left a house?'

'A farm, actually. But yes, she had.'

'I'm not following,' Poe said.

'What do you know about inheritance tax, Sergeant Poe?'

'Not much.'

'Elcid Doyle did,' she said. 'And with the help of our firm he made arrangements to ensure that, within the law, he reduced Estelle's tax burden when he died.'

'By gifting her a farm?'

'No. This was the late addition. It had been a farm tenancy and Elcid's previous will had left it to the long-term tenant – a family who had lived there for three generations.'

'What happened?'

'The farmer died without having anyone to leave the tenancy to.

Elcid added the farm to what Estelle would inherit.'

'But he'd made arrangements prior to that?'

'Very shrewd arrangements,' Ania said. 'Were you aware you can avoid paying inheritance tax on a property if you give it to someone at least seven years before your death?'

'Vaguely,' Poe said.

'There's more to it than that, obviously. If you want to stay in the property, you have to pay rent and bills and tick a few other boxes, but Elcid complied fully with the law when he passed on the family home – we made sure of it.'

'And how much is it worth?'

'I can't discuss my client's financial circumstances, but I can say it's worth considerably more than the farm. Add in ten years of rent, which had been held in trust for Miss Doyle, and the addition of the farm in the new will accounts for—'

'Five per cent of her inheritance.'

'Exactly.'

'Do the CPS know this?'

'We haven't told them.'

'Why not?'

'Case strategy,' Ania explained. 'If we tell them, they won't use it. This way, when they bring it up we can quickly discredit it. Makes the prosecution look unsafe right from the start.'

'Clever,' Poe admitted.

'Motivation is case tinsel,' she shrugged. 'It's not where this will be won or lost.'

Poe knew she was referring to the snow.

'I assume you'll be presenting an alternative explanation?' he said. 'That an unknown intruder killed Elcid Doyle and framed Estelle?'

She nodded. 'That will form the basis of the defence statement we are required to submit,' she said. 'We still need plausible explanations for the gunshot residue, the delay in calling 999 and the fact there were only her footprints in the snow.'

'If this gets as far as court, we lose,' Poe said.

'Agreed. And even if we win, we lose.'

Poe allowed himself a wry smile. Flynn had said the very same thing last night. The damage to Doyle's reputation would be irreparable.

'We need to get the case discontinued,' he said. 'Make sure it never sees the inside of a courtroom.'

'How?' Ania said.

'By blowing down their house of cards.'

His phone rang. It was Flynn.

'Excuse me,' he said to Ania. 'Boss?'

'We need you in London, Poe.'

'What's up?'

'It wasn't the wine.'

'I'm on my way,' he said.

Chapter 23

'It *has* to be the wine,' Poe said. 'Tilly says the fugu neurotoxin works within fifteen minutes and Cummings was in the bath longer than that.'

'It's been triple-checked,' Flynn replied. 'It isn't.'

They were in a heated mobile command and control centre. It was parked at the end of Cummings's street. The rat-tat-tat of rain on the roof was giving Poe a headache, but at least they were dry. He had asked why they weren't allowed in the building and Detective Chief Superintendent Alice Mathers, the senior investigating officer, had told him the residents were already complaining about the police presence in their area. Poe got the impression this was a street with connections. He didn't blame her for moving. Some battles weren't worth winning, never mind fighting.

'Everything else in the bathroom has been checked?' Poe asked, sipping tea from a mug stamped with a Metropolitan Police Service logo.

Flynn nodded.

'Even the soap?'

'Custom made and very expensive, but there was nothing wrong with it. All of his toiletries were checked.'

'His razor? Maybe he nicked himself, put it into his bloodstream that way.'

'That seems unlikely, Poe. This guy warned Cummings he was going to be poisoned – I doubt he was relying on a shaving cut.'

Poe sighed. 'Yeah, I know.'

'But we checked it anyway,' Flynn said.

'And?'

'Clean. Everything in the bathroom was clean. Everything in

the *flat* was clean. I'll get you a copy of the inventory but you won't find anything.'

Poe considered what that meant. Decided only an unpalatable truth remained. 'Someone on his residential security detail slipped him a Mickey then,' he said. 'It's the only thing left.'

'I thought that would be the conclusion you came to.'

'Because it's where you ended up as well?'

Flynn nodded.

'How were they selected for this job?' Poe said. 'Were any of them volunteers?'

'We don't think so. It seems they were assigned.'

'By?'

'By someone we're checking out,' Flynn said. 'I've asked Tilly to draw up profiles on anyone who had prior contact in any capacity with Harrison Cummings.'

'Where is she?'

'Where she always is – trying to find a wi-fi signal.'

'Anything come out of the PM?'

'The only thing in his stomach was the wine, and the toxicology report confirmed it was tetrodotoxin found in the livers of fugu pufferfish that killed him.'

'Have we had sight of Kane Hunt's PM report yet?'

'We have,' Flynn said. 'Same shit. Other than the hyoscine there was nothing of note in his system. Not even sildenafil.'

'Which is?'

'Viagra. Hunt had suffered from erectile dysfunction since his twenties. Morgan Soames hit him with it during her interview.'

'No wonder he hated women.'

'What are we going to do if it isn't someone on the security detail?' Flynn said. 'How do you catch someone who can walk through walls?'

'Why would we try to catch him? I'm slipping him some names.'

'This is exactly the type of thing I don't want to hear!' a voice snapped from behind them.

Poe turned. A stocky woman stood in the trailer's doorway. She was wearing a cheap suit and no makeup. The laminated badge hanging from her lanyard said she had access Level B, whatever that meant. She glared at him.

'My name is Catherine Wilson and I'm a special adviser with the Department of International Trade.'

'Ah,' Poe said. 'You're a SPAD.'

'Excuse me?'

'Isn't that what special advisers get called?'

'Only if someone's trying to be rude.'

'How can we help you, SPAD Wilson?' Poe said.

'That's enough, Poe,' Flynn cut in. 'I'm DI Flynn and this is Sergeant Poe, ma'am. We're with the Serious Crime Analysis Section. What can we do for you?'

'You can start by telling me how a member of Her Majesty's Government was murdered, despite being forewarned and surrounded by supposedly competent guards.'

'I'm working on it,' Poe said.

'Seems to me you're just drinking tea and making wisecracks.'

'I'm a slow starter.'

'Has his Westminster office been searched?' Flynn asked, shooting Poe a warning look.

'It has,' Wilson replied, deliberately turning her back on Poe. 'A bottle of whisky, a couple of pornographic magazines and a mobile-phone charger. Everything else was official, not personal.'

'Can you make sure nobody touches it until the police collect it?'

'Already done. His office has been sealed. Tell me what you have so far.'

Flynn did. It wasn't a long briefing.

'I thought SCAS were supposed to be the experts?'

'We investigate the murders others can't,' Flynn replied. 'You say we're nowhere, I say we've already identified a number of ways it *wasn't* done. Whether you like it or not, that's progress. To catch someone this secretive, this cautious, is going to take time. It might take weeks, months even—'

The door burst open. Bradshaw marched into the command trailer. 'DI Flynn, you won't believe what the Mole People have just . . . Oh, hi, Poe. I didn't know you were back. How is Estelle

85

Doyle? What is the food like in a police station? Was there a vegan opt—'

'Tilly,' Flynn said. 'Focus.'

'What? Oh yes. I think we've found someone.'

Chapter 24

'Who the hell is Brian Price?' Flynn said.

Wilson the SPAD unlocked her iPad and opened a file. She flipped the screen so they could see it. It was a vetting document.

'Detective Constable Brian Price,' she said. 'Been with Protection Command for ten years, attached to Parliamentary and Diplomatic Protection for the last three. Accredited and authorised to carry a firearm operationally. He was with the Met before he moved across. Has Developed Vetting clearance, pretty much the highest you can have as a police officer. As with any job like this, the team was asked to disclose any conflicts of interest before selection was confirmed.'

Flynn opened her file and checked something. 'The rota says Brian Price wasn't on duty when Cummings died,' she said. 'Wasn't due for three hours, and as they were on twelve/twelve shifts, he'd not been around for nine.'

'We need to speak to the shift commander,' Poe said. 'See if there were staffing changes not recorded on the rota.'

Flynn nodded and started thumbing a text to someone. Poe heard the 'whoosh' as it was sent.

'What did the Mole People find, Tilly?' Poe said. 'What did vetting miss?'

'The vetting didn't miss anything, Poe,' Bradshaw said. 'But that's because they only checked connections to Harrison Cummings. *We* checked for connections to Kane Hunt as well.'

Poe looked pointedly at Wilson.

'Oh, for God's sake, man,' she grumbled. 'His protection detail was put together in two days. You can't possibly expect us to have thought of everything.'

'Why not?' Poe said. 'Tilly did, and she's had far less time on this than you.'

'You are an insufferable man, Sergeant Poe! As soon as this is over I'll be having words—'

'They made a mistake, Poe,' Flynn said, clipping Wilson mid-sentence. 'Let's not make it worse. What's Brian Price's connection to Kane Hunt, Tilly?'

'Natasha Price, his daughter,' she said. 'She was being abused online by one of Hunt's so-called bodyguards after she refused to speak to him on a dating site. I have screenshot printouts of their interaction.'

She handed them all copies. Poe read his.

> Ashley3782:   Hi, I'm Ash, a gentleman looking for long-term friendship, possibly romance. Would you like to talk?
>
> Natasha: No thank you, Ash.
>
> Ashley3782:   Fuck you then! What you even doing on this site, you frigid bitch.

'He seems nice,' Poe said. 'I wonder why he's single.'

'Ashley McCall kept up the abusive messages for three weeks,' Bradshaw explained.

'Threats?'

'Insults mainly, but lots of them. Eventually she reported him to the administrator and he was banned from the site.'

'It didn't end there, I take it?'

Bradshaw shook her head.

'The site wasn't using a symmetric 128-bit block data encryption technique—'

'Which is?' Wilson cut in.

'I find it best not to ask questions like that,' Poe said. 'Tell us what happened, Tilly.'

'The site's lax security meant that before he was banned, he was able to identify her on other platforms. He began abusing her. It turns out they are both from Wigan. That's a town in the north-west of England, Poe.'

'I know where Wigan is, Tilly.'

'When she discovered he lived nearby she reported him to the police.'

'That was when her dad found out?'

'Yes, Poe.'

'Did he breach any data protection laws checking on him?'

'He didn't, Poe.'

'So what *did* he do?'

'Nothing that we can see.'

'What are the odds against someone on Harrison Cummings's security detail also having a personal connection to Kane Hunt?'

'High, Poe.'

'How high?'

'Enough for it to be a remarkable coincidence.'

Poe looked at Flynn. 'Boss?'

Flynn paused but not for long. 'I'll have him picked up,' she said.

She went off to make her phone call, returning two minutes later.

'Price didn't report for his shift and his phone is switched off,' she said. 'A sergeant from the Territorial Support Group is on his way. They've been tasked with finding him.'

Poe grunted. TSG, the unit that replaced the controversial Special Patrol Group, got all the unpleasant jobs. They were good, though. Tough men and even tougher women. Had to be: their primary role was responding to public disorder, from bar fights to fully fledged riots.

After Flynn had briefed the sergeant from TSG, she returned to the command trailer. She was carrying two cups of coffee and a doughnut. She handed Poe a cup then took a bite from the doughnut. Raspberry jam squirted out the side and on to the back of her hand. She licked it off.

She saw him watching. 'Get your bloody own,' she said.

SPAD Wilson entered the trailer. 'Thank you,' she said.

89

'We haven't caught him yet,' Poe said.

'But you will. There are over thirty thousand police officers in the Met and they're all looking for Brian Price. It's only a matter of time.'

'It's what we do,' Flynn said.

'I'll be going back to work now but here's my card if you need to get in touch.' She handed Flynn a gold-trimmed business card then left.

'I thought this case was going to get all funky, Poe,' Flynn said. 'Finishing it quickly makes a nice change for once.'

Poe sipped his coffee and said nothing.

Chapter 25

Bradshaw left to oversee the forensic examination of Price's computers. Poe didn't expect her to find a step-by-step blueprint of how he had done it, but Price was a cop, not a scientist. He would have had to research something.

'What do you want to do now?' Flynn said.

'Have a poke around Cummings's flat, I suppose.'

'The search team were pretty thorough. What we looking for?'

'Whatever it is they missed.'

'Where do you want to start?'

'The bathroom.'

Flynn snapped on a pair of rubber gloves.

'Let's get started then,' she said.

The crime scene manager's video hadn't done Cummings's bathroom justice. It was even more ostentatious than Poe had thought, a mish-mash of clashing styles and ideas. Like some Roman and Greek and Spanish designers had put glue on the walls then kept spewing taps, spigots and mirrors until enough of them had stuck.

Poe checked the medicine cabinet first. It was empty. CSI had taken everything. The shelf under the vanity mirror was empty too.

'You got a list of what was in the cabinet?'

Flynn read from her phone. 'Spare toothpaste. Floss. Spare soap. Spare shampoo. Aspirin and antacids. Some fungal cream. Box of pills. Few other odds and sods. Usual shit.'

'What pills?'

'Statins,' Flynn said. 'The family had a history of cardiovascular disease.'

'They've been checked?'

'They have. Clean. As soon as he received the death threat he chucked the ones he had and sent one of his security detail out with a new prescription.'

'Wasn't Price who collected the prescription, was it?'

'Nope. Someone else.'

'What about the candles? Maybe there was something in the wax or on the wick . . . Candle burns down and poof – dead Member of Parliament.'

'Tilly says that's impossible, but CSI took them all.'

'Just leaves this monstrosity then.'

The sunken bath was bigger than Poe's bathroom but was surrounded by so many vases, candles and tat it looked cramped. It dominated the room and was clearly more than just something to sink into at the end of a long day.

'The water he died in has been collected and tested?'

'Along with the shampoo and that ridiculously expensive soap,' Flynn replied. 'Even his dressing gown and towels were taken away.'

Poe, who had never paid more than fifty pence for a bar of soap in his life, said, 'How much is "ridiculously expensive"?'

'At least a hundred quid.'

'Just when I thought I couldn't dislike him more.'

'Hideous, isn't it?' Flynn said. 'The best you can say about him is he didn't deny himself anything. He was an out and out hedonist.'

'Can I get in?'

'In what? The bath?'

'Yeah.'

'But you're not even dirty.'

'Ha ha,' Poe said.

'Seriously, why?'

'Because if the poison wasn't in the soap, the shampoo, the water or the wine, and if it's as fast acting as Tilly says, then something sharp might have been put in the bath. Something he could nick himself on.'

'Pathologist didn't find anything on the body.'

'The pathologist wasn't Estelle Doyle,' Poe said. 'He could have missed something. The wound could have been little more than a scratch and the bathwater would have washed away the blood.'

'And I suppose Price could have set it up when he was on shift, knowing he'd be miles away by the time Cummings actually took his bath.'

'Exactly.'

'Get in then,' Flynn said. 'But, Poe?'

'What?'

'Keep your clothes on, eh?'

Chapter 26

'What do you think?' Flynn asked.

Poe was lying in the bath in the same position Harrison Cummings had been discovered. Head leaning on the rim, feet underneath the gold-plated lever taps.

'Dunno yet,' he replied. 'Just trying to get a feel for what he might have done while he was in here. He took a bottle of wine in with him so he obviously planned on staying a while. What else do you do when you're in the bath?'

'Read. Listen to music.'

'Anything else?'

'You're not having a wank, if that's what you're thinking. Not while I'm standing here.'

Poe didn't answer.

'What is it?' Flynn said.

'He had a bottle of wine with him.'

'You've just said that.'

'No, you don't underst . . . Look, I don't drink wine, but how long to finish say . . . two glasses?'

She shrugged. 'Wine this expensive is to be savoured,' she said. 'Not glugged down like a three-quid carton of gut-rotter.'

'How long?'

'Maybe quarter of an hour a glass.'

'So he was in here at least half an hour.'

'Probably longer, Poe, but we have no way of knowing when he got in. As soon as his detail confirmed the flat was empty, they stayed outside and left him alone.'

'I'm not bothered about that,' he said. 'It's the fact he was in the bath for a while that's interesting.'

'Why?'

'What happens when you stay in the bath for longer than twenty minutes?'

'You go wrinkly.'

'And what happens to the water?'

'The bubbles go flat.'

'And?'

'It gets cold?'

'Does it though? How many times have you sat in a cold bath? The water *cools*, but it doesn't get cold. And it doesn't get cold because we top it up with hot water.'

'Agreed,' Flynn said. 'Unless you've emptied the hot water tank.'

'And how do you warm up the bath?'

'By adding more hot water, obviously.'

'Show me. Carefully.'

Flynn frowned but leaned forwards and reached for the hot water tap.

'Stop,' Poe said. 'You're already in the bath, remember.'

Understanding dawned on her face. 'I'd lift the tap with my foot,' she said.

'Exactly. He'd have put his foot underneath the tap and pushed up. It's why most baths have lever taps, rather than spigots.'

He sat up.

'Careful, Poe,' Flynn said.

Poe got to his knees and gingerly felt under the hot water tap lever. Ran his finger up and down, feeling for something sharp or irregular. Anything that could have snagged the skin.

His index finger touched something.

He twisted round and lay on his back, head underneath the taps. He couldn't see anything but he'd definitely felt it. Something small but sharp. Probably a bit of swarf, a metal shaving that had survived the fitting process. As sharp as a razor and virtually impossible to see. But, if you knew it was there and you knew Cummings took long baths, you'd know he would keep topping up with hot water. And that he would lift up the tap with the top of his foot. The bit between the toes and the ankle. Where the skin was very thin. If you knew the swarf was there you could set a trap.

'We need CSI and we need a plumber,' he said.

'We'll get it checked . . .' Flynn cocked her head. 'What the hell's going on outside?'

'You can't go in there,' someone said.

'My name is Matilda Bradshaw and I jolly well am going in there, thank you very much. I have important information for Detective Inspector Stephanie Flynn and Detective Sergeant Washington Poe.'

'Whatever,' the same person said.

'Let her in,' Flynn called out.

A few seconds later Bradshaw stepped into the bathroom.

'You'll never guess what's just happened, DI Flynn,' she said. 'Someone has just . . . Whatever are you doing, Poe? I thought you preferred showers?'

'I'm not having a bath, you berk. I've got my bloody clothes on and the boss is standing right next to me.'

'Well, what—'

'What's happened, Tilly?' Flynn said.

'The poisoner,' she said. 'He's just been on the phone.'

Chapter 27

Detective Chief Superintendent Mathers drove them to the nearest police station that had a cyber and digital crime unit. A man in jeans and an Iron Maiden T-shirt was waiting for them.

'The call came in to the hotline an hour and a half ago,' Mathers said. 'In total, the conversation lasted just under eleven minutes. After our cop suspected the caller knew details we'd been keeping back from the press, he let his sergeant know. A copy of the call was sent to tech support for analysis. We now have different versions of it.'

'It's Price?' Poe said.

'I don't know the man but someone's coming in who does. He'll be here soon.'

'Can we hear the original version first?' Flynn said.

The man in the Iron Maiden T-shirt pressed a button and the killer's voice filled the room . . .

'Is this the hotline for the man who killed that politician?'

'You're through to PC Matt Griffiths, how can I help you today, sir?'

'I believe I might be the man you're looking for.'

'And what makes you say that, sir?'

'Because I killed Kane Hunt with hyoscine from the mandrake plant and Harrison Cummings with tetrodotoxin extracted from the fugu fish. I sent them both a poem and a pressed flower.'

'All this was widely reported, sir, and I'm obliged to warn you that these calls are recorded. Anyone wasting police time will be prosecu—'

'And on the back of each envelope I drew a scientific drawing of a plant.'

'One moment please.'

There was then a minute-long gap as Griffiths made some checks.

'He hadn't been told what had been kept back from the press?' Poe asked.

'That circle is extremely small,' Mathers replied. 'The hotline room commander knew but that was it.'

'Sorry about that, sir, I was required to confirm some details with my line manager. Could I take your name?'

'One of the papers called me the Botanist this morning. That will do for now.'

'My name's Matt, sir. Are you OK to talk?'

'I'm in no hurry.'

'Good.'

'I must warn you though – I'm on an unregistered phone and where I am now there is no CCTV.'

'That's good of you to let me know, sir, but we aren't tracing this call.'

'Were you?' Poe said.

'Of course,' Mathers said. 'But he was right – his phone was unregistered and when we triangulated it, he was in the middle of rural Wales.'

'I doubt he lives there. Probably drove there so he knew he had some time.'

'Yep.'

'Can I ask why you're doing this, sir?' Griffiths asked.

'Why? Why? Isn't it obvious why?' the Botanist replied. 'A man who is so sexually dysfunctional, so afraid of women, that his hatred of them shines through in everything he does. A politician so morally bankrupt his own daughter has disowned him. And you ask me why they had to die?'

'I suppose I'm asking why you think you have the authority to act as judge, jury and executioner, sir.'

The pause lasted several moments. When the Botanist spoke again his tone was less measured.

'Did you know there are more narcissists in the world now than ever before, PC Griffiths?' he said. 'Never in recorded history has there been more people without empathy. We used to rely on the young to rebel for us, now they're so self-absorbed they don't even resent authority any more. And has there ever been a more boring generation than the millennials? The hipster generation, with their flat whites and their selfie sticks and their never-ending search to find something to be offended by. Is it any wonder people like me are starting to appear?'

The Botanist's tirade went on for another five minutes. Incoherent lunacy, Poe thought. He'd get Bradshaw to analyse it when they were done. She might be able to pull something useful. Start building a profile.

'You have strong views, sir,' Griffiths said after the Botanist had simmered to a finish.

'We need these views, PC Griffiths. It's not just evil that flourishes when good men do nothing, it's banality. People like me remind us of what we've lost.'

'It's a serious subject, sir, and one we don't have time to do justice right now. I have to ask you – are you prepared to come into a police station to talk to someone?'

'It's funny you should say that,' the Botanist replied. 'There *is* someone I'm willing to speak to. Would you be able to do me a favour, PC Griffiths?'

'If I can, sir.'

'I'd like you to get in touch with someone for me.'

'Who's that, sir?'

'A man called Henning Stahl,' the Botanist said. 'He's an ex-journalist. Out of favour right now, but you shouldn't have too much trouble finding him.'

'And you'll talk with Mr Stahl?'

'I will.'

'When?' Griffiths asked.

'Right after I kill someone.'

Chapter 28

'Who the hell is Henning Stahl?' Poe asked.

'He's a disgraced journalist,' Bradshaw replied. She was reading from her tablet. 'He was implicated in the 2005 phone-hacking scandal. Became the public face of it. He was the nasty pasty who disclosed the actor Dominic Denly's son had leukaemia.'

'That was him?' Poe said.

'Yes, Poe. He'd been listening to their voicemail messages.'

'Where is he now?'

'According to this article, he disappeared.'

'Abroad?'

'His passport isn't recorded as going through a UK border.'

'He's hiding then.'

'I think it's more likely he's keeping a low profile.'

'Any idea where we can start looking?'

'You can't live off the grid in this country – he'll be on a database somewhere. I'll find him, Poe.'

'Why does this Botanist idiot want to speak to him specifically?' Flynn said. 'You say he was the public face of the hacking scandal, but I'd never heard of him. He certainly doesn't have the profile of Kane Hunt or Harrison Cummings.'

'He might just want to talk to someone.'

'Why?'

'Guess we'll have to wait and see,' Poe said.

Poe wanted to be the one who picked him up. Stahl was such a random person to choose, there had to be a connection somewhere. They needed to know what that was.

'He was an investigative journalist, Tilly?' he asked.

'He was, Poe,' Bradshaw replied. 'A good one, until he went bad.'

'Can you draw up a list of the stories he reported on? Maybe the answer's in there somewhere.'

'I've already asked the Mole People to do this, Poe,' Bradshaw said. 'They'll have something for us tomorrow.'

'Good. Any idea on who the next victim is?'

'No one has come forward,' Flynn said. 'Chief Superintendent Mathers is thinking about holding a press conference. She wants to warn the public.'

Poe grunted.

'You don't think that's the right call?' she said.

'Cummings was under the protection of the best trained guards in the world and he's still dead.'

'Yeah, but he can only do the poisoned-tap trick once. It isn't something he can replicate.'

'When do we get the results back on that?'

'It was rushed through, so any time now I imagine.'

'Any word on the search for Price?'

'Only that he's not where he normally is. TSG are still looking.'

'And what about that bloke who knows him? We could do with someone saying whether it was Price's voice on the hotline.'

Flynn shrugged.

'All they told me was that he's on his way.'

'He went a bit off-script in the middle, didn't he?' Poe said. 'Completely wigged out.'

'Who?' Flynn said. 'The so-called Botanist? Just a bit.'

'No, he didn't,' Bradshaw said.

'No? What do you mean, no?' Poe said. 'He lost the bloody plot halfway through. I mean, no one likes millennials, but even I thought he was being a bit harsh on them.'

'There were two distinct phases to the conversation, Poe. The first was when he responded to PC Griffiths's questions. These were unrehearsed as he didn't know what he was going to be asked. The second phase was what you call him "wigging out". I believe he was in complete control in this part. Although it may appear to be unstructured and spontaneous, I would be very surprised if he hadn't been reading directly from a script.'

'How can you tell?'

'I've reduced the ambient noise and listened to his speech pattern. In the first section it was free flowing, but in the shouty bit there were regular pauses. Almost immeasurable, but I have a program that can spot them.'

'Pauses?'

'The kind of pause you get when reading from a page. When the eye has to move from the end of one line to the start of the line below, there's a tiny delay as the eye moves from right to left.'

'Why would he read from a script though?' Flynn said.

Poe considered it, but only for a moment. 'To give the appearance of someone who isn't in full control,' he said.

'That's concerning.'

'Very.'

A knock on the door made them all turn. A tall, beady man had entered the room. He was in plainclothes but was clearly a police officer. Cops looked like cops even when wearing a bear outfit at a fancy-dress party.

'Ah, you must be the person who's going to tell us if it was Brian Price who called the hotline earlier?' Flynn said.

'No, ma'am,' he said. 'I *am* Brian Price. I heard you were looking for me.'

Chapter 29

'Stay right there!' Poe ordered. 'Don't touch anything and don't put your hands in your pockets.'

Brian Price stood still.

'How the hell did you get in here?' Flynn said.

'Through the staff door, same as always,' he said. He had a Brummie accent. 'I'm on shift soon. Heard you were looking for me.'

'Chief Superintendent Mathers!' Poe yelled. 'A moment, please!'

It took a few seconds for Mathers to make her way to the cyber and digital crime unit's IT suite.

'What's up?' she said. 'I'm in the middle of the search for . . . Is that . . .?'

'It is,' Poe said. 'Can you cuff him, please? I seem to have left mine at home.'

Two minutes into the interview and Poe knew they had the wrong man. Price's accent was wrong for a start. The man on the hotline recording had sounded flat and monotonous, eminently forgettable. Price's accent was pure Birmingham. When he said his name for the tape, 'Price' rhymed with 'choice'. His demeanour was wrong, too. Poe had interviewed more serial killers than was decent and, although he knew they evolved and mutated, the two things they all had in common were a compulsion to kill and pride in what they had done.

Price was polite, attentive and nervous. He'd clearly done something wrong, but Poe didn't think he'd killed anyone.

'Where have you been, Detective Constable Price?' Poe asked.

'Why?'

'You know how this goes. I ask the questions, you *answer* the questions, we all go home and eat sausages dipped in mustard.'

'I've been to see my daughter.'

'She lives in Wigan, right?'

Price furrowed his brow. 'How do you know that?'

Poe didn't respond.

'Why do you know where my daughter lives, Sergeant Poe?'

'We checked with her, Detective Constable Price. She hasn't seen you. And, now she's had police turning up at her home, she's worried. The sooner you answer, the sooner you can call her. Let her know you're OK.'

'She wasn't in.'

'That might account for some of the time you've been missing, but it doesn't account for all of it. So, I'll ask again – where have you been?'

'Unless you tell me what's happened, I'm not saying another word until my federation rep gets here.'

Poe sighed. Recognised it was a cop on the other side of the table. Decided he'd earned a bit of respect. 'Mr Cummings is dead,' he said.

'I know. But I wasn't on shift.'

Irrelevant, Poe thought. The hot water tap could have been tampered with at any time.

'Do you know a man called Kane Hunt? Apparently he's been on TV.'

Price stiffened. His eyes narrowed and his lips pursed.

'I'll take that as a yes,' Poe said.

'I know of him. I don't *know* him.'

Poe picked up the slim file on the table. Pretended to read from it. 'Would it surprise you to learn you're the only person we've identified with confirmed links to both victims? You were assigned to Cummings's security detail and your daughter was being abused online by one of Kane Hunt's lackeys.'

'What's your point?'

'My point, Detective Constable Price, is that right now we don't have anyone else for this—'

He was cut short by a rapid knock on the door. Flynn entered the room. She handed Poe a bit of paper then took the seat next to him. Poe quickly read it. He glanced at Flynn, who nodded.

'Seems we have the wrong man, Detective Constable Price. A colleague of mine has compared your voice to the killer's and she assures me you are no match.'

'I can go?'

'I'm afraid not,' Poe said. 'Because there's something else on this piece of paper. A message from Lancashire Constabulary. Apparently, Ashley McCall, the wanker who was abusing your daughter, was found beaten to a bloody pulp last night. Two broken arms, ten broken fingers. Ruptured spleen and a jaw that'll never again line up properly.'

Price didn't answer.

'Detectives from Lancashire are coming down to speak to you,' Poe said. 'You'll be held in custody until then. Can I make a suggestion?'

'Please do.'

'Take your own advice: don't say a word to anyone until you've spoken to your rep.'

Price nodded. Pretended to zip up his lips.

After he had been led out of the interview room, Poe said, 'Guess that's what happens when you mess with the wrong person's daughter. Do Lancashire like him for it?'

'They do. Don't think they can prove it, though.'

Poe was oddly comforted by that.

'We're back to square one,' he said. 'We have absolutely no idea who's doing this.'

'That's not the only bit of bad news,' Flynn said. 'The results are back from the tap on Cummings's bath.'

'And?'

'Negative.'

'You're joking? I was so sure.'

'No trace whatsoever. Whatever poisoned Cummings, it wasn't a tampered hot water tap.'

'Why do I feel like I'm in a John Dickson Carr novel?' Poe said.

'Who?'

'American crime novelist. Arguably the greatest locked-room

mystery writer who ever lived. We have a killer in London who warns his victims yet still gets to them, and up north someone murdered Estelle Doyle's father and walked away from the crime scene without treading on a single fucking snowflake.'

'It's not all bad news,' Flynn said. 'Tilly's found an old address for Henning Stahl. Let's go and be detectives for a while.'

Chapter 30

'How did Tilly even find this address?' Poe asked.

'How does she do any of these things?' Flynn replied. 'And I wasn't going to ask her in front of Chief Superintendent Mathers in case I had to arrest her.'

Poe chuckled. When it came to the internet, what others called an absolute right to privacy, Bradshaw called a grey area. She'd exploit the slightest loophole in a site's user agreements, the tiniest chink in someone's settings. She went where she wanted and left no trace. If she weren't so useful there'd be very little reason not to put her in prison.

'Where are we?' Poe asked.

'Plaistow,' Flynn said, pulling into a recently vacated on-street parking space.

'Never heard of it.'

'Why am I not surprised? According to you, all urban areas suck.'

Poe didn't like London. He preferred living somewhere with a horizon, somewhere it got dark when the sun went down. Like all major cities, London seemed to flash and blink and turn neon.

'To be fair, most Londoners struggle to locate Plaistow,' Flynn continued, 'but it's actually a really cool area. Bit rough around the edges, but vibrant and diverse. The hospital employs translators who speak one hundred and thirty languages.'

Poe got out of the car and took it in. His nose was immediately battered with food from all over the globe. It was almost 6 p.m. and the fast-food joints and restaurants were opening. From where he was standing he could see Indian and Bangladeshi curry houses, a Jamaican jerk chicken place, a Korean barbecue, a Russian deli and two Chinese takeaways.

'I'm hungry,' he said.

'We'll get something after we've checked this address.'

'And as Tilly isn't here, can we have something nice?'

'There's a Vietnamese nearby and it's excellent. We'll eat there.'

'Where's this clown live?'

Flynn checked her phone. 'We're on the right street,' she said. 'According to Tilly, Henning Stahl used to live in a basement flat.'

'Renting?'

'Everyone in London rents, Poe.'

'So he might not still be there?'

'He almost certainly *isn't* there, but it's somewhere to start and it gets us out of the station.'

The basement flat Henning Stahl was, or had been, renting was symbolic of an unregulated housing market. Poe was no friend of bureaucracy, but, if he'd had the powers, he'd have stepped in and condemned the basement without even entering. It was dank, dark and an inch of stagnant water puddled against the front door. Flynn point blank refused to risk the green, algae-smeared steps.

'I'm not going down those,' she said. 'I'll fall on my arse.'

'What if *I* fall on my arse?'

'You're right. Give me a second.' She removed her phone from her jacket pocket and pointed it at him. 'Make sure you cry out if you hurt your back.'

'Ha ha,' he said, but he took extra care going down the steps. The last thing he wanted to be was the star of a murder investigation blooper reel.

Poe rapped on the door. Paint flaked off and floated down to the standing water. There was no answer so he risked an ear infection and put the side of his head to the decaying wood. He couldn't hear anything, just his own breathing. He moved to the only street-facing window. It was protected by heavy bars and was so dirty that even when he'd wiped away some of the grime with his handkerchief, he still couldn't see inside.

'I think that's tobacco staining,' he called up. 'Is Stahl a smoker?'

'How the fuck would I know?' Flynn replied.

'Fair point.'

He carefully navigated his way back up to street-level. 'He's out, good at being quiet or he's dead,' he said.

'Don't say that.'

'He might be, boss. All this "I'll only talk to him" bollocks could simply have been this wanker's way of pointing us to his body. People who die in basement flats like this don't get discovered until the rent's due or the cat finishes eating them.'

'What can we do?' Flynn said. 'He's not a suspect and as far as we know he's not broken the law. We can't just barge in.'

'Maybe I found the door unlocked? Went in to do a welfare check?'

'*Did* you find it unlocked?'

'No,' Poe said. 'But I doubt it'd take much to open it. Thing's rotten at the hinges.'

Flynn took a moment to consider this. 'Let's go and eat,' she said. 'We'll come back afterwards. If he's still not in, we'll have a rethink.'

Chapter 31

Flynn had ordered steamed sea bass with ginger and lemongrass; Poe had gone for the beef *pho*, a spicy, flat noodle soup that had him reaching for the water after his first spoonful.

'Any obvious candidates for the third victim?' Poe said. With no television, and his DAB radio permanently tuned to *Test Match Special*, popular culture was something that happened to other people. He had no idea who the tabloids were currently vilifying.

'You mean, are there any more obnoxious arseholes out there?' Flynn said. 'How much time do you have?'

'That many?'

'I hate to say it, but this prick has tapped into the country's zeitgeist. Chief Superintendent Mathers is worried that if she starts getting canny with the press, she could start a tidal wave of copycat attacks.'

'Really?'

'We're in the age of populism, Poe.'

'Is she going ahead with her press conference?'

'When we thought he'd smeared the neurotoxin on Cummings's hot water tap, that's exactly what she was going to do. Now we're back to not having a clue how he's doing it, she plans to wait.'

'But if no one comes forward?'

'She'll have to, I guess. But the media have covered it fairly accurately so far. If someone gets a poem and a pressed flower, they'll get in touch.'

Poe wasn't convinced it would be that straightforward. As he had said many times before, humans were bloody weird. There was no second-guessing what they might do. And even if they were to identify the third potential victim, so what? Hunt was killed on live television and Cummings was being guarded by cops.

'What do you think's really happening with Estelle Doyle, Poe?' Flynn said, expertly picking up a piece of fish with her chopsticks.

Poe put down his spoon. Glad she had raised it. 'I'm convinced she's being set up,' he said. 'There's too much evidence against her, if you know what I mean?'

Flynn nodded thoughtfully. 'OK,' she said. 'Let's run with that for a while. Apply the principle of *cui bono*.'

'Who benefits?' Poe said. 'Well, Estelle does. Her defence team can counter the main thrust of the CPS's motivation, but there *is* still some material gain. A fraction of what they think, but even so, put inheriting a farm in front of a working-class jury and it might convince them she had motive.'

'No one else waiting in the wings?'

'She's an only child.'

'Who gets it all if she goes away for murder?'

'The forfeiture rule applies. According to her solicitor, a murderer cannot inherit from the person they have killed. She thinks it will all go to the Crown.'

'Her dad was an only child too?'

'Apparently. And his wife died a long time ago.'

'Estelle isn't being framed for her dad's money then.'

'Nope.'

'Any ideas?'

'Honestly, boss, I've been thinking of nothing else, and the only thing I've come up with is that it's someone she helped put away. Maybe a case in which she was visible.'

'You mean one where she was an expert witness?'

'Yep.'

'That's what you think is happening here?'

'No. But it's the only thing I have.'

He ate some more beef *pho*. Noisily sucked up a noodle.

'What evidence are you most worried about?' Flynn asked.

'The snow. I can explain the firearms discharge residue, although it'll sound like a trick, but I can't explain the snow.'

'Maybe the killer was hiding in the house?'

'It was searched top to bottom. And, as they were looking for the murder weapon, it was done properly. The killer wasn't in the house.'

'But according to the fresh snow, the killer didn't *leave* the house either?'

'You can see why I'm worried,' he said. 'And I know we're full-on right now, but is there any chance I can get back up there? I need to start knocking on doors. Speak to witnesses. Cops up there think they have her cold, so aren't looking for anyone else.'

'I'll clear some time for you.'

'Cheers. Because if I can . . .' He trailed off.

Flynn looked up from her fish. 'What's up?' she said.

'Show me that photograph of Henning Stahl again.'

'Why?'

'Because I think he's just walked past the restaurant window.'

Chapter 32

Poe left Flynn to pay the bill – she had an NCA credit card, he had never been trusted with one – and made his way out of the restaurant. Henning Stahl was one hundred yards ahead, shuffling along, oblivious to what was happening behind him. Poe eased into a jog and caught up with him near his basement flat.

Stahl heard him and swung round. He held a full plastic bag protectively against his chest.

'Get away!' he snarled. 'You're not having it!'

'Calm down, Mr Stahl,' Poe said, trying not to wince at the man's sour breath. 'I'm a police officer.' He slowly removed his ID and held it up.

Stahl leaned forwards and squinted. He smelled like a week-old beer towel. His shoulders were stooped and his ginger hair was lank and thinning. Poe could see his scalp. Week-old stubble covered his chin and throat like a rash. He was pale, even paler than Bradshaw and she avoided the sun like a Scottish vampire. And Stahl's skin looked shiny, like he had a fever. Poe glanced in his carrier bag and was unsurprised by its contents – eight cans of premium-strength lager and a cheap bottle of vodka.

'I'm with the National Crime Agency,' Poe continued. 'I'd like to ask you some questions.'

'I have nothing more to say. Everything I knew, I told. Everything I did, I paid for. I just want to be left alone now. I made a mistake, but I wasn't the worst.'

'I've got no idea what you're talking about, Mr Stahl.'

'He thinks we're here because of the phone hacking, Poe,' Flynn said, coming up behind him.

'Who's this?' Stahl said.

'This is my boss, DI Flynn,' Poe said. 'And we're not here because of the phone hacking, we're here for something else.'

'Oh?'

'Have you heard about the man who calls himself the Botanist?'

He held up the carrier bag full of booze. 'I'm an alcoholic, not an idiot,' he said. 'He's the one who's been killing all those vile people. What's that got to do with me?'

'Because, Mr Stahl,' Poe said, 'for some reason he's chosen you as his conduit.'

Stahl's eyes narrowed. A cunning look flashed across his face. 'Has he now?' he said.

'And understandably, we're wondering why.'

'You'd better come in then.'

'Do we have to?' Flynn said.

Poe had optimistically hoped that Stahl's flat might be like a grease-spattered kettle – filthy on the outside but sparkling on the inside. He was wrong. If anything, the interior was worse than the exterior.

The discoloured carpet was littered with crushed beer cans, vodka bottles and containers from what looked like every takeaway in Plaistow. A teetering stack of empty pizza boxes reached for the tobacco-stained ceiling like a cardboard stalagmite. Scattered rodent droppings made it look as though someone had dropped a packet of raisins.

And the smell . . . It was somehow both cloyingly sweet and acrid. Although Poe could smell vomit, urine and faeces, the over-riding smell was stale alcohol. It seemed Stahl had hit rock bottom, then taken the elevator down a few more floors.

Poe's eyes began to sting. Flynn put a tissue over her mouth and nose, didn't even try to hide her disgust.

'It's the maid's week off,' Stahl said.

He slumped into a sagging armchair and reached for a plastic tumbler, one of the tacky promotional ones that came with meals at burger chains. The logo *Frozen* was printed above a snowman and two princesses. He upended it, shook out a cigarette butt and blew away the ash. He unscrewed the new bottle of vodka and filled the tumbler to the brim. He took a long drink, shut his eyes for a moment, then reached for the vodka bottle again.

Poe grabbed it first. 'After we've spoken,' he said.

'Fine,' Stahl muttered, reaching for his cans of lager.

Flynn stepped on the bag's handles. 'He said, "After we've spoken."'

'Bastards,' he muttered, scratching himself vigorously. He opened a pack of cigarettes and tapped one out. 'OK if I smoke, or is the nanny state going to stop me doing that as well?'

Poe ignored the jibe and studied Stahl. The man was clearly an alcoholic, had been for some time judging by the broken capillaries on his nose and the red splotches on his face. And given how yellow his skin was, and how much he was scratching, he obviously had liver damage.

Stahl tried and failed to light his cigarette – his hands were trembling too much. Ordinarily Poe would have assumed it was nerves, but in this case he put it down to sustained alcohol abuse.

'Need help?' Poe said, reaching down to steady the hand holding the cheap lighter.

'Thanks,' Stahl grunted after he'd taken a long drag. 'Now, what can I do for you?'

Poe took his phone out and sent a text to Bradshaw. As soon as he got her reply, he called her. She answered on the first ring.

'Ready?' he said.

'I am, Poe.'

He held out the phone so it was close to Stahl's head. 'Please can you say, "I'm on an unregistered phone and where I am now there is no CCTV," Mr Stahl?' Poe said.

'Er . . . why?'

Poe stared at him.

'Fine,' Stahl said. 'I'm on an unregistered phone and where I am now there is no CCTV. Happy?'

'You get that, Tilly?' Poe said.

'I did.'

'Is it enough?'

'Give me a few minutes. Don't accept any food from him until I've got back to you.'

Poe watched a cockroach scuttling towards a discarded bit of pizza crust.

'What did she say?' Flynn asked.

'Don't let him feed us.'

'Aw,' she said.

Chapter 33

Bradshaw rang back ten minutes later. Poe jumped, so did Flynn. Stahl had his eyes shut. Poe couldn't tell if he was asleep or dead.

'We good, Tilly?' he said.

'I've compared intonation, fluency, individual vowel and consonant pronunciation, Poe, and I am one hundred per cent certain that Henning Stahl is not the man who rang the Botanist hotline.'

'OK, speak soon.' He pressed end call and slipped his phone back into his coat. 'We're good, boss,' he said. He leaned over and shook Stahl. He woke with a start and immediately reached for his vodka.

'Mr Stahl,' Flynn said, 'a few hours ago the man claiming to be the Botanist called the police hotline and said he wanted to talk to you.'

'Sergeant Poe said as much outside,' Stahl replied. 'He didn't say why though.'

'We were hoping you might have some insight into that.'

Stahl gestured at his living room. 'Just how clued up do you think I am in world affairs right now?'

'We'd like you to come with us,' Flynn said. 'Right now you're the only lead we have.'

'I'm not going anywhere.'

'Why, what else have you got going on?'

'I have a plan.'

'And what's that, Mr Stahl?'

'I plan to see what kills me first: lung cancer or cirrhosis of the liver.' He paused then added, 'How much do you need me?'

Poe said nothing.

'A lot then,' he continued. 'If that's the case we need to establish some ground rules.'

'And what are they?' Flynn said.

'I get put up in a five-star hotel with mini-bar privileges.'

'Four-star and *no* mini-bar privileges,' Flynn said. 'Next.'

'You can confirm this with my GP, but as you might have gathered, I have a slight drink problem.'

'Gosh, really?'

'And that means if I don't have a certain amount of alcohol every day I go into withdrawal,' Stahl said, ignoring the sarcasm. 'I want money to buy vodka and a room to drink it in.'

Poe snorted.

'Agreed,' Flynn said. 'I'll consult a force FME and float you enough to buy a medically responsible amount of alcohol every day.'

'Really?' Poe said. 'If I get a letter from my doctor, can *I* have—?'

'No, you can't. What else do you want, Mr Stahl?'

'Complete and exclusive access to the investigation,' he said. 'I want copies of all available files and I want to sit in on any interviews.'

'No,' Poe said.

'No?'

'Of course not, you little tit.'

Stahl slumped back into his armchair.

'But,' Poe continued, 'if you sober up, you're bound to pick up stuff your old colleagues would pay good money for. And as long as it doesn't compromise case integrity, we may even slip you the occasional nugget of information. While you remain useful, that is.'

'It's the best offer you're going to get all year, Mr Stahl,' Flynn said. 'A chance to be relevant again. Maybe give your liver a bit of a rest.'

'OK,' he said.

'OK?'

'I'll help you with whatever you need. And any insight into the investigation will be gratefully received.'

He offered them his hand. Against his better judgement, Poe shook it. It was like touching raw meat. Flynn pretended she hadn't noticed.

'Let's go,' she said. 'We'll put you up in the same hotel we're in.

119

I'll even stump up for some new clothes if you have nothing clean to take with you.'

'Thank you,' he smiled. His teeth were chipped and discoloured, like a bag of broken Smarties.

'Is there a dog or a cat we need to think about?' Poe said.

Stahl took another swig of vodka. Drained a third of the bottle. 'The cat died weeks ago,' he said. 'In fact, can you give me a hand? I think it's still in the kitchen somewhere.'

'Yeah,' Poe muttered, 'you're going to be a great help.'

Chapter 34

Before they took Stahl to their hotel, Flynn said she would nip into Primark and get shirts, trousers, underwear and socks. She asked Poe to get him toiletries and a new pair of shoes. Poe was about to complain but he could see Flynn wasn't in the mood.

'Fine,' he said. He spotted a Clarks on the street corner. Remembered his dad used to take him to a local store each year before the new school term started. 'We'll go in there.'

'See you in thirty minutes,' Flynn said.

'You'd better wait outside,' Poe said to Stahl at the shop's entrance. 'What size are you?'

'Ten. Should I not try some on?'

'You smell like a goat, mate. Try on shoes in there and they'll have to burn them afterwards. No, you stay outside and I'll get you something comfortable. And you're not putting them on until you've had a bath.'

Poe approached the nearest assistant. He flashed his ID card and said, 'I need to keep that man in my sight at all times. Would you be able to get me a pair of size ten shoes? Bring them straight to the till?'

'What are you looking for?'

'Something like mine – cheap, sturdy and comfortable. Maybe a pair of trainers as well?'

'And you have no colour or style preference? We have a nice Italian loafer that's proving popular.'

'Look at him. What do you think?'

She did. 'I'll be right back,' she said.

'Thank you.'

During the time it took the assistant to find something suitable, out on the pavement three people tried to give Stahl some money and one of them bought him a sandwich.

Poe, Flynn and Bradshaw met in the small meeting room that SCAS's office manager had arranged to be at their disposal.

'Where's Stahl?' Flynn asked.

'Where do you think?' Poe said, throwing a thumb over his shoulder. 'He's in the bar, drinking like a pirate.'

'You let him?'

'If he doesn't drink he can't function.'

'Jesus,' she muttered.

'Have you told Chief Superintendent Mathers we have him?' Poe asked.

'I have. I haven't told her we're getting him pissed though.'

'And?'

'I think she's happy we're shouldering some of the responsibility.'

'Does she think he's a potential victim, DI Flynn?' Bradshaw said. 'Because he doesn't fit either the Botanist's previous target group or his methodology.'

'Poe?'

'I don't think he's a victim, boss. He has nowhere near the visibility of the other two and he says he hasn't received a poem or a pressed flower. And if the Botanist wanted him dead, all he'd have to do is wait a few weeks.'

'Is he dying, Poe?' Bradshaw asked. 'Gosh, that's so sad.'

'Suicide by bottle.'

'I don't underst—'

'He's an alcoholic, Tilly. Has been for years.'

Bradshaw made a note on her laptop.

'So why choose him as his media contact then?' Flynn said.

'Two options.' Poe held up a finger. 'One: he wants someone at rock bottom, someone desperate to get back in the game. A person like that might be easier to manipulate. Willing to do things that more established investigative journalists wouldn't.'

'And the second option?'

'Stahl knows him.'

122

'Is that likely?'

'He was a journalist for twenty years,' Poe said. 'The amount of stories he's been involved in will be in the thousands.'

'Tilly needs to turn his life upside down then,' Flynn said. 'See if he's led on stories featuring anyone with an expertise in botany or chemistry or something like that. That doable, Tilly?'

'I'll work on search parameters tonight and run them by you in the morning. But, I must warn you, DI Flynn – Oxford University alone has dozens of undergraduate degrees and PhDs in its prospectus that would qualify as relevant.'

The door opened and Stahl joined them. He was wearing his new clothes but they were mismatched and ill fitting. He still looked like a homeless person, but at least he no longer smelled like he lived in a wheelie bin.

'Looking sharp, Henning,' Poe said.

'Cut it out, Poe,' Flynn said. 'And I got him the sizes he asked for.'

Stahl shrugged. 'I must have lost weight recently,' he said.

They took their seats at the conference table.

'My name is Matilda Bradshaw, Henning Stahl,' Bradshaw said. 'It is very nice to meet you. Poe says you're an alcoholic.'

She held out her hand. They shook.

'Yuk,' Bradshaw said. 'You have very sweaty hands, Henning Stahl. Please don't touch any of my computers.'

Poe sniggered.

This bit was going to be fun.

Chapter 35

'Poe tells me there were rat droppings on your living-room carpet, Henning Stahl,' Bradshaw said. 'Is that because the deteriorating planning and organisational skills associated with alcoholic dementia meant you couldn't figure out how to dispose of your dead cat?'

Stahl stared at her.

'Is this strictly necessary, Tilly?' Poe asked, hiding a smile.

'Not a bit,' Bradshaw replied.

'Then why . . .?'

'You said I needed to work on my small talk.'

Poe gave her a double thumbs-up. 'You're getting really good at it,' he said.

'I understand you were born in London, Henning Stahl,' Bradshaw said.

'Tottenham,' he nodded.

'But Henning is Germanic in origin.'

'And Scandinavian.'

'I discounted Scandinavia because Stahl is also Germanic.'

'I was an army brat,' Stahl said. 'My dad was in the Royal Signals and he met my mother in a town in Germany called Paderborn. Brought her back to the UK. When they got divorced my mother returned home and took me with her. She reverted to her maiden name and changed mine too. I stayed in Germany until I started university.'

'What was your surname previously?' Poe said.

'Mitchell.'

'OK. Tilly's going to take you through some of the stories and investigations you were involved with. See if we can work out why the Botanist chose you as his conduit.'

'You think we've crossed paths?'

'You weren't chosen for your personal hygiene.'

'And if it's *not* a story I was involved with?' Stahl said, ignoring the sarcasm.

Poe didn't respond.

Bradshaw did.

'The alternative is that you were selected because your alcoholism and lack of moral fibre makes you uniquely pliable. Presuming you can still construct a semi-cohesive sentence, and presuming you wish to be a journalist again, it could be that the Botanist thinks you will be willing to do things others won't.'

'More small talk?' Poe said.

'No. That's a précis of what you said before Henning Stahl entered the room. Do you remember, Poe? You said that Henning Stahl was a complete . . . urine-head, who would do something rude to a homeless person for some alcohol.'

'I didn't think you were listening.'

'I'm *always* listening, Poe.'

'What did he actually say, Tilly?' Stahl asked.

'Poe said you would W-A-N-K off a tramp for a bottle of turps.'

Stahl let out a throaty laugh.

'He also said that you would be as much use as a waterproof teabag.'

He laughed even harder.

'Yeah . . . sorry about that,' Poe said. 'Been a long day, etcetera.'

'Don't worry about it,' Stahl said, waving away his apology. 'And he's not wrong, Tilly. But I *do* want to change.'

Chapter 36

Bradshaw spent the rest of the night taking Stahl through any story he had been credited with that had even the remotest link to what was happening now.

Flynn had disappeared to assist in the search for the Botanist's third victim, but Poe stayed behind. He didn't trust Stahl. He wasn't the Botanist – the effects of his alcohol abuse were real and debilitating and couldn't be faked – but anyone who thought that someone's son having leukaemia was newsworthy wasn't the type of person he wanted left alone with Bradshaw.

He sipped a beer while Stahl walked her through his career. Its downward trajectory was depressing. In his early years he'd been a talented journalist. He had reported from warzones and he had lived with London Yardies. He had told human stories from the Malaysian Nipah virus infection and he had exposed the board-approved cancer-causing practices of a major petrochemical company. Poe wondered what had happened to him.

'Do deep-dive profiles on those last two stories, Tilly,' Poe said. 'The Botanist hasn't used a virus yet, but he might, and that petrochemical company will have been packed with scientists. Maybe one of them lost his job and is out there seeking redemption.'

'I will, Poe.'

'But not now. It's almost midnight and we all need some rest.' He faced Stahl. 'I'm under no illusion you don't sleep well, Mr Stahl. If you want a nightcap, go and get it now. Although this hotel's secure, once you're in your room I'm putting an armed cop outside.'

'I wouldn't mind a small brandy,' he said.

Stahl returned ten minutes later. He needed a tray to carry all the booze.

'For fuck's sake,' Poe muttered.

Chapter 37

It was as if they had never left the meeting room. Poe, Flynn and Bradshaw had enjoyed an early breakfast then had a quick chat about what they needed from Stahl. Flynn asked Bradshaw to lead, with Poe asking follow-ups. Flynn was going to be away again for most of the morning.

'We ready?' Flynn said. Poe and Bradshaw nodded. 'I'll go and get him then.'

She returned fifteen minutes later. She didn't look happy.

'He awake?' Poe asked.

'He is now.'

'What's up?'

'Have you any idea how expensive these hotel mattresses are?'

'Do you want me to find out, DI Flynn?' Bradshaw asked, opening her laptop.

'It's OK, Tilly. I'm sure the hotel bill will be very clear.'

'He pissed it?' Poe said.

Flynn nodded. 'He's sleeping in the bath tonight,' she said.

Stahl appeared an hour later. He had a glass of clear liquid with him. It could have contained water but Poe knew it was vodka. He drained half the glass, noticed Poe was watching him, and shrugged in a what-you-gonna-do kind of way. If he was embarrassed about wetting his bed, he didn't show it. Poe imagined it was a semi-regular occurrence.

'I'd like to talk about the phone-hacking scandal now, Henning Stahl,' Bradshaw said. 'If the Botanist's interest in you isn't because of one of your investigative reports, then perhaps it was because of your involvement in that?'

'What are the odds, eh?' Stahl said.

'Seventy-two per cent, Henning Stahl.'

'What is?' he said.

'The odds of the Botanist's interest in you being related to phone hacking.'

'How could you *possibly* know that?'

'I did the maths. Obviously the Frequentist probability model didn't apply, as there were no repeatable objective processes—'

'Obviously,' Stahl said.

'I know, duh, right? So I tweaked the Bayesian interpretation, where probability expresses a degree of belief in an event. And clearly—'

'Can we do this later, Tilly?' Poe said. 'We don't really have time now.'

'Of course, Poe. We can discuss it during our evening meal. Have you read *Bayesians Versus Frequentists: A Philosophical Debate on Statistical Reasoning*, or should I prepare a briefing?'

'Which edition?'

'Well, obviously not the second . . .' She frowned. 'Oh, you're joking. Very funny, Poe. Ha ha.'

Poe smiled at his friend. He faced Stahl and said, 'I think you'd better tell us how you went from being a well-respected, hard-hitting investigative journalist to an absolute disgrace.'

Chapter 38

'I had wanted to be a writer for as long as I can remember,' Stahl said. 'When I was eight I had my mother send off for correspondence courses in how to construct novels, how to write poetry, how to . . . write. And I devoured them. Thought I'd take off when I was a young man. Drive Route 66 during the day, write the Great American Novel at night.'

'Why didn't you?'

'Apart from the fact that *everyone* was driving Route 66 while trying to write the Great American Novel?'

Poe nodded.

'A classmate told me a girl he knew had scored higher on her exam than he had on his,' Stahl explained. 'And you've got to understand, this guy was a real brainbox, always finished top.'

'But he was beaten by a girl and he didn't like it?'

'He wasn't moaning. But it awakened something in me, something I didn't even know existed.'

'Your inner, nosey-needs-to-know?'

'Something like that. So I looked into it. Found I had a talent for seeing where the real story was. Realised it was something I could maybe do for a living.'

'And?' Bradshaw said.

'And what?'

'What happened with the exam result?' Bradshaw didn't like loose ends.

'Oh that?' Stahl said. 'The teacher had been shagging the girl. No crime had been committed as she was seventeen, but I found a pattern of him favouring students he was in a sexual relationship with. I went to university, got a degree in English then applied for a job with the local rag.'

'Where was that?' Poe asked.

'Peckham.'

'Lovely jubbly.'

'Excuse me?'

'Doesn't matter.'

'Yes . . . well, I was put on the crime beat so I got to hone my interview techniques. Got used to asking open questions. Using the pause, not being afraid of silence.'

Poe nodded. Interview skills were the same for journalists as they were for cops. 'And that's when you made the step up to Fleet Street?'

'I'd interviewed the wife of a man who'd murdered a girl collecting money for the air ambulance. And something appeared off, right from the beginning. She wanted money for the story – I mean, they all did – but there wasn't much with the local paper. More of a whip round than a budget. She'd asked, off the record, if she told me something that hadn't come out in court, would it make a difference to her payment. I was honest and said no, not with my paper. But if it were juicy enough, the nationals would pick it up. There might be money on the follow-ups.'

'What did she tell you?'

'Nothing. She correctly guessed that if she bypassed me and went straight to the *Sun* she stood a much better chance of being paid.'

'So you dug in?'

'I did. Spoke to her neighbours, her friends, anyone who knew her.'

'You found it?'

'Turns out she *knew* her husband hadn't killed the girl. He'd been having an affair with a married woman and his wife had been watching them that night. Was going to confront them both but bottled it. When the police arrested him, the married woman denied all knowledge of the affair. He was left without an alibi and the jury convicted him.'

'She could have cleared his name?'

'Absolutely.'

'You got her to admit this?'

'Not her, the woman her husband had been having an affair with. By then I think she'd started to feel guilty and was glad to talk.'

'What happened to his wife?'

'Nothing,' Stahl said. 'Which coincidentally is exactly how much money she got.'

'Nothing?'

'Police couldn't prove she knew about the affair. And she couldn't get any money for the story without admitting there *was* a story.'

'Bet that pissed her off.'

'Not half as much as when her husband was acquitted on appeal, and he and the woman he had been seeing sold *their* story, made a bundle and bought a house in Provence.'

'Tilly, profile the woman who missed out on the money. I doubt she's involved, but it's something we weren't aware of yesterday.'

'I'll do it tonight, Poe.'

'And that got you a place on a national newspaper?'

Stahl nodded.

'What went wrong?' Poe said.

Chapter 39

'The first generation who didn't play outside are adults now, Sergeant Poe,' Stahl said. 'Some of them are management and they see the world differently to you and me. If something doesn't have an electronic footprint, it doesn't have a value. I'd made the big league by then, and for a while it was everything I'd thought it would be. We were given serious budgets, told to put serious exclusives on the front page. We had weeks, even months to follow leads, develop stories.'

'But it changed?'

Stahl nodded.

'The moment papers went online was the moment real journalism stopped. Investigative journalists were the dinosaurs, unneeded relics of the golden age of Fleet Street. Clickbait was king now. Likes and shares more important than exposés and Pulitzers. The didn't-go-outside-to-play generation wrote attention-grabbing, advertising-friendly headlines and journalists were told to find, twist or plain make up stories to fit them. Churnalism we called it, as we were expected to churn out meaningless story after meaningless story. Getting it online was more important than getting it right. They were hammering chequebook-journalism too. Outbidding the other papers for scandals about fading celebrities, half of which were planted by the celebs themselves.'

'You went along with it?'

'I resisted for a while, but by then I was used to a certain standard of living. We all were. So it was either do their bidding and debase myself, or pack it all in and find a new career.'

Poe finished his coffee. Asked Stahl if he wanted another one.

'I'll get some more water,' he said.

'We have some here, Henning Stahl,' Bradshaw chipped in. 'Poe doesn't drink enough so I always order bottles for any room he's working in.'

Stahl glanced at Poe and shrugged.

'You haven't got the kind of water Mr Stahl likes, Tilly,' Poe said.

'Oh? But I've got sparkling and still. Unless he wants flavoured, I don't know what else there is.'

'It's vodka, Tilly. Mr Stahl's drinking vodka.'

'For *breakfast*?'

Stahl sloped out of the room, embarrassed.

'What a loser,' Bradshaw said.

'He's not well, Tilly.'

'You were telling us how news had been replaced by clickbait, Mr Stahl,' Poe said.

Stahl was back, a glass full of vodka in front of him. Poe calculated that in the last hour he'd had nearly a pint of the stuff. Despite that, his eyes were clear and his voice was steady.

'There were still pockets of serious journalism going on, just not at the paper I worked at.'

'You couldn't transfer?'

Stahl shook his head. 'Get a reputation for clickbait stories and that's who you are. I applied for a job with the *Guardian*. Didn't get past the front door.'

'Was that when you started drinking?'

'It was always a hard-drinking profession. I suppose most jobs are when you finish work in the middle of the afternoon. But it was when I started drinking too much.'

On cue, he drained half his glass. Above him, the clock showed nine o'clock in the morning. Poe said nothing. Bradshaw tutted.

'And then some morally bankrupt chancer decided we could cut out the middleman. Stop paying journalists to develop stories and hire private investigators to steal them instead. Ask *them* to find out what it was the celebs didn't want found. Pay them a fraction of what we were paid. And because they were technically freelance, we could turn a blind eye to their methods.'

'Methods like phone hacking?'

'Among other things.'

'You knew it was going on?'

'We all did. We listened to the tapes.'

'Which was why people went to prison.'

'Not the *right* people,' Stahl said.

'Talk me through hacking a phone,' Poe said.

'Hacking's such a grandiose term. It was essentially taking advantage of the lazy and the technically incompetent. In those days mobile voicemail was new and exciting. You could leave messages for people and they could access them wherever they were. Remote access it was called. Godsend for people like us.'

'What equipment did you need?' Poe said.

'Nothing. That was the beauty of it. All you had to do was ring their number. If they didn't answer, you entered their personal identification number, or PIN, which gave you full access to their messages.'

'How did you get their PINs, though?'

'Most people were either too lazy or didn't know how to change them. Their PIN was invariably the four-digit factory-set number you needed to enter. One, two, three, four, or four zeroes, or if it was Vodafone, three, three, three, three.'

'It was that easy?'

'You can see why it was so tempting. A chance to listen to the private lives of anyone. Senior politicians, A-list celebs, anyone.'

'The parents of murder victims?'

'Yes,' Stahl said quietly. 'And that's not even the worst of it. To stop other journalists getting the same story, it was common practice to change the PIN once you had got in. That way, no one but you had access to the messages, not even the intended recipient. That part was underplayed in court but it always bothered me.'

Poe nodded thoughtfully. Wondered if there was an angle to this that no one had considered. Maybe it wasn't a hacked message, maybe it was a message no one had listened to. He'd get Bradshaw to go through all Stahl's hacking victims, even the ones where no stories emerged.

'And it was you who hacked Dominic Denly's voicemail?' Poe said. 'You listened to the message about his son's leukaemia?'

'Technically, it was my private investigator, but I'd hired him so, yes, it was me.'

'You weren't named on the byline,' Poe said. 'Why's that?'

'I didn't write the story. Didn't even show what I had to my editor. I knew we had crossed a line – Denly's boy was eight years old and he was dying. I was immoral, but I wasn't a monster.'

'You didn't want to run it?'

'I did not.'

'How did your editor get hold of the voicemail?'

Stahl shrugged. 'That's the problem working with people whose only motivation is money,' he said. 'If they think they can get more, that's what they'll do. In hindsight, what happened was entirely predictable.'

Poe skipped ahead a couple of pages. 'When the PI realised you hadn't used his information, he went to your editor?' he said. 'Tried to get paid again?'

'And, as it was the paper that had paid the PI, it was technically their information to use. I begged him not to run it, but my editor couldn't risk the PI going above his head. I refused to have anything to do with it so he asked one of the gossip writers if they fancied writing it.'

'They did?'

'Jumped at the chance. And why not? It was a guaranteed front page, all the work was done and she was using information she'd been handed by her editor. *She* hadn't hacked anyone's voicemail. Absolute no-brainer for someone young and ambitious.'

'And it was one of the stories that broke the scandal,' Poe said.

'Which was exactly what I'd told my editor would happen. After I'd tried and failed appealing to his sense of decency, I told him that a story like that would bring the world crashing down on his head. On *our* heads.'

'But he ignored you.'

'You've got to understand, the editor of a big paper is in an impossible position. He gets shit off his reporters for trimming their budgets and he gets even more shit from the owner who wants increased sales with fewer overheads.'

'They ran the story,' Poe said.

'And they made a mistake.'

'Which was?'

'Journalism 101: protect your source,' Stahl said. 'That doesn't just mean not giving them up; it also means providing a plausible explanation if the real source is illegal. You certainly can't admit you were listening to a private voicemail.'

'How do you get around that?'

'Simple. Once you have the story through voicemail hacking, you work backwards and confirm it. You speak to sources, offer money, go through bins. Basic journalism skills, unfortunately.'

'And this gossip reporter didn't do that?'

'Didn't even know she was supposed to. Her stories were handed to her on a silver platter. Publicity-hungry celebs, desperate for exposure. The inbox of a gossip reporter is never empty, believe me.'

'So she just wrote it?'

'She did.'

'And Dominic Denly went to the police?'

'Can you blame him?' Stahl said. 'He told the detective that the paper had shared confidential medical information. There was already a low-key hacking investigation going on by then, but the Met had never had such a blatant example. Dominic Denly's case really speeded things up.'

'Spin forward a bit,' Poe said. 'The first arrests are made. How long until they got to you?'

'The day after they'd arrested the gossip reporter who wrote the story. She gave up the editor and he denied knowing where the information came from.'

'He denied knowing about the voicemail?'

'You've never seen a bigger example of collective amnesia, Sergeant Poe. Everyone could see where this was going, so it all came down to plausible deniability. My editor had told me to hack voicemails, but he wasn't stupid – there was nothing in writing.'

'But the money led back to the PI?'

'Who, when facing a prison sentence, couldn't name me fast enough.'

'And you had no one to trade up?'

'Buck stopped with me on the Dominic Denly story.'

'You didn't go to prison, though?'

'By the time of my trial, people knew the bigger picture. That it was endemic across the whole paper. My solicitor argued that the pressure put on me to come up with stories meant I'd been effectively coerced into doing it. I was found guilty but spared prison. Got a year's probation and three hundred hours community service.'

'What happened then?' Poe asked.

'Do you know who Pearl Rigby is, Sergeant Poe?'

'No.'

'She's the girl who broke the internet.'

Chapter 40

'Pearl Rigby was a thirty-three-year-old advertising exec from Chicago,' Stahl explained. 'She was flying to Australia to visit family and, during a layover at Amsterdam, she tweeted what she'd thought was a funny joke – "Don't like airplane food so going to eat some fried chicken to remind me of home while I wait. Just kidding. I'm from River North, not Englewood." She then got on a twenty-one-hour flight to Sydney. Some bloke retweeted it and, unbeknownst to her, while she was in the air the tweet went viral.'

'I assume Englewood is a predominantly black area of Chicago?' Poe said.

'Over ninety per cent.'

'Blimey.'

'There was even a hashtag, Poe,' Bradshaw said. '#HasPearl LandedYet.'

'You know about this?'

'Duh; it happened on the internet.'

'Tilly's right,' Stahl said. 'That Pearl was oblivious to her predicament became a form of entertainment. I've read articles that said people had refused to leave bars until she'd landed in Sydney. They were waiting for her to turn on her phone and realise her life was ruined. The next day she was fired and for a while she became unemployable. She had to go to East Africa to find redemption.'

'So?'

'Rigby's comment *was* offensive, but you have to admit there's a disconnect between her transgression and the severity of her punishment.'

'You have a point, I take it?' Poe said.

'Can you imagine what it was like for me?' Stahl said. 'Pearl

Rigby almost ruined her life with a racist joke. *I* was the man who'd hacked the parents of a dying child. That I hadn't done it personally, or that I'd refused to write the story, was irrelevant. For a while I was the most reviled man in the country. I couldn't go home and I couldn't book into a hotel. I had to withdraw my life's savings and basically go on the run. Went to Blackpool and rented rooms in the most disgusting B & Bs you can imagine. Blended in with the down-on-their-luck crowd. Started drinking even more. And once a week I had to schlep down to London to answer police bail, where my former colleagues, half of whom had also been hacking voicemails but hadn't been caught, were waiting to photograph me.'

'Alcohol became your crutch?'

'Wasn't long before it was the only thing I had in my life.'

'When did you move back to London?'

'I was sentenced in London so my probation officer was from here. Did my community service here. I could have applied for my case to be transferred to Lancashire Probation's Blackpool office, but that would have made me a celebrity up there. The one good thing about London is the anonymity. It's a curse for some but I welcomed it like a friend. Hugged and cherished it.'

'And now a serial killer wants to talk to you.'

'Apparently so.'

Stahl paused to finish his vodka. Poe drained his coffee. Bradshaw made some notes on her laptop.

'What happens now?' Stahl asked.

'Based on what you've told us, and what Tilly has uncovered, she'll now task the Mole People with drawing up profiles on anyone she thinks might be holding a grudge against you.'

'Good luck with that,' he grunted.

'Thank you,' Bradshaw said.

'No, I meant there must be hundreds of people who fit that criteria.'

'That's incorrect, Henning Stahl.'

'It is?' he said. 'That's a relief, I suppose.'

'Because I'm including the family and friends of the people who can legitimately hold a grudge against you, the actual number is in the thousands.'

Poe laughed. Stahl didn't.

The door swung open and Flynn stormed into the room. She was carrying a laptop and didn't look happy. She put it on the table. A paused video filled the screen.

She pressed play and they watched in silence.

When the video had finished, Poe said, 'What's this bullshit?'

Chapter 41

'Has she taken leave of her senses?' Poe said. 'And what the hell is a KRC?'

'Her name's Karen Royal-Cross,' Flynn said. 'She refers to herself as KRC.'

'Like the fast-food place Tilly's banned me from going to?'

Flynn glanced at him. 'Huh?'

They were in the back of a police minivan. Detective Chief Superintendent Mathers had arranged transport and support, but had asked Poe and Flynn to make first contact. See if Karen Royal-Cross really was the Botanist's intended third victim. She lived in London, as had all the victims so far, but on the other side of the river to where their hotel was. In Cumbria, the trip would have taken Poe ten minutes. They'd been in the minivan for over an hour.

'Put the video on, boss,' Poe said.

'Again? We've watched it three times.'

She pressed play, though. Everyone in the back of the van crowded round the screen.

A heavily made-up woman leaned back from what Poe assumed was her laptop. She'd obviously just pressed record on her webcam. She was wearing a low-cut T-shirt, white with red lips on the front. Her hair was blonde – too blonde to be natural – and her eyebrows were thick and black, like they'd been drawn on with a Sharpie.

'This is KRC again,' she said. 'And do I have a story for you.'

She reached for something off-screen and returned with a pressed flower. It was small, green and spiky. It had a prominent red stigma, the part of the flower that receives pollen. Bradshaw hadn't been able to identify it yet but the video had been sent to Kew Gardens. They were expecting an answer within the hour.

'The statue-destroying libtards are at it again. This time they're trying to intimidate me with, of all things, a pressed flower and a third-rate poem.'

She reached for a piece of paper this time and pretended to read it. Unfortunately, the camera didn't pick up what was on it. Poe hoped she hadn't destroyed it.

'And it's nonsensical,' she said, shaking her head in feigned disgust. She leaned into the camera and whispered, 'I know it's not PC to say this, but I don't think English is this guy's first language, if you know what I mean.'

Poe pressed pause. 'What *does* she mean?'

'She's jumped on the far-right immigrant-bashing bandwagon,' Flynn said. 'According to her the only good asylum seeker is a drowned one.'

'Nice.'

Poe pressed play.

'I mean it *does* rhyme,' Karen Royal-Cross admitted, 'but the words don't make sense. There's even something about snails. Probably a delicacy where they come from. And while he's here, free to threaten British citizens, our soldiers are banned from wearing poppies and saying Merry Christmas.'

'Very subtle,' Poe said.

'And I know the snowflakes will have another go at me for saying this, but you know it and I know it: each time someone like this' – she waved the poem in the air – 'is allowed into our country, the purest bloodline in the world gets polluted that little bit more.'

Flynn pressed stop.

'What a fucking dummy,' Poe said.

'It's what she does, Poe,' Flynn said. 'She's good at finding things to manipulate on social media.'

'Why bother?'

'She's jumping up and down, trying to get noticed by one of the American cable news shows, apparently. Wants to be an alt-right commentator.'

'Are her targets always asylum seekers and liberals?'

'Usually, although she doesn't like fat people either. Says they're a burden on the NHS.'

'She has a weight management problem she doesn't want to deal with.'

'Probably,' Flynn agreed. 'What do you think?'

'I think too many people have got used to posting shit online without getting punched in the mouth.'

'But you can see why the Botanist has set his eyes on her, though? Some racist dickheads might kick up a fuss, but the rest of us will have street parties.'

'Oh, yeah,' he said. 'She's ideal. I wonder if she's realised just how much danger she's in?'

The driver looked at them through his rear-view mirror and said, 'We're here.'

Chapter 42

'Have you seen the news recently?' Poe asked Karen Royal-Cross.

'Why, was I on it?' she replied, her eyes lighting up.

'Why would you be on it?'

'Because I'm a well-respected political commentator. I'm frequently on the news.'

'You are?'

'I am,' she nodded.

'Which papers do you write for? Which news programmes do you appear on?'

She tried to frown but couldn't. Too much Botox in her forehead, Poe thought.

'I'm more interested in social media these days,' she said. 'I can speak directly to my supporters without being censored by the lamestream news. But, I did have regular columns before the lefties took over.' She handed Poe a well-thumbed scrapbook. 'Have a look at that if you don't believe me.'

It was full of press clippings. Some of the early ones were from local and national news, but more recently they all seemed to be from far-right fringe publications.

'According to YWNRU,' she said, 'I'm England's Conscience.'

'YWNRU?' Poe said. 'The white supremacist slogan "You Will Not Replace Us"?'

'Oh, my poor darling,' she sighed. 'White supremacists? How can someone as world-weary as you be so gullible?'

'Oh do fuck off,' Poe said.

'Pack it in, Poe,' Flynn warned.

'Thank you, DI Flynn,' Karen Royal-Cross said. 'It's time people like him realised diversity is just another name for white genocide.'

Flynn glared at her.

'Oh do fuck off,' she said, leaving the room.

The problem was this: Karen Royal-Cross, aka KRC, simply didn't believe she was in any danger. She would seize on the smallest thing as proof that 99 per cent of the population loved her. She showed them her last tweet – something about Black History Month being another example of white oppression – and directed them to the number of comments, likes and retweets.

'There's a silent majority in this country who are as sick of the radical left agenda as I am,' she explained.

'Jolly good,' Poe said. 'But if we can get back to the matter in hand?'

'That's just fake news, darling,' she said. 'These loser snowflakes are always up to something. I try not to take them too seriously. They won't actually do anything, not while this country pays them to smoke bongs all day.'

'You must have taken some of those threats seriously; you've moved three times.'

She rolled her eyes. 'When I get to be too much of a nuisance, the government hires crisis actors to protest outside my house,' she said. 'Probably the same lot who do the mass shootings in America.'

'Crisis actors?' Poe said before he could stop himself.

'As if all those high-school massacres are real,' she laughed. 'The deep state stage a shooting every time they want to draw attention away from immigration. If you look carefully, you see the same actors over and over again. They change their clothes but the proof's there, if you're prepared to follow the breadcrumbs.'

Flynn walked back into the room.

'Do we *have* to save her, boss?' Poe said. 'She's a fucking pinhead.'

'I'm calling your superior officer!'

'Has she found the poem yet?' Flynn asked, ignoring the now beetroot-red Karen Royal-Cross.

'Still looking. She thinks it's in with this lot somewhere,' he said, pointing to a stack of gossip and celebrity magazines on the floor.

'Excuse me,' Karen Royal-Cross said. 'I *am* still here.'

'It's the envelope we really need. Without it we don't know if this is a genuine threat or a copycat. Everything on the video has been in the public domain for a while now. Easy enough thing to replicate.'

'It's already happening,' Flynn said. 'There's been a spate of poems and pressed flowers posted to celebrities.'

'Any scientific drawings on the back of the envelopes?'

'No. Thank God we kept that bit out of the press. Tilly says public support for the Botanist is building.'

'Ten minutes in this idiot's company and I can see why.'

'Who's an idiot, Poe?' Bradshaw said, entering the room.

'You'll see soon enough.'

'I need to make a phone call,' Flynn said. 'Let Mathers know we haven't been able to confirm Royal-Cross is a potential victim yet.'

Flynn left the room and Poe had an idea. So far, neither he nor Flynn had managed to get it through to Karen Royal-Cross just how much danger she could be in. She was half-heartedly looking for the poem and the envelope, hampered by her obsession with filming herself as she did. Each time he tried to impress upon her how important it was, she laughed it off and said it was fake news.

She seemed to live in a self-replicating bubble of toxic shit.

But Bradshaw had a way of cutting through shit. She was unintentionally direct, had no embarrassment threshold and missed 90 per cent of nonverbal cues.

'Tilly,' Poe said, 'can you please brief this silly woman on what's been happening, and why she should be more worried than she is?'

'Of course, Poe,' Bradshaw said. 'Please sit here, Karen Royal-Cross.'

'Er, it's KRC.'

'No, that's your online persona. Your real name is Karen Royal-Cross and that is how I shall address you.'

Karen Royal-Cross folded her arms and scowled. She turned to Poe and said, 'I'm not listening until I'm shown the respect I deserve.'

'I don't think that's possible,' Poe replied. 'Not unless we can find some faeces to fling at you.'

'Excuse me?'

'You heard. Now listen, you dumb piece of sh . . .' Poe took a

146

breath and composed himself. 'Mrs Royal-Cross, I don't know if you're the Botanist's intended third victim or not, and frankly I don't care. The world would be a far nicer place without you in it, but we're cops and that means we don't get to pick and choose who we try to save. So, you're going to listen to Tilly's briefing and if you say one nasty thing to her, I'm going to shave off one of your eyebrows.'

'You wouldn't dare!'

'Try me.'

'I want to speak to your line manager.'

'What's he done now?' Flynn said, walking back into the room.

'He's being rude and aggressive.'

'Poe?'

He shrugged.

'Tilly?' Flynn said.

'Poe said that she was dumb – which she is – and that the world would be better off without her – which it would. He also said he was going to shave off one of her eyebrows, which I thought was rather kind of him. They look very silly.'

'Poe?'

'Boss?'

'Stop being rude and aggressive.'

'Yes, boss.'

'Happy?' Flynn said to Karen Royal-Cross.

'Of course I'm not happy! I want him sacked.'

'You worked out who the idiot in the room is yet, Tilly?' Poe said.

'Karen Royal-Cross isn't a well woman,' Bradshaw said. 'I've been reviewing her online videos and she has a textbook case of histrionic personality disorder.'

'You sure? She barely *has* a personality.'

'I'm sure, Poe.'

'What is it?'

'I most certainly do *not* have a personality disorder!' Karen Royal-Cross snapped.

'It's one of the classic PDs, Poe,' Bradshaw said. 'It's characterised by excessive attention-seeking behaviour. Karen Royal-Cross displays all the recognised traits: manipulating people so she remains the centre of attention, egocentrism, persistent longing for appreciation and approval. She blames others for her failures and has an unrealistic view of her successes. Her neurotransmitters aren't functioning correctly.'

'Stop it!' Karen Royal-Cross yelled.

'How much more is there, Tilly?' Poe asked.

'Lots, Poe. I'm only just getting started.'

'You have two choices then,' Poe said to Karen Royal-Cross. 'I send out for popcorn while Tilly explains what's wrong with you for the next two hours, or you listen to her briefing.'

'Fine,' she sighed. 'Tell me your fake news briefing. I'd rather be dead than listen to any more of that.'

'That's the spirit,' Poe said.

Chapter 43

'Kane Hunt isn't dead, my dear,' Karen Royal-Cross said. 'That man's the grandmaster of the publicity stunt and you could see his chest going up and down when he pretended to fall off his chair.'

'But he didn't die on *The Morgan Soames Hour*, Karen Royal-Cross,' Bradshaw said. 'He died in hospital three days later.'

'And I'm sure that's what you believe.'

'You're a very silly woman.'

Karen Royal-Cross frowned. 'Has anyone told you that you need to work on your people skills?'

'Poe tells me almost every week,' Bradshaw said. She moved her tablet so Karen Royal-Cross could see the screen. 'Now, please, look at these photographs.'

'And I thought Sergeant Poe was a stupid . . .' She trailed off. 'What the hell is that!'

Poe glanced over her shoulder. Kane Hunt was on the slab, rib-cage open. He didn't look well.

'That's one of Kane Hunt's post-mortem photographs, Karen Royal-Cross. The Botanist used hyoscine to murder him. I can assure you, it was not a publicity stunt.'

Karen Royal-Cross stared at the tablet in horror.

'But I thought—'

'Now, please look at this,' Bradshaw said, clearly not giving a monkey's what Karen Royal-Cross thought. 'This is Harrison Cummings in the bath. I've pixelated out his penis, but as you can see, he's dead. This time the Botanist used a neurotoxin found in the fugu pufferfish.'

'And here's the best bit,' Poe added. 'So far, we haven't got a clue how he's doing this . . .'

'But why me?' Karen Royal-Cross sobbed. 'What have I ever done to anyone?'

Poe caught Bradshaw's eye and shook his head. As tempting as it was, now wasn't the time to list the myriad reasons people were queuing up to kill her.

'We need that envelope,' Poe urged. 'The poem will tell us the poison he's planning to use, and the envelope will confirm whether or not it's a copycat.'

She had thrown the pressed flower away so the poem and envelope were all they had. Kew Gardens hadn't yet identified the plant from the video clip she had posted.

'I need you to think,' Flynn said. 'Where could you have put it?'

'I can't remember.'

'Do you recycle, Karen Royal-Cross?' Bradshaw asked.

'Of course I don't. Climate change is a global conspiracy started by the Chinese steel industry.'

'Can we get a search team up here, boss?' Poe said quickly. The last thing anyone wanted was a three-hour presentation from Bradshaw on how fast the icecaps were melting and why future generations might need gills. 'If the envelope's here, they'll find it.'

Karen Royal-Cross's eyes widened. 'A search team?' she said.

'Yes,' Poe said, immediately knowing he was on to something. 'I hope there's nothing illegal in here.'

'I've just remembered where I put it.' She reached under the cushion she was sitting on and handed him the crumpled envelope. Poe put on a pair of forensic gloves and took it from her. He flipped the envelope and saw the scientific drawing. It was in black ink and was exquisitely detailed.

'It's him,' he said. He showed Flynn the intricate picture. 'Kew Gardens shouldn't have any problems identifying what we're dealing with now.'

'I'll email a photograph to Chief Superintendent Mathers,' Flynn said, reaching for her phone.

Poe opened the envelope and carefully removed the poem. It was on expensive paper. Fourteen lines:

To make the terminal bean
To make it cruel and mean
The things you will need
Are puppy dog tails and dandelion weed
The tongue of a quail
And the slime from a snail
The tears of a crone
Or maybe just acetone?
Mash until sleek
Then leave it a week
Be careful not to touch
As it doesn't take much
Because you know there's no vaccine
Once you've had the terminal bean

He reread the first and eighth lines. 'Everybody out!' he ordered. 'Now!'

'One moment, ma'am,' Flynn said into her mobile. 'What is it, Poe?'

'We need specialists, boss.'

'Why?'

'The poem's about a poison bean.'

'So?'

'It also mentions acetone.'

'Shit,' Flynn said. She began urgently whispering into her mobile.

'What is it?' Karen Royal-Cross said. 'You're scaring me. Why's acetone important? It's just the stuff they use in nail-polish remover.'

'Ricin,' Poe said. 'Acetone is used to make ricin.'

Chapter 44

'She was wanting to sell it to the press after we'd left,' Flynn said into her phone. '. . . Yeah, she *is* a moron. Wasn't until we mentioned the search team that she remembered where it was . . . OK, I'll sort it. See you soon, ma'am.' She slipped the phone back into her pocket. Turned and faced the room. 'Well, what are you waiting for?' she said. 'Everybody out. Now!'

The room began to clear. Karen Royal-Cross walked past Poe. He grabbed her arm.

'Not you,' he said.

'I'm not bloody well staying here,' she said.

'What's the problem, Poe?' Flynn said.

'We have no idea how he administers his poisons. She could be unwittingly carrying it now, for all we know. We can't risk exposing anyone else.'

'We can't leave her here on her own, though.'

'I'll stay with her,' he said. 'At least until the hazmat guys clear her and the flat.'

'Why you?'

'You need to coordinate the response and Tilly will probably bore her to death with statistics about climate change.'

Bradshaw stuck her head around the door. 'I heard that.'

'Am I going to die, Sergeant Poe?' Karen Royal-Cross asked.

Lying wasn't the best option right now. He needed her scared. Scared people did as they were told.

'Maybe,' he said.

She sighed. 'Well, my mother used to say there isn't a problem in the world that can't be solved with a nice cup of tea. I'll put the kettle on.'

'Have you been listening to *anything*? He's threatening you with ricin. That's a death sentence. There isn't a cure. There isn't a vaccine. If it gets into your system, you die. It's that simple.'

'What are you saying?'

'I'm saying, you're not putting the bloody kettle on.'

'I assume you don't have a problem with me taking my medication?' she pouted.

'What medication?'

Hunt had been using sildenafil for erectile dysfunction and Cummings had managed his high cholesterol with statins. Their tablets had been tested and come back clean but . . .

'It's private,' she said.

Something embarrassing then.

'Suit yourself,' Poe said. 'The search team will find it anyway.'

She reached into a garish, sequin-covered handbag and brought out a small cardboard box. He could see the white sticker all dispensed medications were required to have. She handed it to Poe.

He still had his forensic gloves on, but he struggled into a second pair. Doubling up was good practice. Karen Royal-Cross was being prescribed orlistat. Poe read the patient information leaflet. It was a lipase inhibitor, a drug designed to treat obesity. It prevented the absorption of one-third of the fat in your meal.

'You think I'm fat, don't you?' Karen Royal-Cross said.

'I don't think about you at all,' Poe replied.

'Charming.'

'Who prescribes this?'

'I order it online.'

'Your GP prescribed it first, though?'

'She did. Although she suggested I try Slimming World instead.'

'You refused?' he said. 'Went straight to the easy solution.'

'You're bloody right I did. Can you imagine what the papers would have said?'

'Where do you collect your prescription?'

'I tick the home delivery box and a couple of days later they pop through my letterbox. No idea who delivers them.'

'When did you last take one?'

153

Poe doubted it was her medication – ricin worked quickly and she still looked annoyingly healthy.

'I had one after my evening meal.'

'And you're feeling OK?'

'You think it's my pills?'

'If it was, you'd be in a coma by now.'

'You really need to work on your bedside mann—'

Poe's phone rang. It was Flynn.

'You still alive in there?'

'Hanging on.'

'And how's KRC?'

'Still annoying.'

'I have good news,' Flynn said. 'Chief Superintendent Mathers has come through. She's got that idiot a bed in the Royal Free Hospital's high-level isolation unit. They usually treat viral haemorrhagic fever but Mathers convinced the consultant there's a genuine public safety risk. She'll be put into a specially designed tent with controlled ventilation. Staff from the infectious diseases unit will provide her care.'

'Great idea. Cummings and Hunt must have ingested their poisons while at home, we just haven't figured out how. The safest way to do this is to take her *out* of her home and *into* an environment we can control.'

'That's almost word for word what Mathers said. An ambulance will collect her. Both the paramedic and the driver will be cops.'

'Why?'

'There hasn't been time to vet anyone.'

'Clever,' Poe said. 'She securing the ward with cops?'

'She is. She's already lost an MP so she's not skimping. We all need to change our clothes and go through a hazmat wash, but after that we'll meet Mathers in the command post she's set up in the isolation unit.'

Poe couldn't think of anything more that could be done. If the Botanist managed to get to Karen Royal-Cross in an isolation ward surrounded by cops then he reckoned they'd have to call in a Catholic priest – the only remaining explanation would be that a ghost did it.

'What's happening?' Karen Royal-Cross asked after he had hung up.

Poe flashed her an evil grin. 'Have you ever seen the *Seinfeld* episode "The Bubble Boy"?'

'I have, actually.'

'Good, because you're about to star in the British version.'

The high-level isolation ward took up half the infectious diseases unit, although in an emergency, the remainder could be converted for category four use. The ward included the bed unit; the tightly restricted area where the patient was isolated, and a doffing area where nurses and doctors could safely remove their PPE. There were laboratories and anterooms and nurses' stations, everything a modern hospital needed to treat highly contagious patients.

The bed unit was a square room dominated by the bed. A metal frame encased in transparent plastic made it look like the bed was inside a high-tech polytunnel. A filtration unit provided negative air pressure, ensuring airborne pathogens were contained inside. Sleeves built into the plastic sheeting allowed doctors and nurses to deliver clinical care. A smaller tented unit was attached to the end of the bed. It was used to pass through food and drinks, and anything else the patient required. Anything coming back out, including human waste, would be rendered safe in an autoclave, a high-pressure chamber that subjected everything to pressurised, saturated steam.

Although Karen Royal-Cross was perfectly healthy, the infectious diseases consultant, an Asian with a cultured Glaswegian accent called Doctor Mukherjee, was managing her as if she were contagious.

'Even if this turns out to be nothing, at least we can practise policies and procedures,' he said. 'Fail to prepare, prepare to fail.'

Which meant Poe and the rest of the cops were restricted to monitoring Karen Royal-Cross via the ward's advanced video and telecommunications system. Only doctors and nurses were allowed on to the bed unit.

Doctor Mukherjee entered the room they were using as a

command post. He popped a can of Coke and took the seat beside Poe.

'We'll check her urinary biomarkers for ricinine every time she urinates,' he said.

'What's that?'

'It's an alkaloid in the castor bean plant. It's why we have her drinking lots of water – the more she urinates, the more we can check.'

'What will you do if the Botanist gets to her?' Poe asked.

'I don't see how he could.'

'Humour me.'

'You think she's in danger, don't you?'

'So far he has a one hundred per cent hit rate,' Poe admitted. 'We have no idea how he administers his poison, so we have no idea how to stop him.'

'But she's being watched twenty-four hours a day.'

'So was Harrison Cummings.'

'In that case, we would help her breathe. Fill her with fluids. Manage her seizures and low blood pressure.'

'Then what?' Poe asked.

'Then we would watch her die,' Mukherjee replied.

Chapter 46

'How long have they agreed to keep her, ma'am?' Flynn asked Chief Superintendent Mathers.

'If no genuine cases come in, a fortnight. We'll contribute to the costs and they'll put it down as a joint training exercise.'

'And worst-case scenario, everyone gets to think about a ricin attack in the capital,' Poe said.

'Do you think he's stupid enough to make a move here, Sergeant Poe?'

Poe looked around the adapted command centre. It was in a sectioned-off area of the nurses' station. Anyone going into the bed unit had to pass through Mathers's handpicked cops. Their IDs were scanned then a member of staff vouched that they worked on the ward. The medical team routinely monitored the bed unit's video and telecommunications system, but now cops had their eyes on the screen as well.

'I don't see how he possibly can,' Poe admitted.

'But?'

'But I'd have said the same thing about Harrison Cummings. The Botanist got to him and he was in Specialist Command's security bubble.'

'That's what I'm afraid of. I don't feel as confident as I—' A burp of static from her radio stopped Mathers. She tilted her head, pressed the transmit button and said, 'Say again.' She listened then frowned. 'OK, thank you. You did the right thing.'

'Problem?' Flynn said.

'The Botanist has been in touch again.'

Poe got out of his chair. He didn't know why. 'And?' he said.

'He wants to speak to Henning Stahl. The sergeant he spoke to gave him the command centre's number. He's calling back in two hours.'

'Why so long?' Flynn asked.

'He knows where we are and he knows where Stahl is,' Poe said. 'He knows we'll have to collect him.'

'He's watching us?'

'Or second-guessing what we'll do. I'll go and get Stahl.'

'Get uniform to drive you. I'll authorise blues and twos to make sure you aren't held up.'

Chapter 47

'We can't let him speak to the Botanist in this state,' Chief Superintendent Mathers said. 'He's too drunk.'

She wasn't wrong. Poe had found Stahl in the hotel bar, surrounded by empty glasses. It looked like he'd been having a party.

'What choice do we have?' he said. 'Yes, he's pissed, but so what? If the Botanist knows him, he'll also know he's an alcoholic. If he doesn't know him, we can send him a scan of his liver.'

'DI Flynn?' Mathers said.

'You're right to be cautious, ma'am, but Poe's also right. If we delay he might not call back. I think it's a risk worth taking.'

'Where's Stahl now?'

'Couple of rooms away,' Poe said. 'Doctor Mukherjee's put an IV in him. He's topping up his water, blood sugar and vitamin levels.'

'That'll sober him up?'

'No idea. But he took one look at him and said he wanted to treat him for alcohol poisoning.'

Mathers put her head in her hands. 'What a bloody mess,' she said.

'We have to at least try,' Poe said. 'You haven't seen what's happening out there. There are whackjobs on the street marching in support of him. Queuing up to buy Botanist T-shirts, like children waiting to see a garden-centre Santa.'

'We know about the T-shirts. Amazon has agreed to remove anything with the Botanist on, but you know how entrepreneurial third-party sellers get on there. They're avoiding the Amazon ban by selling T-shirts that don't mention the Botanist at all. "Public Service Isn't Murder" and "Send That Man A Poem" are the highest selling items of clothing today.'

'And if he keeps choosing unsympathetic victims it's only going to get worse. He has a cult following now, imagine what'll happen if he gets to Karen Royal-Cross? Most of the country will rejoice.'

Mathers groaned. 'Fine,' she said, 'we'll let Stahl talk to him.'

'And we have to change the narrative,' Poe said.

'How?'

Poe thought about what the Botanist was doing. He was targeting high-profile dickheads, something the UK had an unending supply of. The public wouldn't turn on him unless he made a mistake and killed the wrong person. And so far he hadn't put a foot wrong. Given what he was doing, that seemed unlikely.

'I'm not buying the story he's feeding, ma'am,' he said. 'I don't want to big him up, but he's been flawless so far. Hasn't left a shred of evidence and has killed exactly who he said he would.'

'So?'

'So, how the hell did he get so good?'

Mathers looked at him shrewdly.

'He rehearsed,' he continued. 'That's how. He practised on people who wouldn't be missed.'

'And given how connected the UK is, it wouldn't be here,' Mathers agreed. 'While we do have a homeless population, people would notice if some of them went missing. Plus, where would he do it?'

'Exactly. I live in one of the most sparsely populated corners of the UK and even there someone would notice if human experiments were going on. That's too much risk for this guy.'

'He rehearsed abroad then.'

'That's my guess. Somewhere remote.'

'I'll get a blue notice drafted. Get it circulated today.'

Poe nodded his approval. An Interpol blue notice was a request to locate, identify or obtain information on a person of interest in a criminal investigation. It would go out to almost two hundred countries. If the Botanist had left breadcrumbs abroad, a blue notice was the first step towards finding them.

The designated phone rang. They all looked at each other.

'We ready?' Mathers asked.

Poe and Flynn nodded.

She pressed answer and the voice of the Botanist filled the room.

Chapter 48

'This is Detective Chief Superintendent Mathers,' she said. 'Who am I speaking to?'

'You know who I am,' the Botanist replied. 'Is Mr Stahl there?'

'He's with a doctor right now. I can get him, though.'

'There's no need to bother him if he's receiving medical attention.'

'Oh. I thought you wanted to speak to him?'

'I do, but not over the phone. I'll be meeting with him face-to-face.'

'Face-to-face?' Mathers said.

'Yes.'

'Even though we'll arrest you on sight?'

'That's my problem, not yours.'

'Why would you do this?'

'Henning Stahl was a good journalist once,' the Botanist said. 'Perhaps he could be again.'

'When?'

'Tomorrow.'

'Where?'

'Aha,' the Botanist said. 'You nearly got me with your cunning police tricks there. I'll let you know "where" a bit nearer to the time.'

'Is that all?'

'For now.'

'No,' Poe said, loudly.

Mathers stared at him in horror.

Flynn hissed, 'Poe! What the hell are you doing?'

'Who is this?' the Botanist asked.

'Detective Sergeant Washington Poe.'

'What do you mean "no", Sergeant Poe?'

'Look, I'm not being a prick about this,' Poe said. 'This isn't some weird negotiation tactic. I said no because you don't want to meet Henning Stahl tomorrow.'

'I don't?'

'No. You picked Stahl for one of two reasons: you either want him to write your story . . .'

'Or?'

'Or you want to kill him.'

'Go on.'

'If it's the first reason, I've got to tell you that Mr Stahl is a wreck right now. He's a serious alcoholic. Has untold liver damage and when the blood tests come back, I suspect he'll have the hepatitis alphabet as well. He's drunk by nine in the morning and he only gets drunker. If we withhold alcohol from him before the meeting he'll get life-threatening withdrawal symptoms.'

'And if I want to kill him?'

'He's trying to drink himself to death,' Poe said. 'Just how much satisfaction will you get from that? The poor bastard will probably welcome it.'

The Botanist didn't respond.

Mathers nodded appreciatively at Poe. 'Good job,' she whispered.

'I have a solution though,' Poe said.

'I thought you might.'

'Give me a fortnight.'

'And what will that buy you?'

'I can get him ready in two weeks,' Poe said. 'I've spoken to a doctor and he tells me Mr Stahl's alcohol addiction is so advanced it requires a medically supervised detox. He'll be treated as an in-patient and will be sober when he comes out.'

'Mr Stahl has agreed to this?'

'He hasn't been told yet, but I think he will.'

'You have ten days,' the Botanist said.

The phone went dead.

Chapter 49

Doctor Mukherjee arranged for Henning Stahl to go to an addiction centre outside London. Mathers had a police convoy transport him there. He went willingly. Poe thought Stahl had recognised that, for whatever reason, the Botanist had thrown him a lifeline.

'What now?' Mathers asked. 'Karen Royal-Cross is under twenty-four-hour observation and Stahl's about to have the worst forty-eight hours of his life. We have ten days to plan for an operation that could take place anywhere in the country. Have I missed anything?'

Poe didn't think she had. Bradshaw shook her head.

'Your team will keep working the evidence?' Flynn said.

'What there is, yes.'

'Can I stand my lot down for a couple of days? We've been at this non-stop and I wouldn't mind seeing my son.'

'Take longer, if you need. I have your mobile numbers and I'll copy you in on anything relevant.'

'That OK with you, Poe?'

'It is, boss. I'll head up north.'

'Are you planning on seeing Estelle?' Flynn said.

'I am.'

'And the crime scene?'

'Northumbria haven't released it yet.'

'Tell her I'm thinking of her.'

'I will.'

'Tilly, what will you do?'

'I'm going with Poe. He wants me to review the evidence against Estelle Doyle, DI Flynn. He says I might have "science answers", whatever that means.'

'It means he's stuck, Tilly.'

Poe nodded. 'I hate locked room mysteries,' he said.

Chapter 50

Poe left immediately and was back in Cumbria by midnight. He dropped Bradshaw at the Shap Wells Hotel then quad-biked across the fell to Herdwick Croft.

He was dog-tired and the two cases were beginning to merge in his thoughts. Both impossible, both time-sensitive. Someone who could levitate over fresh snow had murdered Estelle Doyle's father and the Botanist was killing with impunity. He couldn't begin to explain either and the stakes were being raised daily.

As he crested the last peak, black against the starlit sky, he thumbed a text to Mathers, asking for an update. She responded immediately. No change in the health of Karen Royal-Cross, no breakthroughs on any line of enquiry. She ended the text telling him to get some rest and come back refreshed.

Fat chance, he thought. He was up here to work.

Poe turned on his generator and fired up the wood-burning stove. He wasn't hungry, but he opened a bottle of Spun Gold and drained it in one go. He took another bottle upstairs to drink in bed. The irony wasn't lost on him. Henning Stahl was probably strapped to a gurney somewhere, sweating, withdrawing, IV lines pumping medication and fluids into his alcohol-ravaged body, while he was drinking beer in bed.

He raised the bottle, took a swig and said, 'Get well, mate.'

Ania Kierczynska, Estelle Doyle's solicitor, had arranged for Poe and Bradshaw to see Estelle as official visitors. It meant they'd see her in a private room rather than the communal visiting area.

HMP Low Newton was an all-female, maximum-security prison in the village of Brasside, County Durham. Past inmates included

Rosemary West and the serial killer Joanna Dennehy. It was a serious prison.

Poe hadn't been there for years and the process of getting inside had changed dramatically. Last time he'd flashed his ID card and been waved through. This time he had the ignominy of sitting on the BOSS chair, the Body Orifice Security Scanner. Satisfied he hadn't 'plugged' a mobile phone up his rectum, he'd been given a laminated pass and told he was good to go. He turned and waited for Bradshaw. She was deep in conversation with the prison officer operating the chair.

Poe frowned and walked back over.

'What's the problem?' he asked. 'Don't tell me Tilly's had a positive reading?'

'Why would I have metal up my bottom, Poe?' Bradshaw replied. 'I was asking this lady if the low intensity magnetic field that the BOSS chair uses to detect conductive metal is configured in a Mach–Zehnder interferometric arrangement.'

'It's true,' the prison officer said. 'She *did* ask that.'

'I'm sure I read somewhere it does, Tilly,' Poe said. 'Come on, Estelle's waiting for us.'

Chapter 51

Estelle Doyle wasn't a convicted prisoner; she was on remand. That meant, among other things, she didn't have to wear the prison uniform. Poe doubted she'd ever worn an outfit like this, though. A shapeless jumper, and jeans so baggy she had to hold them up with her left hand. Straight out of the prison spares cupboard, no doubt. She looked like a child who'd lost her school uniform. When she reached across the table to shake their hands with her right, Poe held her hand a little longer than he was comfortable with. Her thin, strong fingers, gripped him back. He looked down and saw blue veins visible under her translucent skin. He turned her wrist slightly and checked her lower arm for bruises. There weren't any.

'Don't worry, Poe,' Doyle said softly. 'They call me Doctor Death in here. My cellmate, a lovely heroin addict called Britney, was, in her words, "clucking like a C-word" last night. She used a sharpened toothbrush on the inside of her thigh, just to get away from me. Nicked her femoral vein. I tried to help, apply pressure to the wound, but she was so scared of me she pressed the panic button. I think she survived.'

Poe let go of her hand and sat on one of the four moulded plastic seats. The Formica-topped table was scarred with cigarette burns. A tinfoil ashtray was the only thing in the room that wasn't bolted to the floor. The cubicle smelled of body odour, industrial disinfectant and despair.

'It's better to be feared in here,' he said.

She held him in an intense gaze. 'I disagree,' she said finally.

'May I hug you, Estelle Doyle?' Bradshaw asked.

'I think I'd like that, Tilly.'

Bradshaw walked around to her side of the table. The two women held each other for a long time, long enough for the prison officer monitoring the official visits suite to get interested. Poe shook his head at him. 'It's OK,' he mouthed.

When they'd finished embracing, Doyle sat down. Poe could see her eyes were glistening. He pretended not to notice. Sometimes Bradshaw's innocence was exactly what people needed.

'Shall I ask for the wine list, Poe?' Doyle said.

'He only drinks beer, Estelle Doyle,' Bradshaw said.

Doyle smiled. Poe did too.

'What?' Bradshaw said.

'Your solicitor tells me she's knocked down the CPS's motivation,' Poe said. 'That your father's new will didn't materially change that much.'

'So I've been told.'

'Without motivation our alternate theory holds more water.'

'And what alternate theory is this?'

'Someone is setting you up.'

'That's your theory?'

'No,' Poe said. 'It's *our* theory.'

'I'm a doctor and a pathologist. I'm not in a position to make enemies like this.'

'You'd be surprised how easy it is for someone to work up a good grudge. Tilly's profiling people you've given evidence against.'

'If this is true, some—'

'It is.'

'—Someone's gone to an awful lot of trouble,' Doyle said. 'If they hate me that much it almost seems rude to fight it.'

Poe considered this. 'Sod that,' he said.

'How long are you up here?'

'Another three days. I'm hoping Northumbria will release the crime scene before we have to go back down south.'

'I'd prefer it if you didn't go to my father's home, Poe.'

Which took him by surprise. 'Why ever not?'

Doyle didn't respond.

'Why not, Estelle?' he repeated. 'I need to see where it happened.'

'I don't want you seeing where my father lived,' she said eventually.

'Is it because he was poor?' Bradshaw said. 'Because Poe doesn't care about things like that, do you, Poe?'

'You do know I've seen photographs of his study?' he said to Doyle. 'And Elcid wasn't poor, Tilly. Far from it; he was quite wealthy.'

'I still don't want you seeing where he lived, Poe.'

Poe didn't understand. He knew he worked best when he'd seen everything for himself. When he had a visual image running in the background, day in, day out. Ruining his sleep. Doyle had known him long enough to know this. She wasn't telling him something.

He folded his arms. 'As soon as that crime scene's released, I'm going inside.'

'You're a stubborn, stubborn man, Poe,' Doyle sighed.

'I'm not putting your future in the hands of some dipshit CSI photographer and an ambitious SIO. You're the villain of their piece and they aren't considering other explanations. And if they aren't considering other explanations, that means the only things they photographed were the things that fit their narrative. I want to look at the things they *didn't* photograph.'

'But—'

'I'll be honest, Estelle,' Poe cut in. 'Tilly's going to science the shit out of the positive firearms discharge residue test. By the time she's finished rubbishing it, inmates on Florida's death row will be filing appeals.'

'There's a point to this uplifting tale, I assume?'

'Unfortunately there is.'

She tilted her head. Her lips curved in a quarter-smile.

'We can't explain how someone can cross fresh snow without leaving a footprint,' Poe continued. 'And that's the whole ball game. If we can't put someone else at the scene, we're all going home.' He replayed what he'd just said. Spotted his error. 'Well, you won't, obviously, but you get my point.'

'And you think this conundrum will be defogged by your visit?'

He hesitated before answering. Lack of hope was a killer – literally – in prison, but he also needed to prepare her for what was likely to happen. They could knock down as many of the CPS's building

170

blocks as they wanted, but unless they explained away the foundation of their prosecution, Doyle was going to be convicted of her father's murder. No ifs, no buts; it was happening. Poe chose his words carefully.

'I know you didn't shoot your dad, Estelle,' he said. 'And that means someone else did. That someone wasn't in the house when the police arrived, and there's no evidence to support him or her having left before you arrived. Unless Tilly can explain away the snow, there's got to be something in the house that Northumbria have missed. And I won't be able to find it by looking at photographs.'

'And if you can't find it?'

'Then you're spending the next twenty years in here.'

She took a silent moment then said, 'Thank you, Poe.'

'For what?'

'Your honesty.' Doyle faced Bradshaw. 'So, Tilly, *can* someone walk across snow without leaving footprints?'

'Legolas could,' she said. 'Humans can't.'

They both looked at Poe. Doyle fought a smile.

'Ha! I actually know that reference,' Poe said. 'He's an elf in *Lord of the Rings*. I read it at school.'

'Yes, Poe. A Sindarin Elf from the Woodland Realm.'

'Dork,' he said.

Chapter 52

'Tell me what you're working on,' Doyle said. 'It'll take my mind off things.'

'You've heard of this Botanist?' Poe said.

'Just snippets. My fellow inmates prefer *Geordie Shore* to the news. They also seem to enjoy shouting "slag" at the women on the show for some reason, but that's a discussion for a different day, I fear.'

Poe spent five minutes giving her a brief outline of where they were. Bradshaw chipped in with the Latin names of the poisons and some of the more technical stuff.

When they'd finished Doyle said, 'What do you know about poisons, Poe?'

'Probably not as much as I should.'

'Tell me what you *do* know.'

'It's long-arm murder,' he said.

'I'm not familiar with the phrase.'

'Murder from afar. The murderer doesn't have to be present when the victim takes the poison.'

'What else?'

'You can drip-feed small amounts over a period of time or you can do what our guy must be doing – give them one big unsurvivable dose.'

'A "guy"? I know it's a myth that most poisoners are women, but you seem surer than you ought to about the killer's gender.'

'Poe's spoken to him, Estelle Doyle,' Bradshaw said.

'You have?'

'He's a showboat,' Poe said. 'You should see it out there, Estelle. Loads of dickheads wearing T-shirts. Going on the news saying it's the start of the revolution.'

'Why?'

'He chooses unsympathetic victims – Kane Hunt was an appalling misogynist and Harrison Cummings was a corrupt MP. We got to the last one in time, but arguably she's the worst of the lot – she's monetised racism.'

'How did you get to her in time? I thought you said he gave them unsurvivable doses?'

'Because, believe it or not, he warns them first. Sends them a poem and a pressed flower in the post. Both connected to the poison he's planning to use.'

This didn't elicit the surprise Poe had anticipated.

'I assume the dead men were being protected at the time they died?'

'The MP was,' Poe said. 'We didn't know about Kane Hunt's death threat until he collapsed on live television.'

'He's planting the poison *before* he warns them then. Gets them to take it themselves.'

'Where?'

'It'll be something simple.' Doyle looked thoughtful. 'What do we do every day?'

'Eat. Drink. Sleep. Brush our teeth. Shower.'

'Charge our laptops, phones and tablets,' Bradshaw said.

'The usual stuff, in other words,' Poe said. 'But we've pretty much ruled that out. Anything the victims might have touched has been checked.'

'Poe even got in the bath and checked underneath the taps in case Mr Cummings had cut himself when he used his foot to add hot water.'

'He's not bribing or threatening someone to bring the poison in?'

'We can't rule that out,' Poe admitted.

'But?'

'But I don't think that's how he's doing it. This guy's careful. Bribing someone leaves too many variables.'

'And you don't think he's somehow forcing them to take it themselves. Threatening to expose a shameful secret?'

Poe snorted.

'Cummings didn't possess the shame gene,' he said. 'And Hunt was a shallow gobshite. And if you threatened to expose one of Karen Royal-Cross's secrets she'd just start yapping about fake news and how it was all the fault of immigrants.'

'Well then,' Doyle said, 'it seems it's a case of waiting your whole career for an impossible crime and two showing up at the same time.'

'I swear, I'm one bad mood away from declaring it black magic and going home.'

He checked his watch. They'd been allocated two hours for the visit and he wanted to use it all. Doyle being out of her cell, talking about something normal, for her at least, was probably preferable to being in her cell trying to read indecipherable graffiti. Also, her brain was as big as Bradshaw's – discussing a case with her was always time well spent.

'Tell me about poison,' he said.

'All things are poison and nothing is without poison,' she said automatically.

Poe leaned forward.

'Explain,' he said.

Chapter 53

'It's part of a famous quote, Poe,' Doyle said. 'A man called Paracelsus is believed to have said it in the sixteenth century. It ends on, "Surely it is the dose that determines that a thing is poison."'

'What's that mean?'

'Would it surprise you if I said that in the right dosage, fruit can be poisonous?'

Poe glanced at Bradshaw. 'Told you,' he said.

'For example, the potassium in bananas is a naturally occurring radioactive isotope. Eat enough and you get radiation poisoning.'

'You're joking?'

'Tilly?'

'She's right, Poe,' Bradshaw said. 'In an infinitesimal amount obviously. If you give me a second . . .' She shut her eyes and began muttering under her breath. Poe and Doyle stared at each other. Poe shrugged in a no-idea-what-she's-doing kind of way. In less than a minute Bradshaw's eyes opened. 'I estimate you would have to eat one hundred million bananas in a twelve-hour period to get a lethal dose.'

'I need to go to hospital then,' Poe said. 'I had one hundred million bananas for breakfast.'

Doyle laughed, the first time she had since they'd been there. 'And before you start gloating about your diet,' she said, 'even cheese can be poisonous.'

He paused, then said, 'Even cheddar?'

'I'm afraid so. It's called tyrotoxism.'

'*Cheese* is poisonous?'

'My point is this. You have to think round corners when it comes to intelligent poisoners. Gone are the days when cutting-edge medicine was using dried eel skins as elasticated bandages. Scientists are doing extraordinary things now. They're editing the genes of crops to make them drought resistant, the genes of babies so they don't inherit hereditary diseases. And tomorrow's science is today's magic, don't forget. Or *black* magic, as you put it. What's to say there isn't someone out there making single-use, designer poisons? Untraceable at source, only reacts when it's in the body, designed to mimic a known poison.'

'You think that's what's happening?'

'I have no idea,' she said. 'But, as you've run all your tests, followed your murder manuals, you need to start thinking creatively – he certainly is.'

'Will you help me?' he said.

'From in here?'

'If I can get you copies of the post-mortem reports?'

'How will you do that? I understand that some poor soul has to read every inmate's mail. PM documents will be marked as contraband, Poe. You could get in trouble.'

'You may as well have dared him, Estelle Doyle,' Bradshaw sighed.

'Well, if he gets caught, he can always share my cell. Britney won't be back any time soon and it gets very cold at night. What do you think, Tilly? Is that a good idea?'

Uncharacteristically, Bradshaw giggled and blushed.

Poe shook his head in exasperation. 'You two will be the death of me,' he said.

Doyle smiled. 'Pretty sure you're going to live forever, Poe.'

He considered that for a moment. 'What a horrible thought,' he said.

Thinking creatively was on Poe's mind as they made their way back to the car park. Specifically, how he could get post-mortem reports to someone in a high-security prison. He was concentrating so much, when someone shouted his name it didn't immediately register.

Bradshaw nudged him. 'Poe, I think that man wants to speak to you.'

'What man?'

She pointed to the other side of the car park. 'The one shouting your name.'

The man jogged towards them. He looked familiar although Poe couldn't place him. He was obviously a cop – the rubber-soled shoes were a dead giveaway. He was in his early thirties and looked as keen as Tabasco. Bright of eye and ruddy of cheek. Poe was glad he didn't have to work with him.

'Sergeant Poe,' he smiled, pushing out his hand. 'We haven't officially met. I'm Detective Constable Robert Bowness. I was one of the first detectives at the crime scene that night.'

He had a strong Geordie accent. Poe shook his hand. 'Haven't I seen you before, Robert?'

'I'm part of the Elcid Doyle murder investigation. I was in the custody suite in Newcastle when you visited Miss Doyle. You've caused quite a stir.'

'Gosh, that *is* surprising,' Bradshaw said.

Poe ignored her. 'I did? How?'

'By reputation,' Bowness said. 'I know Detective Chief Inspector Tai-young Lee has had to have meetings about your involvement.'

'She has?' he said, aware he wasn't sounding too awesome right then. 'Why?'

'I would imagine they're worried about you. Trouble seems to find you, Sergeant Poe. She's got us going back through the evidence, triple-checking everything. I don't suppose finding out that you've been visiting Miss Doyle in prison will help improve her mood.'

Poe grunted. He had some sympathy for Tai-young Lee. He wouldn't like another cop looking over his shoulder, telling him where he was going wrong. But Doyle was his friend and Northumbria Police *had* got it wrong.

'What are you doing here?' Poe asked. 'I assume I'm not being followed?'

'Nothing like that,' Bowness laughed. 'Just going in to see Miss Doyle. Part of the triple-checking the chief inspector wants.'

'It's *Professor* Doyle,' Poe said. 'And you're triple-checking what?'

'Sorry. And it's all in the defence bundle. I assume you've seen it?'

Poe didn't answer.

'Right,' Bowness grinned.

'You say you were one of the first on the scene?'

'I was.'

'You got anything that isn't in the defence bundle? First impressions that didn't get reported?'

'Everything went in my report.'

'Everything?'

Bowness dropped his gaze for a moment, long enough for Poe to sense there was something he'd omitted.

'What is it?' he asked. 'What didn't you put in your report?'

'It's nothing really,' he said, reddening. 'Certainly not the type of thing you'd put in writing.'

'Tell me.'

'Cricket bats, Sergeant Poe. That's what I didn't put in my report.'

Poe frowned. 'There was a cricket bat in Elcid Doyle's office?' he said. 'I don't remember seeing that on the list.'

'No, you misunderstand. When I went into his office I thought I could *smell* cricket bats.'

'What are you, a fucking bloodhound?'

Bowness shrugged. 'You can understand why I didn't mention it. And it was linseed oil I could smell really. But my dad used the stuff to condition his cricket bat, so that's where the association came from.'

Poe didn't respond.

'Told you it was nothing.'

'Maybe not, Detective Constable Robert Bowness,' Bradshaw said. 'Of all the senses, smell has the longest evolutionary history. It goes back to how single-celled organisms interacted with their surrounding chemicals. It explains why we have over one thousand types of smell receptors but only four light sensors. It's the only sense that bypasses the thalamus. Scents go straight to the brain's olfactory bulb, which is directly connected to the amygdala and the hippocampus. It's why smells trigger such detailed memories and emotions.'

Bowness stared at her in surprise. Poe saw his expression change as understanding dawned on him. 'You're Tilly Bradshaw,' he said.

'I am very pleased to meet you, Detective Constable Robert Bowness.'

'We didn't know you were involved as well. The chief inspector's going to be bloody thrilled about this.'

'That's nice,' Bradshaw said.

'This linseed oil,' Poe said, 'did anyone else notice it?'

'If they did, they didn't say. Do you think it's important?'

'I don't see how it possibly can be.'

Bowness shrugged. 'You asked if there was anything I didn't put in my report.'

'I did, and thank you,' Poe said. Something dawned on him, something he couldn't share with the young detective. 'Anyway, nice to meet you, Robert, but Tilly and I have a meeting we need to get to. Can you let Detective Chief Inspector Tai-young Lee know I'm up here?'

'She'd sack me if I didn't.'

'Good man.'

After he'd gone, Bradshaw said, 'What meeting are we going to, Poe? I have nothing in my e-diary.'

'No meeting, Tilly, I just wanted rid of him.'

He unlocked the car and retrieved his phone from the glove box. He scrolled through his recent contacts, found the name he was looking for and pressed call.

'How can I help you, Sergeant Poe?' Doyle's solicitor said.

'When are you next due to visit, Estelle, Ania?'

'Tomorrow morning. I have some documents for her to go through.'

'And she's allowed to keep legal documents in her cell, right?'

'She is. And they're privileged. The prison staff aren't permitted to go through them.'

'Would you be able to slip something in for me?'

'What?'

'Post-mortem reports from the case I'm working on. Estelle's agreed to look at them.'

'And why would I do that?'

'I'd say because I'm out here trying to prove Estelle's innocence, but she's my friend and I'm going to do this even if you say no. And you know that.'

'So, why should I?'

'Because it'll help her feel normal,' Poe said. 'It's a madhouse in there. Last night the woman she's padded up with almost killed herself with a toothbrush. I'm worried about her and I think having something to focus on will do her good.'

Ania didn't respond.

'Also, I'm completely stuck.'

'And I thought people were exaggerating when they said you were dangerous, anti-authoritarian and had a discipline problem.'

'You'll do it?'

'I will. I'm concerned about Estelle's wellbeing, too. Email me everything. That way I can print it out on our stationery. Should be enough to fool a casual observer.'

'Don't do that,' Poe said. 'If she gets caught, I'll say I smuggled it in. I'm the discipline case, you have a bright career ahead of you.'

When he'd hung up, Bradshaw said, 'Where are we going now, Poe?'

'We'll get a bite to eat, then I want to time the journey from Estelle's workplace to her dad's house. We may as well check the discrepancy in the timeline. And although the crime scene hasn't been released, we might be able to peep through the windows.'

Chapter 54

Poe was lost. He hadn't expected to be, as he thought he knew the Corbridge area reasonably well. It had a good bookshop and a microbrewery, pretty much two of his favourite things. The satnav said he'd reached his destination a mile down a narrow country lane. He didn't like satnavs. He wasn't stupid enough to drive into a river because a robot told him to, but he was forever typing in the wrong postcode. But Bradshaw had entered Elcid Doyle's address and it was therefore correct. She didn't make mistakes like that.

So far, the journey time from Doyle's workplace – the Royal Victoria Infirmary – to the address on the satnav had been within Bradshaw's margin of error.

'I don't think Northumbria Police made a mistake with the time discrepancy, Poe,' she said. 'There are forty minutes we can't account for.'

Poe grunted his annoyance. He hadn't thought Northumbria had made a mistake, but was disappointed anyway. He now had to find an alternative explanation.

He stopped in front of the intricate, wrought-iron gates of what he assumed was the entrance to a stately home. There was another car parked a couple of hundred yards ahead of him. A red Volvo. It had pulled up on the side of the road as well. Its warning signal was on. Poe reckoned they were lost too. Unsurprising really – he hadn't seen a signpost for miles.

Poe tried to get his bearings. If the estate were on the map he would have a reference point to work from. He searched for the estate's name, but the arching canopy of trees cast the entrance in shadows. The gates were black. Poe could see bubbles of rust erupting, like lava, on the thick vertical bars. They were being maintained, but not expensively. A new padlock and chain ensured they couldn't be opened. No one lived there then. The drive twisted up an incline and into the distance, meaning Poe couldn't see the house.

Cumbria and Northumberland had hundreds of sprawling estates like this. They seemed to be propped up by subsidies and organised shoots. Deer and game mainly.

Poe was fundamentally opposed to inherited wealth, although he'd never put a finger on why. His father owned several properties and they'd never discussed what would happen when he died. He had no desire to inherit a property portfolio, but he was damned if the government were getting hold of it. Something to stew over.

'What's Estelle's dad's address again, Tilly?'

She told him.

'And I've been tracking our journey on my phone,' she added. 'We aren't lost, Poe. The house just isn't where we were told it would be.'

He went back to studying the map. 'What's it called again, Tilly?' he said

'Highwood, Poe.'

'And we were given no other directions?'

'No. Just the house name and postcode.'

'I'll call Estelle's solicitor,' Poe said. 'She'll know where it is. Her firm has represented the family for generations.'

He took a moment to digest his own words. 'That's odd, isn't it?' he said.

'What is, Poe?'

'Who has a family firm of solicitors these days?'

'I don't know, Poe. I do all my own legal work. I find it therapeutic.'

Poe glanced at her. 'You're very strange, Tilly. But my point is that normal people engage solicitors when they're buying a house, getting divorced or when someone dies.'

'I haven't thought about it, Poe.'

He shrugged. It was probably nothing. He found Ania Kierczynska in his contacts and called her.

'Ania,' he said when she answered. 'We can't find Highwood. The satnav has taken us to the middle of nowhere. Are there any directions you can give me?'

'Why do you want to see Highwood?' she asked. 'The police haven't released it yet.'

'We've been timing Estelle's journey.'

'I have news on that, as it happens. My assistant found something buried in one of the police statements.'

'Helpful?'

'Possibly.'

'What is it?'

'When Estelle left work she discovered she had a flat tyre. She had to get it changed before she went to her dad's.'

'Surely the police took that into account?'

'The CPS contend her journey took the usual time and she used the extra time to stage the burglary.'

'So, it's possible that when Estelle told them how long her journey had taken, she assumed they'd included the time it had taken to change her tyre.'

'It's possible.'

'Which statement was it on?'

'One of the first. She was still a witness at that point so the police officer was letting her talk. She mentioned the flat tyre when he asked her what time she'd left work.'

'And it wasn't mentioned again?'

'We can't see it anywhere.'

Poe hadn't been able to quiz Doyle about her journey the first time he'd seen her. He'd wanted to ask if she'd stopped off for a bottle of whisky or something on the way to her dad's, but Tai-young Lee had warned him not to interfere in the investigation. And he'd just plain forgotten today.

'Can you send it to Tilly?' he asked Ania.

'I'll do it now.'

'Thanks. Who did she use to change the flat tyre?'

'Said she did it herself.'

'No video?'

'RVI staff car park doesn't have CCTV.'

The flat tyre was troubling. If someone was ultra-cynical, they might have suggested Doyle had dropped this into an early interview so it was on record. During a trial she could make it appear as if the CPS barrister had been hiding things, and the more she could do that, the less believable everything else became. Reasonable doubt – that was all she needed. He put the thought out of his mind. Doyle was being framed. He was sure of it.

'Anyway,' Poe said. 'We've managed to get lost. We're where the satnav told us to be, but we can't find her dad's house.'

'Where are you now?'

'Outside some stately home.'

'Does this stately home have black gates? They'll be mounted on stone pillars, green with algae.'

'It does. They're padlocked shut. Are we near?'

'Is there a sign on one of the stone pillars?'

It took a few seconds for Poe's eyes to adjust to the gloom, but there was a sign. It was old and wooden. The creep of green algae had covered both the pillar and the sign. No wonder he'd missed it earlier. Words were engraved into the wood but they were illegible.

'Yes,' he said.

'What does it say?'

'I can't make it out from here.'

He got out of the car and stood in front of the sign. 'Ah,' he said. '*This* is Elcid Doyle's house? This massive estate?'

'Highwood is the Doyles' ancestral home, yes.'

'Why didn't she want me seeing it?'

'Your opinion of her is very important, and she's aware of your views on the aristocracy. She didn't want you to think less of her.'

'But . . . why would I think less of her? Just because her dad's rich? That's stupid. *My* dad's rich.'

'Nevertheless.'

'Just how big an estate is it?'

'Almost eighteen thousand acres of prime farming land. Numerous tenants. One of the best grouse moors in the country.'

'And the house?'

'Comparatively modest,' Ania said. 'Just fifteen bedrooms and a few reception rooms. Elcid's office, obviously. Why, is that important?'

'It could be,' Poe replied. 'When the police said they'd searched the house to make sure the killer wasn't still on the premises, I thought they were referring to a two-up, two-down. I didn't know they were searching a bloody mansion. What if the killer was a world champion hide 'n' seek player? There are hidden servant entrances, priest holes, all sorts of stuff in these old houses.'

'They used search dogs,' Ania said.

Poe hadn't known that. He thought about how easily Edgar found him when they played together. It didn't matter how well he hid, the spaniel always knew where he was. Something Ania had said finally filtered through.

'What do you mean, "She's aware of your views on the aristocracy"?'

'I thought you knew?'

'Knew what?'

'Elcid Doyle's formal title was Lord Doyle, the Marquess of Northumberland.'

'What the hell's a "marquess"?'

'I understand it's the hereditary rank between duke and earl.'

'Hereditary? You mean it's passed on.'

'Yes, Sergeant Poe; that's what hereditary means. Estelle is now Lady Doyle, the Marchioness of Northumberland.'

'Bloody hellfire.'

'She's asked me to tell you that she's never had anything to do with her aristocratic rank, or the privilege that came with it.'

Bradshaw joined him outside.

'What did Ania Kierczynska say, Poe?' she said.

'The Doyles are richer than that short-arse off *The Apprentice* and from now on every time we see Estelle we have to bow.'

'I don't understand.'

'Nor do I, Tilly,' he said. 'But it seems we're not trying to help Estelle Doyle any more.'

'We're not?'

'No, we're now trying to help *Lady* Doyle, the Marchioness of Northumberland.'

Understanding rippled across Bradshaw's face. 'So that's what she was scared of telling you,' she said.

'Excuse me?'

'Nothing. What else did Ania Kierczynska say, Poe?'

'Estelle had a flat tyre before she left work. It's possible that's where the time discrepancy came from. Ania's sending you an email.'

'I'll check now. What are we going to do? If the journey time has been explained, this has been a wasted trip, hasn't it?'

He looked at the padlocked gates and said, 'Maybe not.'

Poe walked up to the gates and gave the chain a rattle. He held the lock and peered into the keyhole.

'Have you ever tried to pick a lock, Tilly?'

'Don't be absurd, Poe.'

'I haven't either,' he said. He removed a pen from his pocket and broke off the clip. He stuck it into the padlock's mechanism. 'But really, how hard can it be?'

'Yeah, I don't know how to do this,' Poe said ten minutes later. 'For all I know I'm making it more locked.'

'At least you tried, Poe.'

He let go of the padlock. 'Do you think I can climb over that gate, Tilly?'

'Why would you want to do that, Poe?'

'Yes, Poe,' a voice behind him said. 'Why would you want to do that?'

He spun round.

It was Detective Chief Inspector Tai-young Lee.

Chapter 55

'What are you doing here, Sergeant Poe?' Detective Chief Inspector Tai-young Lee said.

She was wearing jeans, a thick coat and an over-the-shoulder bag. It looked like she was on her day off. Probably hadn't had time to get changed into her power suit.

'I could ask you the same thing,' Poe said.

'And if you did, I'd say that when Detective Constable Bowness called me at home to inform me that you and Miss Bradshaw had visited Professor Doyle at Low Newton, I thought to myself, what would be the stupidest thing Sergeant Poe could do next? I then drove here and waited.' She pointed at the car up the road, the one Poe had thought belonged to another satnav victim. 'That's my Volvo.'

'I'm that predictable?'

'I've done my research. So, I'll ask you again: what are you doing here? Because I know you aren't reckless enough to enter a crime scene without my permission. I don't want to pick a fight with the NCA by arresting one of their sergeants, but I will if you set foot in the grounds of Highwood.'

'We should go, Poe,' Bradshaw said, tugging his arm.

'I'd listen to Miss Bradshaw if I were you,' Lee said.

Poe didn't move. 'I don't think so,' he said.

'You know I could arrest you just for being here.'

'All I've done is park and ask for directions. Good luck getting me on that.'

'Maybe it won't stick. But it *will* inconvenience you and it will protect my crime scene.'

'Maybe,' Poe nodded. 'But, when I arrest you for suppressing evidence to influence a CPS charging decision, I bloody well know *that* will stick. Perhaps you'll get a good rep and keep your job. Not a chance you'll keep your rank, though. How's that for being inconvenienced?'

'What the hell are you talking about?' Lee snapped. 'I've run this investigation by the book. I had to – Professor Doyle's almost one of our own.'

'And yet I've just had a discussion with her solicitor about her extended journey time. She had a flat tyre before she left work. That's why it took her longer. And yet you didn't mention this to the CPS.'

'We don't know anything about a flat tyre,' she said. 'And it's convenient she's only remembering this now.'

'Tilly?'

'Yes, Poe?'

'Can you show the chief inspector the email you've just received?'

'I will, Poe.'

Bradshaw opened her tablet and navigated to the screenshot of the cop's statement. She opened her fingers to expand the screen and passed it to Lee.

'You see, ma'am,' Poe said. 'You *did* know about her flat tyre. You've known all along.'

Lee paled. Withholding evidence from the CPS was a career killer. She'd be forever tainted with it. Either she'd known about the flat tyre and was corrupt, or she hadn't known and was incompetent. Those were the only options the inevitable disciplinary board would be able to consider.

But Poe had a mutually beneficial third option in mind.

'Tomorrow morning, Estelle's solicitor will lodge a complaint with the IPC. Tell them you deliberately withheld the evidence to positively influence a CPS charging decision.' Poe paused a moment, enough time for it to register. 'Or you can convince me you made a mistake in a fast-moving case and you're now doing your best to rectify it.'

'What do you want?' Lee sighed, resigned and deflated.

Poe nodded at the locked gates.

'I want to see the crime scene.'

Chapter 56

Tai-young Lee removed a key from her pocket and unlocked the padlock that Poe had unsuccessfully tried to pick.

'As you're blocking the drive, we'll go in your car,' she said to Poe.

'Can't we walk?'

'It's a quarter of a mile to the house.'

'Fair enough.'

Highwood's drive was only wide enough for one car, although there were plenty of purpose-built passing places. It was flanked by a gentle, undulating meadow. Individual oak trees broke the clean lines. If they had been planted by design, it was by a landscape artist long dead. They were well over one hundred years old. The grass was fairway-short and glistened with dew. Sheep grazed freely. Not the scrawny Herdwicks Poe was used to; these were plump – and in his opinion, pampered – lowland sheep. Probably a breed that sounded like posh cheese. Charollais or Ryelands, maybe. Wool so fine it was sent to the Japanese futon market rather than the makers of unwearable scratchy jumpers. A herd of animals skirting the edge of a wood caught his eye. Red deer, if he wasn't mistaken. The UK's largest native land mammal. Pretty, but destructive if not managed properly. No wonder the grass was short. Poe stopped the car and watched them for a while. They didn't seem bothered. He wondered if they were resident at Highwood.

'I haven't got all day, Poe,' Lee said.

Poe put the car back into gear and started driving again. He crested a small incline and Highwood came into view.

Estelle Doyle's ancestral home was an impressive building, but it wasn't as big as he had expected. Ania had said it had fifteen bedrooms and in Poe's mind that was huge. And it was, but it wasn't *Downton Abbey* huge. It was an unfussy design. Rectangular, without wings or turrets. Windows all the same size. Three chimneys. A large door in the middle. The type of house a child might draw.

The road eased into a half-moon gravel drive. It extended round both sides of the house. Poe hoped it didn't wrap Highwood like a moat. He hoped there were overhanging trees or a fence at the back that the killer could have reached without his feet touching the ground. Anything a jury might accept as an explanation for the footprint-free snow. A stream gurgled in the distance. Big enough for rainbow trout, too small for salmon.

The expansive double door was protected by a portico. Four fluted columns and a sandstone roof with a triangular pediment. The capitals, the topmost part of the columns, were decorated with curling leaves. A single uniformed cop sheltered underneath. 'Ma'am,' he said, as they approached.

'I need to go inside, Andy,' Lee said.

'It's not locked, ma'am,' he replied, standing aside.

To Poe's surprise, Lee didn't ask them to don forensic suits. She explained that CSI had finished with the house the day before and it would soon be released. Poe ignored the unsaid, *So you didn't need to resort to blackmail to get access.*

She pushed open the doors and led them through the vestibule into an open reception room with a plush red carpet. Poe saw a huge curved stairway, oak-panelled walls and high ceilings with ornate crown mouldings. Portraits of long-dead ancestors hung under carefully positioned picture lights. Corridors stretched into darkness. Furniture that went *up* in value. It looked as though the air hadn't moved in centuries. There were even suits of armour. Shafts of low winter sun sliced through gaps in the heavy drapes like lasers.

The house smelled of wax polish and history and tradition.

'Very Agatha Christie,' Poe said.

'What do you want to see first?' Lee said. 'The whole house has been cleared so you can go where you want.'

'Everywhere, but we'll leave the study for last.'

Chapter 57

They began on the first floor. Poe counted the bedrooms. Doyle's solicitor was right – there were fifteen of them. Most now served as storage rooms, packed with heavy furniture covered in dustsheets.

'You checked all this, I take it?'

Tai-young Lee nodded.

'I gather you sent spaniels in?' Poe said.

'A search and rescue Belgian Malinois, actually,' she said. 'We asked for one as soon as we realised the killer couldn't have left and the house was large enough for someone to hide in. It searched all the rooms, including the attic and crawlspaces.'

'And the perimeter was watched while the dog was inside?'

'It was. No one left.'

'Was the dog interested in any of the rooms?'

'Just the study.'

'That'll have been Elcid Doyle's corpse,' Poe said.

A resourceful person could have found somewhere to hide from the police, but not from a Belgian Malinois. They had one of the keenest senses of smell of any breed in the world, keener than English springer spaniels. They were even used to smell prostate cancer.

'Can I see Elcid's bedroom?' Poe asked.

Lee led them along a corridor. They watched themselves in a gilded mirror as they approached.

Elcid Doyle's bedroom was spacious but sparsely furnished. A four-poster bed, a chest of drawers and a wardrobe. A bedside table with a lamp and a selection of magazines. *Shooting Life* and the *Field* mainly. An armchair with clothes strewn across the back, probably where Elcid had put stuff that was not yet dirty enough for the wash. It was what Poe did. Something occurred to him.

'Who cooked and cleaned for him?' he asked.

'He did his own cooking but someone from the village came in a couple of times a week to clean.'

'They've been interviewed?'

'They have. Nothing. They were working in another house at the time.'

'Does Estelle still have a bedroom here?'

'Sort of.'

Poe raised his eyebrows.

'I'll show you,' Lee said.

She guided them down yet another corridor, right to the end where there was a door with a handwritten sign. It said, 'Keep Out!'.

'This is Estelle's childhood bedroom, isn't it?' Poe said.

'It is.'

Poe wasn't sure he wanted to go inside. This was an echo of her past self. It would be like stepping inside her private diary. Something very personal.

He opened the door anyway.

It looked like any teenage girl's room. A bit gothier, judging by the band posters decorating the wall. The Sisters of Mercy. The Cult. Bauhaus. Siouxsie and the Banshees. Joy Division. A record player with a stack of vinyl beside it. A corkboard pinned with photographs and gig tickets. A dressing table with lots of black and red makeup. A pair of Dr. Martens.

There were also hints of the woman she would become. A Cambridge fencing 'Blue'. Thick books on biology and chemistry. A walnut box containing a microscope and a tray of glass slides. A shelf with rocks and geodes. A periodic table duvet cover. There was nothing to suggest the adult Doyle had ever lived in the room.

'OK,' he said.

'Don't you want to search it?' Lee said.

'No. It wouldn't be right to. Estelle didn't want me to come here – I won't rifle through her backstory. Not until I have her permission.'

'Fair enough.'

Poe spent ten minutes looking through Highwood's first-floor windows, desperately hoping for something that could explain the unblemished snow. A tree that could be reached with a ladder. Telephone wires. Anything he could sell to a jury.

But there was nothing.

The drive wrapped the house and it was ten metres wide. The killer couldn't have jumped out of a window without leaving a mark in the snow. Poe's mood blackened.

'What next?' Lee asked.

'I'd like to see Elcid Doyle's study.'

Chapter 58

Elcid Doyle's study was at the back of the house. It was a wonderfully sunny room. Warm rugs and a flagstone floor. Bespoke, floor-to-ceiling bookcases hugged the walls on the left and right. The wood was dark and old. Teak, Poe thought. There was even a rolling library ladder so Elcid could reach the uppermost shelves. Poe had never seen that in a private residence.

The wall opposite the door had windows overlooking the grounds and a stone fireplace in the middle. A shovel, poker and tongs hung from a brass stand. Logs were stacked either side of the fire.

The fourth wall, the one they'd walked through, showcased a collection of original oil paintings. Poe put on his reading glasses and studied them. They were all British game birds. There were ring-necked pheasants, snipes, woodcocks and partridges. Some mallard ducks. The majority were grouse, though. A pair of red grouse resting in purple-flowering heather. A black grouse 'lek'– a site where males display their tail feathers to attract females. Red grouse being flushed from cover by a black Labrador. Black grouse flying over the waiting guns. Ania said Elcid Doyle had owned one of the best grouse moors in the country and it was clear the game bird had been his passion.

A magnificent mahogany pedestal desk centred the room. It had a green leather inlay. Poe imagined Elcid sitting behind it, glancing up occasionally to admire his paintings. He ran his fingers over it. It was warm and smooth. The only items on the desk were an antique banker's lamp, a sheaf of expensive paper, a blotter pad and a Montblanc fountain pen.

The desk chair was missing. Elcid Doyle had died sitting down and Poe assumed the chair had been taken away for further analysis.

He remembered being told about the old days. There would have been a ring of ash circling the body as cops walked around it while smoking. Not here, though. All he could see was evidence of a thorough CSI investigation.

There was a small, low table in front of the fire. A Chesterfield high wingback chair was positioned to catch the last of the evening light. There were slate coasters, an ashtray and a cigar cutter on the table. Elcid probably lived in this room. Spent the day working at his desk and the evening in front of the fire, sipping Scotch and reading.

One of the bookcase walls had a door. Poe opened it. It was an en suite shower room. A modern cubicle, a toilet and a hand basin. A shelf with a traditional shaving kit. A classic design straight razor, badger-hair shaving brush, soap and balm. The kit looked decades old but lovingly cared for.

The bathroom had another door. It was a small airing cupboard. Slatted shelves loaded with towels and spare toilet rolls. Given the dimensions of the two rooms, it was a bit smaller than Poe had expected. He suspected a new water heater was behind it. The shower was too new to run off the house's original plumbing.

Poe turned and noticed something.

'Can you come in here please, ma'am,' he said.

'What is it, Poe?'

He pointed at the frosted window. 'The latch. It's unlocked.'

Tai-young Lee bent down and studied it.

'You can still see aluminium fingerprint powder,' she said. 'The tech must have forgotten to lock it after he'd finished. If it'd been unlocked when he dusted it, he'd have highlighted it to one of the guys.' She pulled a tablet out of her shoulder bag, found a file and turned it round. 'We can check, though. This is the video walk through of the office. It was taken before anything was processed.'

The video was three minutes long and the CSI tech hadn't missed anything. It ended in the office's en-suite. As Lee had said, the window had been locked.

Poe considered where he wanted to look next. Highwood had been a bust so far and he was running out of things to check.

His phone rang.

It was Flynn. He frowned. She was supposed to be spending time with her son.

'What's up?' he asked.

'It's Karen Royal-Cross,' Flynn replied. 'The bastard got to her.'

Chapter 59

Poe glared at the isolation ward's video monitor as if it were personally responsible. It wasn't hyperbole – the Botanist *had* got to Karen Royal-Cross. She was dying. Twenty-four hours earlier, a urinary biomarker had tested positive for ricinine, the alkaloid in the castor bean plant, and the only reliable way of verifying ricin poisoning. Within two hours she'd started to vomit and her bowel movements became looser and more frequent. Her temperature spiked and she developed a cough. She was now at the stage where her lungs were filling with liquid. Her skin had taken on a bluish pallor as the blood gradually became deoxygenated.

'She's deteriorated sharply in the last couple of hours,' Doctor Mukherjee said. 'We're still doing everything we can. She's being pumped with fresh blood, saline. A few other tricks we learned during the COVID crisis.'

'Can you save her?' Poe said.

'No. She has multiple organ failure. She'll be dead by the end of the day.'

Flynn was in a meeting with Detective Chief Superintendent Mathers and Bradshaw was copying the infectious diseases unit's video files to her computer. It meant that when Karen Royal-Cross died, they could decamp and let the unit return to their day job. Doctor Mukherjee was keen to help. The only people who had been in contact with the patient were his staff. He didn't want them falling under suspicion.

Poe decided to review the footage of the last twenty-four hours. He wasn't expecting to see anything, but he couldn't think what else there was to do.

Contact with Karen Royal-Cross had been kept to a minimum. Partly because it was an ongoing police operation and partly because she wasn't being treated for anything. Essentially, the doctors and nurses were feeding her and monitoring her urine. Each time someone entered the isolation ward, Poe paused the screen before they had masked up. He then compared their face against the corresponding photograph on the hospital's HR database. He checked them all on the way in, all on the way out and saw nothing suspicious.

The first sign that something was wrong with Karen Royal-Cross was when she said the shepherd's pie she had eaten for lunch had given her an upset stomach. Doctor Mukherjee had immediately asked her to urinate. As soon as the urinary biomarker tested positive, the infectious diseases unit kicked in with their protocols.

Despite the near-hysterical Karen Royal-Cross refusing to acknowledge she was ill – it was more fake news – a doctor had managed to insert a drip and was able to start flushing her system.

But it wasn't long before the gravity of the situation became apparent to her. She begged for help. She issued threats to sue, threats of violence, even some racial slurs. Inside the isolation ward, the doctors and nurses remained calm. They spoke to her in relaxed, measured tones. They told her she was ill, but they would be doing everything possible to keep her alive. It was what they were trained to do – stress reduced the body's immune system. *Outside* the isolation ward was a different matter entirely. Not panic, more a sense of disbelief. Like they'd been told a well-liked colleague had been crushed to death by a block of frozen urine ejected from a jumbo jet's toilet.

Mathers had detectives checking the kitchens in case the Botanist had somehow managed to slip something into Karen Royal-Cross's meal before it had arrived on the ward. Poe didn't think that was what had happened. Her meals were standard hospital slop, plated under the watchful eye of a detective sergeant. Her custard was ladled into her bowl from a big vat, her shepherd's pie was spooned from a tray. None of the other patients had fallen ill, so it hadn't been tampered with at source. It was possible the Botanist had got to her meal after it had been dished up, but Poe didn't think he played that way. It was too ... close. Too immediate. Poe didn't think the Botanist was anywhere near his victim when the fatal dose was delivered.

Doctor Mukherjee slumped in the seat beside him.

'How is she?' Poe asked.

'Deteriorating. I expect her liver, spleen and kidneys to stop working any time now. She's on a ventilator as she can't breathe on her own.'

'How long?'

'Minutes, not hours. She's been given a large dose. Death is inevitable.'

Poe didn't doubt it. Ricin was one of the few poisons without an antidote. Accepted treatment was to provide supportive medical care. Fluids for dehydration, mechanical assistance for breathing. Drug therapy to treat seizures and low blood pressure. After that, the body was on its own.

'How easy is it to make ricin?' Poe asked. Bradshaw had explained the science, but the complexity was subjective. She'd said it was easy, but he shouldn't try it.

'You need castor beans, obviously,' Doctor Mukherjee said. 'A solvent to extract it. Some basic lab equipment. I'm told it's not a difficult process.'

'Could you do it?'

Doctor Mukherjee frowned.

'I'm not asking if you did,' Poe explained, 'I just want to know who could. I need to understand what level of expertise is needed.'

'With the right equipment, yes,' Mukherjee said. 'I believe I could make ricin.'

'Who else?'

'Anyone with access to the internet.'

'That's not true though,' Poe said. 'Because of the Counter Terrorism and Border Security Act, detailed instructions aren't as readily available as you might imagine. And the security services routinely monitor who's accessing sites that do still have recipes.'

'Let's think about this logically then. Anyone employed in a discipline where a working knowledge of chemistry is a prerequisite would understand the theory.'

'Chemical engineers?'

'Almost certainly.'

'Veterinarians?'

'Biochemistry forms part of their training, so yes.'

'Who else?'

'Any branch of biology.'

'Such as?'

'Too many to list, but off the top of my head: genetics, biophysics, cytology, biotechnology, virology, bacteriology, protozoology, mycology, toxicology, pathology, some of the zoology disciplines.'

A junior doctor poked his head around the corner.

'What is it, Ben?' Doctor Mukherjee asked.

'It's time,' Ben replied.

Mukherjee eased himself out of the chair. 'Do you want to come, Sergeant Poe?'

'What's happening?'

'Karen Royal-Cross is about to die.'

Chapter 60

Poe had seen people die before. Too many times. Perceived wisdom was that police officers became desensitised to death, but he wasn't sure it was true. It certainly wasn't for him. The dead stayed with him. Haunted his dreams and occupied his waking thoughts. They were the soundtrack to his life and the day he couldn't hear them would be the day he handed in his warrant card. Poe needed to live among the dead. It was how he protected the living.

But doctors, particularly ones who had a few years in, like Mukherjee, came across death on a daily basis. Desensitisation would be the only way they could cope. Same for nurses.

Even so, for the men and women gathered around the bed of Karen Royal-Cross, this death would hit them hard. They looked shell-shocked, but there was something else as well. Shame, maybe? This woman, this vile racist, had been admitted to their care fit and healthy, but would leave in a waterproof body bag.

Karen Royal-Cross was no longer under the isolation tent. The only sound in the bed unit was the ventilator breathing for her. It sounded like Darth Vader standing next to a ticking clock. Poe scrutinised the machines monitoring her vitals. He didn't know the optimum numbers for blood pressure, oxygen saturation and respiration, but he knew when a temperature was dangerously high and a heart rate far too low.

Without warning, a series of alarms sounded. None of the medical team moved. Mukherjee stepped forwards and took Karen Royal-Cross's pulse. He then lifted her eyelid and shone a torch into her eye.

'Time of death is ten p.m. exactly,' he said. 'Record this, please.'

Junior doctor Ben made a note on a form while a nurse began

unplugging Karen Royal-Cross from everything to which she had been connected. Another nurse turned off the ventilator. The bed unit fell silent.

Mukherjee filled it.

'This woman might have held unpleasant views, Sergeant Poe, but she was still someone's daughter. I spoke with her mother and father earlier today and now I have to tell them she is dead. Please, catch this man before another doctor is forced to make such a call.'

'I'll catch him,' Poe promised.

His phone vibrated in his pocket. It was a text from Bradshaw.

'Speak of the devil,' he said. 'He's on the phone now.'

Chapter 61

'He'll only speak to you, Poe,' Chief Superintendent Mathers said. 'He's calling back in' – she checked her watch – 'two minutes. They'll patch it through to me.'

Poe couldn't tell if she was annoyed or relieved. Probably a little from column A and a little from column B. Annoyed she'd been reduced to a spectator in her own case, relieved someone else was sharing the burden of responsibility. Now that Karen Royal-Cross was dead, the infectious diseases staff needed to get back to their day jobs. Mathers had taken over a small room off the main ward while her team dismantled the temporary command centre they had set up. The isolation ward's bed unit would remain a crime scene for now, although Poe doubted CSI would find anything useful.

'Did he say anything?' he asked.

'Nothing useful. Just an instruction to get you.'

'Why me?'

'We assume after your last exchange that he sees you as someone who won't bullshit him.'

'He's wrong then,' Poe said, Mukherjee's words still echoing in his head. 'I'll do whatever it takes to catch this prick.'

'The psychologist thinks you should stick with the same level of aggression as last time. If he thinks you're a "straight talker", we might gain a small advantage.'

'At SCAS we prefer the term misanthropic arsehole to straight talker, ma'am,' Flynn said, walking into the room. Bradshaw was with her.

'You got anything?' Poe asked.

'Maybe,' Flynn replied. 'Tilly, can you tell them?'

'Certainly, DI Flynn,' Bradshaw said. She produced a tablet and flipped it to the landscape position.

Poe craned his neck and stared at the screen. It was a chemical formula, all parentheses, letters and subscript numbers – $(CH_3)_2CO$.

'What's that, Tilly?' he asked.

'It's acetone, Poe.'

'One minute,' Mathers warned.

'And what's the significance?'

'Infinitesimal traces of it were found in the samples we sent to Estelle Doyle's lab from Karen Royal-Cross. I know she's in that horrible prison, but we thought if—'

'Who's this "we", Tilly?' Flynn snapped.

'I explained to DI Flynn that if Estelle Doyle works for a laboratory they must be very good.'

'Cost me a fortune,' Flynn grumbled. She looked at Mathers expectantly but got no help. The put-upon chief superintendent had budget problems of her own with all the overtime she'd had to authorise. She wasn't paying for lab tests unless she was forced to.

'So it *was* acetone he used to make the ricin?'

'It was, Poe.'

'Anything else?'

'Possibly,' Flynn said. 'Acetone can be used to make explosives so it's on something called a precursor chemicals list. It's difficult to buy in bulk without ID.'

'Why do we think he bought it in bulk?'

'We don't, but at least we'll be doing something.'

Poe thought about that. Decided Flynn was right. Investigations stalled when detectives were left idling. Following up meaningless leads was useful because it kept people busy. Busy people's brains worked faster.

'So, unless he stole the acetone, or bought it in small amounts, he might be on a database somewhere?' he said.

'Yes.'

'Along with tens of thousands of others, I imagine,' Mathers said. 'An unmanageable number basically.'

Poe and Flynn smiled.

'We have an app for that, ma'am,' Poe said.

'An app? What app?'

'It's called Tilly, and the larger the number, the happier she is.'

Bradshaw nodded vigorously. 'I've already started thinking how we can do this, Poe. First of all we . . .'

The phone Mathers was holding rang. Everyone jumped.

'You're on, Poe,' she said.

Chapter 62

'This is Sergeant Poe. Who am I speaking to?'

'Can you update me on Henning Stahl's detoxification programme, please?' the Botanist replied.

'I don't have that information to hand. He's undergoing a medical procedure and there are rules about confidentiality.'

'You've not spoken to him?'

'This isn't the only case I'm working.'

'So I gather.'

'Excuse—'

'Is Karen Royal-Cross dead yet?' the Botanist cut in.

Mathers shook her head.

'Just now,' Poe said. He covered the handset. 'This is how I build on any trust he has for me, ma'am.'

'So now we move on,' the Botanist said. 'I am prepared to sit down with Henning Stahl. At this meeting you will try to catch me and I will try to evade said capture. Am I close?'

'We'll have Henning Stahl wired for sound too.'

'Helicopter surveillance?'

'If I had the authority to direct satellites, we'd be watching from space.' He covered the handset again. 'We can't direct satellites, can we, Tilly?' he said.

'The majority of satellites are only capable of taking twenty-five-centimetre resolution pictures, Poe. That means each pixel represents twenty-five centimetres on the ground. Individual details will be indiscernible. We would need to task an advanced government spy satellite capable of taking one-centimetre resolution pictures, and even then we'd only be able to see the top of his head.'

Poe uncovered the handset.

'The top of your head doesn't have any distinguishing features does it, Mr Botanist?'

'The top of my . . .?'

'Yeah, like a tattoo or something. Maybe an amusing birthmark.'

'Sergeant Poe, I have absolutely no idea what you're talking about.'

'Poe, stop mucking about!' Flynn hissed.

Poe covered the handset for a third time. 'He's rehearsed what he wants to say,' he said. 'I want him improvising.'

'Really? Because it sounds a lot like you're taking the piss.'

'Trust me.' He uncovered the phone again. 'I've just had word from Henning Stahl's doctor. He's not ready yet. I don't know what the medical term is, but I understand he still has the shakes.'

'Delirium tremens,' the Botanist said automatically. 'And, even in the most extreme cases, they only last ten days.'

Mathers's eyes widened.

For the fourth time, Poe covered the handset. 'Told you I could knock him off his game,' he said. 'And now we know he's medically trained.'

Chapter 63

'OK,' Poe said. 'Let's say Henning Stahl *is* fit to meet with you; I assume you have a plan?'

'I'll call with a location. We'll be meeting at eleven a.m. the day after tomorrow.'

'That's a Sunday.'

'It is.'

'We're meeting in London, I assume?'

'The most surveilled city in the world? I hardly think so. No, you'll need to get in your cars and head north.'

'And where do we stop?'

'You stop when you get home, Sergeant Poe,' the Botanist said. 'I'll be meeting Henning Stahl in Cumbria.'

The phone went dead.

'Tilly?' Poe said. 'Anything?'

She shook her head.

'He's using a different phone each time and he either calls from a high-population area or somewhere very rural. I can tell you he's just called from Covent Garden, but we can't narrow it down any more than that.'

'Why the hell does he want to meet in Cumbria?' Poe said. 'And what did he mean when he said, "So I gather," when I told him I was working on another case?'

'Perhaps he's watching you,' Mathers said.

'Why?'

'No idea,' she shrugged. 'We can talk about this later but right now I need to let Cumbria know we'll be operating in their area on Sunday. Anyone I should speak to up there? We could do with an ally.'

'Detective Superintendent Jo Nightingale,' Flynn said. 'We've worked with her before and she's good. She'll help if she can.'

Mathers nodded her thanks and left the room.

'I suppose I'd better go and collect Henning Stahl,' Poe said. 'Meet back in the hotel bar?'

'Is that wise?' Flynn said. 'What if he relapses?'

'After a day?'

'We're cutting his treatment short, Poe.'

'I'll speak to his doctors. See what we can and can't do.'

'And ask them if he's still pissing the bed every night,' she said. 'If he is, I'm buying him a multipack of TENA adult nappies.'

Chapter 64

The difference in Henning Stahl was remarkable. The first thing Poe noticed was that you saw him before you smelled him. That alone was worth the detox unit's exorbitant fee. He was wearing clean clothes and he'd had a shave. His hair was washed and combed. And while he wasn't yet bright of eye and rosy of cheek, at least he no longer looked grey and blotchy.

Poe shook his hand. It was dry, not wet.

'You look better, Henning.'

'We need to talk,' Stahl replied.

'What do you mean, "The old price isn't the new price"?' Poe asked.

They were driving back to London and Poe had been stuck in first gear for twenty minutes. He thought there might have been an accident, although it was the tail end of rush hour so the reason for the delay was anybody's guess. His mood hadn't improved with Stahl's statement.

'I want something,' Stahl said.

'Of course you do.'

'Look, I'm aware that your intervention probably saved my life, Poe, but I feel I have more cards to play now.'

'It's not a game, Henning.'

'No, it's not. And this is why I deserve more.'

'What do you want?' Poe sighed.

'Exclusive access to the investigation.'

'And why would we do that?'

'Because it's the right thing to do.'

'It is?'

'This man has killed two people so far and—'

'Three,' Poe said. 'Karen Royal-Cross died this morning.'

'He got to her in hospital? Despite all the security you'd put in?'

'Yep.'

Stahl said, 'I'm sorry to hear that, but it makes my request more reasonable, I think.'

'Go on.'

'You say you don't know why he's chosen me.'

'We don't.'

'But you agree there are other, less . . . compromised journalists he could have sought out?'

'That's an understatement,' Poe said.

'So if he could have chosen someone—'

'Who isn't an arsehole?'

'I was going to say more suitable, but we'll go with your definition if you prefer. If he could have chosen someone *who isn't an arsehole*, he would have, and that means either he knows me or he wants to kill me. You're an intelligent man; I know you've already arrived at this conclusion. And yet, you still want to go ahead with the meeting. That means, to a certain extent, you think I'm expendable.'

'That's a bit harsh.'

'Would you let Tilly meet with him?'

Poe didn't answer.

'I'm under no illusions my passing will not be mourned,' Stahl continued, 'but I have a second chance here, Poe. How many people can say that? The doctors got me clean and I'm taking Antabuse. I'm grabbing life with both hands.'

'What's Antabuse?'

'My medication. If I have alcohol, even a tiny amount, I'll feel very ill, very quickly. It's both a physical and psychological deterrent. I take it in the morning, when I have the most motivation, and it lasts all day.'

Poe glanced at Stahl, not sure whether to believe him. Antabuse sounded too good to be true. He'd check with Bradshaw later. It was important that Stahl was sober on Sunday. A drunk Stahl might let something slip, and, although most of the police operation would be hidden from him, there were certain things he would have to be told.

'And what are you planning to do with this newly negotiated exclusivity?' Poe asked.

'I'm going to write a book about this case. I'm going to write a book and that book is going to win awards. And with the money and recognition that comes from said book and awards, I'm going to rebuild my career. And in return you'll get my full cooperation. From now until it's over.'

Although it wasn't an attractive offer, Poe knew Mathers would go with it. She wouldn't have a choice. It was possible the Botanist knew Stahl personally so they couldn't risk putting in a double. Hoping he didn't notice the old switcheroo until it was too late. And they couldn't force Stahl to meet him – as he'd quite rightly said, the Botanist might try to kill him.

'I'll ask Detective Chief Superintendent Mathers,' Poe said. 'See what she says. You're not getting live access to the investigation, though. You'll get access when it doesn't compromise anything. But I think we can work out something on exclusivity.'

'Good enough,' Stahl said. 'As long as I get to write the book before anyone else does.'

Chapter 65

Flynn and Bradshaw were waiting in the hotel bar. To Poe's surprise, Mathers was there as well. She didn't look happy. Neither did Flynn. Bradshaw was fidgety, a clear sign she was worried about something.

'What's up?' he said, taking a seat.

Mathers threw a newspaper across the table. It was a copy of the *Chronicle*, Newcastle's daily newspaper. It was upside down. He could see a story about a recent football match on the back page.

'What's this?'

'Turn it over.'

He did.

And saw himself on the front page.

TOP COP COMPROMISED!

DETECTIVE SERGEANT WASHINGTON POE TAKES BREAK FROM SEARCH FOR BOTANIST – COMPROMISES INVESTIGATION INTO MURDER SUSPECT FRIEND!

Detective Sergeant Washington Poe, the famed National Crime Agency officer, has been taking time out of the search for the serial killer known as the Botanist to conduct a private investigation into the circumstances around his friend's arrest. Estelle Doyle, 39, was recently charged with the brutal slaying of her father. She is currently remanded at HMP Low Newton in Durham. Sergeant Poe and a mystery brunette were spotted in the prison car park. It is believed he was visiting Doyle. Sergeant Poe is no stranger to controversy . . .

It continued into a hit piece. A summary of the high-profile cases he'd been involved with. No mention of the killers he'd put behind bars, but plenty about the complaints lodged against him. Northumbria Police had declined to comment. And when the journalist had called the NCA, he'd been told Poe was 'unavailable'. Which, while factually accurate, had been reported in such a way to make it sound as though Poe was hiding in a caravan somewhere.

The accompanying photograph was of him and Bradshaw in HMP Low Newton's car park. Judging by the shadows, it was after their visit with Doyle, not before. Looked like it had been taken a few moments before Robert Bowness, the detective who had smelled a cricket bat in Elcid Doyle's office, had approached them. Bowness must have taken the picture to show Chief Inspector Tai-young Lee. She must have slipped it to a friendly journalist. Retaliation for forcing his way into her crime scene.

'You OK, Tilly?' Poe asked.

'I am, Poe. I'm not named in the article and the photo of me is blurry.'

'I didn't know you were a brunette.'

'I certainly didn't know I was a *mystery* brunette, Poe.'

'This is serious!' Flynn snapped.

'It really isn't, boss,' Poe replied. 'I was visiting a friend during a few days off. If Chief Inspector Lee is annoyed by my presence she should raise it with you, not go sneaking to the paper.'

'The director *has* demanded an explanation from Northumbria's chief constable,' Flynn admitted.

'And?'

'Chief Inspector Tai-young Lee denied it was her.'

'I bet she did.'

'Regardless. The fact remains that Detective Chief Superintendent Mathers is facing unsurpassed scrutiny as it is. The press are baying for her blood and articles like this make it look as though she's lost control.'

'I'm sorry, Poe,' Mathers said. 'But Stephanie and I are in alignment – to protect the Botanist investigation, you need to stay away from Estelle Doyle. If she's innocent, the truth will out.'

214

'Is this an order?' he asked.

'It is, Poe,' Flynn replied. 'Staff at HMP Low Newton have been instructed not to let you in.'

Bradshaw put her hand on his arm. Kept it there until his breathing returned to normal. 'It's OK, Poe,' she said. 'We've seen everything we need to. We can keep investigating from here. I'll help you, I promise.'

'Fine,' he said eventually.

Flynn and Mathers were right. He *had* compromised the investigation. Whether he liked it or not, effective media relations were important in managing a high-profile murder. He was annoyed he'd been taken off the board with an underhand trick, but Bradshaw was right: visiting Doyle in custody was a luxury, not a necessity. If he needed further information, the quickest way to get it would be through her solicitor.

'The story's above the fold,' Stahl said.

'What's that mean?'

'Physical newspapers are folded and displayed so only the top half of the front page is visible. Anything above the fold is therefore the most important story. Which is strange.'

'Why?' Poe asked.

'If you read through the flashy headlines and the filler, there isn't a story here. A man visits his friend in prison on his day off. So what? That isn't front-page news, not even on a local rag like this.'

'You saying . . . actually, what are you saying?' Poe said.

'I don't know. It just seems odd. There's no story so there's no reason it should be on the front. It might mean they have a bigger story, but don't have the legal cover to run it. Local papers sometimes put something on the front page hoping one of the nationals will pick it up and pay them for the extra information. And if it's something salacious, it won't have come from a police officer. Too easy to check.'

'You think there's more?'

'That's what it looks like to me.'

'But there isn't anything.'

'You sure, Poe?' Flynn asked.

'Positive. And, now I think about it, I have a problem with Chief Inspector Lee being responsible.'

'Why?'

'We caught a mistake she made. She wouldn't have gone to the press in case I returned the favour and ruined her career.'

He told them about Estelle's flat tyre and how it hadn't been taken into consideration when explaining the discrepancy in the journey length.

'Poe said she did it on purpose to influence a charging decision,' Bradshaw explained. 'He pretended to be cross so she'd let us have a look at Elcid Doyle's study.'

'You've seen the crime scene?' Flynn asked.

'Yes, DI Flynn. Poe tried to pick the padlock first, but he gave up when he realised he didn't know how to do it. He was then going to climb over the gate but Detective Chief Inspector Tai-young Lee had been spying on us and she caught him. She threatened to arrest Poe and then Poe threatened to arrest her. She said what for, and then I showed her the evidence she'd missed as it was on my iPad. After she read it she let us into Estelle Doyle's ancestral home.'

Flynn stared in astonishment.

'Unfortunately, that's exactly what happened,' Poe said.

'You tried to pick a lock?' Flynn said. 'At a crime scene?'

'It was the outside gate. I wasn't going to break into the house.'

'And you wonder why Detective Chief Inspector Lee thinks you're interfering . . .'

Poe noticed Stahl scribbling in his notebook. 'And what the hell are you doing?'

'You said if I secretly recorded Tilly' – he flipped back a few pages and read from his notes – 'you would "pull my fucking ears off and stick them up my arse". I assumed this was hyperbole, but I understood the general point. I am therefore dusting off my short-hand skills and writing down all your conversations.'

'No, you bloody aren't,' Poe said.

Chapter 66

'You've spent the most time with him, Poe,' Mathers said. 'Do you think he's up to this?'

Stahl and Bradshaw were in the bar. Stahl was buying himself a Coke and Bradshaw was making sure he didn't put Jack Daniel's in it.

'I have no idea,' Poe replied. 'You can see the improvement in him physically, but he's been an alcoholic for years. He has to have psychological scars we don't yet know about.'

'Is he clean?' Mathers said.

'Says he's on Antabuse, which Tilly says gives him an acute sensitivity to ethanol. He'll basically get the world's worst hangover as soon as he takes a sip and there'll be no hair of the dog – he won't be able to drink it away. The more he has, the worse it'll get.'

'How sure are we he's taking it?'

'There's an easy way to find out,' Poe said.

'How?'

'I could put a splash of vodka in his drink when he isn't looking.'

'That would work,' Mathers nodded. 'Obviously I'd have to immediately arrest you for unlawfully administering a noxious substance with intent to cause harm, but at least we'd know.'

'He was joking, ma'am,' Flynn said. 'You were, weren't you, Poe?'

Poe shrugged. 'Of course,' he said. 'Look, as long as we can keep him out of the bar for a few hours, we should be able to get him through this. He's not our problem after that. If he's drunk, he doesn't get access.'

'Gut view?' Mathers asked.

'I think he's sober.'

'DI Flynn?'

'He's sober now. Whether he has the motivation to sustain it, I don't know. But Poe's right, long-term sobriety is Stahl's problem, not ours.'

Mathers tapped out an email.

'We're on then,' she said. She threw her phone on the table and sighed. 'Come on then – cards-on-the-table time. What do we think's really happening here? Why did he ask for Stahl and what can we expect on Sunday?'

'I don't know,' Poe said. 'He doesn't smell like a goat any more, but I can't shake the feeling we're about to tether him like one.'

Chapter 67

The drive north was straightforward. The ten-car convoy left at 7 a.m. exactly and arrived at Carleton Hall, Cumbria Constabulary's headquarters building in Penrith, six hours later. They were ushered towards a sectioned-off area of the car park.

Detective Superintendent Jo Nightingale, the head of Cumbria CID, greeted them. SCAS had previously worked a few major cases with her. They knew her well. She was shrewd, intuitive and one of the few senior managers Poe had time for.

'You can set up in Conference Room A,' she said after introductions had been made. 'I take it he hasn't been in touch with a location?'

'We're expecting something tomorrow,' Mathers replied. 'I doubt we'll get much notice.'

'We're pretty central here. With blues and twos it's an hour to Barrow and fifteen minutes to Carlisle. West Cumbria might be problematic as the roads aren't always great and communication can be patchy.'

'Air support?'

'The National Police Air Service have moved three EC135 Eurocopters to their Newcastle base. From six a.m. tomorrow, at least two will be hovering above Cumbria at any one time.'

'And on the ground?'

'One hundred uniformed officers, fifty more in reserve. All CID leave has been cancelled and, unless they are actively involved in a case, they will be strategically placed in all towns and larger villages. We undertook a mock exercise last night and believe we can throw a ring around any location within twenty minutes.'

'That's thorough,' Mathers said.

'It is. Which is what's worrying me. Why risk the exposure? He must know we'll put in every measure we can.'

'Maybe he won't show. Could just be a way of getting the core investigators out of London.'

'Is that what you think, Poe?' Nightingale asked.

'I think he will show, ma'am.'

'So he wants to be caught?'

'No, ma'am,' Poe said. 'I believe he thinks he can meet with Henning Stahl *and* evade arrest. I'm not saying he will, obviously, just that he thinks he can.'

'Why Cumbria? Up until now, every case has been in London.'

Poe shrugged. 'No idea,' he said. 'It's rural up here, but so is Wales, and that's much closer to London. I assumed he'd want somewhere crowded, somewhere he could meet Stahl then melt away into a crowd. I've been racking my brain and I can't see any tactical advantage to Cumbria. None whatsoever. And that means there's something we haven't thought of.'

'You're not filling me with confidence, Poe,' Nightingale said.

'That's because I'm not confident. I reckon there's a one in ten chance tomorrow.'

'Of him evading us?' Mathers said. 'I suppose I can live with those odds.'

'You misunderstand me, ma'am,' Poe said. 'I think there's a one in ten chance we catch him.'

Chapter 68

Poe hadn't wanted to risk going back to Herdwick Croft so he took a room at the North Lakes Hotel with the rest of the team. It also meant he could keep an eye on Henning Stahl. So far the journalist was doing everything asked of him, including having a small patch of his hair shaved off so a mic could be attached to his scalp. It had been Flynn's idea. The Botanist knew Stahl would be wired for sound, and having a second, less obvious, mic in case the first was found seemed a good idea. Poe thought it was superfluous – the Botanist wanted to be heard – but didn't raise any objections. Mathers had raided Counter Terrorism Command's toy box and brought a small, flat, flesh-coloured listening device that, when glued to Stahl's head, would be almost undiscoverable.

'You OK about this?' Poe asked.

'I feel like that guy from the *Mission Impossible* films,' Stahl replied.

'You're nothing like Ethan Hunt, Henning. Maybe Ethan *Cu*—'

'Don't be vulgar, Poe,' Flynn said.

Poe said, as he was staying at the hotel, he might as well bunk up with Stahl. Make sure he didn't sneak out for a drink during the night. Mathers readily agreed and sent someone off to change the room booking to a twin.

'I'll post a team outside your window and door,' she said. 'Just in case this has all been a ruse to get to him tonight.'

Poe slept fitfully and woke early. Stahl was already up, sitting at the dressing table, making notes again.

'You're an aggressive sleeper, Sergeant Poe,' he said.

'I am?'

'You are. You were tossing and turning all night. Cried out once.'

Poe touched his T-shirt. It was damp and his skin felt clammy. 'You get the nightmares you deserve, I guess.'

'And there's the title of the book,' Stahl smiled, turning back to his notebook.

'Just put the bloody kettle on.'

'You had any overnight insight?' Poe asked over the rim of his coffee mug. 'Something you haven't shared yet?'

'Trying to take my mind off what's about to happen, Sergeant Poe?' Stahl replied.

'I'm that obvious?'

'Don't worry. I appreciate the gesture.'

'Nevertheless.'

'I've thought about nothing else. True, my mind was fogged up with vodka and self-pity before, but it's clear now. I've stared at the list Tilly gave me, the one with all the stories I was involved in, until I can see it in my sleep.'

'And?'

'Nothing. The people I wrote about in my later career were celebrities, and, while I did do some decent investigative journalism back in the day, you've seen the same names I have. There's no one with either the motivation or skills to pull off something like this.'

Poe's phone rang. It was Tilly. He wondered if she'd actually been to bed.

'Are you dressed, Poe?' she said.

'We are. Having a brew before we meet you all for breakfast.'

'May I come in? I have something to show you.'

Chapter 69

The 'something' was another list. Bradshaw and the Mole People had contacted every supplier of acetone in the country and got the names of everyone who had made a bulk purchase in the last five years. It ran to almost ten thousand names.

'And this is just the UK,' Bradshaw explained. 'If he brought it in from abroad he won't be on here.'

'Neither would he be if he borrowed it, stole it or just happened to have some in his shed from years ago.'

'I don't have confidence in the list either, Poe. It would be out of character for him to leave his name on a database somewhere.'

'And even if he had, this is unmanageable. We can't possibly check every name. Is there any way we can narrow it down?'

'If you're confident about his gender we can remove all women—'

'He's a man,' Poe cut in, 'but we can't remove women in case someone bought it for him.'

'You think he has an accomplice?' Stahl asked.

'Unlikely, but acetone isn't something dodgy. Asking someone to get you some isn't going to raise any alarms. Can you get hard copies for me, Tilly?'

'That's a lot of paper, Poe.'

'I get seasick if I stare at a screen for too long.'

'Also, you don't know how to work computers. You're the only person in SCAS who still has a filing cabinet.'

'My filing cabinet never gets viruses.'

'But you're always losing your key. You've broken into it so many times it won't lock any more. DI Flynn has someone check it every night to make sure there's nothing confidential in it. She has them put everything back first thing in the morning.'

'Really?'

'Yes, Poe.'

'I'm putting mousetraps in it when I get back then. See how they like that.'

Stahl stared at them. 'You guys are nuts,' he said.

The hotel room phone rang. Bradshaw picked it up. 'Good morning, this is Matilda Bradshaw speaking, not Detective Sergeant Washington Poe. I repeat, this is not Washington Poe.'

Poe gave her a double thumbs-up and a 'way-to-go' nod.

'OK, I'll tell him,' Bradshaw said, putting the phone down.

'Was that reception? I'd asked for an alarm call and I forgot to cancel it.'

'It wasn't reception, Poe. That was DI Flynn. The Botanist has called – he wants to meet Henning Stahl at eleven a.m. in Carlisle.'

'Looks like you're up, Henning,' Poe said.

Chapter 70

'He hasn't said where in Carlisle yet?' Poe said.

Conference Room A, the bigger of Carleton Hall's two incident rooms, was packed with officers from London and Cumbria. Poe was wedged between Bradshaw and Nightingale. Mathers had just started her briefing.

'Not yet,' she said.

'Was it a text this time?'

'It was. How did you know?'

'Because he's already near the meeting place,' Poe said. 'He didn't call in case sound gave away his position. He'll be watching the area to make sure it's safe.'

'I agree,' Mathers said. 'We'll get the phone's location but it won't be until later today. We need a fresh warrant for each phone and he's using burners. Linda, can you take everyone through the logistics?'

A plainclothed cop got to her feet. Poe had seen her in London, on the periphery of the main investigation.

'At nine o'clock we move, in convoy, up to Durranhill, which I understand is Carlisle's headquarters building,' she said. 'We then split into our assigned teams as per last night's briefing. We don't expect the Botanist to give us the final location until just before eleven. Detective Superintendent Nightingale will have a team of fifty officers in vehicles to be used in reserve should we need them, and air support is already above the city. Sergeant Poe from the National Crime Agency will walk Henning Stahl to the location and try to keep eyes on him at all times. Detective Chief Superintendent Mathers will be in overall strategic command as the gold commander. Detective Superintendent Nightingale, with her local expertise, will manage the operation on the ground. This is as much planning as we can do, given we don't yet have a location. Are there any questions?'

There were a few. Not many, as the previous briefing had been thorough.

'Are you OK, Mr Stahl?' Mathers asked. 'What do you think of all this?'

'I think I picked a pretty stupid week to give up drinking.'

Which was exactly the right thing to say to a room full of jumpy cops. After the laughter had died down, Mathers said, 'Don't worry, one way or another, this will all be over by lunchtime.'

Poe frowned.

Chapter 71

Unlike most territorial forces, the Metropolitan Police has five ranks above chief superintendent: commander, deputy assistant commissioner, assistant commissioner, deputy commissioner and commissioner. Poe reckoned almost all of them were facing Mathers across the long table. Like the world's worst job interview. He hadn't seen so much back covering since the Jimmy Savile enquiry. Mathers would do well to come out of this 'exploratory panel' still wearing her crown. Everyone was back in London, but only Mathers had been invited to attend.

'Talk us through it one more time, Detective Chief Superintendent Mathers,' the commander asking the questions said. He had a wart on his eyebrow and a pockmarked face. His name was Ratfield, although Poe was referring to him as Ratface.

'It was a disaster from start to finish, sir,' Mathers said.

'Where the hell is Chance's Park?' Mathers asked, clambering into the back of the command vehicle. Poe and Henning Stahl got in beside her. By the time Poe had shut the door, the four-by-four was already moving.

The Botanist had called with the location at five minutes to eleven.

'West of the city, not far away, ma'am,' Poe said. 'It'll take longer than five minutes to get there, but not much.'

'Anything I need to know about it?'

'Only that it makes no sense as a location.'

'Why not?'

'Chance's Park isn't on the outskirts of Carlisle, it's hemmed in by city. It's well maintained and has lots of paths and formal garden areas. Not many trees. Absolutely nowhere to hide. Once he's inside, we can put a ring around it.'

'Why's he doing this then?'

Bradshaw put her hand in the air. 'I think I know, Detective Chief Superintendent Mathers.'

'Why do you think he changed his modus operandi?' Commander Ratface asked. 'The old one was working well for him. Support was growing exponentially.'

'No, sir, it wasn't,' Mathers said.

'I've seen MOPAC's data, Detective Chief Superintendent. His support *is* growing.'

'I had access to the data Miss Bradshaw provided. She'd been tracking it carefully and had concluded it was actually shrinking.'

'And you trust the word of a single data analyst over that of MOPAC's Evidence and Insight Unit?'

'Yes, sir.'

MOPAC, the Mayor's Office for Policing and Crime, was a functional body of the Greater London Authority. It was responsible for the oversight of the Metropolitan Police.

'The Evidence and Insight Unit is internationally respected,' Ratface said.

'Yes, sir.'

'And she's just one analyst.'

'Yes, sir. Tilly . . . I mean Miss Bradshaw says they got it wrong. That there was a definite decrease in social media engagement. She says if the Botanist didn't do something different, he would find himself in a cycle of diminishing returns. Essentially, the public will get desensitised and move on to the next new thing.'

'So, Chance's Park was all about keeping him trending on Twitter?'

'Yes, sir.'

'OK, we'll come back to this later,' Ratface said. 'As I understand it, despite being a couple of minutes past eleven, you got to Chance's Park first?'

'That's correct, sir. We thought we might have missed him but

Detective Superintendent Nightingale, the silver commander from Cumbria, thought it unlikely. She said we had got there as quick as possible.'

'It was you who made the decision to send in Henning Stahl?'

'Yes, sir.'

'It's now or never, mate,' Poe said to Stahl. 'Step out of this car and you're on your own. I know from experience that's not a nice feeling.'

'You'll be watching me?' he said, his voice little more than a whisper.

Now it was time, the enormity of what was being asked of him had dawned on Stahl. He was trembling, he was blinking rapidly and his breathing was fast and shallow. He looked like a man who could use a drink.

'Like a hawk,' Poe said. 'And not just me. All three helicopters are overhead now. As soon as he makes an appearance we'll surround the park and put undercovers in. Take him when he tries to leave.'

'And my microphone is still working?'

Poe glanced at the tech. Received a confirmatory nod. 'It is. And remember, if he tries to take the one taped to your chest, let him. It's a real mic but it isn't transmitting. The live one is on your head. Hopefully he won't think to check there.'

'Do I go now?' Stahl said.

'If you're ready?'

'I am.'

'And you can see the picnic table he wants you to sit at?'

'The one next to the ha-ha,' he said, pointing towards a sunken ditch.

'That's right.'

Stahl stepped out of the car and offered Poe his hand. 'In case something goes wrong, Sergeant Poe,' he said, 'I've enjoyed watching you work.'

Poe shook it then watched as Stahl crossed the road and entered Chance's Park.

'Good luck, Henning,' he said to himself.

'How long did Henning Stahl wait before anything happened?' Commander Ratface asked Mathers.

'Six minutes, sir.'

'Was that unexpected?'

'Yes, sir. The Botanist had been extremely punctual with his communications up until then.'

'Did you consider calling it off?'

'I did, sir. Chance's Park was far too quiet for a Sunday.'

'So why didn't you?'

'After consulting the senior managers on the ground I made the decision to press ahead. Up until then we hadn't caught a single break and this seemed like our best chance.'

'When did you first suspect things were about to go wrong?' Commander Ratface asked.

'When I saw the lady in the pink T-shirt, sir.'

Poe watched Stahl through his binoculars. From car to picnic table, he hadn't taken his eyes off him. Not for a second. Stahl still looked horror-stricken, but he was doing what they'd advised – he wasn't looking around, craning his neck to see what was happening. He was simply looking straight ahead with his hands palm down on the table.

'Who the hell is she?' Mathers said.

The woman was wearing a garish pink T-shirt and leggings. She was jogging on the spot. She stopped, and with her legs straight, she bent forwards at the hips, lowering her head to the floor. She then reached behind, grabbed the back of her calf muscles and held the position. A standing hamstring stretch, Poe thought it was called. It looked like she was getting ready for something. As he watched, another woman joined her. Then a man. Then a group of five jogged in.

It wasn't long before there were fifty of them.

'Oh shit,' Poe said.

***

230

'No one had thought to check if there were any public events in the park that day, Detective Superintendent Mathers?' Commander Ratface asked.

'No, sir.'

'If you were sitting on this side of the table, would you class that as a failure in planning?'

'I would, sir.'

'Very well. What happened next?'

'Who the hell are these clowns?' Mathers said. 'Surely they can't be part of it?'

Nightingale's voice crackled over the radio. 'It's a parkrun.'

'Why didn't we know about this?'

'They usually happen here on Saturdays and there wasn't time to check the events schedule given how short the notice was,' Nightingale replied calmly.

'Why are they all dressed in pink?'

'We can't read the T-shirts from here.'

'I can,' Poe said. 'There's a logo on the front. It's either a brain or an upside-down testicle. Has letters underneath: ABBS. Does that make sense to anybody?'

'Never heard of it,' Flynn said into his earpiece.

She was on the other side of Chance's Park. He doubted she had seen the runners yet. She would soon, though; there were hundreds of them now. Poe could still see Henning Stahl but he wasn't sure for how much longer. The runners continued to pour in and they were starting to congregate around Stahl as they moved further into the park to make room for everyone.

'Can you hear me, Tilly?' Flynn continued.

'I can, DI Flynn,' Bradshaw said. She had stayed at Durranhill, but was monitoring the operation.

'Find out what ABBS stands for. Poe says he can see a brain or a testicle logo. I doubt it's testicular cancer as they're wearing pink. Start with neurological disorders.'

'I'll do it now.'

Poe pressed the transmit button on his radio. 'I'm going to lose visual soon,' he said. 'If anyone has better eyes on Stahl say so now, because . . . right, I've lost him.'

A sea of pink stood between Poe and Stahl. He estimated there were at least five hundred people in the park. He got the occasional flash of the ex-journalist as he was the only one not dressed like a flamingo, but he could no longer tell if he was alone.

'Quebec callsigns,' Poe said. 'Do you have eyes on Stahl?'

Quebec 251, 252 and 253 were the police helicopters. They were hovering above the three main entrances to the park.

'This is Quebec 253,' a voice crackled. 'We have eyes on the target. He's surrounded by people in pink but he appears to be on his own.'

'I want an update every thirty seconds, guys,' Poe said.

'Roger that.'

'This is Matilda Bradshaw from the National Crime Agency; please may I talk now, Poe?'

'Go ahead, Tilly.'

'ABBS stands for acquired Breeg–Bart syndrome. It's a neurode-generative disorder, an extremely rare variant of amyotrophic lateral sclerosis, one of the motor neurone diseases. Have you heard of Lou Gehrig's disease?'

'I have.'

'It's like that but ten times worse. It was jointly named after the first person to be diagnosed with it and the doctor who identified the variant.'

'And this is a regular thing?'

'It's the first one in Carlisle, Poe. The group who arrange the events concentrate on one motor neurone disease a year. They visit a city or large town each Sunday.'

'Of all the bad luck,' Mathers said.

Poe frowned. The Botanist didn't rely on bad luck. He'd known this was happening. 'I don't think—'

A klaxon sounded.

'What the hell was that?' Mathers said.

***

'The organisers sounded a klaxon for the run to start, sir,' Mathers told the panel.

'But by then you'd been told the event wasn't contained to Chance's Park?' Commander Ratface asked. 'Just the first part.'

'Yes, sir. It seems that after the run there was a reception in the grounds of Carlisle Castle, with the High Sheriff and Lord-Lieutenant.'

'How long were the runners in Chance's Park?'

'Just under half an hour, sir.'

'And it was towards the end that the Botanist made his move?'

'Yes, sir.'

'Who's that?' Quebec 253 said.

'We're blind here,' Mathers said, craning her neck in a vain attempt to see over the multitude of pink. 'Describe what you see.'

'Henning Stahl isn't on his own any more. Someone is sitting opposite him. He's wearing a brown hat and a tan coat.'

'I've gone dead,' Poe said, realising he could no longer hear the beating feet of the runners. He pressed his headpiece hard into his ear. 'I've got nothing.' He turned to the tech guy. 'Now is not a great time for a malfunction.'

'It's not us!' the poor man replied, frantically checking his systems.

Poe didn't doubt it – the Botanist had somehow found a way to jam their signals. Other than the Quebec callsigns, they were deaf, dumb and blind. They couldn't hear Henning Stahl, they couldn't speak to Henning Stahl and they couldn't see Henning Stahl.

'The Botanist used the cover of the crowd to move into the park, sir,' Mathers said. 'He had a radio frequency jammer with him.'

'This was one of the things he left with Stahl?'

'Yes, sir. It was a modified walkie-talkie. He'd altered the circuit board so the transmit button activated a jamming signal. Only about ten yards range but enough to render redundant the listening device on Henning Stahl.'

'What happened then?'

***

Poe had been a policeman a long time. He had seen operations go sideways before. He'd even been on an operation when one undercover unit arrested another undercover unit. But he had never seen an operation go from complete control to total chaos. Not this quickly.

'Quebec callsigns, do you have eyes on the target?' Mathers urged.

One at a time, Quebec 251, 252 and 253 confirmed they had.

'We need to get Henning Stahl out now, ma'am,' Poe said. 'He'll be able to tell us what the Botanist looks like, but only if he's alive.'

'What he *looks* like? You don't think we're going to arrest him?'

Poe shook his head. 'He's ten steps ahead of us here. I don't know what his escape plan is, but I do know he has one.'

'We go in then,' she said. 'Grab the bastard before he has a chance to play his fancy tricks. You OK with this, Jo?'

'You're gold commander, ma'am,' Nightingale replied.

Mathers nodded to herself. Decision made. She pressed the transmit button again.

'Sixty seconds then. Everyone into position, please.'

'But before the ground teams were able to move in and apprehend the suspect, the wheel turned again?' Commander Ratface said.

'Yes, sir. Quebec 252 said the man sitting opposite Henning Stahl had passed an envelope across the table.'

'Which was when Sergeant Poe shouted—'

'—Don't fucking touch it!' Poe screamed at the monitor.

The tech beside Poe jumped. So did Mathers.

Stahl, in the process of reaching for the envelope, sharply pulled back his hand. He looked in Poe's direction.

'Has he just heard me?' Poe said.

'*Could* Henning Stahl hear Sergeant Poe?'

'Yes, sir. The Botanist must have taken his hand off the radio jammer to pass Stahl the envelope. We could hear Mr Stahl and he could hear us.'

'But it was a short-lived victory, I understand?'

'It was, sir.'

'And why was that?'

'Because the parkrun finished.'

A second klaxon sounded and the drumbeat of footsteps changed tempo as five hundred people moved from gallop to canter to trot. The run had obviously finished.

'Now what?' Poe muttered, his eyes fixed to his binoculars again.

'The suspect is standing up,' Quebec 253 said.

Poe flicked his head towards the live helicopter feed. The man opposite Stahl was indeed getting to his feet. Poe also noticed the runners had started to leave Chance's Park. They were using the eastern exit.

'Cancel my last order,' Mathers said. 'I say again, cancel my last order. Suspect is about to leave the park. We'll arrest him on the street as originally planned. Quebec callsigns to advise if he uses a different exit to the runners.'

Poe went back to his binoculars. Back to Plan A, he thought. He wondered how long it would last. Not very, he imagined.

'This is the bit I've struggled with, Detective Superintendent Mathers,' Commander Ratface said. 'You had three helicopters watching the suspect, you had every exit covered and your communications had been restored.'

'Yes, sir.'

'Yet you still managed to miss him. How is that possible?'

'The Botanist had one last trick to play, sir.'

'What's he doing?' Mathers said. 'He's taking off his . . . oh shit!'

Poe span round to watch the helicopter feed. Saw the Botanist remove his coat, roll it up and wedge it in the waistband of his tracksuit bottoms. Saw what he was wearing underneath. He joined Mathers with an 'Oh shit.'

'And what was the suspect wearing underneath his coat, Detective Superintendent Mathers?'

'A pink T-shirt, sir.'

'Similar to what the park runners were wearing?'

'No, sir.'

'No?'

'It was *exactly* like the T-shirts the park runners were wearing.'

'But the Quebec callsigns were still able to see him?'

'Yes, sir. The Botanist joined the runners as they swarmed out of Chance's Park but he was still wearing his hat, so we didn't lose sight of him.'

'What happened next?'

'There's a large oak tree by the exit the runners were using, sir. The Botanist, who was among them by then, passed under the tree's canopy wearing his hat and came out the other side without it. Became just another person in the sea of bobbing pink. The Quebec callsigns tried to follow the crowd but it was an impossible task, sir.'

'Why?'

'The organisers hadn't sought permission to shut down Castle Way,' Mathers replied. 'That's the road to Carlisle Castle. There were five hundred runners all trying to get to the reception. When Castle Way's pavement got clogged up they used alternative routes. Almost twenty in total.'

'You lost him?'

'We did, sir.'

'"We"?'

'*I* lost him, sir.'

'And the hat?'

'Recovered in the mop-up operation, along with the radio frequency jammer.'

'DNA?'

'No, sir. We think he was wearing a wig. And we know he was wearing gloves as Henning Stahl told us he was.'

'Tell me we have enough for an E-FIT?'

'No, sir. Stahl says he was wearing a mask.'

'I've read the witness statements,' Ratface said. 'Why is it that no one can recall seeing a man in a mask? Doesn't that strike you as odd?'

'In this case? Not really, sir.'

'Very well,' Ratface sighed. 'Please tell the panel what was in the envelope he passed Mr Stahl.'

'What the hell?' Poe said.

It was two hours after the botched operation. Specialists had examined the envelope and declared it safe to open. Henning Stahl was in an interview room being debriefed. Chance's Park was now a crime scene.

On the off-chance the Botanist had licked the glue, Mathers opened the envelope at the opposite end to the gummed seal. She'd then upended it. A single sheet of paper fell out. On it was a series of typed letters and numbers.

Fhwfhtdnfyt70d52nfvlh8srwb347cbrkbplm64n6y8vngs
b96fgsb36db.onion/

'It's a dark web URL,' Bradshaw said, already unlocking her tablet. 'You can tell because it has an onion TLD.'

'TLD?' Mathers said.

'Top level domain, Detective Chief Superintendent Mathers.'

'Gotcha. You want me to read it out, Tilly?'

'Why would I?'

Poe suppressed a smile. 'Tilly has a photographic memory, ma'am,' he said.

'Don't be ridiculous, Poe. There hasn't been a single documented case of a photographic memory. What I have is an *exceptional* memory.'

She finished typing the URL into her browser and pressed enter.

They stared at the screen in astonishment.

'Well, this has just got a whole lot weirder,' Poe said.

'It was a poll?'

'Yes, sir,' Mathers replied. 'It seems the Botanist has moved away from the flowers and poems and gone for an online poll this time. It goes live in two hours.'

'I think you'd better elaborate, Detective Chief Superintendent.'

***

'I think you'd better elaborate, Tilly,' Mathers said. 'This is a website where people vote on who the Botanist should kill next?'

'Out of the two people listed, yes,' Bradshaw replied. 'It's a simple enough system. The website captures your IP address so you can only vote once, although if you have more than one device, like me, you could technically vote again. Most people have a laptop, a smart-phone and a tablet so some double-voting will be inevitable.'

'So, in twenty-two hours this thing goes live and anyone in the country can—'

'Anyone in the *world*.'

'Anyone in the world can effectively condemn one of these two to death?'

'Yes, Detective Chief Superintendent Mathers. The poll will be up for seven days, after which the person with the most votes dies.'

'And given he managed to sneak into a hospital ward that was under twenty-four-hour surveillance, does anyone doubt he can do exactly what he says?'

Flynn shook her head. She pointed at the thumbnail pictures of the two potential victims.

'Who are they?' she said.

'And more importantly,' Mathers said, 'can we shut this website down?'

'*Can* we shut it down?' Commander Ratface asked.

'Tilly says as soon as it goes live, she could do it quite easily. Something to do with the onion router not being as private as people think it is. She believes she can trace it back to the host server and either ask the authorities in whichever country it is in to do it on our behalf, or, failing that, she can simply send a code that she's devel-oped directly into the server. She says it will fry it.'

'Why can't she do that now? Stop it going live in the first place?'

'The website you have in front of you is the beta version, sir. We think the Botanist developed it with two purposes in mind: as proof of concept and to demonstrate what's about to happen.'

'We ask Tilly to shut the real site the moment it goes live then. Problem solved.'

'It's not as simple as that, sir,' Mathers said. 'There are clear instructions on what will happen if the website is tampered with.'

'As bad as the public voting on who dies next?'

'Worse, sir. The instructions say, if the vote doesn't run its course, the Botanist will kill ten innocent people. He will then let it be known that the Metropolitan Police "chose the life of one rich asshole over the lives of ten members of the public." His words, not mine.'

'Is there anything we can do?'

'Other than arrest him before the seven days are up, no, sir, we don't think we can. For obvious reasons, I don't feel this is a decision I can make on my own.'

'Do you need a comfort break?'

'I'm OK, sir.'

'Have a comfort break so we can talk about you behind your back, please, Chief Superintendent Mathers.'

'Yes, sir.'

'What do you have on Chrissie Stringer and Douglas Salt, Tilly?' Mathers asked.

Bradshaw had asked for ten minutes to draw up basic information packs on the two people selected for the death vote. She was ready in eight.

'Chrissie Stringer is the fashion designer who campaigned against modern slavery,' she said.

'She's *that* Chrissie? The one from the *Guardian* exposé?' Flynn said.

'Yes, DI Flynn. The *Guardian*'s investigative journalist found that while she was campaigning against slavery, her firm had been using indentured labour. She denied any knowledge of it, of course, even sacked her entire overseas executive team, but the *Guardian* had held back an audio tape where she not only approved the practice, but also suggested ways dissenters in the workforce could be made examples of.'

'Indentured labour?' Poe said. 'Isn't that just another way of saying slavery?'

'Except it's not illegal, Poe. Her firm encouraged Bangladeshi and Nepalese migrants to move to Qatar, promising them six hundred dollars a month. They were told there would be an administration fee of three hundred dollars, but after that had been paid back they would be sending home more money than they'd ever seen. Unfortunately, the administration fee was three *thousand* dollars, not three hundred, and they also had to pay back the cost of the flight. It took the average worker well over two years to pay back what they owed, and even then, at Chrissie Stringer's instruction, they would be fined for some arbitrary misdemeanour and the process would start again. The *Guardian* found some workers had been there five years, toiling for over a hundred hours a week under the most appalling conditions, without being paid a penny.'

'I'm voting for her,' Poe said.

'I assume they couldn't leave?' Flynn said.

'They had no money for flights, no passport and, under Qatar law, it's illegal to be in the country without a work sponsor,' Bradshaw explained. 'They had two options: work in the factory for free or go to jail. As Poe has just pointed out, they were effectively slaves.'

'OK,' Mathers said. 'She's a monster. Who's Douglas Salt? Is he better or worse?'

'He's the CEO of Salt Pharmaceuticals, Detective Chief Superintendent Mathers,' Bradshaw said. 'He's not well known in the United Kingdom, but he has a high profile in the United States of America.'

'He's a Yank?' Poe said.

'British with dual citizenship, Poe. He splits his time between London and New York.'

'And what's he done to piss off the Botanist?'

'His company makes a great deal of money acquiring the rights to old, neglected drugs and turning them into high-priced speciality drugs.'

'What the hell does that mean?'

'Well, just recently, his company bought Adetensine, an old drug used to treat multi-drug-resistant tuberculosis. It had previously been available for three hundred dollars for twenty-one pills. The day they acquired it, Salt Pharmaceuticals raised the price to nine thousand dollars. They said it was due to the investment needed to make the supply of the drug reliable.'

'Which was bullshit?'

'Yes, Poe, it was bull . . . poo. They lobby hard to stop cheaper, generic versions being imported from Canada, and Adetensine's distribution is tightly controlled, which makes it all but impossible for American-based companies to access the samples they need for testing.'

'That's decentralised procurement and private healthcare for you,' Flynn said. 'How much does the NHS pay for the drug, Tilly?'

'Nine pounds exactly, DI Flynn.'

'See?'

'OK,' Poe said. 'So he's an arsehole as well. The question is, who will the public vote for?'

'I assume you think it's Chrissie Stringer who's most at risk of winning, or should I say *losing*, the public vote?' Commander Ratface said. 'She's responsible for an actual atrocity, Douglas Salt just took advantage of a loophole and a flawed healthcare system.'

'That's what I think, sir.'

Ratface frowned. 'But not *we*?'

'No, sir. Tilly says Douglas Salt will get the most votes.'

'Really?'

'She says it's a rigged vote and Salt will win by a landslide.'

'That seems . . . counterintuitive.'

'It does, sir. She's basing this on how the location of an event dictates how much media coverage it gets. She quoted a *New York Times* editor who said, "One dead fireman in Brooklyn is worth five English bobbies, who are worth fifty Arabs, who are worth five hundred Africans".'

'That can't be true, surely.'

'It isn't, sir. Tilly says, from the perspective of the news media in the west, five hundred Africans have nowhere near that value. She also quoted' – Mathers checked her notebook – 'someone called Stephen Barnett from 2006. He said, "One death in your street is worth ten in the next town, one hundred in a European country and ten thousand a long way away".'

'She's saying that Douglas Salt had more media attention? I've never heard of him. Chrissie Stringer, on the other hand . . .'

'The Botanist is a British serial killer, sir, but this is a global vote. The PR firm Chrissie Stringer hired was successful at changing the narrative to one of a woman having to be ruthless in a man's world, whereas Douglas Salt was the lead on the news for weeks in the States. And Americans have died as a direct result of his actions. Miss Bradshaw says he's winning the media coverage by a factor of ten.'

'But really it's flip-a-coin time?'

'Yes, sir.'

'What are your next steps?'

'Excuse me, sir?'

'You still have our confidence, Detective Chief Superintendent Mathers. There will be a couple of things we'll want to review later, but, on the whole, there isn't anything you could have done differently. You remain in charge of the investigation.'

Mathers picked up her dress hat and got to her feet. 'Thank you, sir,' she said. 'I'd better get back.'

'I understand you have handpicked the officers guarding Chrissie Stringer?'

'I have, sir. She's in a safe house and no one with prior involvement in the case is on her protection detail.'

'And Douglas Salt?'

'He refused to leave his house, sir.'

'Why?'

'Says it's more secure than anywhere we can provide.'

'You're protecting him there?'

'Sergeant Poe is, sir.'

'But with our support?'

'No, sir.'

'No?'

'It's all very unorthodox, sir, but, given the circumstances, I think it's exactly the right move . . .'

Chapter 72

Douglas Salt's house was the strangest Poe had ever seen. In Hemel Hempstead, it was unapologetically modern. It was one storey high, but had three subterranean levels. There were no bricks and mortar above ground, just steel and fortified glass. All rectangles and squares and other shapes not found in nature. The computer-controlled solar panels on the flat roof tracked the sun's progress throughout the day. An eight-foot wall ringed the house. It was topped with wicked-looking razor wire. The gardens were landscaped and extensive. A blue Jaguar I-PACE and a green Porsche Taycan were parked in the drive. A small, eave-mounted camera followed their progress. Poe winked at it.

'He might be a greedy bastard, Tilly,' he said, pointing at the cars, 'but at least he cares for the environment. Both of these are electric. Probably why he keeps them outside. Needs the good publicity.'

After Poe had explained his plan, Flynn had met with their boss, Director of Intelligence Edward van Zyl, to discuss the resources he'd requested. In the meantime, she had asked Poe to make contact with Douglas Salt. He had taken Bradshaw and no one else. Working on the assumption Flynn would persuade Van Zyl, he had already made the required calls. Everyone had said yes.

Salt's front door was polished steel, more like the entrance to a vault than a home. It had a keypad and a biometric scanner. Poe pressed the discreet intercom button. He wasn't surprised to get an immediate answer.

'Identification, please,' a man's voice said. 'There's a camera built into the door. Hold them up.'

They did.

'Well, this *is* curious. Why would the National Crime Agency be bothering a private citizen? Please wait while I validate your identities. I have already photographed your faces; if you're not who you say you are, you *will* be arrested for impersonating police officers.'

'Dickhead,' Poe muttered.

'This intercom is incredibly sensitive and records all conversations, Sergeant Poe. I do not appreciate being called a "dickhead".'

'Whoops,' Poe said. 'Please accept my apology.'

'I *would* accept your apology, Sergeant Poe, if I wasn't watching you doing the masturbating gesture.'

Poe reddened. 'Who is this clown?' he whispered to Bradshaw.

'My name is Douglas Salt,' the voice said through the intercom.

'Oh for God's sake,' Poe said.

After five minutes Salt said, 'Your IDs have checked out. Now, please tell me what you want? I assure you I have broken no laws.'

'We're here to save your life, Mr Salt. Can we come in?'

'I arrange my own security, thank you. Death threats are an occupational hazard in my line of work. Now, please, if you don't mind leaving—'

'Have you heard of a man called the Botanist?'

'No.'

'Well, he's heard of you.'

The door opened a fraction. Douglas Salt peered through the crack. He was frowning. He clearly *had* heard of the Botanist.

'You'd better come in,' he said.

Chapter 73

Douglas Salt was too tall for his build. If he'd been four inches shorter he might have got away with it, but at six-foot-five he just looked weird, like he'd been put through a pasta machine. He had compensated as best he could. His face was tanned and symmetrical and his teeth were whiter than snow. Poe suspected his tan came out of a bottle, surgeons had sculptured his face, and his teeth had been bleached until they were down to the quick. His hair was ordered and neat. He wore cream chinos, a polo shirt and, despite being indoors and in his own home, he had a pink jumper slung over his shoulders. For some reason, he reminded Poe of American cheese.

The front door opened directly into a sunken living area of uninspired monotony. The floor was polished concrete and the walls were glass. The ceiling was twenty feet high. The kitchen area had a futuristic oven and other gadgets Poe recognised from a previous case. The only organic thing in the house was the Bonsai tree on the granite coffee table. The room's central column, the only thing supporting the roof, housed a built-in fire and a flatscreen television. *Citizen Kane* was playing.

'Welcome to my humble abode,' Salt said.

'Cosy,' Poe replied.

'Now, what's this Botanist nonsense? I assure you I've done nothing—'

'You need to pack a bag, Mr Salt. We leave in five minutes.'

'And where are we going?'

'Somewhere safe.'

'Am I under arrest?'

'Have you done anything illegal?'

'No.'

'Then you're not under arrest.'

'I read the news, Sergeant Poe. I watch TV; why do you believe the Botanist has shown interest in me?'

'We don't believe he's shown interest in you, we *know* he's shown interest in you. Tilly, can you show Mr Salt the website?'

Chapter 74

'Can you shut it down?' Salt said. 'If you don't have the technical skills, I assure you my people do.'

'No,' Poe said.

'Have you tried?'

'This is the demonstration site. The actual site isn't live yet.'

'You'll shut it down then?'

'Still no.'

'Why?'

'There's a penalty clause.'

'Which is?'

'Ten innocent people will die if we do.'

Salt frowned. 'I don't want to appear insensitive, Sergeant Poe, but my company literally saves lives.'

'You're saying we should sacrifice them to save you?'

'It's the logical choice.'

'It's funny,' Poe said. 'If anyone else had suggested this, I'd have been appalled. Why is it with you I sort of expected it?'

'If you won't shut it down, I will,' Salt said.

'You don't have anyone capable,' Bradshaw said.

'Don't be stupid.'

'He's using the TOR network, has hardware and software firewalls and he's protected it from distributed denial-of-service attacks. If you think of website security as like the layers of an onion, the beta version's onion would be bigger than this house.'

'Could *you* breach it?'

'Of course. But I won't unless Poe asks me to.'

'I'll make you rich.'

'I'm already rich and Poe doesn't care about money.'

'You've been working with the wrong sort of people for too long, Mr Salt,' Poe said.

'I'll sue you.'

'For refusing to sacrifice ten members of the public? I think I'd enjoy that.'

Salt slumped into an uncomfortable-looking, weirdly designed chair. 'I'm not leaving my home, Sergeant Poe,' he said. 'I can have my legal team contact the National Crime Agency if you need me to.'

Poe sighed. He reminded himself that *everyone* was entitled to protection from serial killers. 'Fine, we'll do it here,' he said.

'Do what here?'

'Prevent the impossible, Mr Salt.'

Chapter 75

'Change of plan, ma'am,' Poe said into Bradshaw's laptop. He and Mathers were on a Zoom call, whatever the hell that was. 'He's refusing to leave and we can't make him.'

'And he caught Poe pretending to shake some dice, didn't he, Poe?' Bradshaw chipped in. 'Mr Salt mistook it for a rude sign.'

'Thank you, Tilly,' Poe said. 'That was very helpful.'

'You're welcome, Poe.'

'How does this affect your plan?' Mathers said, failing to completely cover a smirk.

Poe looked around the minimalist living room. At the glass walls. At the polished surfaces. At the lack of places to hide . . .

'I'll make it work,' he said. 'We'll set up here and let everyone know.'

'OK. Stay in touch.' Mathers reached forward and ended the call.

'Tilly, should we work from here?' Poe said, pointing at the granite coffee table. 'We'll have views of the door, the stairs to the lower levels and we can see through all the windows.'

'I'll piggyback his wi-fi, Poe. I'll have everything running in fifteen minutes.'

'Mr Salt, before my team arrives we're going to run through some precautions,' Poe said.

'Very well. But, like I said, I've been arranging my own security for years. This place is impregnable.' He held up a small tablet. 'The whole house is controlled by this. No one gets in who shouldn't.'

'I'm here.'

'Yes, but you're . . .'

Salt took a step back. Reached for his phone.

'That's good, Mr Salt,' Poe said. 'You're thinking now. And don't worry, we *are* here to protect you. From now on, though, I need you to assume that anyone I haven't personally vouched for is here to kill you.'

'It can't be that bad, surely?'

'You say this place is controlled by that tablet?' Poe said, ignoring the question and asking one of his own.

'It is. It's configured to my palm print and it can't be hacked.'

'Tilly?'

'I'm in, Poe.'

'Don't be ludicrous!' Salt said. 'A contact at the Pentagon installed this system for me. It isn't even officially out yet.'

'Tilly?' Poe said again. 'A demonstration.'

'Certainly, Poe.'

She typed some commands into her laptop and pressed enter. The ceiling lights flashed on and off. 'Tin Soldiers' by Stiff Little Fingers, a song Bradshaw knew Poe liked, started playing through the concealed speakers. The kettle began to boil. The television switched from *Citizen Kane* to a news channel.

'But . . . how?' Salt stammered. 'This isn't poss—'

'Are there any physical locks in this house, Mr Salt?'

'No, the whole system's electric.'

'Pick a letter then.'

'Excuse me.'

'Pick a letter. A to Z.'

'A.'

'For fu . . . Pick a *different* letter. And if you say Z I'm going to punch you.'

'H, then.'

'Tilly, find a security business beginning with the letter H and put an order in for their best stuff. Tell them we want modern, physical locks on every potential entrance point. It's coming out of Detective Chief Superintendent Mathers's budget, so pay any same-day surcharges. I want it done before it gets dark. And you'd better explain that whoever they send will be watched the entire time they are here.'

250

'I'll do it now, Poe.'

'I'll make us some hot drinks,' Salt said. 'Is Japanese green tea acceptable?'

Poe grabbed Salt's arm. 'Mr Salt, from now on you don't put anything in your mouth that hasn't been handed to you personally by me or my team.'

'This isn't good for my blood pressure, you know.' He reached into his pocket and removed a blister pack. 'I assume it's OK to take my Norvasc?'

'No, of course it isn't OK,' Poe said. 'Tell me what it is and I'll get you a new prescription. One of my guys will get it filled.'

He took the medication from Salt and sealed it in an evidence bag.

'This is all a bit over the top, isn't it?' Salt said.

'How familiar are you with the Botanist?' Poe asked.

Salt shrugged. 'I'm a busy man.'

'Let me tell you what's happened so far. He killed his first victim before anyone knew who he was, so we get a pass on that as far as I'm concerned. We don't for the next two, though. Parliamentary and Diplomatic Protection were camped outside Harrison Cummings's flat and he still managed to kill him. And Karen Royal-Cross was in a high-level isolation unit under twenty-four-hour observation. I've reviewed the tapes and I have no idea how he got to her.'

'Poe says he's one bad mood away from declaring it black magic,' Bradshaw called out. She was setting up monitors and computers and a whole bunch of stuff Poe didn't recognise.

'I want you to sit here while I go downstairs with a bin bag. Anything disposable is getting chucked. We'll bring in shampoo, soap, food, toilet roll—'

'You *are* joking? Toilet roll?'

'He's getting to his victims somehow, Mr Salt, and I'm told it's most likely that they poison themselves. And wouldn't toilet paper be a perfect delivery system? You use it, you infect yourself, you flush away the evidence.'

'No one has been tampering with my toilet paper, Sergeant Poe.'

'Mr Salt, I don't think I'm getting through to you. If you lose

251

this vote, and Tilly assures me you will, we put your chances of survival at six per cent.'

Salt opened his mouth, but no sound came out.

'So, yes, I'm changing your fucking bog roll,' Poe added.

There was a knock on the door. Poe looked at one of the monitors Bradshaw had set up. He smiled.

The cavalry had arrived.

Chapter 76

'That looked rough, ma'am,' Poe said to Mathers when she finally got away from Scotland Yard.

'You've seen it?'

'Tilly was given access to your systems when she was analysing Spring-heeled Jack's freerunning moves. She never leaves a system without installing a backdoor. We watched it live.'

'Might have known,' she grinned. 'And it wasn't rough. Not really. We're in a command and control organisation and something went wrong. Investigating why is an important part of what we do.'

'Ratface didn't need to be such a dick about it though.'

'Who?'

'The guy asking the questions.'

'Commander Ratfield? He's OK. Where is everyone?'

'Tilly has gone to get some equipment she needs and the boss is downstairs with Douglas Salt. Henning Stahl is on his way back from his Chance's Park debriefing. Thought it best to keep him with us. I doubt his part is over yet.'

'I think that too,' Mathers agreed. 'Anyone could have taken delivery of that envelope. How's Salt taking it?'

'Not well. Keeps going on about his bloody shareholders.'

'He taking it seriously?'

'I had to tell him what we estimated his chances of survival were.' She nodded. 'Is your security detail here?'

'They are.'

'I think I'd better meet them then.'

Poe had said the definition of being a dickhead was doing the same thing over and over again and expecting a different result. Flynn had congratulated him on bastardising Einstein's famous insanity quote. Bradshaw had said the quote had been misattributed to Einstein and it was now widely accepted as coming from a novel written by Rita Mae Brown in 1983. Poe had asked how she could possibly know that.

'Because I don't just read books by Carl Hiaasen, that's why, Poe,' she'd said.

'Whatever,' he'd replied. 'The point is, when Harrison Cummings and Karen Royal-Cross died they were being protected by people we didn't know. We trusted them because we were told they were trustworthy.'

'And your point is?' Flynn had said.

'Would you trust a stranger to babysit Scrapper?'

Scrapper was the nickname he'd given Flynn's son. He was born under the most appalling circumstances and the name had stuck. He wasn't entirely sure he could remember his *actual* name. He thought it might be Adam. Zoe, Flynn's partner, glared at him every time he said Scrapper out loud.

'Zoe and I occasionally pay for professional childminding,' she had replied. 'We don't always know who they'll send.'

'Fair enough. But would you still trust an agency if you knew the child snatcher from *Chitty Chitty Bang Bang* was in the area?'

'Well, no, not then obviously. If we had to have childcare, we'd ask family or friends . . . Ah, I see. Who do you have in mind?'

Poe had grinned.

'Ma'am, let me introduce you to Douglas Salt's bespoke security detail,' Poe said to Mathers.

They had assembled in Salt's subterranean movie theatre. It had three rows of vintage cinema seats, even a popcorn machine. One of the team had asked if he could turn it on.

'Of course you can,' Poe had said. 'I mean, the most cunning poisoner in history is trying to kill Mr Salt, but sure, go ahead, eat some of his popcorn.'

The machine remained unplugged.

'We'll do the residential detail first,' he continued. 'You know

Detective Superintendent Nightingale from Chance's Park, of course.'

'Nice to see you again, Jo,' Mathers said.

'Let's hope for a better result this time, Alice.'

'This is Ian Gamble, Detective Sergeant Andrew Rigg and Detective Constable Anne Hawthorne,' Poe said. 'All from Cumbria. Ian was head of CID before he took retirement. I trust them implicitly.'

'Pleased to meet you,' Mathers said. She gestured towards a group of men dressed in jeans, T-shirts and heavy boots. They were covered in tattoos and attitude. 'And who are these mean-looking desperadoes?'

'My external security, ma'am. This is Jefferson Black. He and his men are all ex-Parachute Regiment, ex-Royal Marines Commandos, even ex-regiment.'

'Regiment?'

'SAS. Jefferson's team will be in the surrounding area performing close target reconnaissance. Two of them are in Salt's garden now, but you won't see them. They'll be our early warning system. If the Botanist thinks he can sneak in without being noticed, he's in for a very bloody shock.'

'Are you staying in the house when you're off shift?' she asked Jefferson Black.

'This will be the last time the two details meet, ma'am,' Poe explained. 'We want to limit the door being opened.'

'We can put you up somewhere, if you want?'

'No, thank you,' Black replied.

'Best not to ask too many questions, ma'am,' Poe said. 'You may not like the answers. I don't know these guys, but I trust Jefferson and he trusts them.'

'There's a Duke of Wellington quote that seems apt,' Mathers said. 'Something about not knowing what effect they'll have on the enemy, but, by God, they frighten me.'

Poe nodded. He felt the same. Bringing in Black was a risk. He had moved seamlessly from being a top chef to an organised crime boss in the space of a few years. He had removed the competition

255

in a bloodless coup and, as much as it was possible, had civilised the drug and prostitution trade in Cumbria. Drugs were no longer sold near schools and the girls were protected and well paid. But, although he owed Poe a favour, he was still a criminal and so were his associates. On the flip side, there was no way the Botanist could have predicted a move like this.

Mathers addressed the two teams.

'Thank you for coming at such short notice,' she said. 'Sergeant Poe thinks the Botanist is killing his victims by compromising someone protecting them. He believes it must have been arranged in advance. By handpicking people the Botanist could have no way of knowing about, we're hoping to have an edge for the first time. If he can't compromise someone in this room, he may have to take risks he's so far managed to avoid. We're aware this theory doesn't work all the way to the end, but right now it's all we have.'

With Salt and Flynn squirrelled away in a basement room, and the residential team sleeping, eating or watching television, Poe and Bradshaw settled down to wait for the countdown timer to run down on the Botanist's beta website.

It was like waiting for a microwave meal. You knew it was going to be awful, but you watched the clock anyway. Waiting for the ping that said your horsemeat lasagne was ready.

Henning Stahl joined them. He had arrived back from his Chance's Park debriefing in a taxi. Poe had asked why he hadn't had a police officer bring him. He'd said he needed some time on his own. They settled down on the sofa to watch the countdown. It was less than a minute now. Stahl opened his notebook.

'How are you feeling right now, Sergeant Poe?' he said.

Poe ignored him, kept his eyes on the timer.

Thirty seconds now.

'Are you nervous? Excited?'

Twenty seconds.

Ten.

Five.

Zero.

The website on Bradshaw's screen dissolved. It was replaced by two words.

Game on

Chapter 77

'Now what?' Poe asked.

'Just a moment, Poe,' Bradshaw replied. She reached across him, ran her finger across the laptop's trackpad and moved the cursor above 'Game on'. 'I think this is probably a link to the live website.'

She clicked it.

A new window opened. Poe stared at the screen. 'Shit,' he muttered.

The Botanist's website was black with red writing. It looked disturbingly professional. It was a single-page site. There was no menu, no 'about', 'home' or 'contact us' pages to explore. He had written a short intro.

A note from the man you call the Botanist

You are my people and I work for you. So far it has been a privilege to punish on your behalf. The misogynists, the corrupt, the morally bankrupt – all have been tested and all have failed. But, my friends, I was being selfish. Greedy, even. Why should I choose who faces judgement? I am but a man and I have foibles and prejudices like everyone else. I see you wearing your T-shirts and I read what you say on the internet. So, my friends, from now on it is *you* who will decide who dies, not me. #getoutthevote #wehavethepower #stringerorsalt

'Self-aggrandising bullshit,' Poe said.

Underneath the introductory paragraph were two photographs, screenshots of newspaper articles. Chrissie Stringer's was from the *Daily Express*, and Douglas Salt's was from the *New York Times*.

Both headlines screamed, 'Monster!' Under each photograph was a 'Vote now' button and a counter. So far, both were reading zero.

'People haven't discovered it yet, Poe,' Bradshaw said. 'But they will. They always do. If he knows what he's doing, and it looks like he does, given how this is set up, he'll have used SEO to increase the visibility when people search for him online.'

'SEO?' Poe said.

'Search engine optimisation. He'll have added frequently used keywords to the webpage's meta data. And people will vote. They like to think they're part of a movement.'

'He's just another serial killer, Tilly.'

'That may be so, Poe, but this site *will* give his popularity a boost.'

'Yeah? Well, wait until the Interpol blue notice coughs up some info.'

'I didn't know we'd sent a blue notice.'

'Chief Superintendent Mathers did.'

Poe talked her through their reasoning. That the Botanist must have practised on people who, in his eyes, were disposable. It was the only way he could have hit the ground running.

'Anyway, we'll know . . .'

He stopped. The first vote had been cast.

Douglas Salt: 00000000

Chrissie Stringer: 00000001

'It's started,' Henning Stahl said.

Chapter 78

Bradshaw checked her watch. 'It's about right. Voting will rise exponentially as people discover the website and begin to share the link
and talk about it online.'

'And you're certain Salt is going to win?' Poe said.

'I am, Poe.'

'But he's losing now.'

'This time tomorrow over a million votes will have been cast.'

'Really?'

'If I'm right.'

'And if you're wrong?'

'I'm not wrong, Poe. Douglas Salt will win this by a margin of at
least three to one.'

The counter clicked again.

Douglas Salt: 00000000

Chrissie Stringer: 00000002

'OK, well there's nothing to be gained from watching this all
night,' Poe said. 'I'm going to do my rounds. Make sure there are
no teething problems. And then I think I'll go through Estelle's file
again.'

'Do you want me to help you, Poe?'

'Yes please, Tilly. We still can't explain the impossible.'

'Which is?' Stahl asked.

'How someone levitated over fresh snow.'

'This isn't a mathematical equation with no solution, Poe,'
Bradshaw said. 'You'll get there.'

He asked her what she meant.

'It happened, so there is an explanation. It's like this case. The Botanist can't walk through walls and he isn't practising something phooey like black magic. He has a way of getting to the victims that we haven't discovered yet. That's all.'

Stahl opened his notebook and said, 'Phooey.' He wrote it down and shook his head. 'Classic Tilly.'

Poe glared at him.

His phone rang. It was Jefferson Black. He was only supposed to ring if he had something.

'A car's just driven past slowly,' Black said the moment Poe answered the call.

'Suspicious?'

'The driver slowed as he drove past then sped up.'

'You get his registration?'

'We did,' Black said. 'It's . . . Hang on, he's on his way back . . . He's stopped now. Driver's getting out. Do you want us to detain him?'

'I'll be right out.'

Poe ended the call and said, 'Tilly, can you go and find the boss? Jefferson Black's boys have got someone.'

Chapter 79

'Who the hell are you?' Poe said to the terrified man who Jefferson Black and a brute of a man in a maroon T-shirt were restraining.

'I'm James Godfrey, sir. Matilda Bradshaw asked me to come. I have a delivery for her.'

'Could you go and get Tilly, Jefferson? See if she knows this clown.'

Black darted into the house, returning a few seconds later with a worried Bradshaw. She took in the situation. Tilted her head to see who was being restrained.

'James? I thought I told you to call first?'

'You did. But my phone died so I thought it would be OK to just turn up.'

'But I said if you tried to get in without calling ahead, a bunch of tough men would stop you.'

'I thought you were exaggerating. And I know karate.'

'And how did that work out for you?' Poe said.

'I tried to sweep this man's legs and he punched me in the throat.'

Poe turned to Bradshaw. 'He says he has a delivery for you.'

'Actually, it's for you.'

'It is?'

'It's the hard copies of the lists of people who made bulk orders of acetone. I had to use a courier as there are boxes of them. I selected a firm at random then Skyped the driver so I'd know what he looked like.'

'Seems everything's OK, Jefferson,' Poe said.

Jefferson Black and Maroon T-shirt Man slunk back into the shadows. At least the eyes and ears part of the operation was working, Poe thought. Which was more than could be said for James's throat, judging by how red his face was. He was glad Flynn had stayed with Douglas Salt. She would have had views on this.

'We'd better get all this inside then,' he said. He pulled three twenty-pound notes out of his pocket and handed them to James. 'For your troubles. I don't imagine you'll be reporting this?'

James looked at where Maroon T-shirt Man had been standing.

'Er, no . . . Like Tilly says, I should have called first.'

'Good man,' Poe said.

Chapter 80

The incident with James had taken less than ten minutes, yet during that time the voting had accelerated.

Douglas Salt: 00000467

Chrissie Stringer: 00000489

'Chrissie Stringer is still winning, Tilly,' Poe said.

'Wait until later tonight, Poe.'

'Why? What happens then?'

'The Americans will be commuting. That's always when there is the highest traffic on social media. By midnight, Douglas Salt will be comfortably ahead.'

Henning Stahl was peering inside one of the boxes that James the courier had delivered.

'What's this?' he asked.

'Bit of light reading,' Poe replied. 'Five years' worth of people who have bulk-purchased acetone.'

'But there must be thousands of names in there.'

'This is ninety-nine per cent of what I do.' Bradshaw cleared her throat. 'This is ninety-nine per cent of what Tilly does,' he continued without missing a step.

'May I take a look?'

'Wait until Tilly's put them into piles first. And please don't use any of these names in your book. Acetone is widely used and it's unlikely our guy was stupid enough to use his real name when he bought it.'

'So why bother?'

'Investigations are like sharks, Mr Stahl: if they don't keep moving forwards they die.'

Stahl opened his notebook again and wrote something down. 'You're the gift that keeps on giving, Sergeant Poe.'

'You can help me sort them into piles if you want, Henning Stahl?' Bradshaw said. 'Poe and DI Flynn will review the lists once I've prioritised them.'

'How will you do that, Tilly?'

'As the Botanist wouldn't have needed much, and so far he's used a different poison each time, I'll start with people who made single bulk purchases and I'll sort them into size; smallest to largest. I'll sort the rest into individuals or companies that purchased large quantities of acetone more than once. There will be sub-lists relating to dates and logistics, of course, but I imagine these will be the main three.'

'I assume the companies that bought it more than once will be businesses that use it in a manufacturing process?'

'Yes, but Poe wanted them left in.'

'What did Poe want, Tilly?' Flynn said, entering the room. Douglas Salt was on her heels. Salt looked angry, Flynn looked bored.

Bradshaw told her how she planned to triage the acetone lists.

'What you been up to?' Poe said. He'd insisted that Salt was shadowed at all times. Flynn had drawn the first shift. Gamble, Nightingale and the others were relaxing in the myriad subterranean rooms. Every now and then Poe heard the click of pool balls and the occasional cheer. He assumed Salt had a games room that he hadn't seen yet.

'We've just watched the new Bond movie and now Mr Salt says he's hungry.'

'I have a *côte de boeuf* chilling in the fridge,' Salt said.

'And what's that?' Poe said.

'It's a cut of vintage beef that's been stored in a ventilated negative cold room since 1998. I'll fire up the Konro grill while I bring it up to room temperature. I'm sorry, but I only have the one.'

'No, you don't,' Poe said.

Salt frowned. 'OK, I do have more in the freezer, but they're imported from Saint-Mihiel at eight thousand euros per kilo. Please don't take this the wrong way, but the palate of the average police officer won't be sophisticated enough to appreciate an artisanal steak of this quality.'

'Why on earth would I take that the wrong way?' Poe said. 'And I said no, because you do not have a massively overpriced ribeye in your fridge. And nor do you have any in your freezer. Not any more. They were thrown away, along with everything else.'

'How dare—'

'A poisoner has threatened you, Mr Salt, and no one here likes you enough to taste your food.'

'Eating meat is unhealthy, Douglas Salt,' Bradshaw said.

'It's not all bad news, though,' Poe said. 'I'm treating everyone to a nose-to-tail goat later. There's a Moroccan place nearby that dry rubs a whole one with five types of chillies before it's basted in its own fat for twenty-four hours. Comes with the works: preserved lemons, toasted almonds, the lot. If you stop moaning, you can have one of the eyeballs.'

'You're disgusting,' Salt said. He spun on his heels and stomped back down the stairs. Flynn, suppressing a grin, followed him.

Poe smiled. That had been fun.

'He's right, Poe, you *are* disgusting,' Bradshaw said.

'You ever seen a goat, Tilly?'

'Of course.'

'In real life?'

'Gosh, no. I imagine that would be very scary.'

'Well, *they're* disgusting, not me. Did you know, bucks masturbate then ejaculate on their own bellies and beards?'

'Who told you that?' Bradshaw said sceptically.

'Victoria Hume. She tried keeping them once. Said they're the sex offenders of the farmyard and people should be paid to eat them.'

Poe made himself a cup of coffee then picked up Doyle's file. For the next hour he reread everything, including his own notes. Bradshaw and Stahl were on their hands and knees going through the acetone lists. They were talking quietly, trying not to disturb him.

The last section of the file was where he'd placed copies of the CSI photographs. His phone rang. It was Doyle's solicitor, Ania Kierczynska.

'Estelle has asked to see you, Sergeant Poe,' she said after they had exchanged pleasantries.

'She has? Why?'

'She wouldn't say. Just that it was important.'

'I'm going to struggle to get away,' Poe said.

'I thought she was your priority?'

'She is. I'm reviewing her case file right now.'

'What's the problem then?'

'You saw the newspaper coverage of my last visit?'

'I did. Estelle said it wouldn't scare you off, though. Don't tell me she was wrong.'

'She's not wrong, Ania, but I'm under strict instructions to keep away from Northumberland right now. It's beginning to compromise the case down here. And I've seen everything I need to for now. If there's an answer, it'll be in my file.'

Ania didn't respond.

'Did you get the post-mortem reports to her?' Poe asked.

'I did. Do you think that's why she wants to see you?'

'Possibly. Can you ask her? Because if it is, I can justify seeing her.'

'I'll pass it on,' Ania said. 'You'll keep me updated?'

'I will.'

Poe picked up the file again. Returned to the photographs of the office. Of Elcid Doyle, dead in his chair. The fresh snow with only one set of footprints. Estelle Doyle's arrest photographs. Side on and facing the camera. She looked defiant but vulnerable. There were pictures of her hands, including a couple taken after they had been bagged to preserve the firearms discharge residue evidence. He paused on the photograph taken *before* the paper evidence bags had covered her hands. There was something wrong with it but he couldn't work out what. It was just a hand. A delicate hand. A hand skilled with a scalpel. Pale with blue veins. Crimson nail polish, flawlessly applied. He flicked back to a picture of her face and confirmed the nail polish was the same colour as her lipstick.

'You got a minute, you two?' he said to Bradshaw and Stahl.

They got up off their knees. He showed them the photograph of Doyle's hands.

'You notice anything odd about this?'

'Who is it?' Stahl said, taking a pair of reading glasses from his top pocket.

'They're Estelle Doyle's hands, Henning Stahl,' Bradshaw said. 'She's a pathologist who Poe likes to work with. She's on remand for murdering her father but Poe says she didn't do it. He's asked me to explain how someone could have travelled across fresh snow without leaving footprints. If I can't, then Estelle Doyle will be found guilty.'

'Have a look at this photograph,' Poe said. 'Tell me what you see.'

Bradshaw studied it. Stahl went back to checking the acetone lists.

'Nothing curious, Poe,' Bradshaw said after a few moments. 'Do you think they might be someone else's hands?'

Poe frowned. He didn't think that was it. He'd spent a lot of time watching Doyle's hands as she sliced into the cadavers he sent her. They were definitely hers. And, although he was certain she was being set up, he had no reason to suspect a Northumbrian cop was behind it.

'They're her hands, Tilly,' he said. 'No doubt about that.' He put the photograph back in the file and closed it. 'I'm tired, it's probably nothing.'

'You have good instincts, Poe,' Bradshaw said. 'We'll have another look when we've finished with the acetone purchases, won't we, Henning Stahl?'

But Stahl didn't answer. Poe glanced at him. He seemed transfixed by one of the pages. He was holding it like it was radioactive.

'What do you have there, Henning?' Poe asked quietly.

He looked at him blankly.

'What does Mr Stahl have in his hand, Tilly?' Poe said.

'It's a page from the box of people who made a one-off purchase of acetone.'

'And?'

Stahl came out of whatever fugue state he was in. He jabbed his finger at one of the names on the list.

'I know this man,' he said.

Chapter 81

Poe turned in the passenger seat and faced Henning Stahl.

'Tell me again,' he said. 'Start from the beginning, leave out nothing.'

They were in a black Range Rover, racing through the Hemel Hempstead suburbs. Stahl was sitting beside Mathers in the back. Mathers's driver, a detective called Cat Baker, had her blues on but didn't need the twos yet. That would change when they hit north London. Mathers had her phone glued to her ear as she took in constant updates from her team on the ground. Flynn and the rest of the team had stayed with Douglas Salt. Poe didn't want to leave Salt exposed.

'His name is Doctor Frederick Beck,' Stahl said, 'and he was a pharmaceutical scientist with Straikland Industries.'

'Doing what?'

'Identifying new compounds that could be used to treat diseases. Developed drugs from lab to shelf. That type of thing.'

'And he was good?'

'Brilliant, apparently. He's named as a significant contributor on the licence of at least three drugs being used today.'

'You said "*was* a pharmaceutical scientist". What happened?'

'I suppose this is where I come in,' Stahl said. 'I was drafted in to help with background research on Straikland Industries. The deep swimmer the paper had planted—'

'Deep swimmer?'

'An investigative journalist who goes all in. Stays in role for months, even years.'

'We use the same term for our undercovers, Poe,' Mathers said. Her phone was still pressed against her ear. 'I'm on hold, would you believe? The most important manhunt since the Yorkshire Ripper, and some moron at the UK Border Agency has me listening to "Copacabana".'

'The border agency?'

'A computer check showed Beck hasn't used his passport recently, but I wanted someone senior to confirm this. Tracing his movements will be easier if we know he hasn't been abroad. Means . . . Hello, yes, no problem.' She mouthed sorry and went back to her call.

'Carry on,' Poe said to Stahl.

'Our journalist was called Fiona Musgrave and she'd penetrated Straikland at the highest level. Uncovered systemic unethical practices.'

'Such as?'

'Scientists cutting corners in human trials. Falsifying data. A couple of other things. It's a cut-throat business and it does happen occasionally, but this was different.'

'How?'

'Because it wasn't limited to ambitious scientists. Fiona discovered that when Straikland's senior management team were informed of illegal practices, instead of conducting root and branch reviews of policies and safeguards, they would quietly dismiss the offending employee after getting them to sign non-disclosure agreements. Fiona found it had happened at least six times.'

'Including Frederick Beck?'

'Yes. For conducting unauthorised human trials. He'd replaced the placebo drug on a randomised clinical trial for a new anti-obesity drug, with one he'd been developing outside of work.'

'And it was brought to Straikland's attention?'

'One of Beck's research assistants turned whistleblower.'

'What did Straikland do when they found out?'

'What they always did,' Stahl said. 'Paid him off, had him sign an NDA and pretended it hadn't happened. Gave him a seven-figure payout.'

'Why so much?'

'Because the drug he was privately developing, the one he'd been substituting for the placebo, actually worked. He got a seven-figure lump sum and Straikland kept his research.'

'What was his drug used for?' Poe asked.

'That, I *can't* remember,' Stahl said. 'Probably something to do with his wife. She was extremely ill and he became obsessed with finding a cure. I do know that when the story broke, he came across sympathetically. His research had egregiously breached medical ethics, but he'd done it with good intentions.'

'What did he do after Straikland?'

'Got a job for another of the big firms. He was there when the story broke. They let him go as well, said they were unaware of what he'd done. Even started legal proceedings against Straikland for not telling them, although everyone knew it was a PR stunt. Big pharma's a revolving door when it comes to top research scientists – they knew why Straikland had let him go. Knew and didn't care.'

'And after the story broke? Where did he work then?'

'No idea. Someone will have snapped him up, though.'

'Really? He wasn't struck off or something?'

'Like I said, Beck was brilliant,' Stahl said. 'And, due to the principle of autonomy and the laws of consent, animals have more protection than humans when it comes to health-related services. You have to be a registered veterinarian to provide treatment to an animal, but there's no law against who can treat humans. And that includes surgery. It's why it isn't illegal for any shyster to get a Harley Street address and set themselves up in the cosmetic surgery or laser eye treatment racket.'

'I really hope that isn't true,' Poe said. 'But the thing—'

'It is true. You can check—'

'—But the thing I don't understand, Henning, is why Tilly didn't uncover this when she was researching the stories you'd been involved in. Seems like this would have been an obvious place to start.'

'That's easy to explain,' he said. 'My name was never attached to the story when it broke.'

'Why not?'

'Like I said, I was only involved in background research on Straikland Industries.'

Poe considered what he knew about journalists. Someone of Stahl's stature would have insisted on his name being on the story somewhere. Maybe not on the first-day exclusive, but definitely in one of the follow-up features.

'Nah,' he said. 'There's something you're not telling me.'

Stahl said nothing.

'Henning?'

'OK!' Stahl snapped. 'The hacking scandal was about to break. The paper didn't want my name on anything. I was *persona non grata* by the time the story was published so my research was attributed to Mark Dare. Mark didn't actually exist, it was just the name they used when a journalist's real name had to remain confidential.'

Poe nodded. That had the rare stench of truth. Something occurred to him. 'Why do you think he chose to meet *you* in Chance's Park?' he said. 'If this is about revenge, surely the woman who broke the story would have been a more obvious choice?'

Stahl considered this. 'It doesn't make sense,' he said. 'Fiona was the one who exposed Beck, stopped him continuing with his life's passion, but she's a bit of a boy scout. An irritating over-achiever, but essentially a good person. Killing her would have alienated the public, I suspect. I, on the other hand, *would* have made an acceptable target, but I wasn't substantively involved in the story.'

Mathers finished her call. 'SCO19 are in position,' she said. 'Just waiting for my go order.'

'You going to give it?'

SCO19 was the Met's specialist firearms unit. Mathers wasn't taking any chances.

'How long until we get there, Cat?' Mathers asked her driver.

'We're here now, ma'am.'

Chapter 82

North London

The address on Frederick Beck's driving licence was straight out of the dodgy-part-of-town starter pack. Pawn shops, derelict factories, sketchy pubs, and takeaways with names like Bob's Burgers, Quick Wings and A Slice of Heaven. Beck was renting both flats above a fried chicken shop. SCO19 had named them Alpha and Bravo. Checks with the landlord confirmed Beck was up to date with his payments. The flats were accessed through a keypad-controlled door at street level.

Poe followed Mathers out of the vehicle but hung back. This part of the operation was all hers and he didn't want to prove a distraction. Henning Stahl joined him.

'Get back in the car,' Poe said. 'These are armed police. The last thing they need is you stumbling into their line of sight.'

'The agreement was that I'd have full access.'

'Access, yes. Being part of the breach team, no. Now, do as you're told and sit in the bloody car.'

Mathers beckoned Poe over. 'Anything you want to say before I give the order, Poe?' she asked.

'Hazmat is on standby?'

'They are. We'll record the scene, but we won't move or touch anything, not until it's been declared safe.'

'Is he in there?' Poe asked.

'We can't see him, but it's late. He could be in bed.'

'Nothing more from me then.'

Mathers turned to the armed cop standing next to her. He was wearing a black baseball cap with white chequered banding and Police written on the front. He had a Heckler & Koch MP5 slung across his chest and a Glock strapped to his thigh. He was chewing gum and seemed calm.

'We ready, Sergeant Holder?' Mathers asked.

'Just waiting for your order, ma'am.'

'I'm handing you temporary control then,' she said. 'Please go when you're ready.'

Poe made his way back to the Range Rover. By the time he'd opened the door the shouting had started.

Frederick Beck wasn't in bed. SCO19 cleared both flats in seconds. Poe listened on Cat Baker's radio. They opened the front door using the keycode the landlord had provided, then sprinted up the stairs screaming 'Armed police!' They simultaneously smashed open the doors to Alpha and Bravo and started clearing them. Two bedrooms, two living rooms/kitchenettes and two bathrooms – six rooms in total. SCO19 went through them in thirty seconds.

'Anything, Sergeant Holder?' Mathers said when the noise had subsided.

A pause.

'I think you'd better come and see for yourself, ma'am.'

Chapter 83

Poe followed Mathers up the tight staircase. They were togged out in full barrier clothing: white paper suits, hoods, face masks, gloves and overshoes. Like nurses during a pandemic.

With the exception of Sergeant Holder, SCO19 were outside forming a perimeter.

'What do we have?' Mathers asked.

'He's used every room, ma'am. There's a single bed in Bravo, and a lot of stuff on the walls. Looks like he was using the rooms in Alpha as laboratories.'

'Thank you, Sergeant Holder. Good job.'

After he had joined his colleagues, Mathers asked her crime scene manager to start recording. CSI would be there at least a week. The TV shows consistently got it wrong – processing a crime scene was laborious, painstaking work. It couldn't be rushed.

The architectural plans showed the two flats were mirror images of each other. The front doors were thin and flimsy and had been kicked off their hinges by SCO19. They entered Alpha first, the flat Sergeant Holder had said contained laboratories. The front door led directly into a cramped living room. On the wall opposite the window was the kitchen area. Little more than a stove and an oven, both electric, both fed by the meter fixed to the wall.

The landlord's cheap furniture had been pushed aside to make room for objects seldom found on any furnishings and fittings inventory. Poe couldn't identify most of them, but he knew what they had been used for.

He followed Mathers as she moved methodically from living room to bedroom to bathroom, pointing out things she needed the crime scene manager to record. No emotion, no opinions, just facts.

The video might form part of the prosecution one day and it was important to keep emotion out. This part of the investigation was all about evidence recovery.

They left Alpha, crossed the landing and entered Bravo. Sergeant Holder hadn't been exaggerating when he'd said there was stuff on the walls. There wasn't a spare inch. The living room was dedicated to the three victims: Kane Hunt, Harrison Cummings and Karen Royal-Cross. Press clippings, long-distance photographs of them and their homes, research on their friends, families and neighbours. Details of their vehicles and what public transport they used. Freedom of information requests. Medical histories and information on their hobbies. The pubs and restaurants they frequented, the gyms they used, where they shopped.

The poems he'd sent, the poisons he'd killed them with . . .

They waited for the crime scene manager to video everything then moved into the bedroom. The bed had been pushed against the wall. It was neatly made. A clean duvet and a single pillow. A bedside table and a lamp. No personal items whatsoever. Like the rest of the rooms, the curtains were drawn.

Mathers turned on the light.

'Bloody hell,' Poe muttered. 'Where's he getting all this?'

Chrissie Stringer and Douglas Salt's lives were laid bare on two of the walls. A third wall was dedicated to the website. The server Beck was using, the hashtags he hoped would make the vote go global. Measures he'd taken to ensure it couldn't be taken down. The last wall was all about the parkrun. An estimate of the number of people who would attend. Start and end times. A circuit diagram of the radio frequency jammer he'd used to render Stahl's microphone redundant. There was even a photograph of the tree he stood under when he removed his hat, the simple trick that ensured air surveillance couldn't track him. Poe had been on army ops with less planning. If he hadn't been appalled, he'd have been impressed.

With both flats documented, Mathers let the crime scene manager leave so he could brief his team. She turned to Poe and said, 'Is this guy taking the piss?'

Poe nodded. 'This isn't a crime scene,' he said. 'It's an exhibition.'

Chapter 84

'It's the most blatantly manufactured crime scene I've ever come across, boss,' Poe said into his phone. 'Little more than a love letter to himself.'

'What do you mean?' Flynn replied.

'He knew we were coming. Planned for it. It's probably why he made such a large purchase of acetone and why he used his real name. He *wanted* us to find this place.'

'And this isn't just you, you know . . .?'

'What?'

'Being you?'

'Chief Superintendent Mathers spotted it as well. We'd assumed Beck had slipped up when he used his own name to purchase the acetone. He hadn't. It was entirely deliberate.'

'Talk me through everything.'

'I can do better than that,' Poe said. 'I shot a video on my phone and I've sent it to Tilly. Call me back when it's on her laptop.'

'It's a chromatography column, Poe,' Bradshaw said. 'It's a piece of equipment used to separate chemical compounds.'

The object on the video was a cylindrical glass tube. It was about two feet tall, had a built-in tap at the bottom and was clamped in the upright position. It was filled with a solid material.

'The solution is poured into the top, and as it passes through the absorbents in the column, the individual compounds react differently to the packed material. Because of this they reach the bottom at different rates, allowing them to be separated,' Bradshaw continued. 'They'll have to check the trace evidence, but it wouldn't surprise me if he used the chromatography column to extract the ricin from the castor bean oil. It's what I would have used.'

'I assume they're widely available?' Flynn asked.

'You can get them on Amazon for fifty pounds, DI Flynn.'

Flat Alpha looked like a sixth-form chemistry lab. Some of the equipment, like Bunsen burners, test-tube racks and a microscope, Poe recognised from school. Glass beakers, crucibles and Petri dishes. Funnels and stirring rods. Other equipment Bradshaw had to talk them through.

As well as the chromatography column, she had identified a centrifuge, an analytical balance, which Poe guessed was just a fancy way of saying scales, an incubator and a mobile fume cupboard. There was a digital refractometer to check the purity of his poisons and a laboratory fridge to store them in.

'There's nothing here that would raise any concerns, Poe,' Bradshaw continued. 'Other than the acetone, this can all be purchased without leaving your details.'

'What's that grey thing?' Poe asked. 'Looks a bit like a deep fat fryer.'

'It's a dehydrator. I imagine he used it to dry out the flowers he sent to his victims.'

'Why not use a flower press?'

'A dehydrator is more reliable, Poe.'

'It's a fully equipped, modern lab then?'

'Every poison he's used so far could have been manufactured to a high quality in there. Absolutely no question.'

'OK. Henning Stahl established that Beck has both the pedigree and the motivation,' Poe said. 'We've now established he has the facilities. You see why I say it's a staged crime scene, boss?'

'It's *absolutely* a staged crime scene,' Flynn agreed. 'Everything is about the poisons and victims we already know about. There's nothing about how he's getting it into his victims, or who he wants to kill when the Douglas Salt/Chrissie Stringer phase is over. Nothing at all that will help us catch him.'

Chapter 85

With Mathers taking charge of the hunt for Frederick Beck, Poe asked if he could return to Douglas Salt's house. He would ask Bradshaw to winkle out a more recent picture of Beck to assist with the nationwide manhunt. All Mathers had now was a twenty-year-old DVLA photograph and an even older one from the Passport Office. All wild hair, Brian Blessed beard and horn-rimmed spectacles. With contact lenses, a shave and a haircut he would waltz past them unnoticed.

Mathers wanted Poe to stay at the crime scene, see if something jumped out, but he was feeling anxious about Salt's safety. Beck had wanted the flats to be found. His latest move might look like another jigsaw puzzle within a jigsaw puzzle, but Poe believed it meant something. Maybe the start of a new phase.

She reluctantly agreed to let him go.

'Before I leave, ma'am, should we remove something from the crime scene?' he said.

'I wasn't planning to. Why?'

'This is the highest profile case in years. It's making headlines across the world. Are you absolutely certain the crime scene photographs won't get leaked? The tabloids will pay five figures to see the inside of this mad bastard's hidey-hole. If you remove something before the place is photographed, you'll be able to weed out the cranks later on.'

'You got anything in mind?'

'Tilly says the flats are equipped like any high-school lab, so there's nothing in here that someone with a rudimentary understanding of extracting and refining poison couldn't guess would be here.' He walked over to the dehydrator. 'Except this. We'd assumed he'd been using a flower press for the petals, so this might be enough of a curveball.'

Mathers nodded.

'Can you get this bagged up before you start photographing the scene, please?' she asked the crime scene manager.

He was hovering in the doorway, eager to get started. He scuttled back down the stairs to get an evidence bag, returning a few moments later. They watched as he photographed the dehydrator. He opened the lid and reached inside with a pair of tweezers. He gently removed a flower petal. It was as dry as peanut skin. He carefully put it into a bag, sealed it, then made a note of the reference number. He then did the same with the dehydrator.

Poe's phone vibrated. It was Henning Stahl.

'What you got in there?'

Poe told him.

'I want a photograph,' Stahl said. 'And not the sterile crime scene ones, I want a *before* shot as well.'

Poe frowned. The agreement they'd made was that he could have access. But Poe couldn't let him tramp around a live crime scene. He told Mathers what Stahl wanted.

'Sod him,' she said.

'How about we let him up to the doorway? Let him use his phone to take a couple of photographs. I'll email them to Tilly then we'll delete everything. He can get them back when this is over, and if something *is* leaked, we'll know it wasn't him.'

'OK,' she said. 'But I want one of my guys to delete it all from his phone. No disrespect, Poe, but Tilly tells me you're as much use as the Pope's balls when it comes to the technical stuff.'

'She said that?'

'No, I was paraphrasing. What she *actually* said was, "Don't let Poe touch anything electronic. He'll press a weird combination of buttons that'll make the battery explode."'

'That only happened once,' he said.

Chapter 86

'How's the public vote going, Tilly?' Poe asked as soon as he walked through the door. 'Is Salt winning?'

'He's up by almost a million now, Poe,' Bradshaw replied.

'That many? Where is he?'

'Downstairs, sulking.'

'Why?'

Bradshaw reached for the remote and turned on the television.

'It's almost ten p.m.,' she said. 'Why don't you watch for yourself?'

'We'll now go to Maria Dorey for a full update,' the news anchor said.

Maria Dorey was standing outside the police cordon on Frederick Beck's street. There was a fine drizzle in the air. She'd obviously been waiting a while for her cue as her head was wet.

'Thank you, Charles,' she said. 'There was chaos earlier today when armed police raided an address on this street . . .'

A report heavy on supposition but light on facts followed. It was clear that, while the press knew there had been a breakthrough, no one had been briefing them. They didn't even have the Botanist's name. Poe suspected that Dorey's wilder claims were simply an attempt to get someone to put the record straight.

She gave a quick update on the public vote before introducing pre-recorded biographies of Douglas Salt and Chrissie Stringer. Poe now understood why Salt was sulking. His bio was particularly unpleasant. The station's American correspondent had spoken to families who had lost loved ones to multi-drug-resistant tuberculosis. They were only too happy to vent against the man who had hiked up the price of the drug that could have saved them.

The report went on for a couple more minutes before she started to wrap it up for the night.

'This, of course, follows on from the bungled police operation in Chance's Park in Cumbria. As the Botanist's popularity grows, confidence in the police's ability to apprehend him is at an all-time low—'

Bradshaw turned off the television. 'Douglas Salt says we're deliberately overreacting as revenge for him being a successful capitalist,' she said. 'He told DI Flynn that we had to leave.'

'What did the boss say?' Poe said, grinning.

'She told him to stop being so immature. DI Flynn and Ian Gamble are asleep now, as their shift has finished. Detective Sergeant Andrew Rigg and Detective Constable Anne Hawthorne have taken over.'

'Is there any goat left? I'm starving.'

'You're joking, aren't you? No one's touched it. In fact, we had to put it in the garden as it was making the house smell yucky.'

'What did you have instead?'

'Jefferson Black went to McDonald's. I had a vegan wrap.'

'You? You had a McDonald's?'

'I did. And I shan't be having one again.'

'Horrible, aren't they?'

'It's the worst thing that's ever been in my mouth,' she agreed.

'You can't eat a whole goat, Poe.'

'I can and I will.'

'But you'll suffer from crapulence.'

Poe didn't immediately respond. 'Potty mouth,' he said eventually.

'Crapulence isn't a derivative of the Middle English vulgarism "crap", Poe. It means sickness or indisposition from excess eating or drinking.'

'All I know is I'm eating my goat,' he said. He leaned forwards and took in the aromas coming from the grease-stained takeout bags. The smell was intoxicating. 'You're about to witness something very special here, Tilly.'

Bradshaw sighed. 'Before you start, I need to tell you something.'

'If this is about how unhealthy—'

'You know how Detective Chief Superintendent Mathers said Frederick Beck hasn't left the country since he was exposed in the newspaper article?'

'The UK Border Agency have confirmed it,' Poe nodded. 'If he has been rehearsing, it was in the UK somewhere.'

'I think he has two passports.'

Poe looked at his takeaway goat.

'Shit,' he said.

Chapter 87

'He has two passports?' Poe said.

'That I know of,' Bradshaw replied. 'One under his real name, the other under the name Stuart Rich.'

'How did he get the second one?'

'It's perfectly legal to have more than one passport, Poe.'

'It is?'

'Yes, Poe. If your job involves a lot of international travel you might need more than one passport so you can send one off for a visa while you're using the other. It's quite common.'

'But not in two different names, surely?'

'No, that's less common. But you can apply for a second passport using a document like an affidavit, a deed poll or a statutory declaration. All he would have needed was evidence that he was using his new name.'

'*Did* he use his new name?'

'He did, Poe. After the exposé in the newspaper, despite being a leader in his field, he struggled to find work—'

'Or he didn't want to draw attention to himself while he planned all this?'

'I hadn't considered that, but keeping a low profile makes much more sense. Anyway, he ended up in a small flat in Kenilworth, near Coventry. He used his council tax forms to apply for a passport in his new name. As soon as it was issued he left the country.'

'How did you find him?'

'It was on the HM Passport Office database.'

'And how did you . . .? You know what, it doesn't matter,' Poe said, electing for plausible deniability. 'We'd better get someone to check out that address in Coventry.'

'It's been rented out several times since then, Poe.'

'Where did he fly to?'

'Leonardo da Vinci Airport in Rome.'

'Damn,' Poe said. Da Vinci was a hub airport, servicing forty-five million passengers a year. From Rome you could fly anywhere in the world.

'Did you track him after that?'

'He didn't use a connecting flight, Poe.'

'He didn't?'

'Perhaps he acquired another passport?' Bradshaw said. 'An illegal one this time.'

That wasn't so unlikely. He remembered seeing an NCA bulletin a few years ago about a batch of faulty Italian passports. Thousands had been on their way to be pulped when they'd been stolen. You could buy one, complete with supporting documents, for around ten thousand euros. And in Sweden you could lose your passport six times a year and get six replacements. Europe had a massive problem with passport fraud.

'I'd better call Detective Chief Superintendent Mathers,' he said. 'It might help with her Interpol blue notice.'

He was searching through his recent contacts when Mathers called him.

'What's up, ma'am?' he said. 'I was just about to ring you.'

'I need you and DI Flynn back here.'

'The boss has just finished her shift, ma'am. I'll wake her if it's important, but she's been putting in some serious hours over the last few days.'

Mathers paused. 'Just you then.'

'What is it?'

'We think we've found something.'

Poe looked at the slow-roasted goat again. 'I'll be right there,' he sighed.

Chapter 88

'We found this in Flat Bravo,' Mathers said, pointing at a single-page document. 'It hasn't been processed, so don't touch it.'

She told Poe it had been hidden in a cheap clip frame, one of those with an MDF back and an acrylic front. The acrylic and MDF were held together by four stainless steel clips. The document had been slipped between the board and a watercolour print of a sailing ship and a buoy. The same picture hung on the wall in Flat Alpha. It was almost certainly the stock picture that came with the frame. The landlord had probably bought them in bulk and put them in all his flats.

The diagram showed a repurposed bug fogger, a specialised aerosol can used in pest control. Sometimes called 'bug bombs', they were filled with pressurised insecticide and were for indoor fumigation. The diagram showed a 'total release' fogger, a one-shot use-and-discard can. It had a nozzle on the top like a can of shaving foam. But, unlike a can of shaving foam, once the nozzle was pressed, the fogger emptied its contents like a smoke grenade; you didn't need to keep your finger pressed down.

The diagram had accompanying instructions. Poe read them in growing horror.

- Take fogger to Whippendell Woods. Empty safely.
- Remove valve from bicycle tyre.
- Drill 1 x 2 mm hole and 1 x 5 mm hole into side of fogger.
- Solder bicycle valve over 5 mm hole.
- Inject 200 ml of solution into fogger via 2 mm hole.
- Seal hole with spot solder.
- Using bicycle pump, re-pressurise fogger through the bicycle valve.

Poe gulped. With a single press of the repurposed fogger's nozzle, Beck could fill a large room with whatever he wanted. And Poe knew from Bradshaw's briefing that ricin was deadly as a mist.

'We found a bicycle tyre in his dustbin,' Mathers said. 'The valve's been removed. He's actually made this thing.'

Poe didn't answer. Step-by-step, Beck had detailed how he had made a device capable of killing dozens of people. Poe didn't understand why. Beck was a precision killer. Mass murder didn't fit with what he was trying to do, or the image he was trying to project.

'I think I have to bring in CTC now,' Mathers said.

Counter Terrorism Command was the Met's anti-terror unit.

'Before you do, ma'am, can we have a chat about what this means?'

'Which part?' she said. 'The weapon of mass destruction or the fact that we're still ten steps behind this prick?'

'The fogger plans,' Poe replied. 'Why did we find them?'

'He forgot to take them with him.'

'Then why were they hidden? Nothing else is.'

'He made a mistake?'

'This guy doesn't make mistakes,' Poe said.

'Well, he has now.'

'What if he hasn't?'

'You're saying he wanted us to find it?'

'Everything else in here has been carefully staged,' Poe said. 'Why not this? And, while we're on it, repurposing this fogger isn't a complex task. He certainly wouldn't have needed detailed instructions. What was it? Empty the can, drill two holes and fit a valve over one of them. Fill it with poison and pump it up with a bicycle pump. He's even drawn us a picture, for God's sake.'

'You have a theory?'

'I think this is his equivalent of a suicide vest, ma'am. A warning about what happens if he's cornered.'

Mathers stared at the diagram. Read everything again. 'I think you're right, Poe,' she said. 'I'll still need to inform CTC, but I'll ask to stay in charge. Now, what was it you wanted to speak to me about?'

'Excuse me?'

'When I rang, you said you were about to call me.'

'Beck has a second passport, in the name of Stuart Rich. Used it to fly to Rome. He could have got new papers in Italy, which would have allowed him to travel anywhere he wanted.'

'Well, isn't today the day that keeps on giving?' Mathers sighed. 'You'll email me the details?'

'Tilly already has. And why don't you head home for a few hours? Nothing is going to happen right now, and we need you fresh . . .' He trailed away.

'What is it, Poe?'

Poe had been watching one of the CSIs photographing the carpet. He had assumed it was a stain of some kind, but after she had recorded the carpet from a number of angles, she plucked something from the weave with a pair of forensic tweezers. Poe strained his eyes to see what it was. Tweezers were only used when something was too small to be picked up by hand. And if it was that small, it might not be part of the manufactured scene.

'What's that?' he asked.

'A couple of bits of thread,' the CSI replied. 'Probably nothing, but they looked a bit out of place as the carpet is blue. Maybe he walked it in.'

They were cotton. One thread was white, the other was red. They were about four inches long.

And they looked familiar.

Nothing recent, but he'd seen threads like them before. Snatches of memory resurfaced. A detail from years ago, nibbling at the edges of his memory. He cast his mind back to his army days. He thought that was where the answer was.

'What is it, Poe?' Mathers asked again.

Poe ignored her. 'Can I smell them, please?' he asked the CSI tech.

'Smell them?'

'Yes.'

The tech looked at Mathers for confirmation. Mathers shrugged then nodded. She held out the tweezers.

Poe leaned in and took a deep breath. His eyes snapped open. 'Cricket bats,' he said.

A huge piece of the puzzle had just dropped into place.

And someone he cared about was in imminent danger.

Chapter 89

'Linseed oil, boss!' Poe shouted into his phone. 'Tilly knows what I'm talking about!' He was running to his car, desperate to get back to Salt's house.

'Well I don't, Poe,' Flynn snapped. 'Either calm down and tell me, or shut up until you get here.'

'Hang on.'

Poe threw himself into the driver's seat and pulled on to the road without checking his mirrors or signalling. He Bluetoothed his mobile to his car's system. He was now hands-free.

He caught his breath and said, 'When Tilly and I went to see Estelle at HMP Low Newton, we spoke to one of the cops who'd been first on the scene. I asked him if there was anything he hadn't put in his report.'

'And he said linseed oil?'

'He actually said cricket bats, but yes, we narrowed it down to linseed oil. Tilly said some science stuff about why smell triggers such detailed memories.'

'Go on.'

'At Flat Bravo, one of the crime scene techs has just lifted two threads out of the carpet. One white, one red. They triggered a memory.'

'Of linseed oil?'

'No,' Poe said, 'of guns.'

'Guns?'

'I'm certain the threads are from a roll of cloth patches used to clean gun barrels.'

'That's weirdly specific.'

'Hear me out. Keeping your assault weapon clean in the army

was a critical task. You were taught to clean it before you were taught to fire it. Dirty weapons jam, clean weapons don't. Simple as that.'

'Makes sense. Lots of moving parts on modern weapons.'

'Exactly,' Poe said. 'And because of carbon fouling, the most important thing to clean was the barrel. If the barrel remains dirty, over time, the weapon becomes inaccurate. And to clean the barrel you use a pull-through.'

'A pull-through?'

'It's a length of cord with a narrow weight at one end and a small loop at the other. You thread a patch of cleaning cloth through the loop, drop the weight down the barrel then pull it through. Do that a few times and the barrel is spotless.'

'And you think these threads are from a cleaning patch?'

'I do. And the reason I do is that British squaddies can be stupid. Time and time again they'll use cloth patches that are too big, thinking it's a short cut. The bigger the patch, the sooner the barrel will be clean.'

'But it doesn't work that way?'

'It does. Sort of. The problem is, if you use a patch that's too big it gets stuck. And then squaddies panic. They either snap the pull-through or they try to hammer it out with a thin rod. Jammed pull-throughs cause barrel bulges or scratches, or any other number of problems.'

'I take it the army found a way around this?'

'They did. The rolls of cloth patch are white, but they're sectioned off every five centimetres by a single red thread. If you tear off one patch and it gets stuck, it's not your fault. You were using the right size. If you use more than one patch and it gets stuck, you're in deep shit.'

'I'm still not seeing the link, Poe,' Flynn said. 'I assume you didn't use linseed oil in your barrels?'

'No, we used gun oil. Came in little plastic bottles. But the thing is, the whole gun industry started using white cleaning rolls with red cutting lines. Up in Cumbria, all fishing and sporting goods stores sell them.'

'Poe, can you get to the—'

'Elcid Doyle owned the biggest grouse moor in the north of England, boss. His study was full of game bird paintings. I'll confirm it with Estelle's solicitor, but he had a shotgun. I guarantee it. Probably had a collection. And they'll have been valuable. Hundreds of thousands of pounds worth, probably.'

Flynn didn't respond.

'I think he was cleaning his shotguns when he was murdered,' Poe continued. '*That's* why his office smelled of linseed oil. It isn't the oil we used in the army, but it will be the oil used on the woodwork of antique shotguns.'

'So?'

'Elcid Doyle will have been cleaning shotgun barrels for decades – he wouldn't have cut his cleaning patches with scissors. He'd have torn them off. That's why there were loose threads on the carpet for someone to stand in.'

'Someone like Frederick Beck? You think the two cases are linked?'

'I absolutely do. For reasons unknown, Beck killed Elcid Doyle while he was cleaning his shotguns. Tried to frame Estelle to conceal the fact he's been operating up north as well. During the commission of the murder he gets some cleaning cloth threads stuck in the treads of his shoes and unwittingly drags them back to London.'

'Why though? It doesn't fit at all with his need for attention.'

'It doesn't, does it? Elcid Doyle's murder is part of his plan, but for some reason it's not something he wants the public to know about.'

'It's pretty thin, Poe.'

'It is.'

'It's just a couple of threads.'

'Agreed.'

'Elcid Doyle may not even have kept shotguns.'

'He did. Trust me on this.'

'Then where are they?'

'Don't know.'

'You're going up there, aren't you?'

'I am, boss,' Poe said. 'To catch the Botanist, we first have to solve Elcid Doyle's murder.'

Chapter 90

Poe thought about calling Detective Chief Inspector Tai-young Lee in Newcastle, but decided against it for now. He would need her help in the search for the missing shotguns, but now wasn't the time to speak to her. He hadn't yet confirmed that Elcid Doyle had owned shotguns and he was still hyped after discovering a potential link between the two cases. When he called Lee he wanted facts to dominate, not emotion.

He pulled up beside Salt's Porsche and leaped out. Flynn and Bradshaw were waiting by the front door.

'I'm surprised you bothered to stop, Poe,' Flynn said.

'I came to collect Tilly, boss,' he explained. 'Tai-young Lee is going to baulk at releasing Estelle. I'm going to need more than a theory about linseed oil and missing shotguns to get her onboard – I'll need to explain away every bit of evidence.'

'You think Tilly will be able to do this?'

'I know I can't.'

'I'm sorry, Poe, but things are critical here,' Flynn said. 'I need Tilly to monitor the website and do all the other stuff she does. I can't release her on a half-baked theory. Get me something solid. Is that OK, Tilly?'

Bradshaw didn't answer. Poe could see why. Over Flynn's shoulder he could see her throwing laptops and tablets and cables and adaptors into two canvas bags.

'Oh, for God's sake,' Flynn muttered.

A few moments later, Bradshaw appeared at Flynn's shoulder. She was weighed down with all the equipment she was carrying. Poe grabbed one of the bags from her.

'I've left everything up and running, DI Flynn, so you can keep an eye on the vote. Douglas Salt will win though, in line with my projections.'

'I want an update every hour, Tilly.'

'Yes, DI Flynn.'

'And Poe?'

'Boss?'

'Please remember Detective Chief Inspector Lee isn't your enemy. Please don't turn this into a turf war.'

'When do I ever?'

Chapter 91

Mathers answered on the first ring.

'Poe, what's happening?'

'Tilly and I have just passed Luton.'

'You're convinced your case is linked to mine?'

'Absolutely. I don't know why, I just know it is.'

'And the fact DI Flynn has let Tilly go with you must mean she's thinking that way as well?'

'That's exactly what happened.'

'No, she—' Bradshaw started to say.

'What's up, ma'am?' Poe cut in. There was no point in advertising that sometimes they were an unmanageable rabble.

'I have news,' Mathers said. 'I've just told DI Flynn that the Interpol blue notice has had a hit.'

'It has? Where?'

'Japan.'

'Japan?'

'Specifically, Iriomote Island.'

Poe glanced at Bradshaw.

'It's one of the Yaeyama Islands, Poe,' she said. 'It's actually nineteen hundred kilometres from the main islands of Japan, but only three hundred from Taiwan. Ninety per cent of the island is covered by jungle and mangrove swamp.'

'What was the hit?' Poe asked, wondering not for the first time how on earth Bradshaw knew these things.

'We got a call from the Japanese National Police Agency,' Mathers said. 'Local police were called to a long-abandoned ammunition dump that was built to defend against the American invasion. A Brit had been supervising a group of tourists on a jungle trek and he took them to one. It was a thing he did, apparently; let them think they'd stumbled upon something no one had seen for years.'

'It wasn't abandoned any more?'

'No. Instead of the empty underground bunker, they found a makeshift hospital ward. Ten beds, all covered with the remains of isolation tents. A DIY version of what Karen Royal-Cross was in.'

'What else?'

'Each bed had a dead body chained to it,' she said quietly. 'Looks like they were victims of medical experiments. Evidence suggests all ten were Han Chinese, rather than Japanese.'

'So no one on the island would miss them,' Poe said.

'Exactly.'

'Do we know what type of medical experiments?'

'You have to understand that the doors had been deliberately left open so the jungle animals could get in. There wasn't much left of the victims.'

'But?'

'A toxicological analysis of their hair – pretty much all that was left of the poor bastards – showed they had all been poisoned.'

Poe shuddered. 'With?'

'Four of them with hyoscine and four of them with tetrodotoxin.'

'The mandrake root poison and the fugu fish poison,' Poe said. 'Beck was testing his doses.'

'He was.'

'And the last two victims?'

'You don't need me to tell you, Poe,' Mathers said.

'Ricin?'

'Exactly.'

'He only needed two test subjects as there's no antidote for it.'

'Again, that's our conclusion.'

'It's him then.'

'It is. You were right. He didn't get brilliant straight away, he got brilliant by practising. By testing his doses, by monitoring the results.'

'And becoming desensitised to murder.'

'The sick bastard,' Mathers said.

'He'll have had easier access to the fugu poison as well,' Poe said. 'I never bought him obtaining it in London. Somebody would have remembered. But Tilly tells me there are still ten thousand restaurants selling it in Japan.'

'I've already scaled back the number of detectives working the private supper club angle.' Mathers paused. 'I'm thinking of releasing this at a press conference. What do you think?'

'He's containable right now, ma'am. Remove his celebrity status and he becomes an unpredictable loser with a weapon capable of killing dozens of people. I'd think very carefully about a press conference, if I were you.'

She didn't respond. Poe liked that about her. She wasn't fixated on her own ideas. She made the decisions, but only when she had all the available information.

'I'll pass that up to my commander,' she said eventually. 'But this investigation has been a one-way street of humiliation so far: the advance notice he gives, the Chance's Park debacle, the press deliberately getting the wrong end of the stick with that photograph of you and Tilly outside Low Newton. They may not want to sit on this.'

'It's your call,' Poe said.

'Is Douglas Salt still safe?'

'Yep. Everyone's staying put. The boss'll make sure nothing happens to him.'

'And you'll keep me updated?'

'I will.'

'Let me know if you need pressure put on anyone.'

'I'm hoping it won't come to that. And, in the meantime, there's a slow-roasted goat going spare if any of your guys are hungry.'

'Not any more,' Mathers said. 'DI Flynn called the council and had someone collect it for disposal.'

'That cost me over two hundred quid!'

'I think she told them it was a dead dog.'

The phone went dead.

Poe scowled; Bradshaw sniggered.

***

He had two more phone calls to make before he got up north. The first was easy. He needed to speak to Estelle Doyle's solicitor, Ania Kierczynska. Bradshaw dialled the number for him. It went to voicemail.

'Ania, it's Poe. Can you call me back when you receive this? I need you to make a judge in chambers bail application for Estelle.'

A JiC was an application for a Crown Court judge to consider bail. The defendant's solicitor had to complete a two-page form and submit it twenty-four hours before the matter was heard. A judge would then consider it in his chambers. For a JiC to be successful there needed to be a significant change in circumstances. Poe briefly outlined the linseed oil and the red and white cotton threads found in the Botanist's flat.

It sounded weak, even to him. He was hoping that by the time Ania met with the judge, they'd have something more persuasive. He ended the call and hoped she had enough faith in him to do as he had asked.

'Now for the tricky one,' he said.

He scrolled down his contacts, found who he wanted and pressed call.

'What the fuck do you want now, Poe?' Detective Chief Inspector Tai-young Lee snapped.

Chapter 92

The call with DCI Lee was unexpectedly smooth. Poe told her his theory and she was surprisingly amenable to letting him test it. Perhaps a bit *too* amenable.

'Talk me through it one last time,' she said. 'Just so I have the SOE straight for the assistant chief.'

Poe ran through the sequence of events. How Henning Stahl had recognised Frederick Beck on the list of people who had made a large acetone purchase. How that had led them to flats Alpha and Bravo. He explained that the two threads of cotton embedded in the weave of Bravo's carpet had smelled of linseed oil, and how one of her cops had told him he'd smelled cricket bats in Elcid Doyle's office.

'So it's DC Bowness's fault I'm on the phone at four a.m.?'

'Sorry, ma'am.'

'Tell me again what you think this all means,' she said.

'I'm waiting for confirmation, but I'm sure Elcid Doyle would have kept shotguns. And that he was cleaning them, or had just finished cleaning them, when he was murdered.'

'Hence the forensic transfer of the threads from Doyle's office in Northumberland to the flat in north London?'

'Exactly.'

'And you're wondering what happened to the shotguns?'

'I am,' Poe said. 'There was no mention of them in the evidence you recovered.'

'That's because we didn't recover any.'

'Which doesn't make sense. You saw his office – he had a passion for game birds, he owned the biggest grouse moor in the north of England and we know his office smelled of linseed oil. I'll get confirmation soon, but trust me, Elcid Doyle had guns.'

Lee didn't immediately respond. 'OK, I'm interested,' she said. 'You are? Why?'

'Because Elcid Doyle *did* have a shotgun certificate, and therefore the lack of guns is an anomaly. And if for no other reason than I don't want to be ambushed at court, we'll conduct another search of the property with a different firearms detection dog to last time.'

'A different one?' Poe said. He knew a Belgian Malinois had been through the house in case the killer had been hiding somewhere; he *didn't* know they had also searched Highwood with a firearms detection dog.

'A Labrador. It only barked in Elcid's study, which isn't surprising. *I* could smell a gun had been used to kill him.'

'The one you haven't been able to find?'

'That one, yes.'

The missing weapon was still a major hole in the prosecution's case. Elcid Doyle had been killed with a small-calibre gun and, as the CPS planned to say the footprints in the snow proved Estelle hadn't left the house, not having the gun was problematic. It wasn't insurmountable – there was firearms discharge residue on her hands and there were no other suspects – but Poe knew they would be concerned.

'The CPS plan to say she flung it out of a window and into the trout stream where it was washed away,' Lee said.

'The stream?' Poe said. 'The stream that's almost seventy yards from the house?'

'From the top floor, it would be possible.'

'If you're a track and field Olympian.'

'I'm letting you into the house again,' Lee said. 'Take the win, Poe.'

He sighed. She was right. It was the missing shotguns that were important, not the CPS's implausible explanation.

'Thank you, ma'am,' he said. 'Can I ask you something?'

'As long as it's not about our tactics at court. I've already told you too much.'

Poe didn't think she had. He thought she was as unhappy as he was that the CPS intended to say Estelle Doyle had somehow managed to throw a handgun seventy yards.

302

'Why are you being so helpful?' he said. 'I've been a bit of a dick and—'

'A bit?'

'OK, a lot. My point is, I've done nothing to warrant any cooperation whatsoever.'

'I'm a cop, Poe. You're a cop. Ultimately it's about finding out what really happened in that house. Everything else is bullshit.'

Something occurred to him. 'You said you had already confirmed that Elcid Doyle held a firearms licence.'

'Excuse me?'

'When I asked why you were interested in this, you said you'd already confirmed that Elcid Doyle held a shotgun certificate.'

'So?'

'Why did you check?' Poe thought about the question. Decided he already knew the answer. 'DI Flynn's already called you, hasn't she?'

'Yes, she has,' Lee said. 'She was worried you might have had trouble explaining your position.'

Chapter 93

Detective Chief Inspector Tai-young Lee met them at Highwood at 7 a.m. She took one look at Poe and said, 'When was the last time you slept? You have eyes like a racing dog's bollocks.'

Poe laughed. 'You've been in Newcastle too long,' he said.

'PD Bailey will be here soon.'

'PD Bailey?' Bradshaw asked, stifling a yawn. 'What's that?'

'Police Dog Bailey,' Lee replied. 'He's the firearms detection dog we're using this time.'

'Aww, I bet he's so cute!'

'He's a working dog, Tilly,' Poe said. 'So don't feed him any treats.'

'I won't, Poe.'

'And if either of you have had a toot of something to stay awake, I advise you to say so now,' Lee said. 'Bailey's also a drugs detection dog.'

'I don't even know what "toot" means, Detective Chief Inspector Tai-young Lee,' Bradshaw said, 'but neither of us takes drugs, if that's what you mean. Poe won't even take medicine when he's supposed to. He's been prescribed codeine for an abscess in his tooth and I found the unfilled prescription a fortnight ago in a book he was reading. He'd written a list of his favourite sausages on the back.'

'Thanks, Tilly,' Poe said.

'OK then,' Lee said. 'Shall we go in? We can have a look around before PD Bailey gets here.'

PD Bailey was a cocker spaniel. His coat was blue roan and, like all spaniels, he had energy to burn. He was wagging his tail so hard that half his body was moving.

'Can I pet him?' Bradshaw asked his handler.

'As long as you don't mind getting licked to death.'

'She doesn't,' Poe confirmed.

After two minutes Bradshaw stood up and said, 'I have two favourite dogs now, Poe. Do you think we could train Edgar to sniff out guns?'

'Guns? Definitely not. *Buns?* Almost certainly.'

The only room to get a positive response for firearms from PD Bailey was Elcid Doyle's study again. The spaniel didn't show a shred of interest in any other room in the house.

'Are you satisfied there are no shotguns on the premises, Sergeant Poe?' Tai-young Lee asked after PD Bailey and his handler had left for another job.

'Dogs' noses can't be fooled,' he admitted.

He was disappointed. He wasn't sure what he'd wanted to find, only that he'd wanted to find something. If Elcid Doyle *had* been cleaning his shotguns when he was murdered, they had to have been in the house. The CPS might convince a particularly moronic jury that someone could throw a small handgun seventy yards, but shotguns were long and awkward and heavy. Poe reckoned he had decent upper body strength but he knew he couldn't throw one more than thirty yards. Yet PD Bailey's nose was one hundred million times more sensitive than a human's – he wouldn't have missed anything. The shotguns weren't in the house. The link between Elcid Doyle's murder and the Botanist case was looking tenuous.

His phone rang. It was Ania Kierczynska.

'Excuse me, ma'am, I'd better take this,' he said, stepping away. 'Ania, thanks for getting back to me. I was going to ask you to apply for a judge in chambers, but my lead hasn't panned out as I hoped it would.'

'I wish you'd told me this ten minutes ago,' she replied. 'I've just emailed it in.'

'Can you cancel it?'

'I'll see if we can get hold of a clerk before the judge starts working his way through his in-tray.'

'Sorry about that. And can you tell Estelle I haven't given up?'

'I will do. And remember she still wants to see you.'

'That might not be politic right now. The chief superintendent in London is still under a microscope.'

'OK, I'll let her know. You wanted information on Elcid's guns?' she asked.

'Just confirmation he had some,' Poe replied. 'DCI Lee has already checked the firearms certificate database though. He did keep shotguns.'

'Yes, we helped him insure them. A pair of gold inlaid J. Purdey & Sons over and unders, whatever that means.'

'The barrels are mounted on top of each other, rather than side-by-side.'

'Well, that means nothing to me, but his insurance policy states the pair is worth one hundred thousand pounds.'

'You'd better tell them they're missing then.'

'Are you sure? They shouldn't be.'

'A firearms detection dog has been through the whole house. We're sure.'

'And they're definitely not in the gun safe?'

Poe frowned.

'What gun safe?' he said.

Chapter 94

Poe could scarcely believe what he had just seen. Under Ania's instruction, he had tugged at one of the bookcases in Elcid's office, not entirely convinced he wasn't being pranked. But, to his astonishment, after slight resistance, no more than it would take to open a fridge door, the bookcase had swung away from the wall. It was flush-mounted on heavy hinges and had rollers concealed under the bottom shelf. He let go of it and it slowly closed. It was weighted to gently swing back to the wall. Poe opened it again and looked behind it. A small magnet was fixed to the back of the book-case. That explained the slight pressure he'd had to apply to open it. He studied the floor. Now he knew what he was looking for, he recognised the faint marks on the flagstones as groove tracks left by the rollers. Elcid must have been opening and closing the bookcase door for years.

Poe let it close again. He stepped back and studied it. There was no way to tell the bookcase was actually a concealed door. The craftsmanship was exceptional.

'Are you kidding me?' he said. 'A secret door. What is this, an episode of *Scooby-Doo*? Should we be looking for an evil janitor?'

'This isn't as uncommon as you might think, Poe,' Bradshaw said. 'They're called Murphy doors and there are several firms in the UK who specialise in them, three within fifty miles of where we are now.'

But Poe had stopped listening. Because as surprising as the hidden door was, he was far more interested in what was behind it.

It was a gun safe.

Except it wasn't a gun safe, it was a strong room. The narrow door was thick with a reinforced frame. It was made of steel, painted dark green and looked impregnable. There was a handle and a mechanical keypad. Poe put on a forensic glove and tried to open it. It was locked. They needed either the code or a locksmith.

'No luck with the safe company, I'm afraid,' Tai-young Lee said, stepping back into the room.

'Why not?' Poe asked.

'This model of door is obsolete. They've offered to bring an engineer out of retirement if we're willing to pay his airfare and put him up in a hotel, but it'll take at least a week for him to get here.'

'That long? I know they're a German firm, but they're in Hannover and Tilly says there are regular flights to London. He could be here in ten hours.'

'He's in a cabin in the Black Forest, apparently. Due back next week and he isn't contactable.'

'And we can't just call a local locksmith? Get someone to bash it in with a hammer?'

'It's two inches thick, Poe,' she replied. 'It's bulletproof and explosive-resistant. The woman I spoke to said not even diamond crown drill bits can penetrate it.'

'A sledgehammer then.'

Chapter 95

Elcid Doyle's late wife hadn't liked being around guns. She had insisted her husband keep them in his study. For a while, he had got away with a standard gun safe, little more than a sturdy filing cabinet. But, after acquiring the pair of J. Purdey & Sons shotguns, his insurance company insisted on something with a higher security rating.

Rather than purchase an ugly safe, the owner of a German company, also an old grouse-shooting friend, had suggested a bespoke, concealed strong room instead.

The Germans had removed a bookcase and knocked through the wall into the back of the airing cupboard in the office's en-suite. They made the airing cupboard smaller and reinforced the strong-room side with interlocking steel panels. They fitted a door that wouldn't have looked out of place in a bank. The Germans then repurposed the original bookcase as a concealed Murphy door. When it was finished, the strong room, which was about the size of a telephone box, was rated for up to two million pounds.

'I can't believe we missed this,' Lee said.

'You didn't know to look for it,' Poe replied. 'Ania said it was never a secret, but the craftsmanship is so good it's unlikely you'd stumble upon it by accident.'

'And the dogs must have been barking at the safe, not the smell of the gun discharge that killed Elcid.'

'Probably both,' Poe said, nodding.

He wasn't out of the game yet . . .

'Ania,' Poe said, 'we don't know the combination to the strong-room door.'

'Elcid didn't write it down?'

'If he did, we can't find it.'

'I'm due to see Estelle this afternoon. I'll ask her if she knows it.'

Poe frowned. This afternoon meant losing time they didn't have. 'Didn't you say you were managing the Doyle account because the senior partner was in his eighties, or something?' he said.

'I did,' Ania replied. 'Mr Howey.'

'Would he have been involved in the installation of the strong-room door?'

'He'd have liaised with the insurance company, certainly. Made sure it met their expectations. Probably negotiated a reduction on Elcid's premium.'

'Can you ask him if he knows the code?'

'I'll see if he's in.'

'Thanks, Ania.'

'But, before I do, I have some bad news.'

'Oh, well, we were due some,' Poe said.

'Yes, very funny. I couldn't get to the clerk and the judge has read our bail application. He'll see us at nine o'clock tomorrow morning.'

After Ania had hung up, Poe told Bradshaw and Lee about the judge in chambers application.

Bradshaw looked at her watch. 'We have less than twenty-fours then,' she said.

'Tick tock,' Lee said.

Chapter 96

Ania called back ten minutes later. The news wasn't great, but it wasn't terrible either.

'Mr Howey doesn't know the code to the strong room, Poe,' she said. 'But, he did say Elcid was scared of his memory fading. His father had suffered from early-onset Alzheimer's, apparently. Mr Howey said if the code isn't written down, there'll be something in the room to jog his memory.'

'Like what?'

'That's all I have, I'm afraid.'

'What we have here, is a puzzle,' Poe said.

Bradshaw and Lee looked at him quizzically.

'Not only that, it's a *number* puzzle,' he continued. 'We have a zero-to-nine keypad. With the star and the hashtag that's twelve buttons Elcid could have used.'

Poe looked at Bradshaw expectantly.

'What?' she said.

'Well, go on then – solve it.'

'Solve what?'

'The safe-room code.'

Bradshaw's jaw dropped. 'Are you simpleminded, Poe! This isn't something I can solve!'

'Why not?'

'Because, even if he's only using a four-digit code, there are still ten thousand possible combinations. And if he's used a six-digit code there are well over a million.'

'Can't be that many, surely?' Poe said.

Bradshaw sighed. 'Poe, did you know that if you shuffle a deck of cards correctly, mathematically speaking, the likelihood of that precise order ever having been seen before is almost zero?'

'But didn't you lecture me the other week about the PIN on my phone being one-two-three-four?'

'I did.'

'And you said lots of people use that PIN.'

'I actually said lots of *idiots* use that PIN. Just over ten per cent.'

'There you are then.'

'There you are, what?'

'Ania said Elcid would have used something easy to remember—'

'I thought she said there would be something in the room to jog his memory.'

'Yeah, but there isn't.'

Bradshaw paused.

'OK then, I'll give it a go,' she said.

Chapter 97

'Do you think Tilly can crack this?' Tai-young Lee asked.

'If she can't, it can't be cracked,' Poe replied.

Poe had dragged a chair from another room and was sitting behind Elcid Doyle's desk. CSI still had the chair he had died in. Lee was in the wingback armchair by the fire. Bradshaw had put a stool in front of the strong room's keypad and was methodically working her way through a list of possible combinations.

'And if we finally get it open, so what?' Lee said. 'The shotguns are either there or they aren't. I fail to see how this helps you.'

She had a point. How *did* the locked strong room help them?

'It's the only thing we have left,' he said eventually. 'Leaving it closed means Estelle gets a life sentence.'

'Why are you so sure she didn't do it?'

'Why are you so sure she did?'

'Because the evidence supports it.'

'Not all of it. Some of it is contradictory.'

'No case is perfect, you know that. There are always unanswered questions.'

'Like, how someone can throw a handgun seventy yards?'

'Like that, yes.'

She took a swig from a bottle of water. She offered it to Poe. He shook his head.

'So,' she said, 'what's *really* going on here?'

'Cards-on-the-table time, is it?'

She glanced over at a muttering Bradshaw. 'It seems we have time,' she said. 'Be honest – are you trying to exonerate Professor Doyle or are you just throwing shit at the case to sow reasonable doubt?'

'What do you think?'

'I've been told you're the last honest cop. That you follow the evidence where it takes you, regardless of the personal cost.'

'What's your point?'

'We both know the Botanist wasn't in this room. What possible reason could he have had? All you've done up here is annoy me and embarrass Chief Superintendent Mathers.'

'Yeah, thanks for that,' Poe said.

'What?'

'It *was* you who leaked that photo of me and Tilly visiting Estelle at HMP Low Newton, wasn't it? I don't actually blame you – if someone was interfering with my case I'd do what was needed to get them to stop.'

'You still think that?' she said. 'I told you, we had nothing to do with it.'

Poe said nothing.

'Seriously, Poe, we didn't. And believe me I checked. All of DC Bowness's phones were forensically examined and came back clean. He didn't take a photograph. And even if he had, we wouldn't have impeded a major investigation in London just to get you to back off.'

'Who the hell did then? You say it wasn't you – OK, I believe you. But it not being you doesn't make sense.'

'No, it doesn't,' she said. 'Unless . . .'

'Unless what?'

'OK, bear with me. And I can't believe I'm floating this. The Botanist will have known whoever was heading the investigation in London would have called in SCAS at some point. Hunting serial killers is the unit's remit and you've gained quite the rep over the last few years. Taken down some big names.'

Poe leaned forwards. 'We have,' he agreed.

'And anyone who can read the headlines will know it's you and Tilly and DI Flynn who are the driving force behind it all.'

'There are a lot of unsung heroes in the unit. Tilly in particular works with a team of—'

'Exactly!' Lee cut in. 'Because anyone who knows how to read

314

behind the headlines will know who you prefer to work with. Tilly's Mole People, as you call them, Superintendent Nightingale—'

'And Estelle Doyle,' Poe finished for her.

'What if someone wanted to mess with the dream team. To borrow a saying from my baseball-crazy father: what if someone wanted to bench one of your star players?'

Poe nodded. It made sense. Sort of. There were other forensic pathologists. The one Mathers was using seemed very good, although he was no Estelle Doyle. But, if the Botanist had really wanted to disrupt SCAS, benching Bradshaw would have been far more effective.

'So you believe me now?' Poe asked.

'I don't . . . not believe you. I have the same problems with the case that you do.'

Bradshaw stood up, knocking over her stool. The crash of wood on stone made enough noise to stop all conversation.

'Sorry,' she said.

'How's it going?' Poe asked.

'I've tried two hundred of the most commonly used four-digit and six-digit combinations and Elcid Doyle wasn't using any of them.'

Poe stood too. 'OK, let's have one last look around the office. See if we can see what Elcid Doyle used as a reminder. Otherwise, we'll have to wait until Ania sees Estelle this afternoon.'

Bradshaw checked her watch. 'We don't have long, Poe.'

'Let's get started then. He was an old man worried about Alzheimer's. It'll be something obvious.'

Chapter 98

'Well it's nothing obvious,' Poe said. 'I knew it wouldn't be.'

Bradshaw rolled her eyes. She was on her hands and knees examining the books on the lower shelf of the Murphy door. Tai-young Lee was standing on the library ladder, pulling out and replacing books on the top shelf. Poe had given up on the idea that the code had been slipped between the pages of a book. He was back behind Elcid Doyle's desk.

'Are you comfortable there, Poe?' Lee said. 'I can't get you a cup of tea or something?'

'Elcid Doyle will have split his day between his desk and the armchair by the fire,' he said. 'If there's something in the study to remind him of the code, he'd have been able to see it from here' – he pointed to the fireplace – 'or from over there.'

'But we've looked, there's nothing.'

'We're overthinking it then. Tilly, you know about PINs – other than the most predictable ones, which you've already checked, what else do people tend to use?'

'Birthdays,' she said straight away. 'But I've tried Elcid's and I've tried Estelle's and I've tried his late wife's.'

'What else do people use?'

'Birth years. And I've tried them.'

'What's next?'

'Anniversaries.'

'When did he get married?'

'June ninth 1977.'

'Did you try that?'

'I did, Poe.'

'What about the day his wife died?'

'Her *death* day? That's sick, Poe.'

'Try it anyway.'

'I already have.'

'You're a monster,' Poe said.

'We're on to something here,' Lee said, climbing down the library ladder. 'Keep going, Tilly. What other numbers do people use?'

'Two-five-eight-zero.'

'Why?'

'Because, from top to bottom, they appear in a single column on a phone or a keypad. And I've tried it.'

'Anything else?'

'The next group of numbers people tend to use are dates that mean something to them personally, but that aren't included in the ones we've already been through.'

Poe considered that. 'The date I bought Herdwick Croft, for example,' he said.

'The day I passed my driving test,' Lee added. 'The day my parents landed in the UK.'

'Things like that, yes,' Bradshaw agreed. 'But without knowing what Elcid Doyle knew, we can't know what was personally significant to him.'

Poe leaned back in the chair and exhaled loudly. The answer would be in front of them and it would be obvious – he was sure of it. He cast his eyes around the office, tried to see it through Elcid's eyes. He had spent his days with his back to the window, but he wouldn't have been looking at his books. They were displayed spine out, and from behind the desk Poe couldn't make out any of the titles. And it wasn't the paintings – Poe had examined them and none of them had numbers on. They were just paintings of British game birds. Ring-necked pheasants, partridges and snipes. Woodcocks. Ducks. Lots of grouse.

Actually, now he was seeing the collection as a whole, rather than individually, he could see that more than half the paintings were of grouse. He clearly loved the bird.

Poe looked at the paintings thoughtfully. Had Ania been right all along? Had Elcid left something obvious to jog his memory? Something hidden in plain sight . . .

'Try one-two-zero-eight, Tilly,' he said carefully.

Bradshaw frowned, but didn't ask why. She tapped in the numbers. There was a small click.

Bradshaw and Lee looked at him in amazement.

'But how did you . . .?' Lee asked.

'It's the Glorious Twelfth,' Poe said. 'The twelfth of August. Start of the grouse shooting season in the UK. Biggest day in the shooting calendar. Elcid Doyle *did* have something to jog his memory in his office – it was his paintings and it was his love of grouse.'

Lee pulled on a pair of forensic gloves.

She lifted the handle, opened the strong-room door and stepped back. They all peered inside.

'Bloody hell,' Poe said eventually.

Chapter 99

'He hid in the bloody strong room, boss!' Poe shouted into his phone.

'You *have* to be joking,' Flynn replied. 'Are we in an episode of *Scooby-Doo*?'

'Ha! That's exactly what I said! We think he must have sent Estelle the text from Elcid's phone, inviting her to dinner. Probably planned to kill him just before she was due to arrive so there would be no time discrepancy between Estelle leaving work and how long he'd been dead. Unfortunately, by the time he'd killed him it had started to snow, so he couldn't leave the house without leaving footprints. He had no option but to hide before Estelle arrived. He locked himself in the strong room and the Murphy door closed behind him. It's weighted to stay in the closed position, a bit like a fire door closes after you've walked through it.'

'And the smell of Elcid's corpse fooled the search dog?'

'That's what we think happened.'

Poe was standing outside, shielding his phone from the fresh easterly wind. CSI were inside, processing the strong room, and Bradshaw was typing everything into a statement that Poe could sign for the judge in chambers bail hearing the following morning. Poe reckoned they now had enough to get Doyle out.

'How big's the bloody thing?' Flynn asked.

'About the size of a telephone box. Not as tall. Big enough to stand in or sit on the floor with your knees hugged to your chest, too small to stretch out.'

'The shotguns?'

'The contents of the strong room match what's on Elcid's shotgun certificate. Nothing's missing. Apart from the gun rack, the rest of the strong room was full of shotgun cartridges, gun belts and Elcid's cleaning kit. Rolls of cleaning cloth. Lots of loose threads on the floor. Must be where he got a couple snagged in his shoes.'

'Was the murder weapon in there?' Flynn asked.

'Nope. Still missing.'

'How long do we think he hid in there?'

'At least two days,' Poe said. 'CSI were in the office for twenty-four hours after Elcid's body was removed. After that, there was just one uniformed cop on the front door. Beck must have waited until he couldn't hear anything, then snuck out of the en-suite window. It's at the back of the house and explains why it was unlocked when we were there the first time.'

The inside of the strong room had smelled. The sour stench of stale sweat. Concentrated urine. Faeces. Poe had wondered why Beck had made no attempt to clean it, but quickly realised he couldn't have risked the exposure. Once he'd opened the door, he'd had to get out of the house. And he wasn't able to douse it with bleach or set it on fire as that would have telegraphed the framing of Doyle. Poe reckoned he had taken a calculated risk that the strong room would remain locked until long after this had ended.

'If it was locked, how the hell did he get out?'

'It has an internal handle. Most safe rooms have them, apparently. Safety feature in case someone gets locked in by accident. Bit like the doors on walk-in freezers in meat-packing factories.'

'Do you think there's enough evidence in there?'

'CSI have already sent samples for DNA matching.'

'And you're certain it's Frederick Beck?'

Poe told Flynn about the conversation he and Tai-young Lee had had about the leaked prison photo.

'I don't think she believes in her own case any more, boss,' he said. 'Beck must have been watching Low Newton to see who visited Estelle. When he saw me and Tilly, he decided he didn't like that. We think it was him who leaked the photo. He didn't want me clearing her.'

'Estelle's good, Poe, but she's not the only pathologist we work with.'

'I know the theory doesn't make complete sense, but it's more convincing than anything else we have so far.'

'We'll know soon enough, I suppose. What are your next steps?'

'Tilly's typing up a statement for tomorrow's bail hearing. As soon as it's ready, I'll drive it over to Estelle's solicitor. Get her to run her eyes over it. Take it from there.'

'OK.'

'How's Douglas Salt?' Poe asked.

'Still a pain in the arse. Threatens to kick us out every ten minutes. He never will though – he's way ahead in the vote. I think it's finally hit home that he's in real danger.'

'If a guy's so committed he'll hide in a strong room while a bunch of hairy-arsed cops are just the thickness of a bookcase away, then yeah, I think he has a problem.'

'I won't tell him that.'

'No. Best not,' Poe said. 'And what about Fiona Musgrave, the woman who broke the story about Beck? Is she safe?'

'She's been taken into protective custody, although we don't think she's at risk.'

'Why not?'

'She's not an arsehole.'

'Fair enough.'

'Call me later?'

'Will do,' Poe said. 'But before you go, do you want to tell me what happened to my slow-roasted goat? Mathers told me you had it removed. Said it was a dead dog.'

'It was attracting rats, Poe.'

Tai-young Lee had stepped outside. She beckoned him over. She looked worried.

'I've got to go, boss,' he said. Poe ended the call. 'What's up, ma'am?'

'We have a problem,' Lee replied.

Chapter 100

'The CPS say nothing has changed,' Tai-young Lee said. 'Not enough for them to support your judge in chambers application.'

'We have overwhelming evidence that the killer hid in the strong room,' Poe said, exasperated. 'What more could they possibly want?'

'Your judge in chambers application says it was Frederick Beck who killed Elcid, not Professor Doyle.'

'It does.'

'The CPS won't support bail until they have irrefutable evidence that the person hiding in the strong room was Frederick Beck. And the DNA results won't be back for thirty-six hours. Their new position is, Professor Doyle took advantage of a burglary, not realising the burglar was still on the premises. She killed her father assuming the thief would take the blame.'

'That's insane.'

'It is,' Lee agreed, 'but that's not the issue.'

'It isn't?'

'The real issue is the positive firearms discharge residue test. The CPS can't support bail until that's explained. Otherwise they risk contradicting themselves in front of the judge. They secured Miss Doyle's remand on a series of facts. To support bail now is to admit they knew the FDR test was irrelevant.'

'So it's about saving face?'

'No, it's about anticipating what the judge will say tomorrow.'

'And they won't accept it's a false positive? That she probably got it when she touched the brake pads when she changed her flat tyre?'

'But we know she didn't get it from her brake pads, Poe,' she replied. 'We had them analysed and the chemical composition doesn't match.'

'Those tests are open to interpretation.'

'Which is an argument for a jury, it's not new evidence for a JiC.' Poe sighed.

'I don't believe Professor Doyle killed her father any more than you do now,' Lee said, 'but she didn't get FDR on her hands from her car's brake pads.'

'What are you saying? That she didn't murder her father, but she *did* fire the gun that killed him? That makes no sense at all.'

'No, it doesn't,' she said, 'but if you want Professor Doyle released tomorrow, you have eighteen hours to find an alternative explanation.'

Poe looked her in the eye. 'Then that's what we'll do,' he said.

Chapter 101

'Cross-contamination is a legitimate defence strategy, Poe,' Tai-young Lee said. 'But again, it isn't new evidence. It's not something you can bring up at a Judge in Chambers bail application.'

Poe pouted. She was right, of course, but it was all he had come up with so far. CSI were still processing the strong room so they had decamped into Elcid Doyle's sitting room to brainstorm how Doyle had ended up with firearm discharge residue on her hands. He and Lee were now talking in circles. Each time he speculated on how it had happened, Lee either disproved it or said it wasn't new information and was an argument for the trial, not a judge in chambers.

The latest theory to be shot down was that the FDR had been transferred from the handcuffs used to secure Doyle after her arrest. Poe had argued that, if they had been recently used on someone who had handled a gun, there could have been cross-contamination. That it wasn't FDR on her hands from the gun that had killed her father, but from another gun entirely. Lee had said her hands had been bagged before the cuffs were put on. He'd said so what, mistakes happen. Which was when she had reminded him that this was an argument for a jury, not a judge in chambers application.

And so on.

'You're being uncharacteristically quiet, Tilly,' Poe said.

'I'm reading an FBI article on gunshot residue, as they call it in the United States of America, Poe,' Bradshaw replied. 'Did you know the following have all given false positives: fireworks, welding, key cutting, even some types of paper?'

'I know, it's unreliable.'

'And that's before you get on to cross-contamination from the back of police cars, holding cells, interview rooms, even police officers themselves.'

'None of which is new information, all of which we'll raise at her trial.'

'I'm sorry, Poe. I don't have anything that can help you.'

Poe frowned. 'You know what?' he said. 'This is bullshit. If she had FDR on her hands—'

'Which she did,' Lee said.

'—Then it was because of something that happened. And that means we should be able to work it out. The fact we haven't worked out how yet means we need a different approach.'

'What are you suggesting?'

'You ever see *Crimewatch*, ma'am?'

'Of course.'

Crimewatch ran on the BBC from 1984 to 2017. It was one of the BBC's largest live factual programmes and was a collaboration between the public and the police. Three or four cases would be profiled each episode. The sixty-minute programme featured interviews with detectives, the victims' families and witnesses. Key evidence like E-pics would be shown. The *Crimewatch* telephone number remained open until midnight the following night. In the years it ran, fifty-seven murderers, fifty-three rapists and eighteen paedophiles were apprehended as a direct result.

'And what was the most powerful tool at their disposal?'

Lee nodded in understanding. 'You want to do a reconstruction,' she said.

Poe turned to Bradshaw. 'You up for being a corpse, Tilly?'

Chapter 102

'One more time, please,' Poe said.

Tai-young Lee groaned but left the room again.

'You OK, Tilly?'

'I'm fine, Poe.'

They were in the drawing room. It was similar in size to Elcid Doyle's study. Like the study, it had south-facing windows and bookcases lining the walls. It didn't have a private bathroom or a secret strong room, but it was a close enough fit for what they needed. They had spent ten minutes arranging the furniture so it was as close as possible to the office layout. Anything surplus was humped outside. They used a dining table as the study desk and moved a coffee table and armchair to where the fireplace would have been. A sideboard was too heavy to move so Poe told Bradshaw and Lee to pretend it wasn't there.

It wasn't perfect, but it wasn't bad.

Three times Lee had entered the dining room and carried out the actions detailed in Doyle's statement, and three times Poe had seen nothing that explained why she'd had firearms discharge residue on her hands.

He moved to a different corner of the room for the fourth attempt. Hoped the fresh angle might offer new insight. Bradshaw checked her tablet and slumped in the makeshift office chair in the same position Elcid Doyle was found. She even shut her eyes and let her tongue loll out.

'We're ready for you, ma'am,' Poe called out. 'Don't forget to hang your coat up before you enter the room this time.'

'Piss off, Poe,' he heard her mutter.

'What was that?'

'I said, I'm hanging up my coat now.'

After a few moments Lee opened the drawing-room door. She called out, 'Dad?' then approached Bradshaw.

'Faster,' Poe said. 'She thought he was asleep when she said "Dad?" but now she thinks he's had a stroke.'

Lee jogged across to Bradshaw then knelt down. She paused – Poe had put that in there as he imagined Estelle would have needed a few seconds to make sense of what she was seeing – before reaching out with her left hand to check for a pulse. Lee then stood, reached into her back pocket for her phone and pretended to dial 999.

'From this point she said she didn't touch anything,' Poe said. 'Said she waited beside her father until the police arrived. Have I got that right, Tilly?'

'You have, Poe.'

'Did you video this reconstruction?'

'I've recorded them all.'

'Let's have a look then.'

They crowded round the table and watched the most recent video. Despite the new angle, Poe couldn't see anything that might explain the FDR on Doyle's hands.

'Let's go through the arrest photographs again,' he said.

Bradshaw brought them up on her tablet. She let Poe swipe through them. By now he had been through them hundreds of times: Doyle in black jeans and an even blacker blouse; Doyle in a paper evidence suit; a close-up photograph of her face; another of her hands, bagged and un-bagged.

'Hang on, her jeans are skin-tight,' Lee said.

'Other than when she's in a post-mortem, she dresses like she's in Siouxsie and the Banshees,' Poe said. 'If it's not jeans, it's pencil skirts and fishnets. I'm sure she does it just to make me squirm.'

'I'm not commenting on her sense of style, Poe. Jeans as tight as the ones she was wearing are uncomfortable at the best of times. Try putting something bulky in the back pocket. It'd be like having a tumour on your arse.'

'That's why I prefer cargo trousers, Detective Chief Inspector

Tai-young Lee,' Bradshaw said. 'They have baggy pockets so I can comfortably carry cables and chargers and my phone. Poe says I look scruffy, but he's one to talk. One time he came to work and he was using string as a belt.'

'It was baler twine. And my belt had blood on it.'

Lee shook her head. 'You two,' she said. 'And my point is this: what if her phone wasn't in her back pocket?'

'And it wasn't in her jacket, as she hung that up as soon as she got in the house. Did she have a handbag with her?'

'No, but she did have a laptop bag. We tested it in case the gun had been inside it.'

'Can you bring that up on your tablet, Tilly?' Poe asked.

Bradshaw did.

It was black and thin with a faux-leather handle. It had zipped pockets and a neoprene shockproof interior.

'Let's see what she had in it,' Poe said.

The photograph had been taken on a white forensic table. The contents were unremarkable. A bunch of keys, memory sticks, charging cable, the bag's unused shoulder strap. A small makeup bag. The laptop itself; a rose-coloured MacBook Air.

'OK,' Poe said. 'She would have used that big pocket for the stuff she didn't need access to all the time, like the cables and the shoulder strap, and the smaller one for her phone, her keys, probably the makeup bag.'

'So she reached into her *bag* for her phone, not her back pocket,' Lee said.

Poe nodded.

'Let's do this again,' he said. 'But this time we'll give you something to carry. You got anything we can use, Tilly?'

'I have a laptop case, Poe. It's not exactly the same size, but it's a similar design.'

'Excellent. And we need to fill the phone pocket with the same things she had in hers.'

Bradshaw donated her keys. Poe donated his phone; Lee didn't want her screen scratched and Poe's looked like he stored his in gravel. They used Bradshaw's pencil case as a makeup bag.

'From the top,' Poe said.

'You've been dying to say that, haven't you?' Lee said.

'Just call me John Sturges.'

'Who?' Bradshaw and Lee said together.

'*Bad Day at Black Rock? The Great Escape? Ice Station Zebra?*'

They looked at each other in confusion. Lee shrugged. 'I've heard of *The Great Escape*,' she said.

'I am very disappointed in both of you,' Poe said.

Chapter 103

Tai-young Lee left the room, turned around and walked straight back in. She repeated the things she'd done the first four times, but this time, instead of reaching into her back pocket for Poe's phone, she rooted through the laptop bag pocket until she found it.

She pulled it out then said, 'Damn it!'

'What?' Poe said.

She held up one of her fingers. 'This polish has lasted me all week and the one night I have a date, I chip a bloody nail on Tilly's keys.'

Poe waited. He didn't understand why a cop would want painted nails, but he was wise enough not to say anything.

'Sorry,' Lee said. 'Where were we?'

'You were about to call the police.'

She mimed tapping a few buttons then pressed it to her ear. Put it down and shrugged. 'I can't see how that made a difference,' she said.

'It didn't,' Poe said. 'But at least we tried.'

They moved into the kitchen and Poe made a pot of tea.

'Sorry, Tilly,' he said. 'It seems Elcid wasn't a modern man. There are no fruit teas here.'

Bradshaw held up her bottle of water. 'I'm good, Poe.'

'Milk and sugar, ma'am?'

Lee didn't answer. She was still scowling at her chipped fingernail.

'Ma'am?' Poe said again.

'Do you have any idea what it's like trying to juggle being a cop *and* a good Korean daughter, Poe?'

'Hard?'

'Impossible. My dad wants me to get a real job, like a doctor or an accountant, and my mum wants me to get married and look pretty all day. And tonight was the night I'd finally agreed to meet her friend's son. She even chose this shade of polish herself. Said it was colourful but didn't make me look like a common *maechunbu*.'

'I'm not familiar . . .'

'A streetwalker, Poe. A prostitute. Mum has very strong views on which colours are acceptable.' She held out her hands. Her nails were a subtle shade of pink. The chipped nail stood out like the last leaf on the tree. 'And now I'll have to redo them,' Lee continued. 'If I don't, Mum will get upset. It means I need an hour more than I'd thought tonight. Thanks a bunch, Poe.'

Poe caught his breath. Bradshaw noticed.

'What is it?' she said, standing up.

'Show me that photograph of Estelle's hands again, Tilly,' he urged. 'The one that's been bothering me.'

Bradshaw unlocked her tablet and swiped through the defence disclosures until she found the one she was looking for. She passed the tablet to Poe.

Estelle's fingers were pale and long, like a classical pianist's. Her nails were blood-clot red. He did the pinch-out thing and checked each one individually.

He breathed out in relief.

He spun the tablet round so Lee and Bradshaw could see the screen.

'What are we looking at, Poe?' Lee asked.

'Estelle's nails. The polish is perfect.'

'So?'

'You chipped a nail getting your phone out of a laptop bag. Do these really look like the nails of someone who's just changed a flat tyre?'

Chapter 104

'Are you now saying she *didn't* have a flat tyre?' Tai-young Lee asked.

'Not at all,' Poe replied. 'I'm saying those aren't the hands of someone who changed it herself.'

'They could be gel nails.'

Poe looked at Bradshaw, who shrugged. 'What are they?' he asked.

'A gel-based polish cured under UV light,' Lee explained. 'Harder wearing than regular polish. I suppose it would be possible to change a tyre without damaging them.'

Poe considered this. Decided she was probably right but that she'd missed the wider point.

'For argument's sake let's say that's true,' he said. 'But on discovering she had a flat in the hospital's basement car park, she replaced it herself then drove straight here. She didn't stop anywhere and she didn't ask for help.'

'That's what her statement said,' Lee agreed.

'I'm quite prepared to accept there's a super polish out there, and it's entirely possible Estelle uses it, but I am *not* prepared to accept that she could have changed a flat tyre without getting so much as a smidgen of oil or dirt on her hands.'

'Agreed. So we go back to my earlier question: are you now saying she didn't have a flat tyre?'

'I don't know,' Poe said. 'But there's an easy way to find out.'

Doyle's car was still in the police garage that CSI had used when they'd searched it for the murder weapon. It was due to go to the secure police pound the following day. Lee arranged for them to see it.

Poe had no idea what Doyle drove, although he doubted it would be anything vanilla.

He was right.

They were taken to a vintage MGB Roadster. The CSI tech told them it was a 1974 model, a rare edition, with blue-purple paint-work called aconite. Wire wheels, polished chrome and a black leather interior. It was sleek and small and sexy. It would growl when it was angry and purr when it wasn't. If Doyle were a car, she would be a 1974 MGB Roadster.

'It's not locked,' the CSI tech said.

Poe put on a pair of gloves and opened the boot. 'Well, she definitely had a flat,' he said.

Doyle hadn't bothered putting the damaged tyre into the MGB's spare wheel cover. No doubt she had flung it into the boot to get repaired later.

'Why would she say she hadn't had help to change it, if she had?' Lee asked. 'Surely this isn't still about her not wanting to appear feckless in front of you?'

Poe didn't answer. He was rooting through the contents of the boot, searching for something, anything that might offer an explanation. He picked up the jack and placed it on the garage floor. He checked his gloves. They had oil on them. He showed Lee and Bradshaw.

'And all I did was lift it out the boot.'

A used Coke bottle filled with coolant joined the jack, as did a small container of engine oil, a first-aid kit and a bag full of spark-plugs and fuses. Doyle also kept a waterproof jacket and a pair of wellingtons in the boot. Poe put them on the floor along with everything else. The only thing left was a box of tissues. He reached in and grabbed them, realising his mistake as soon as he had them in his hand. They weren't tissues in the box, they were disposable gloves. The blue ones doctors and nurses wore. He was about to throw them on the floor next to the jack when something made him pause.

Why were they in the boot at all? He knew some doctors kept a medical bag with them for emergencies, but Doyle didn't appear to be one of those doctors. So why have a box of disposable gloves? And they weren't even new; the gloves were crumpled up as if they had already been worn. He reviewed the contents of the boot again.

Oil.

Coolant.

Spark plugs.

Fuses.

This was a car she loved, but it looked like it needed lots of care and attention. Probably needed ad hoc repairs to keep it running, hence the spare parts she kept in the boot. The disposable gloves were there to protect her hands when she had to work on her car. One of the perks of being a doctor. She would have worn a pair when she changed her tyre – *that* was why her hands were still clean.

And Frederick Beck had gone to extraordinary lengths to frame her.

'Can we check the insides of these please?' he asked Lee quietly.

'What for?'

'Firearms discharge residue.'

Chapter 105

'Will the CPS *now* support our judge in chambers application?' Poe asked.

'If they don't I'll arrest their solicitor for interfering in an investigation,' Lee replied.

Poe gave her a smile, assuming she was joking. Lee didn't return it.

CSI had swabbed the insides of all the disposable gloves in the boot of Doyle's car. They'd recorded a positive result every single time.

'Do you think he fired the gun then put on the gloves to transfer the FDR?' Lee asked.

'Or he wore them inside out when he fired it. Turned them back the right way round then put them back in the box. There were sixteen, so if we assume he wore a glove on each hand, he'd have only needed to fire the gun eight times. I imagine he intended to plant the gun later. Somewhere that would incriminate Estelle.'

'So, he breaks into her boot, sees something he can use and, what, stole them? Put them back once he had the firearms discharge residue inside?'

'Probably didn't need to steal them,' Poe said. 'You can get these gloves anywhere. I suspect he just bought his own then drove somewhere remote. Fired the gun a few times then broke into her car again and swapped his gloves for hers. Old cars like this aren't difficult to get into. They aren't like cars today with their fancy security systems. A car like this is opened with a key.'

'And on the day of the murder, he makes sure she has a flat tyre,' Lee said. 'Maybe he stuck a knife or a sharpened screwdriver in the tyre wall. Had to be a big enough hole so the tyre was flat enough to

335

notice. Professor Doyle puts on a pair of gloves to change it, unwittingly getting the correct composition of FDR on her hands.'

'I think that's exactly what happened.'

'Who the hell is this guy?' she said.

Chapter 106

The judge in chambers bail application hearing was a formality. The judge asked some searching questions of Poe and Ania Kierczynska, but his most barbed ones were aimed at Tai-young Lee and the CPS solicitor. He asked why the murder charge wasn't being dropped, but the CPS solicitor stood his ground and said they would wait until the DNA found in the strong room was confirmed as Frederick Beck's. Lee glared at him, not wanting to be any part of some bullshit face-saving exercise.

'I am ordering Professor Doyle's immediate release on bail,' the judge said. 'I understand she has a property in Newcastle?'

'Yes, your honour,' Ania replied.

'I will bail her to that address then and, in light of the CPS refusing to drop the murder charge, I will require her to be electronically monitored.'

'I'm sure she won't mind wearing a tag, your honour.'

'No,' Poe said. The judge peered over his reading glasses. 'Your honour,' Poe added.

'This is a generous offer, Sergeant Poe. She is only required to be at this address from nine p.m. to six a.m. She can continue with her work, take a walk, eat at a restaurant.'

'It's a death sentence, your honour.'

Poe spent five minutes outlining how Frederick Beck had circumnavigated every security measure they had taken so far.

'Do you have an alternative suggestion?'

'Actually, I do,' he said.

Ania Kierczynska was the only one allowed into HMP Low Newton when they collected Doyle. There had been some paperwork to sort

337

out, but Poe had shouted at the governor until he'd promised to expedite it. Immediately after the judge's ruling, Poe and Bradshaw drove into Newcastle city centre to buy Doyle some clothes, toiletries and a new mobile. Poe didn't want her going back to her flat in case Beck had been there, and nothing Bradshaw owned was suitable. It wasn't a straightforward shopping trip. Poe hadn't realised women's clothing came in sizes more sophisticated than small, medium and large, and Bradshaw bought all her clothes online. In the end, he had sent Bradshaw into a boutique shop that had a mannequin dressed in fishnet stockings and a red corset in the window, and told her to buy five hundred pounds worth of clothes.

Poe had handed Ania a pair of navy-blue jeans, a black T-shirt with a brightly coloured sugar skull design on the front, a pair of Converse trainers, socks and underwear. He hoped it would all fit.

They had a journey to make.

At Poe's suggestion, the judge had bailed Doyle into his care. Until the CPS officially dropped the charges, wherever Poe was, Doyle would have to be as well.

'And she will agree to this?' the judge had asked.

'I think so,' Poe had replied.

'She definitely will,' Bradshaw had said.

'Very well. I hereby bail Professor Doyle to Sergeant Poe's care. You are to let the local police force know the address you're staying at and you must accept planned and unplanned checks. Is this acceptable?'

'It is, your honour,' Poe had said.

It was ten past three when Ania and Doyle finally walked out of the prison gates. Poe was relieved to see the clothes they'd picked for her fitted. The trousers were a bit baggy, and the T-shirt was a bit tight, but he thought they'd done OK.

Ania walked Doyle to Poe's car, hugged her goodbye, then headed back into the prison. She had another client to see. Poe got out and opened the back door for Doyle. She got in without catching his eye. She looked tired, like her battery had been leaching energy.

Poe doubted she'd slept more than two hours a night since being remanded.

He started the engine then adjusted the rear-view mirror so he could see her.

'Ania's explained you've been bailed to my care, Estelle?'

Doyle nodded.

'We need to go back to London,' he continued. 'That case I was telling you about, it's linked to the murder of your father somehow.'

'Ania told me,' she said, her voice low and flat.

She looked down and began to sob.

Poe and Bradshaw glanced at each other, unsure what to do. Poe passed his handkerchief over his shoulder.

'It's clean,' he said. 'Well, cleanish.'

'Thank you, Poe.'

She wiped her eyes and, although they were still wet, Poe saw the defiance he had expected. Prison hadn't broken her. He passed her a brown paper bag.

'You must be hungry,' he said. 'Tilly and I stopped off at that Italian restaurant in Newcastle that you like. There's crostini and some of those rock-hard biscuits. We told the manager it was for you and he refused to let us pay. Said everyone there is missing you.'

She peered into the bag. 'I can't thank you enough,' she said quietly.

But this time she didn't cry.

Chapter 107

'I knew you'd found something, Poe,' Doyle said. 'When the governor came to get me he was absolutely furious. Only you can make someone that angry. I can't tell you how relieved I was.'

'Poe shouted at him this morning when he said he had no one to process you out,' Bradshaw said. 'He made the governor do it himself.'

'Thank you, Poe. I'm not sure I could have coped with another night in there, not after Ania told me my bail had been authorised.'

'He never stopped working on your case, Estelle,' Bradshaw said. 'Even when he was told not to.'

'That sounds out of character, Tilly.'

'And he even tried to pick a lock on your dad's front gate, until he found out he didn't know how to. He was going to climb over instead but Detective Chief Inspector Tai-young Lee caught him and said she was going to arrest him for breaking into a crime scene. Then Poe said he would arrest *her* for withholding evidence, but said he wouldn't if she showed us the inside of your ancestral home.'

Doyle smiled at her. Bradshaw's innocence was a tonic. 'It sounds like you've been busy.'

Poe caught her gaze in the mirror. 'You didn't think we were going to leave you in there, did you?'

'What else did Poe do, Tilly?' Doyle said.

'Lots of things, Estelle. He also said you're a lady now, but we shouldn't bow as you wouldn't like that.'

'You know about that, Poe?'

'I'm a detective,' he said.

'And?'

'And what?'

'What do you think about it?'

340

'I'm puzzled as to why you thought I'd think less of you.'

'You hate privilege, Poe.'

'I hate the *abuse* of privilege, Estelle. And from what I've uncovered, your father was a decent person. And I know you are.'

Doyle let out a breath Poe didn't know she had been holding. For some reason that little exchange had been important to her. He wondered why.

'And even when we were at Douglas Salt's house,' Bradshaw continued, 'Poe was reading your file, not his.'

'Douglas Salt?' Doyle said.

'The Botanist's next victim,' Poe said. 'I've put a team of oddballs together. See if we can do what no one else has been able to and keep him alive.'

'Did you get my message? That I wanted to see you?'

'I did. But that photograph of Tilly and me visiting you in prison hit the front pages for a day. It sort of grounded us in London. What were you after?'

'I read the post-mortem reports you sent via Ania. Thank you for that. It did me good to think about things other than my father and my own predicament.'

'You found something?'

'No. The pathologist did a good job. I wouldn't have done anything differently.'

'Oh, well. It was a long shot.'

'But it got me thinking.'

'About?'

'You, Poe.'

'Me?'

'Yes, you. I often find myself thinking about you, but on this particular occasion I found myself thinking about your mind.'

Poe glanced at Bradshaw. 'I told you she wants my brain left to medical science,' he muttered.

'Yes, hilarious, Poe,' Doyle said. 'But you told me the Botanist case was the most complex you'd ever worked. That regardless of the security measures, he can seemingly walk through walls and get to his victims.'

'Poe says it must be black magic,' Bradshaw said, 'but I believe the answer is scientific.'

'And as usual you're the voice of reason, Tilly. Because Poe is forgetting one thing in all of this.'

'And what is that, Estelle?' Bradshaw asked.

'That he has the finest detective mind I've ever come across,' she replied. 'And that means if the Botanist *did* have some fancy way of getting past him, he'd have worked out how by now.'

'You flatter me,' Poe said.

'It's a fact, Poe, and like Tilly, I deal in facts. So that got me thinking: how would *I* poison someone you were protecting?'

'You have a theory, don't you?'

'I do.'

She told them what it was.

Poe asked questions.

She answered them.

Bradshaw asked better questions. Doyle answered those too.

Poe glanced at the satnav. They were still an hour away from Salt's house and, if Doyle was right, every second counted. He found Flynn in his recent contacts and pressed call.

She answered immediately.

'Boss, we have a problem . . .'

Two minutes later Flynn put her phone down. She glanced at Salt, obliviously stuffing his face with something from the fridge. Everything in there was safe to eat, but if Doyle was right they'd been coming at this from completely the wrong angle.

She cleared her throat.

'That was Poe, Mr Salt,' she said. 'He has some news.'

Salt looked up from his meal. 'Oh?'

'He no longer thinks the Botanist is trying to kill you.'

He leaped to his feet. 'I knew it!' he said, punching the air. 'There's no way this ass-hat could penetrate all this security. I told Sergeant Poe it's state of the art and that the Botanist would eventually have to move on to a softer target.'

Flynn kept her face flat.

The smile dropped from Salt's face. 'What is it?' he asked.

'Poe doesn't think the Botanist is trying to kill you, Mr Salt,' she replied. 'He thinks he already has.'

Chapter 108

In London, Detective Chief Superintendent Mathers met Poe outside the Royal Free Hospital, the same hospital Karen Royal-Cross had died in. They were familiar with the layout and would be able to take advantage of the infectious diseases unit's surveillance system. Whether Salt lived or died, his body was now a crime scene. It needed to be treated as one, which meant from now on everything had to be filmed.

'Where is he?' Poe asked.

'Rushed in on a gurney and taken straight to the infectious diseases unit theatre. Doctor Mukherjee isn't in yet so the consultant anaesthetist will talk Salt through what we want to do.'

'Doctor Mukherjee's doing the operation?'

'He used to be a surgeon and we know him.'

'What's Salt saying?'

'He's terrified. He won't agree to anything until he's spoken to you.'

'Let's go then,' Poe said.

When the anaesthetist had finished explaining the procedure, Salt gulped. 'It sounds serious.'

The anaesthetist shrugged. 'I won't sugar coat it, Mr Salt; emergency surgery like this is one of the most dangerous things we do. If we had the luxury of time we could make it safer, but my understanding is that waiting carries an even greater risk.'

'And there's no other way?'

The anaesthetist looked at Poe for an answer.

'If we're right, there isn't,' he said.

'How sure are you?'

'It's a theory. Nothing more.'

'What would you do in my situation?'

'This is a binary problem, Mr Salt,' Poe said. 'The Botanist has either already killed you or he hasn't. If he has, this is your only option. If he *hasn't*, you'll be undergoing life-altering surgery for nothing.'

'So?'

'So it depends on how lucky you're feeling, I suppose.'

'And?' Mathers asked when Poe walked out of the surgery preparation area.

'Schrödinger's arsehole is being prepped as we speak, ma'am,' Poe replied.

'Well done,' she said. 'And what the hell do you mean by "Schrödinger's arsehole"?'

'Let's find somewhere we can talk – Estelle can explain it better than me.'

Mukherjee's office was still empty so they piled in there. It was functional, rather than aesthetic. Mass-produced furniture and medical textbooks. A photograph of his family seemed to be the only personal item in the room.

Poe and Flynn perched on the desk, Mathers took the seat and Bradshaw sat on the floor. Henning Stahl found a seat in the corner and opened his notebook. Doyle stood in front of a whiteboard. She had already collected some props.

'Poe's told you what I think?'

'Broad strokes,' Mathers replied. 'He was a bit vague on the science.'

'You surprise me,' Doyle smiled. 'The first thing you need to know is that the Botanist hasn't invented something new, all he's done is adapt something that already exists.'

'Which is?'

She picked up a whiteboard marker, sketched a rough and ready diagram of the human digestive system. The throat, the gullet, the stomach, the small and large intestines.

'What do you know about modified-release drug delivery systems?'

Chapter 109

Doyle popped a blister pack of medication and held up something small and white.

'A standard paracetamol tablet,' she said. 'This is nothing more than compressed powder. It's a hard, smooth-coated pill.'

She opened another blister pack. This time she held up something blue and white, about the same size as a jellybean.

'Paracetamol again,' she said. 'This time it's loose powder in a hard-shelled capsule. The outside consists of two halves. The blue half fits inside the white to form a closed casing. They can be filled with anything unpalatable. Some are designed to contain liquids. Now, what these both have in common is they are immediate-release medications. It means they dissolve in the stomach within minutes of being swallowed. This is a safe and reliable way of getting medication directly where it needs to be. Everyone in this room will have taken immediate-release medication.'

Doyle pointed at the stomach on her diagram.

'However,' she continued, 'it isn't always advantageous to have medication dissolve in the stomach. It might cause nausea, for example, or, as the small intestine is the optimal part of the body for nutrient absorption, it might be preferable for the tablet to bypass the stomach altogether. And for this we have the modified-release drug delivery systems I mentioned earlier. Is everyone still with me?'

Nods all round. Bradshaw did so without looking up from her laptop. She was typing furiously. Poe assumed she was still researching what Doyle had told them in the car.

'There are many variants of modified-release drug delivery systems. For example, with painkilling opiates it is preferable to use a sustained-release variant. That way the patient gets the dose spread out over the course of a day, rather than in one big hit. There are pulse-release delivery systems that allow different medications to dissolve at different times. This might be useful in complex treatments where the success of one medication is dependent on another already being in the body.'

'This sounds complicated,' Flynn said.

'It does, but it's not,' Doyle replied. 'These tablets have been around for years. But we're not interested in sustained-release or pulse-release drugs, we're interested in *delayed*-release.'

'Delayed?'

Doyle nodded. 'These are drugs that are designed to target specific parts of the body, or maybe to work only when blood sugar levels are at a specified level.'

'How do these work?' Flynn asked.

'Science is moving forwards all the time, but currently, the active ingredient – say paracetamol – is coated in a barrier. Natural or synthetic polymers usually. Sometimes chitin, although, like I said, this is a field in constant development. Anyway, when the barrier dissolves, the drug, or in your case, poison, is released. Until then it is completely contained. And the beauty of this system is that the rate the barrier dissolves can be set for however long you want. There is no medical reason to have a barrier that lasts more than twenty-four hours, but there is no scientific reason why it couldn't last longer. Theoretically, the barrier could last forever.'

'Like when drug mules swallow condoms full of cocaine then?' Flynn said.

'Same theory,' Doyle said. 'Obviously, a condom that dissolves is, to quote Poe, as much use as mud flaps on a tortoise. Drug runners don't want cocaine being released into their mules after a set period of time.'

'My question is this then,' Flynn said. 'If our victims did swallow something covered with a barrier that doesn't dissolve for three weeks, why didn't they shit it out like a bit of sweetcorn?'

'Eloquently put, DI Flynn. How *does* the Botanist keep his poison in the victim long enough for the barrier to dissolve?'

'You know, don't you?' Mathers said.

Doyle nodded. 'I have a theory.'

Chapter 110

'It can take up to twenty-four hours for food to pass from the mouth to the anus,' Doyle said. 'That's a journey of nine inhospitable metres. And, DI Flynn's right, unless something stops the barrier-coated poison from working its way out, work its way out it will. Through peristalsis, which is basically a series of muscular contractions, the digestive system will process anything it receives. The scientists who needed pills to stay in the body longer than peristalsis would allow, had to develop tablets that could stop the digestive system doing what it is designed to do.'

Doyle filled a clear glass beaker with water. She dropped the white paracetamol tablet and the blue and white paracetamol capsule into it. She swirled the water with a pen. After a few moments the tablet started to dissolve and sank to the bottom of the beaker. A few seconds later, the capsule began to break up.

'As you would expect, the immediate-release medication did what it was supposed to. If this beaker was a stomach, the medication could now be absorbed by the body.'

She then reached into her pocket and removed another blister pack. She popped it and held up a disc-shaped tablet.

'I got this from the hospital pharmacy. It's chlortenoxicam, an anti-inflammatory drug,' she said. 'Now, watch what happens.'

She filled a fresh beaker and popped it in. Nothing happened. It didn't dissolve and it didn't sink. It just bobbed on the surface like a tiny fishing float.

'This is a stomach-specific floating drug delivery system,' she said. 'It's for drugs that need to be absorbed by the stomach, or drugs that don't do well in the intestines.'

'It floats?' Flynn said.

'It does. They have a bulk density less than the gastric juices and are designed to float until the barrier that coats the drug dissolves. They've been around for a long time and are getting more and more sophisticated.'

'So it's like a ping-pong ball in a toilet. It doesn't matter how many times you flush, the ping-pong ball isn't going down the U-bend.'

'Exactly. Now imagine that same ping-pong ball has something inside that will damage the toilet. Until the ball leaks or degrades, it will remain in the bowl, completely harmless. And this isn't science fiction – MIT have just designed a capsule that unfolds into a star shape big enough to avoid the two-centimetre gap that leads into the intestinal tract. They believe it will be able to stay in the stomach for up to a month.'

'What's MIT?' Poe asked.

'The Massachusetts Institute of Technology, Poe,' Bradshaw replied. 'It's a privately run research university in the United States of America. Twenty-six Turing Award winners, eight Fields Medallists and forty-one astronauts have been affiliated with MIT.'

'Big heads,' Poe said. 'And I was at Kendal College at the same time as Stephen Machalepis. He was pretty famous.'

'What did he do?'

'Bit one of the Queen's corgis.'

Flynn sniggered. 'He's sometimes hard to keep on task, Estelle,' she said. 'But if it's floating in Salt's stomach, why aren't we just sticking a camera down his throat? If it's there, why can't we just grab it like we're playing an arcade claw machine?'

'Two reason why we can't, DI Flynn,' Doyle said. 'He's recently eaten, so it's unlikely the surgeon would be able to see it. And even if we could, retrieving it through the oesophagus would be terribly dangerous. While it's true endoscopic accessories now include attachments that can grasp things, I believe the risk would be too high. If I'm right, and I can't see how else it could be done, the Botanist uses a barrier that degrades over a specified period of time. It would be comparatively thick to begin with, but by now it will have the structural integrity of an over-baked croissant.

The endoscopic attachment wouldn't be able to retrieve the tablet without piercing the barrier. And if the barrier is pierced, the tablet delivers its payload.'

'Which is why Salt is being prepped for surgery.'

'Doctor Mukherjee will cut vertically into the abdominal cavity, through the skin, fat, muscles, muscular aponeuroses – they're the tendons that connect muscles to the thing the muscle moves – and the peritoneum. He'll move a couple of things to the side then open up the stomach. Just like he would if the stomach's lymph nodes had to be removed. Once he has access, he'll use a surgical spoon to scoop out the contents.'

Chapter 111

The anaesthetist popped her head into Mukherjee's office.

'Surgery's in thirty minutes,' she said. 'If you need to get set up it will have to be now. Once Doctor Mukherjee's started, he won't allow anyone else in.'

'Thank you,' Mathers said, getting to her feet. 'I need to put a camera in the theatre as the surgery will form part of the evidence if we eventually get to court. It also means you guys can watch it live.'

After Mathers had left, Flynn said, 'I assume we think he found a way to substitute the medication our victims were taking for his own doctored tablets? If I remember correctly, they were all taking something.'

'Kane Hunt suffered from erectile dysfunction so was prescribed sildenafil,' Bradshaw said. 'Harrison Cummings was taking statins for hereditary cardiovascular disease, Karen Royal-Cross was taking a lipase inhibitor to treat her weight problem and Douglas Salt had high blood pressure. He took amlodipine every day to manage it.'

'How easy would it be to do, Estelle?' Poe asked.

'Substitute their medication? That's your field, not mine.'

'No, I mean how easy would it be to manufacture these poison pills? Do we need to begin checking pharmaceutical laboratories or can it be done in a garage?'

'Do you think drug dealers rent time at a lab when they manufacture MDMA?'

'I suppose not.'

'Or independent research companies go to GlaxoSmithKline when they need a small, no-frills batch of a prototype medication? Of course they don't. They make the tablets themselves.'

'Talk me through the process.'

'It's extremely easy,' Doyle said. 'Anyone with five thousand pounds and access to YouTube could do it. For pills, you need a template, but they're available from any laboratory supply company.'

'What do they look like?'

'Like an ice cube tray with pill-sized compartments. You mix your medication into a paste, spread it across the template with a spatula then press them out using the gadget that comes with it. Let them dry for twelve hours and that's it. As you might imagine, capsules are even easier. They are delivered disassembled, so all you need to do is fill one half with powder then press the two halves together. They're designed to lock without adhesive.'

Henning Stahl cleared his throat. Everyone looked at him. Poe had forgotten he was there. Flynn hadn't wanted to leave the journalist at Salt's so she had brought him with her. He had found a seat in the corner and sort of disappeared. Poe suspected it was his ability to be the grey man that had made him such an effective journalist. He saw everything, he forgot nothing. And he was always scribbling in his notebook. 'And, of course, we already know Frederick Beck has these skills,' he said.

Doyle looked bewildered. 'You know who the Botanist is?' she asked.

'Shit,' Poe said. 'I was going to tell you about him on the journey down, see if you knew why he'd targeted you, but your poison pill theory sort of hijacked the agenda. It's been full speed since then.'

'Freddie Beck killed my father?'

'We think . . .' Poe paused. 'Wait, what the hell do you mean "Freddie"?' he said.

Chapter 112

'You know him?' Poe said.

Doyle nodded.

'I've known him a while,' she said. 'Long enough to know he prefers Frederick to Fred, and that he *hates* Freddie.'

'Where did you meet him?'

'Conferences mainly. We always seemed to be competing for funding at the same time. I admired him, but, like everyone else, I didn't like him. He was singularly obsessed with researching acquired Breeg–Bart syndrome. Nothing else mattered to him.'

'Which fits with Tilly's profile,' Poe said. 'She concluded that Beck had devoted his entire life to curing his wife. After the newspaper article made it impossible for him to continue his research, it was as if the whole world was conspiring to kill her. When she eventually succumbed, it pushed him into a cycle of destruction. Turned him into the narcissist we're dealing with now. It also explains why he chose to meet Henning Stahl in Chance's Park instead of a more suitable location. He'd have known there was a Breeg–Bart fund-raising run that day.'

'I'd like to see the profile.'

'Tilly will print one off for—'

'The link to Douglas Salt's surgery is live now,' Bradshaw cut in, pointing at the image on her laptop.

Bradshaw and Flynn sat in front of the laptop, Henning Stahl, Poe and Doyle were standing. They all had a good view.

Mathers was the only non-medical person in the theatre. She had been allowed to set up fixed cameras. One of them was directly above Salt's pale, hairless belly. Another showed the whole theatre.

Poe reckoned there were close to twenty people in there. Doctor Mukherjee wasn't taking any chances.

'Do we have audio, Tilly?' Poe asked.

She nodded and dragged her mouse across a sound bar at the bottom of the screen. Doctor Mukherjee spoke first.

'I will now make the midline incision,' he said. And he did.

Bradshaw paled. 'I think I'll print off that profile now,' she said.

Chapter 113

Although Poe knew about the organs in the abdomen from his attendance at countless post-mortems, he had never really given much thought to how they all fitted together in a living person. He wasn't naive enough to think the inside of a body was like a child's anatomy book, organs neatly organised with space in between, but he hadn't expected it to be a total car crash. When Mukherjee finally used surgical scissors to open Salt's abdominal cavity, all Poe could see was blood and tissue and fat and pieces of flotsam. It was all red and it all looked the same. Abdominal surgery looked remarkably similar to making black pudding, he thought.

Bradshaw came back into the room. She was holding a document.

'What you got there, Tilly?'

'Frederick Beck's profile, Poe. Do you want me to stay in case Estelle Doyle has any ... Oh my gosh. However will Doctor Mukherjee fit everything back in?'

Bradshaw had a point. Salt's abdomen now looked like a burst suitcase.

'It's a jigsaw he's done many times, Tilly,' Doyle said.

'Mr Salt is going to be very sore tomorrow.'

'Hopefully,' Poe said.

Doyle and Bradshaw looked at him.

'If he's sore, he's alive,' he explained. 'And also because he's a prick.'

'Are you staying, Tilly?' Doyle asked. 'I can recap what's happened. Doctor Mukherjee will be accessing the stomach soon.'

'No thank you, Estelle. I've been anticipating what Poe might need next and I have a program running. It's called RipplePlace and I expect the results in approximately ninety seconds.'

'And what's that?'

'It's a search and merge algorithm, sorting key data into lexico-graphical order,' Bradshaw explained, explaining nothing.

And with that she left the room. Doyle looked at the empty doorway in amusement. 'I think she may be my favourite person ever,' she said.

Poe nodded. 'You understand any of that?' he asked.

'Not a word.'

Chapter 114

'Doctor Mukherjee is five minutes away from accessing the stomach,' Doyle said. 'They're getting all the sponges ready so they can mop up the stomach liquid spillage.'

'Gross,' Poe said.

'It's beautiful, actually.'

'Got to agree with Poe, Estelle,' Flynn said. 'It's absolutely gross.' Doyle grinned.

A theatre nurse unwrapped a clamp. Another unwrapped the surgical spoon that Mukherjee would use to empty the stomach. It reminded Poe of something he wanted to ask Doyle.

'What about packaging for his tablets?' he said. 'If the Botanist's fooling his victims into taking the wrong medication, they have to be in professional packaging, surely. If you always get your Viagra in a blister pack and suddenly it turns up in a brown envelope, you're bound to think twice about taking it. I don't care how horny you are.'

'Getting medication into blister packs is even easier than making the tablets, Poe,' Doyle said. 'Hand-operated blister-packing machines cost less than a thousand pounds. They're sort of like miniature trouser presses. And blank blister pack sheets come in every shape and size you might need. Round, rhombic, capsule, you name it. You put the tablets in the empty bubbles then slot the sheet into the machine, along with the soft-temper aluminium foil that comes with the blank blister packs. You pull down the machine's handle and it simultaneously applies heat and pressure. The heat warms up the lacquer coating on the foil and the pressure seals it to the blister pack.'

'But they wouldn't have the correct writing on the foil?'

'Not unless he has access to a machine that prints them at the same time, but I don't think that's the problem.'

'Oh, what is?'

'It's the medication box and the instruction sheet and the chemist's label with the patient's personal information that's the problem. You put a professional-looking blister pack into the right medication box, and no one will notice there's no writing on the foil. Work out how he gets the wrong medication into the *right* box and you've cracked it.'

'OK,' Poe said. 'Assuming he can do all that. And say he's managed to hack the NHS, or something equally unlikely, and say he has a fool-proof system for making his medication look like their medication, there's still a major stumbling block.'

'Which is?'

'How does he get it to them?'

'He posts it, I assume.'

'Doesn't work,' Poe said. 'Let's say you get your regular medication through the mail, and let's say he posts his through your letterbox. What happens when the real medication arrives? Beck's good, but I don't think he's found a reliable way of intercepting the mail. Not one of his victims mentioned duplicate medication and they lived all over London, so we know he wasn't doorstepping postmen.'

'That sounds like a detective's problem,' Doyle said. 'But not one you can discuss now.'

'Why not?'

She nodded at the laptop. 'The stomach's open.'

Chapter 115

Doctor Mukherjee emptied Salt's stomach as if it were a novelty soup bowl. He didn't check what he was removing – that wasn't what he was there for – he simply took a spoonful then transferred it to a stainless-steel kidney dish. He never took too much and he didn't hurry. Poe recognised an exceptional surgeon when he saw one.

'The pulpy stuff in the stomach is called chyme,' Doyle said. 'It's a mixture of gastric juices and partially digested food.'

'It looks like curried porridge,' Poe said.

'If we'd been able to wait for the chyme to pass through the pyloric sphincter into the small intestine, all that would be left in the stomach would be gastric juices,' Doyle continued. 'Recovering the tablet would have been far simpler.'

'If it's there at all,' Flynn said.

'If it isn't, we're condemning him to a lifetime of anaemia, diar-rhoea and weak bones for nothing.'

She looked anxious.

'I wouldn't worry about that, Estelle,' Poe said. 'If it isn't there, his lifetime won't be very long. Beck will get to him eventually.'

Mukherjee scooped out something long and stringy. He lifted the spoon to his nose and sniffed it. 'Has this man been eating goat?'

Poe scowled. 'How long's this going to take?' he asked.

'The stomach isn't like the inside of a balloon, Poe,' Doyle said. 'It's a J-shaped organ, and even though Doctor Mukherjee has cut into the widest part, ridged muscles – called rugae – line it. It's entirely possible the pill has lodged in the mucus that protects the stomach wall. We won't know for sure until it's empty and the lining has been washed and checked. This might take a while.'

Which was when Mathers stepped away from Salt's open stomach, faced one of the cameras and said, 'Got the bastard.'

Chapter 116

'How is he?' Poe asked Mukherjee.

'He'll never eat a large meal again, but he's alive,' he replied.

The tablet was round, about the size of a standard paracetamol, and was stained yellow with gastric juices. Doctor Mukherjee had put it under the theatre microscope to confirm it was still intact. It was now in the hospital lab. Doyle had wanted to examine it herself, but Poe had insisted she stay by his side.

'You should have let me go with it,' Doyle said. 'I could have made sure it's analysed correctly.'

'You being there doesn't add value. The lab are putting it through their gas chromatography–mass spectrometry machine and, in your own words, "Any idiot can do that".'

They were in Mukherjee's office. Flynn and Bradshaw had disappeared somewhere.

'I assume you're going public?' Doyle said.

'I've advised against it.'

'Why?'

'Beck will adapt. We saved Salt because we had advance notice and you figured out his delivery method. If he *stops* giving advance notice, there'll be no more last-minute emergency operations, just a never-ending procession of dead morons. We need to figure out how he's getting his doctored pills into the victim's hands without them suspecting something. That's how we stop him.'

Mathers knocked on the open door and stepped inside.

'We're meeting in one of the hospital conference rooms, Poe,' she said. 'And I'm sorry, but the decision has been made to go public. I relayed your concerns about Beck changing his modus operandi, but my commander feels we have to warn the public. Encourage people, particularly those with negative public personas, to be hyper-vigilant when it comes to taking medication.'

Doyle glanced at Poe.

He shrugged. 'I'm just a sergeant,' he said. 'It's their call.'

Chapter 117

'Toxicology have confirmed the floating tablet found in Salt's stomach contained ricin,' Mathers told the packed conference room.

It was jammed with Met detectives and uniformed cops. Poe was wedged between Doyle and Henning Stahl. Flynn and Bradshaw were still AWOL. He'd tried texting them but hadn't received a reply.

Mathers's commander had just finished his press conference, a pre-prepared statement about Beck's methodology and a plea for information. To Poe's dismay, there was also a brief line about how the investigation had been merged with one in Northumberland. He didn't give details, but he didn't have to. Beck would be watching and he'd know the ruse to frame Doyle was over. Poe made a mental note to not let her out of his sight.

Mathers held up one of the blister packs Doyle had used earlier in her demonstration.

'Professor Doyle says putting tablets into blister packs isn't complex or time-consuming and we know Frederick Beck already has the skillset needed to manufacture the poisons and the delayed-release barriers. And we now suspect he conducted human trials in Japan. We assume this was where he fine-tuned how fast the tablet's barrier dissolved.' She paused to take a drink of water. 'What we don't know is how he's getting his modified medication into boxes that his victims don't find suspicious. We don't know how he knows what medication they take or how he gets it to them while simultaneously diverting their genuine prescribed medication. Questions so far?'

'Are they with the same GP?' a uniformed sergeant asked.

'They all live miles from each other. Not only did they have different GPs, until Karen Royal-Cross and Douglas Salt were treated at the infectious diseases unit, none of them had even been to the same hospital before.'

The same sergeant said, 'Maybe he posts them?'

'Which doesn't answer what happens when the real medication arrives. No one reported receiving duplicates.'

There were more unanswerable questions before Mathers picked up a whiteboard pen and began tasking. 'Greg, we don't think it's anything to do with their GPs, but check again, will you?'

A fresh-faced detective nodded and wrote something in his notebook.

'Chloe, now we know the victims are taking the poison a couple of weeks earlier than we'd thought, you'd better get your team going through the CCTV footage again. I don't know what you're looking for, but I suspect you'll know when you see it.'

A stern-looking, grey-haired cop stood and left the room. Before the door had time to swing shut, Flynn and Bradshaw entered. Bradshaw scanned the room for Poe but it was too crowded. They hurried to the front. Flynn whispered in Mathers's ear.

'Are you sure?' Mathers said.

'Tilly is.'

'You'd better tell everyone then.'

Flynn faced the room. 'We think we know how Beck's doing it,' she said.

Chapter 118

'Temple Express Pharmacy,' Bradshaw said, pointing at the wall monitor she'd just mirrored to her laptop. 'They have an electronic prescription service contract with the NHS.'

'It's a private business?' Mathers asked.

'Yes, Detective Chief Superintendent Mathers,' Bradshaw replied. 'A customer orders medication via their website and Temple request the prescription from the customer's GP. Temple fill the prescription using medication from their warehouse, then deliver it using their own fleet of vans. Repeat prescriptions are reordered automatically. All of our victims, including Douglas Salt, were registered with them.'

'But we checked GP records,' Mathers said. 'We'd have spotted this.'

'We did,' Flynn said, 'but it wasn't supposed to be the medication so we didn't go too deep. And the reason we missed it is because Temple Express Pharmacy have been hoovering up the competition over the last few years. With few exceptions, any private pharmacy with an NHS contract in London was bought out. They streamline the newly acquired company by centralising services like HR and payroll, but keep the original pharmacy's name. It's why the victims' nominated pharmacies all appear to be different.'

'But in reality they're all subsidiary companies of Temple?'

'Exactly. They're the parent company all the others sit under. And one of their core selling points is guaranteed discretion. All their medication is delivered in discreet packaging. For a celebrity with an embarrassing condition, I suspect this is important. For example, we know Kane Hunt was desperate to hide the fact he was impotent.'

'Which DI Flynn has explained to me but I still don't understand,' Bradshaw chipped in, her brow creased. 'Erectile dysfunction is a common problem, particularly among men over forty. It can be caused by stress, excessive alcohol consumption or underlying health problems. It is not shameful. If Poe told me he was unable to maintain a healthy erection I would advise him to drink less and sleep more. If he were still unable to have penetrative sexual intercourse I would tell him to see his general practitioner. Which he probably wouldn't, knowing him.'

'Oh God,' Poe whispered.

Bradshaw sought him out in the crowded room again, but he was at the back and she was short-sighted. He slumped so far down in his seat his feet touched the feet of the person in front.

Doyle raised her hand. 'He's over here, Tilly,' she called out, grinning.

Bradshaw stood on her tiptoes and waved. 'Hi, Poe,' she said. 'I was just talking about you. Did you hear?'

Poe stared at the floor, his face burning. Cops began to snigger. One openly laughed. Another said, 'We should call him Sergeant Woody,' to raucous cheers.

'What?' Bradshaw said.

'This is gold,' Henning Stahl said, scribbling furiously. 'Absolute gold.'

'OK,' Flynn said. 'As much fun as this is, we haven't finished yet. We believe Beck infiltrated Temple Express Pharmacy and checked their database for potential victims. He selects people who require repeat prescriptions of daily medication, and manufactures identical-looking tablets, one of which is actually his barrier-coated poison. He substitutes their blister pack for his and has them delivered the usual way. He waits until they've ordered a repeat prescription before he goes through the charade of the poems and the flowers and the advance warnings. By then he can be confident his poisoned pill is already floating in their stomachs. They've basically swallowed a ticking time bomb.'

'And only he knows how long the fuse is set for,' Mathers added.

'Yep.'

'Kane Hunt wasn't on daily medication though. How does he fit in?'

'The NHS will only prescribe eight sildenafil tablets per month,' Flynn replied. 'And Kane Hunt ordered as many as he was permitted. We think he took them so he could masturbate.'

Mathers nodded. 'This all works,' she said. 'I'll get someone working on a warrant. See if we can get a list of employees.'

'We've already been through it, ma'am.'

'How?'

'Tilly tells me she did it legally,' Flynn said, 'but maybe don't ask how just yet. We have a list of all employees who have access to their secure medication warehouse, and anyone involved in the distribution process. We'll circulate it afterwards, but we've narrowed it down to males between the age of forty and sixty who joined the company in the last eighteen months.'

'How many names?'

'Just three. Robin Barker works as a cleaner in the warehouse, so potentially has access, and Paul Burdis is a qualified pharmacist. Burdis actually fills the prescriptions. The third is a man called Christopher Goodson. He's one of their part-time delivery drivers.'

'I assume you think Paul Burdis is the most likely suspect?'

'Actually we don't,' Flynn said. 'To dispense medication Beck would have had to forge a pharmacy degree and then hope Temple didn't check if he was registered with the General Pharmaceutical Council.'

'The cleaner then?'

'Certainly possible, ma'am.'

'But you don't think so?'

'Beck would need privacy each time he was substituting the victim's medication for his own. Temple run a twenty-four-hour operation so I don't think a cleaner would get that level of freedom.'

'Which leaves the driver.'

'Who *does* have the privacy required to switch the medication. He could simply take it home at the end of his shift, switch blister packs, then deliver *his* medication the following day. No duplicates to worry about. And he'd have access to the client database so he could check addresses and delivery instructions.'

'Do Temple have an updated photograph of him?'

'Bad news there, I'm afraid, ma'am,' Flynn said. 'As they don't actually engage with customers, drivers aren't required to have photo ID.'

'They must have taken a copy of his driving licence though?'

'They did, but it's an old photograph and it's not great. There's an address though, for what it's worth.'

'Almost certainly fake, but we'll check it out anyway,' Mathers said. 'This is excellent work, DI Flynn. Does anyone have anything to add?'

Poe put his head in his hands and groaned softly. Mathers saw him.

'Is there a problem, Sergeant Poe?'

'This could have ended tomorrow,' he said. 'We could have staked out Temple's distribution centre and arrested Beck when he turned up for his shift. But because of that bloody press conference, he now knows we're on to him. My guess is we'll not hear from him until he has a brand new plan.'

Mathers didn't answer. Poe could tell he had hit home though. A uniformed constable entered the room and made his way to the front. He passed Mathers a note.

'It seems you're wrong, Sergeant Poe,' she said. 'Frederick Beck is on the phone. He wants to speak to you.'

Chapter 119

'What do you want, *Freddie*?' Poe said.

'Ha ha, yes, very good, Sergeant Poe. But you sound tense?'

'I asked, what do you want?'

'I called to congratulate you.'

'Me?'

'All of you, Sergeant Poe, all of you. You've ended phase one slightly earlier than I anticipated. In the simulations I ran, you didn't uncover my methodology until I'd killed six.'

Mathers mouthed, 'Phase one?'

Poe shrugged. He doubted Beck had a phase two, but it wouldn't take long to come up with something. He could stop giving warnings, or worse, start switching boxes of off-the-shelf medication in high-street chemists. If he bought a box of regular painkillers and took it home to switch blister packs, he could return the following week, or month, and put it back on the same shelf. A campaign like that would be impossible to stop.

Beck filled the brief silence.

'By now I expect you've worked out my distribution method as well. And while I don't expect you to take my word for it, I can assure you that Temple Express Pharmacy and I have parted ways.'

'Good to know,' Poe snapped. 'Is that all?'

'I imagine it was Professor Doyle who toppled the first domino? She really is quite brilliant. Unfortunately, that's why she needed to be side-lined for a while. If you're listening, Professor Doyle, I'm sorry about your father. It was necessary, but unpleasant. He was a good man and I took no pleasure from his death.'

Poe shook his head at Doyle. Warned her not to say anything.

'I'll pass that on, Freddie,' he said. 'Anything else? Only I haven't eaten for a while.'

'Always the joker, Sergeant Poe. But no, there's nothing else. Just touching base.'

'Goodbye, Freddie.'

Poe had almost put the phone down when Beck said, 'Oh, and Sergeant Poe?'

'Yeah?'

'I can't wait to meet you.'

Poe ended the call.

Chapter 120

'What the hell was all that about?' Poe asked.

'He was gloating,' Mathers replied.

'But he didn't.'

'Didn't what?'

'Gloat.'

'Maybe he likes hearing the sound of his own voice then. Your profile says he's driven by revenge for his dead wife, but it also says he's a narcissist.'

'All serial killers are narcissists. They don't all call for a chat, especially when their plan is unravelling.'

'Maybe he wanted to let us know he has contingencies.'

'Why would he have contingencies? As a concept for murder it was almost flawless. By the time he warned his victims, they'd already taken the floating tablet. And by the time they died, all the evidence had been digested. Of course, now he has to adapt, but he didn't need to tell us that – it's what we would have expected him to do.'

'I'm not sure what it is you're getting at, Poe,' Flynn said.

'Did you notice how he steered the conversation around to Estelle?'

'I'm not surprised – she's the one who worked it all out.'

'Except she was only able to do that because I got a copy of the case file to her in prison.'

'So?'

'So I think he *guessed* it was Estelle who figured it out. He can't have known. Like everyone keeps saying, as brilliant as she is, she's not the only pathologist we work with. I don't think he actually cared if it was her or not.'

'He didn't care?'

'No, I think he asked if it was Estelle because he wants us to think it's why he framed her.'

'But it wasn't?'

'I think that was pure misdirection.'

'So if it's not her pathology skills he's scared of, where *does* Professor Doyle fit into all this?' Mathers asked.

'I don't know,' Poe said. 'But Estelle's met him. Perhaps she knows something he doesn't want us to know.'

'But I don't,' Estelle said.

'Have you had time to read Tilly's profile yet?' Flynn asked.

'Not yet. I've only just been handed it.'

'Someone get that woman a reading lamp, a comfortable chair and a pot of coffee,' Poe said.

Chapter 121

'Estelle Doyle does know I don't have high confidence in Frederick Beck's profile, doesn't she, Poe?' Bradshaw said.

'I told her, Tilly.'

'Because if I'd had more time I could have done a much better job.'

'I told her that too.'

'And his ex-colleagues were curiously reluctant to talk to us.'

'Probably don't want to receive a pressed flower in the post.'

'All I'm saying is the profile of his mental, emotional and personality characteristics is based on incomplete data. I mean, we know he's an organised, rather than disorganised, killer, but even the FBI's Behavioural Analysis Unit could have worked that out.'

'Not a fan of the BAU, huh?'

'And because he hasn't had a footprint in the United Kingdom for several years, the usual sources of information weren't large enough for any statistically relevant data mining. We couldn't use forensic homology as there has been no offender like this before and—'

'She knows, Tilly.'

'She does?'

'Well, I didn't use those exact words, but she got my drift.'

'What words did you use, Poe?'

'I said, "Tilly says it's a bit crap, but it's the best she can do for now".'

'I would *never* use that word, Poe!'

'She knows that too.'

'If I could just have one more day I'm sure I could make it better,' Bradshaw said, biting her lip.

'You can rework it after Estelle's been through it, Tilly. She's actually met the man. She's bound to have some fresh insight.'

'I'm going to talk to her.'

'Sit down, Tilly.'

'But why, Poe? I should be there in case she has any questions.'

'I agree.'

'Why won't you let me go and find her then?'

Poe pointed down the long corridor. Doyle was hurrying along it. 'Because it looks like she's coming to find us.'

Chapter 122

'This profile is wrong,' Doyle said.

'I told you, Poe!' Bradshaw cried. 'I had nowhere near enough data.'

'Calm down, Tilly,' Poe said. Then to Doyle, 'All of it, or just part of it?'

'First of all, Tilly, given what you had to go on, this' – Doyle held up the profile – 'is remarkably accurate.'

'But we've got something wrong?'

'More like you haven't included something you had no way of knowing.'

'Important?'

'It entirely changes Freddie's psychological profile.'

'Frederick Beck was a fussy, self-important man,' Doyle said, 'but his pharmaceutical expertise in exploiting NCEs was unparalleled.'

'NCEs?' Mathers asked.

'New chemical entities. They're sourced through chemical synthesis or through the isolation of natural products. Not including animal venom, which has come on in leaps and bounds recently, there are four main natural products used in medicine: fungi, bacteria, marine, and Frederick's particular expertise, botanical.'

Poe, Bradshaw, Flynn, Mathers and Doyle had grabbed a corner table in the hospital's staff canteen. They all had hot drinks. Despite the late hour, Poe had persuaded the cook to rustle up a bacon sandwich. White bread, no sauce, lots of butter, lots of pepper. Perfect. Bradshaw grimaced each time he took a bite.

'Tilly's profile is entirely accurate in that he was driven by his ego,' Doyle continued. 'In his eyes, there's nothing worse than being anonymous. Now, in the field of pharmaceutical research, a little bit of ego is not necessarily a bad thing – some of the best scientists in the world are driven, but appalling people. Arrogant, sexist, competitive. Belittling and bullying colleagues.'

'Tilly's profile says Beck was all these things,' Flynn said.

'He was. On one occasion he was asked to appear in front of the European Medicine Agency Committee for Medicinal Products for Human Use as he had refused to share credit on a piece of research. A woman had co-authored a paper with him, but before it was submitted he removed her name from the title page. Downplayed her role in the research to little more than a junior assistant.'

'What happened?'

'The company they worked for put pressure on her to withdraw the complaint,' Doyle replied. 'Said in-fighting didn't reflect well on them. What wasn't said was that Frederick had threatened to walk if he were forced to share credit. She was given a six-figure bonus and told to keep quiet.'

'He had that much clout?' Poe asked.

'Motor neurone disease is a multi-billion-dollar market, and, although Frederick's field, acquired Breeg–Bart syndrome, is relatively small, the company that brings the first effective drug to market will make hundreds of millions a year. When Frederick threatened to walk, they were left with a stark choice: insist the woman got the credit she deserved or protect their investment. For a company with shareholders, that's no choice at all.'

'If he was that much of a star, why wasn't he working on one of the better-known motor neurone diseases?' Mathers asked. 'Is it true he sacrificed his career to work on a cure for his wife?'

'We're getting to the nub of the matter now,' Doyle replied. 'He was the leader in his field because he refused to play in anyone else's and he wouldn't let anyone play in his.'

'He'd rather be a big fish in a small pond, you mean?'

'Exactly. He chose to work in acquired Breeg–Bart syndrome so he could be the acknowledged expert. He wasn't interested in being part of a big research push, didn't want to be on a team. If anyone mentioned Breeg–Bart, in whatever context, he wanted Frederick Beck mentioned in the same sentence.'

Poe frowned. 'But surely he chose to work in Breeg–Bart because of Melanie, his wife?' he said.

'Explain the timeline of events as you understand them, Poe,' Doyle replied.

'Which part?'

Doyle opened the profile. 'Page eight,' she said. 'Meeting his wife and the subsequent discovery she had Breeg–Bart. The love story the press obsessed over.'

Poe had read the profile cover to cover and didn't need his memory refreshing. 'Sad story, really,' he said. 'They met while he was a general research assistant at a teaching hospital and she was a patient. I think she had collapsed on a night out. He met her as she was being discharged and they hit it off. I believe they were married within six months. She was diagnosed with Breeg–Bart two years later and that's when he diverted all his energy and expertise into the disease.'

Doyle nodded. Held up the profile again. 'That's certainly what it says here,' she agreed.

'He became a bit of a crusader,' Poe continued. 'And while I have no doubt he took advantage of his wife's condition to win additional funding, I can't really blame him. The profile says he wasn't a pleasant man to work with, but who would be in that situation? When the newspaper article that destroyed his reputation and career was closely followed by his wife's death, it tipped him over an edge he was already quite close to. Turned him into the nothing-left-to-live-for psychopath he is now. But before he was a serial killer, was he not simply a husband trying to do right by his wife?'

'And if all I had was the information you had, that's the conclusion I'd have drawn too.'

'You said you have information we had no way of knowing?'

Doyle nodded. 'Would it surprise you if I said Frederick Beck never loved his wife?' she said. 'And that, far from being the devastated husband everyone thought he was, he married her *because* she had acquired Breeg–Bart syndrome?'

'No, that's not right at all, Estelle,' Bradshaw said, shaking her head. 'She was diagnosed two years *after* they were married. He didn't start his research until after her diagnosis.'

'It was no coincidence he took a job at that teaching hospital, Tilly,' Doyle said. 'Career-wise, it made no sense – cutting-edge research is carried out in the private, not the public sector. No, he'd already chosen the field he wanted to work in by then, he just didn't tell anyone.'

'What are you saying?' Poe said.

'I'm saying, he took a job at that hospital to find a wife. A wife with a very specific combination of symptoms. Working at the hospital gave him access to the test results of all patients. I think he knew what Breeg–Bart's early indicators were by then, and he chose Melanie because she displayed all the right ones. He never loved her, she was little more than a prop to him. Someone to help frame his story. Who do you think the papers wanted to write about – some stuffy, but effective research going on somewhere, or the brilliant scientist desperately working to save his dying wife?'

'That's cold,' Poe said.

'I'm not saying he didn't grow fond of her,' Doyle said. 'Maybe in the same way a vivisectionist might get attached to a rhesus monkey.'

'How do you know all this?' Poe asked.

'His wife told me,' she said. 'She'd had too much to drink at an event and Frederick had ignored her all night. I think I was a shoulder for her to cry on. She said if things weren't going well in his research, or if he hadn't been successful in a grant application, he would rant and rave at her. On a few occasions, he let slip the true motivation behind their marriage.'

'Do you think Beck knows you know?'

'Possibly. He certainly saw us talking as he stormed over. Whether Melanie said something to him later, I can't say.'

'*This* is why Beck tried to frame Estelle,' Poe said. 'He's obsessed with his public image and he doesn't yet know we've found his Japanese research site. The only threat to the image he's cultivating is the story of how he married his wife because he knew she was going to become ill. In his mind, Estelle's a threat to his celebrity status.'

'So he tried his little bit of misdirection,' Mathers said. 'Tried to lead us away from the real reason he framed her. We could neutralise this by releasing the images we've been sent from Japan. A pre-emptive ruining of his reputation?'

'We should,' Poe agreed. 'While he's still the public's golden boy, he has something to protect. He'll be looking at ways to get to Estelle as we speak.'

'You can't,' Doyle said. 'Other than the information about his marriage, the rest of the profile is accurate. If you ruin him now, he's liable to do anything. And Poe tells me he's adapted a bug fogger into something that can kill dozens of people.'

'She's right,' Mathers said. 'We can't release that information. Which means we need to take Professor Doyle into protective custody. She should be safe now we know his method.'

'Wrong,' Poe said. 'We know one of his methods. But who knows what the lunatic will conjure up next? And to borrow a phrase from my anti-terrorist days: he only has to get lucky once; we have to get lucky every single time.'

'We *can* protect you, Professor Doyle,' Mathers insisted.

'No, you can't,' Poe said. 'But I can.'

Chapter 123

'It's going to be OK, Estelle,' Poe said. 'Tilly's putting Beck's photograph through an age-progression program she's written. It can see past the beard and the specs so she thinks she'll get something usable. Chief Superintendent Mathers will get the likeness out as soon as Tilly has finished. Beck won't have time to worry about you, he'll be too busy hiding.'

'I'm not worried, Poe,' Doyle said.

'You're not?'

'No. You're reckless, but not when it comes to the safety of others.'

Poe indicated and overtook a lorry that was overtaking a slightly slower lorry. One of them was hauling mattresses and he was reminded he hadn't slept for twenty-four hours. He probably shouldn't be driving, but he needed to get Doyle out of London. He wanted home ground advantage during the nationwide manhunt that was about to begin.

'And I know you care about me,' she added softly.

Poe kept his eyes fixed on the road, his hands gripping the steering wheel way harder than he needed to. 'I do,' he said eventually.

The silence was excruciating. Poe turned on the satnav, despite heading north on the M6, a journey he'd made an untold number of times. Where was Bradshaw when you needed her? There'd never been an awkward pause she couldn't make worse with an ill-timed phrase or a too personal question. Right then, he'd have settled for another round of erectile dysfunction.

'Have you been shopping, Poe?' Doyle said at last, throwing a thumb over her shoulder.

Poe glanced in the rear-view mirror. Saw the bags on the back seat. He sighed in relief. Finally there was something noncontroversial to discuss.

'The clothes you're wearing aren't all we bought,' he said. 'We got a load of stuff as we didn't want you having to go home.'

'That was very kind,' she said. She reached back and grabbed a bag. Checked the brand. 'This is an expensive shop, Poe. How much do I owe you?'

'Don't worry about it.'

'There are six more bags back there.'

'I said don't worry about it. I'll claim it all back on expenses.'

She opened the bag on her lap and peered inside. Poe glanced across, tried to gauge her reaction to what Bradshaw had chosen. He hoped it wasn't too weird. Doyle smiled, which he took as a good sign.

She reached into the bag and held up something flimsy. 'Is this what you think I wear, Poe?' she said. 'Red crotchless panties?'

'Bloody hell,' he grumbled.

'Were they all out of edible ones?'

'I just gave Tilly five hundred quid and asked her to buy stuff you might like.'

'This really isn't me at all.'

'I'm sorry,' he mumbled. 'I should have checked.'

'Yes, you should have,' she smiled. 'I only ever wear *black* sex clothes.'

Poe went back to staring at the road.

Chapter 124

'I thought you lived in a tiny shepherd's croft?' Doyle yawned. 'This is a farm, Poe.'

'This isn't where I live. We're here to pick up my secret weapon.'

'Oh?'

'It's time you met Edgar. He's been mixing it up with my neighbour's sheep for a fortnight, so the smell alone will be enough to deter Beck. But if that's not enough, he's such a nosey bastard, the moment someone gets within a mile of Herdwick Croft he barks his head off.'

It was four in the morning and they had driven all night, stopping only for coffee. Poe was dog-tired but he knew he wouldn't sleep any time soon. He was already jittery from the caffeine and was now second-guessing his decision to take Doyle away from the protective shield of the Metropolitan Police.

Herdwick Croft was truly isolated. Surrounded by the rolling Shap Fell, it was like an island. During the day, anyone approaching could be seen for miles and at night it was so quiet Edgar heard everything. But Poe was still only one man, and realistically, how long could they stay there? If Beck went to ground, decided to wait out the rush of public exposure, they could be in hiding indefinitely. Poe knew Doyle well enough to know she wouldn't accept that.

He was still mulling it over when the farmhouse door opened and light spilled across the yard. Victoria Hume's silhouette was framed in the doorway. She was holding two mugs. Before she could gesture them inside, a ball of liver and white fur rushed past her. Edgar was so excited he forgot to breathe in – he simply let out one continuous high-pitched shriek of joy. He almost knocked Poe off his feet as he leaped up to his waist. Poe knelt down and let the spaniel slobber all over his face. Edgar then proceeded to sprint round him in a circle, barking wildly, his tail wagging like a twanged ruler.

'That's quite a greeting, Poe,' Doyle said. 'Aren't you going to introduce me?'

'Of course. Edgar, this is Estelle – she's coming to live with us for a few days.'

The spaniel approached Doyle's outstretched hand cautiously. After a few sniffs he gently licked it. He then span round in a circle again.

'I think he likes you,' Poe said.

They drank tea in Victoria's kitchen while they discussed the logistics of turning Herdwick Croft into a Frederick Beck-proof house. Victoria agreed to bring them provisions every week – she had already topped up the generator and stocked the fridge. She also promised to move as many sheep as she could to his part of the fell. Edgar was a good warning dog, but having to navigate his way through a thousand Herdwick sheep might be enough to make Beck think again if he came for Doyle at night.

'I can lend you a shotgun, if you want?' Victoria offered.

'Thanks, but no,' Poe said. 'I don't have a licence and the last thing I need is Estelle being left on her own because I've been arrested.'

'Fair enough,' she replied. 'But I'll make sure I always have one with me when I'm out and about. If he tries anything up here I'll blow his bloody head off.'

He didn't want to leave his car at the nearby Shap Wells Hotel, in case Beck tampered with it, so Victoria agreed to drive them to his quad bike. He left his BMW at her farm.

Poe sped off over Shap Fell, Doyle sitting behind him, her arms wrapped around his chest. Edgar ran beside them. Two bumpy miles later he pulled up outside his home.

'Welcome to Herdwick Croft,' he said. 'It's not much, but I like it.'

Chapter 125

'Edgar can go in first,' Poe said, unlocking the door. 'If anyone's been in there he'll let us know.'

An excited yap told them it was safe. They followed him inside.

'I'll fire up the wood-burning stove so we have hot water,' he said. 'You'll be able to have a shower soon. There should be clean towels in the bathroom. We'll sort out the sleeping arrangements shortly.'

Doyle didn't respond. She was still taking in the single room that was the entirety of Herdwick Croft's ground floor. Her eyes were wide. Poe had never felt embarrassed about his home, and he wasn't now, but he had hoped Doyle would approve.

'It's the safest place I know,' he said, 'but if you don't like it we can have a rethink after we've had some sleep.'

'Like it?' she smiled. 'It's absolutely perfect, Poe.'

While Doyle showered, Poe fixed breakfast. He couldn't remember the last time he'd had a proper meal. Probably the Vietnamese he and Flynn had shared when they were looking for Henning Stahl. Every meal since then had been taken on the fly. It looked like Victoria had stocked his fridge with a little bit of everything the butcher sold. Cumberland sausage rings, bacon, chicken thighs, diced lamb, black pudding. A couple of Ullswater pies. He reached for some eggs and cracked them into a bowl. Whisked in some milk and a pinch of salt and pepper. As soon as he heard the shower stop he heated up his skillet and added some oil. While the omelette was cooking, he found some cheese and spring onions. By the time he had folded it over, Doyle had joined him downstairs. She was wearing black jeans and one of his Clash T-shirts. It was old and thin and had probably been washed fifty times. Poe thought it looked better on her than it did on him.

'You don't mind, do you?' she asked.

'Not at all,' he replied. 'You feeling better?'

'Much. Your water pressure's insane.'

'It's pumped straight out of the ground. You hungry? I've cooked us an omelette. You don't mind if it's a bit rubbery, do you? I know how to start cooking omelettes, but I never really learned when to stop.'

'Are you asking how I like my eggs in the morning, Poe?'

Poe made a show of checking his watch. 'You're slipping, Estelle. We've been here forty minutes and that's your first double entendre.'

'Sorry.'

'No, it's fine. You're holding up remarkably well.'

'You mean for someone who got out of prison twenty-four hours ago only to find a serial killer is after them?'

'I mean for someone who has just lost her dad,' he said softly. 'While all this was going on, something got lost.'

'And what was that, Poe?'

'You weren't allowed to grieve. It doesn't matter how close you were, he was still your dad. So, I would like it if we could sit down and eat our breakfast and drink our coffee. And afterwards I want you to tell me about him. What type of man he was. Stories he told you about his youth. What it was like to grow up in Highwood.'

'I'm not sure I'm ready yet, Poe.'

'Please, Estelle. For me.'

She tilted her head and pursed her lips. 'What's this about, Poe?'

He mumbled something she didn't catch.

'I missed that,' she said.

'I said, "Your father's dead and it's my fault".'

'Your fault? How on earth is it your fault?'

'If I hadn't kept bringing you all our cases, Beck wouldn't have known we worked together. There'd have been no reason to take you off the board.'

'You're a brilliant detective and I'm a brilliant pathologist and we both live in the north,' she said. 'We were always going to work cases together.'

'But that wasn't the only reason I kept coming to you,' he added quietly. 'I brought cases to you even when I didn't need to. Cases way below your pay grade.'

'And why did you do that?'

Poe didn't answer.

'Poe,' she said, 'why did you keep bringing me cases?'

'Because I like working with you,' he said.

'Oh, you poor man,' she laughed. 'How long have you been worrying about this?'

'Ever since you told us about Beck's wife.'

'Well, if that's the case, I killed my father as well.'

'I don't understand. How did you—?'

'Did it ever occur to you, Poe, that I accepted your cases, the ones you say were below my pay grade, because I like working with *you*?'

'Still, if I'd been a bit more profess—'

'Did you shoot my father, Poe?'

'That doesn't—'

'I don't blame you,' she said. 'And I don't blame me. The *only* person I blame is Frederick Beck. And that's the last I want to hear of you feeling responsible. Are we clear?'

'We are. Thank you, Estelle.'

'That's OK,' she said. 'Now, can we please eat? And after we have, I'll do as you asked and tell you about my father. We didn't always get on – he wanted me to become the lady of the manor and I wanted to study death – but it was never dull.'

Chapter 126

'What do you think, Poe?' Estelle said.

'About what?'

'How privileged my childhood was. I didn't ask to be born into the aristocracy but it would be disingenuous to pretend it didn't help my career. University was guaranteed before exams were sat. Placements at teaching hospitals were agreed with my father's favour in mind. And, while I excel in my field, I'm under no illusion my passion and talent were allowed to flourish only because any obstacles were flattened by my family's perceived influence.'

'You have nothing to apologise for, Estelle,' Poe said. 'And stop underselling yourself. You're like Tilly – you have a once in a generation mind in your field. You'd be the top pathologist in the country regardless of your upbringing.'

Breakfast was over, the omelette was eaten.

Edgar, sensing he had a new mark, had sat by Doyle's feet throughout the meal, staring at her plate like the grifter he was.

'I grew up with gun dogs,' she had told him. 'You think you're the first spaniel to try begging from me?' She had speared the last bit of omelette with her fork, popped it into her mouth and said, 'Yum.'

Edgar had whined and slouched over to Poe. He gave him an egg's worth.

'No wonder I'm always hungry,' he complained.

They had eaten outside. The temperature wasn't much above freezing but the low winter sun washed Shap Fell with a pale light and the view more than made up for the cold. Doyle was hunkered down in one of Poe's old army coats. As promised, Victoria had opened the gates in their shared boundary wall and one of her

387

border collies had nipped at the heels of her flock until they were scattered around Herdwick Croft like snowballs on felt.

Doyle yawned. 'I might have a nap, if that's OK?' she asked.

'Take the bed,' Poe replied. 'I have some phone calls to make and then I'll crash out on the sofa. If Beck is going to come, it'll be during the night.'

Chapter 127

'What's happening?' Poe said the second Flynn answered.

'Tilly's sent you an email.'

'I don't have much of a signal up here. I'll walk to my go-to hot-spot and download everything as soon as we're done.'

'How's Estelle?'

'Asleep.'

'Good,' Flynn said. 'She's been through a lot and I doubt she slept much in prison. Don't forget you need to rest too. Are you sure I can't send a surveillance team up there? They'll be discre— I don't know, Tilly!' Poe smiled as he listened to the muffled discussion in London. 'Tilly wants to know if the clothes you bought Estelle were OK?' she sighed.

'Yes, about that. Please tell her that if she wants a pair of crotch-less knickers in future, she can use her own credit card.'

'Excuse me?'

Poe explained what had happened. Flynn laughed for five whole minutes.

'Yeah, yeah,' he said. 'It's not you who's out five hundred quid. No way can I submit my receipt now. It'll be round the unit within a day. Anyway, what's happening?'

'Tilly's age-progression software produced a likeness she's happy with and Mathers has circulated it. It'll be on the news later but we were too late for this morning's papers.'

'Temple Express Pharmacy?'

'We went there as soon as you'd left. Got the MD out of bed and he let us look at everything. We were right, it was Christopher Goodson.'

'The delivery driver?'

'Yes. The MD was shown the age-progression likeness and he confirmed it. Said he was a model employee. Kept himself to himself. Never socialised outside of work but wasn't so much of a weirdo that his colleagues talked about him.'

'And the address they had for him?'

'As we suspected. False.'

'Mathers is staking out Temple Express Pharmacy?'

'For what it's worth. He's never going back there.'

'That press conference was a bloody disaster,' Poe said. 'Exactly what happens when senior managers get involved in operational decisions.'

'You can't blame her, Poe.'

'I don't blame her – I blame her commander. If he'd held his nerve for one more day we'd have had Beck in custody by now. He'd have turned up for his scheduled shift, right into our arms. Game over.'

'She knows. Her commander knows. There'll be an inquiry after all this and because you'd advised Mathers to hold off, she put it in writing. He overruled her and she has the email to prove it.'

Poe grunted in satisfaction. At least the right person would be held accountable.

'Right, I'm off,' he said. 'I'm going to grab a few hours on the couch this afternoon. Make sure I'm rested before the night shift.'

'I want you checking in every two hours, Poe.'

Chapter 128

Poe woke Doyle around 5 p.m. for something to eat: baked potatoes, lamb chops and some steamed leaves he'd thought were kale but turned out to be spinach. She was gritty-eyed and sleepy when she joined him downstairs, but perked up when he put a bottle of cold beer in her hands.

'I don't have any wine, I'm afraid,' he said.

She clinked his own bottle and said, 'This is exactly what I need.'

They ate quickly and quietly, both of them letting Edgar beg the strip of fat they'd removed from their lamb chops.

'Did you get any sleep, Poe?' Doyle asked.

'Few hours this afternoon,' he replied. 'Enough to stop me falling asleep tonight.'

'You're expecting him to come, aren't you?'

Poe carefully considered the question. 'Actually, I'm not,' he said. 'An accurate likeness of him was on the news earlier and it'll be on the front page of every newspaper tomorrow. He'll hole up somewhere and try to ride it out. I don't doubt he'll try to make time for you at some point, but I don't think it'll get that far.'

'No?'

'I don't think Frederick Beck realises just how famous he's about to become.'

After dinner they walked Edgar, and Poe showed Estelle his land.

'It's only a few acres, so nothing in your father's league,' he said. He realised how tactless that was and immediately apologised.

She waved it off. 'He was the biggest private landowner in the north,' she said. 'I suppose that means I am now.'

Poe brewed tea when they got back to Herdwick Croft and they sipped their drinks, staring into the glowing heart of the wood-burning stove. Something was happening between them but Poe couldn't figure out what. They'd been chatting like the friends they were for an hour or so but the atmosphere had recently changed. Subtly, but enough for Edgar to notice. The spaniel whined. Poe reached down and played with his ears.

Doyle yawned. Poe thought it was forced.

'I think I'll go to bed,' she said, looking directly at him.

'OK,' he said.

'What are you planning to do?'

'Me and furball here will watch the door tonight.'

'Won't you get cold?'

'I'll keep the fire going.'

She sighed and threw her hands in the air in an 'I give up' kind of way. She said, 'See you in the morning then.'

And without another word she left the room.

Edgar looked at the empty stairs then back at Poe. He seemed disappointed in him.

'I know,' he said.

He went back to staring at the door, his eyes shrouded, his face a mask of monstrous calm. Only the clench of his jaw revealing the internal struggle he'd just won.

Chapter 129

It was after midnight when Poe heard Doyle get up, and as no one but him had ever slept in his bed, he misinterpreted the footsteps. He thought she was going to the bathroom, so when she said, 'Poe,' he jumped.

She was standing at the top of the stairs. She was still wearing his old Clash T-shirt, but this time her legs were bare. They were long and pale and toned and Poe was reminded that she fenced in her spare time. He didn't know much about the sport but he imagined when you got to her standard, you had to be fit and supple.

'What's up?' he asked. 'Can't sleep?'

'Come to bed,' she said, her voice smoky. 'I don't want to be alone tonight.'

Poe cleared his throat. Tried not to stare at her. 'I can't, Estelle. You've just been through a traumatic experience. You're grieving. It wouldn't be right.'

'Do I not have agency?' she replied. She was smiling now, sensing his resistance was crumbling. 'Am I not in charge of my own mind?'

'You are.'

'Do you *want* to come to bed?'

'Of course I do.'

'Well get up these bloody stairs then. There'll never be a perfect time, Poe, and life's far too short to worry about every little thing. Let Edgar be our eyes and ears tonight.'

He didn't respond.

'Come on, Washington,' she said. 'Come to bed. We both need this.'

And without a backwards glance, she returned to the bedroom.

Poe stared achingly at the space she'd just left, all his reservations melting away. He looked at Edgar, spread out on the couch next to him, head resting on his paws. The spaniel was watching him.

'You reckon you can handle this shift on your own, buddy?'

Edgar whined and thumped his tail on the cushions. Poe got to his feet.

'OK then,' he said.

Chapter 130

One month later, Chapin-Hag Industries

Predictability killed those people, Frederick Beck thought, as he watched his current target.

Their routines, their passions, their *thirsts*. A meticulous man could study a person and know them more intimately than they knew themselves.

It was how he'd known that Kane Hunt, despite being sent a death threat, would continue to guzzle down his sildenafil. His impotence made him predictable.

And Harrison Cummings, warm in the knowledge that regardless how abhorrent his behaviour, the country would protect him the moment he cried foul. His arrogance had made him feel safe.

And Karen Royal-Cross, monotonously unoriginal in the way she viewed the world. He could have sent her a bottle with 'Deadly Poison' printed on the side and all she'd have done was tweet, 'fake news' before throwing another fat-pill down her flabby gullet.

But people like him saw everything.

The things they wanted everyone to see and the secrets they carried in their deepest pockets. For a meticulous man they were low-hanging fruit. There to be plucked at his pleasure. And yes, he had miscalculated how quickly his method would be uncovered, but that was OK – failure was an essential part of scientific discovery.

So, he would adapt and come back stronger. No warnings this time, just death. Creeping across the country, ruthless, inevitable. The likeness they'd circulated had been a decent representation, but he had planned for exposure. His beard was gone, his eyes now hidden behind coloured contact lenses. His hair was a different colour. Botulinum toxin injections in his forehead and around his eyes made him look ten years younger than the man they hunted.

It had been a month since he had failed to kill Douglas Salt. It was time to start again.

But first someone had to die. A nobody. A piece of life's flotsam. Bill Hershaw was a victim of happenstance rather than design, but unfortunately he stood between him and his current goal. Tonight was a vanity project, an unnecessary risk, but he knew if he didn't scratch the itch, whatever followed would bring him little pleasure.

Bill was a security guard, little more than a nightwatchman. Beck had been watching him for two weeks and his routine hadn't varied. He was *predictable*.

He arrived at work exactly five minutes before his shift began and he left twelve hours ten minutes later, exactly five minutes after his shift had ended. He took a cigarette break every two hours and patrolled the facility every thirty minutes. He ate his meal at midnight – always sandwiches and crisps – and did the *Daily Express* crossword up until then. After that he stuck his nose into a trashy novel – he seemed to like American crime writers – and, other than his patrols and the occasional check of the facility's CCTV monitors, he rarely looked up.

I know everything about you, Bill, Beck thought. I know you were discharged from the army after a back injury and I know you live alone. A sad, flavourless life.

He lived alone, but that was by choice. All great men were alone, really, even when they were married. It was a curse and a blessing. He hadn't enjoyed being married. He resented the time it stole. He had pitied Melanie for the way she looked at him, searching for a sign she was more than just a means to an end. Did he use her? Of course he did. She was *selected*. Not only was she his secret weapon in the cutthroat business of medical research funding, she was also a treasure trove of blood and spinal fluid. No need to get regulatory approval for sample acquisition, not while a living donor slept in his bed.

He never hated her though. She'd had the best life she could have. That's what that pathologist bitch hadn't understood. He'd watched them talking that night. Melanie had known she wasn't supposed to mingle, but there they were at the bar, gossiping like fish wives. Later, back in the hotel room, she'd sworn blind they hadn't been talking about him, but he knew a liar when he saw one.

The pathologist couldn't be allowed to put everything at risk. Couldn't be allowed to ruin his newfound reputation. If Robin Hood had married Maid Marion just to gain a tactical advantage, there would be a different statue outside Nottingham Castle. In hindsight, he should have just killed the pathologist. He had the skills to make it appear natural. He'd wanted her alive, though, knowing she was being punished for interfering with his marriage. That was a wound that would never heal. She would scream her innocence, of course, but it would be too late. She'd be just another rich girl who had killed her daddy. The thought had pleased him. But now she was free and interfering in his plans.

After tonight he would turn his full attention to Estelle Doyle.

Chapter 131

Bill Hershaw went through his post-crisp routine of folding the empty packet in on itself until it was a small triangle. Popped it in the bin under his desk. He had been with Chapin-Hag Industries for four years. Four years sitting in his little booth, eating his stale sandwiches and reading his facile paperbacks. A nothing man doing a nothing job. He wasn't murdering him, Beck thought, he was putting him down.

Bill was a stout man, not fat, but not far off. A heart attack by the time he was fifty, if nature was allowed to run its course. Maybe by the end of the night, if things went as Beck expected them to. Bill had a thick beard and even thicker spectacles. Beck's research had been so thorough he even knew the man's prescription: -4.25 in his left eye, -4.00 in his right. Blind as a bat. He wore a stupid security uniform and never took off his peaked hat, not even when he was having a cigarette.

Beck reckoned the best time would be thirty minutes after Bill had eaten. If he was going to feel tired, it would be then. Six in the morning, before the first employees arrived, would have worked as well, but Beck had less reason to be there at that hour. Thirty minutes after midnight he was just another obsessed scientist returning to the lab to check his research. Bill wouldn't recognise him, of course, but Chapin-Hag Industries had international contracts and professionals visiting out of hours wasn't uncommon. He hadn't been able to get the proper ID card, but he knew enough of the right language to deceive Bill.

And if he couldn't, he would simply wait until he was dead.

Beck approached the front door – basically a glass wall, although it would be stronger than it looked – with the confidence he knew people like Bill fell for. Look as though you have the right to be somewhere and the chances were no one would stop you.

Bill looked up from his novel and watched him approach. He got to his feet and met him at the door. He pressed the intercom and said, 'Can I help you, sir?'

'I hope so,' Beck said. 'I was in earlier today working on the AS9 protein breakthrough and I need to recheck some numbers. Make sure the board's report is accurate in the morning.'

'It's very late, sir.'

'I prefer to think of it as very early.'

Bill didn't respond. Maybe he wasn't as dumb as he looked.

'Science never sleeps' – Beck made a show of leaning in to read Bill's name badge – 'Bill. And, as you know, this protein has got us all very excited. We'd previously assumed AS9 was only carried in inheriting patients, but this breakthrough proves that, just because it isn't forming disruptive clumps in the motor neurone cells of *non*-inheriting patients, it doesn't mean it isn't being disruptive.'

And that's how you baffle an idiot.

'Do you have identification, sir?'

'I'm on the oversight committee,' Beck replied. 'We don't carry formal ID, but you're welcome to see my driving licence.'

'I'm supposed to see something official, sir.'

The idiot still wasn't budging.

'Fine,' Beck sighed, faking a frown. 'The chairman knows I'm coming in. Please call him. He can verify me.'

'It's almost one a.m., sir. I don't think I should be waking the chairman.'

'That's your call, Bill, but I need to check those numbers.'

Bill's brow furrowed as he grappled with his predicament. After a few moments he buzzed him in, as Beck had known he would. Exceptionally replaceable people were terrified of coming to the attention of people who could dismiss them like an annoying waiter.

'You'll have to sign in, sir.'

'Of course. What is it you're reading?'

'Excuse me, sir?'

'You were reading a novel,' Beck said. 'I thought I recognised the cover.'

'*A Private Cathedral.* It's by James Lee Burke.'

'Ah, yes. One of the Dave Robicheaux novels. Great book.'

'You've read it, sir?'

'I have.'

He hadn't. He'd simply made a note of what Bill was reading the night before, assuming he would still be reading it tonight. He then went on to a popular crime-fiction review e-zine and read an in-depth review. It was details like this that made him stand out from the crowd. Why he would never be caught.

He was far too meticulous.

He followed Bill to his workstation and wrote the name on his fake driving licence into the signing-in log. He then reached into his pocket and pulled out an exquisite-looking box.

'Can I offer you a piece of *torrone*, Bill?' he said, opening the lid. 'It's made from honey and sugar and egg whites and I import it from Italy.' He paused then added, 'It's sweet enough to stop your heart.'

Bill took a small piece and nodded his thanks. He put it on top of his James Lee Burke novel. A light dusting of icing sugar settled beside it.

'I'll enjoy that, sir. I'll have it after my cigarette break.'

'Thanks for your help, Bill.'

'Do you know where you're going, sir?'

'Any desktop will do,' he said. 'Everything's in the cloud.'

'OK, sir. I'll see you soon.'

No you won't, Beck thought. The atropine in the *torrone* will soon be in your bloodstream. By the time I'm ready to leave you'll be dead.

He threw a wave over his shoulder and made his way into the guts of the facility. He'd never been there before but knew the server room would be on the ground floor and near the centre. A room with no windows and a high ceiling. It wouldn't be hard to find. Chapin-Hag Industries was a small fish in a large pond with a business model of selling minor breakthroughs to major pharmaceutical companies. One or two a decade made it viable.

According to the papers Beck had read, they had stumbled upon the AS9 protein breakthrough by accident. It was clear they hadn't understood its significance.

But he had.

Chapin-Hag Industries thought they had published an interesting fact about an uninteresting protein. But what they didn't know, what they *couldn't* have known, was that the AS9 protein was the key to unlocking the molecular biology of acquired Breeg–Bart syndrome. It wasn't the silver bullet he'd spent his professional life searching for, but it was the blueprint to building one.

Beck planned to download their research and write a paper on its potential applications. He would publish it under his own name. Although he could never re-enter his previous world, he would still be lauded for the breakthrough. And he didn't consider it stealing. If someone didn't understand the value of something, it was the duty of people who did to take it from them.

He found the server room and sat in front of a monitor. He jiggled the mouse and the screen flickered into life. Instead of the login screen he had expected to see – and had a plan for – it opened directly on a desktop. They hadn't even *tried* to protect their research. He found the correct folder, inserted a memory stick into a USB port and dragged the folder across to begin the download. The progress bar indicated it would take less than a minute. He drummed his fingers on the keyboard and idly wondered if Bill was dead yet.

A small 'ting' told him the folder had been safely downloaded. He highlighted the file on his memory stick, right clicked and selected open. He wanted a quick look at what was now his.

He frowned.

The folder didn't make sense. Instead of an index of files and subfolders, neatly organised into projects and listed chronologically, there was just a single Word document. Maybe it was the summary of the research. He must have missed the main folder somehow. He opened the Word document and read it.

It didn't take long.

Look Behind You

'What the heck?' Beck said.

The server room door opened. Light from the corridor spilled in like stage lamps. Bill was backlit in the doorframe. He leaned against it.

'I'm not finished yet!' Beck snapped.

Bill said nothing.

'I'm sorry, Bill,' he continued, 'but I'm going to have to ask you to leave. What I'm doing is confidential and you can't be in here.'

But Bill made no attempt to move. He just carried on leaning against the doorframe, calmly watching him through those jam-jar glasses. Something was wrong. A feeling of dread crept over Beck, like someone had scraped an icicle down his spine.

'Bill, if you want to keep your job, you're going about it entirely . . .'

His sentence crumpled to nothing as Bill took off his peaked cap and removed his glasses.

'My name's Washington Poe, Frederick,' he said, rubbing his eyes. 'I think we may have spoken on the phone.'

Chapter 132

One month earlier

'OK then,' Poe said.

He glanced at the empty stairs. Nervous about walking up them. Other than his friendships with Bradshaw, Flynn and Victoria, he kept people at arm's length. Didn't allow anyone to get too close. He had cultivated a solitary existence, which, while occasionally lonely, was refreshingly uncomplicated. But then Bradshaw had entered his life. Shook it up, as he had hers. The roadblock he had erected was no match for her guileless innocence and unquestioning loyalty. She showed him there was another way to live. That having friends was OK. That relying on others was OK. That being *happy* was OK.

And now Estelle Doyle was upstairs, waiting. A beautiful woman, a *brilliant* woman. A woman he liked. A woman who seemed to like him.

Perhaps it was OK to climb the stairs. See what happened afterwards.

'OK then,' he said again.

He paused halfway and turned back to Edgar.

'If you hear something, you have my permission to go bloody nuts, mate.'

Edgar whined and thumped his tail on the sofa.

Poe reached the top of the stairs and knocked on the door.

'It's your bedroom, Poe,' Doyle said. Her voice was soft, as if she understood what it had taken for him to get this far. 'You don't need to knock.'

He paused a beat then stepped inside.

'Hello,' he said.

'Hello.'

'I doubt Beck will try anything tonight, but if he does I have a cast-iron skillet downstairs. Bash him over the head with that and it's game over.'

He knew he was babbling.

'Poe?' Doyle said, smiling.

'Yes?'

'Shut up.'

Chapter 133

Poe crept up the stairs with two mugs of coffee. He had woken earlier than usual so had let Edgar out for a run while Doyle slept. He nudged open the bedroom door with his hip. She was already sitting up. Her phone was in her hand and he heard the 'whoosh' as she sent a text.

He raised his eyebrows.

'Just informing Tilly she doesn't have to worry about erectile dysfunction,' she said.

Poe's jaw dropped.

'Relax, Poe,' she laughed. 'I was letting my director know I'm out of prison and I'm doing OK.'

'And are you?'

'Am I what?'

'Doing OK?'

She reached across the bed to take one of the mugs. The duvet slipped from her shoulder. She made no attempt to cover herself.

'I think you know the answer to that,' she said, taking a sip of coffee and wincing at the heat. She patted the bed beside her. 'Get in. We have things to talk about.'

'We do?'

'We do. But we'll finish our drinks first.'

'They're very hot.'

'They are, aren't they? Probably be twenty minutes before they're cool enough to drink. Whatever can we do to fill the time?'

This time it was Poe's turn to grin.

There was no awkwardness afterwards. No stumbling. It felt right and Poe thought that might be because it was right. Maybe Doyle had had this planned for a while, maybe she hadn't. Poe didn't care. He recognised he'd wanted it for a long time.

'You said we had things to talk about,' he said.

'We do.' She drained her mug and put it on the bedside table. 'I want to know what your plan is?'

'My plan?'

'Yes, Poe. Your plan.'

'Er ... I'm not sure. I didn't want to be presumptuous, but I thought it might be nice to wander into the village for some breakfast. Stretch our legs a bit.'

'I'm not talking about us, you silly man,' she laughed. 'I want to know what you plan to do about Frederick Beck. You're proactive, Poe, not reactive. You won't sit around waiting.'

'Maybe I've never had anyone to wait with before.'

The nape of her neck flushed. She smiled. 'Still,' she said. 'I think we need to let Poe be Poe.'

'You've given this some thought?'

'Of course.'

'And?'

She reached out and stroked his chin. Gently turned his face so they were looking at each other. 'How quickly can you grow a beard?' she asked.

Chapter 134

A month and ten minutes later

'My name's Washington Poe, Frederick,' Poe said, rubbing his eyes. 'I think we may have spoken on the phone.'

Beck stared, horrified. 'So it *was* a trap,' he said.

'I'm afraid so.'

'Then it seems I underestimated you. I thought the protein breakthrough seemed a little too convenient, but none of my background checks raised any flags.'

'This was a team effort.'

Beck sighed. 'Do you know how much a human body is worth, Sergeant Poe?' he asked. 'Not a human *life*, I'm talking about the physical body. Specifically, the combined value of the elemental components that make up the most advanced organism in the history of the universe. The oxygen, the carbon, the hydrogen and the nitrogen. The iron and the zinc. The trace amounts of gold, uranium and radium we all have inside us.'

'I have no idea,' Poe said.

'One hundred and twenty-two pounds, depending on how the futures markets are trading.'

'Fascinating.'

'I only mention this in case you thought a person like me, a person who knows exactly how much a human *tooth* is worth, wouldn't have a contingency for this exact type of situation?'

'You have no more cards left to play, Frederick,' Poe said. 'The facility is surrounded. Even if you somehow get past me, you won't get past the armed cops outside. Not without taking a few to the torso. By the way, how much value would bullets add to the human body?'

407

Beck didn't answer. Instead he reached into his coat pocket and removed a red aerosol can. 'I assume you know what this is?' he said. 'I left the blueprints for you to find.'

'It's a repurposed, total-release bug fogger. You press the nozzle and whatever you've put in there is released in one continuous blast.'

'And you thought I didn't have any cards left to play. Because from what I can see, I'm holding all the aces.'

'What do you want, Frederick?'

'I want to know how you managed to get me into this room.'

'And then you'll put down the aerosol can?'

'I will.'

Chapter 135

One month earlier

'How quickly can you grow a beard?' Doyle asked.

'A beard?' Poe said.

She nodded. 'You won't catch Frederick Beck by trying to get ahead of him. He's been planning this for years and he's very intelligent.'

'So how *do* we catch him?'

'His ego,' she said. 'We use it against him.'

Poe sat up. 'What do you have in mind?'

'We have a narrow window of opportunity. At the minute, Frederick's regrouping. We've lifted the shroud, shown the world his trick. He'll be planning how he can recapture the public's imagination. That means we have a month, maybe six weeks where he'll be focusing on far too many things at once.'

Poe nodded. Doyle was right. Beck was currently being pushed in a multitude of directions. His bandwidth had to be stretched to the limit right now. Evading an international manhunt. Planning a new campaign while simultaneously trying to keep the public engaged. Wondering how he could keep the truth about his marriage a secret now that Doyle was out of prison. And Henning Stahl had to fit into his plans somehow. Poe hadn't figured out how yet, but Beck had picked him for a reason.

'You want to give him something else to worry about, don't you?' he asked.

'It was something Tilly said that gave me the idea,' Doyle admitted. 'She told me about the time you pressed a load of random buttons on her laptop. Overloaded the CPU and crashed it.'

'I keep telling people, it only happened once and it was a really old computer.'

'She says she couldn't have replicated what you did, not even in lab conditions.'

Poe cleared his throat and checked his watch. 'You said we only have a month?'

'Sorry,' she laughed.

'Tell me what you want to crash his mind with?'

'What's the most important thing to Frederick Beck?'

'Being the centre of attention,' he said without hesitation. 'His career wasn't about developing the best medicines; it was about his status. And I doubt he cared about the things his victims had done, he just wanted the public to adore him. His campaign of murder was about recapturing what he lost when his career was taken from him.'

'So, what's the one thing that could bring him out of wherever he's holed up?'

'I don't know. Revenge, maybe. I go on TV and call him out.'

'Not revenge. Revenge can wait. This would have to be something time sensitive.'

Poe gave it a couple of minutes, but he couldn't think of anything sensible. 'Other than there being a major breakthrough in acquired Breeg–Bart syndrome,' he said, 'it's hard to imagine what else he'd care enough about to press the pause button.'

Doyle stared at him, her eyes twinkling.

'You've got to be kidding,' he said.

'I'm not,' she replied. 'All we have to do is solve the Breeg–Bart riddle and let his ego take care of the rest.'

Chapter 136

'Very clever,' Beck said after Poe had finished.

'We couldn't make a major announcement, obviously,' Poe said. 'If we went too big you'd have smelled a rat. It had to be something subtle, something only a handful of scientists would understand.'

'So you invented something about the AS9 protein?'

'Professor Doyle knew you'd always considered the scientific community wrong in their assumption about disruption in non-inheriting patients.'

'Did you understand any of what you've just said, Sergeant Poe?'

'I don't need to. I work with people who do.'

'It was Professor Doyle who put the article together?'

'She wrote it in such a way that it supported your hypothesis, but made it look like Chapin-Hag Industries didn't really understand what they'd stumbled upon.'

'What about the peer review process?' Beck asked. 'Articles like this aren't published in medical journals without going through a rigorous process.'

'Yeah, we thought that would convince you,' Poe said. 'And that bit was easy. All we did was ask them nicely. Said we were setting a trap.'

Or that's what we will be saying, Poe thought. Bradshaw had planted the article in a couple of minor medical journals after she had sneaked into their systems. After the editorial process, but before the magazines went to the printers. She had offered to do the same in the major journals, but Doyle had said lower profile magazines were more convincing. They would fit better with what they were trying to achieve – a small lab that had failed to grasp the significance of its discovery.

'What about this place?' Beck said. 'Did you ask them nicely too?'

'Professor Doyle knows the owner. They used to work together and she asked if we could use their premises out of hours.'

'And Bill Hershaw?'

'One of my colleague's legends,' Poe said. 'She keeps a dozen or so running at any one time. They have social media profiles, work and medical histories, addresses and credit cards. Enough for her to build a convincing identity in a day or two. She fixed it so Bill had worked at Chapin-Hag Industries for four years. A day before the articles appeared in the journals, me and my beard and my thick glasses and my silly peaked cap started doing the nightshift here.'

'I imagine you think you've won, Sergeant Poe?'

'This isn't a fucking game,' Poe snapped. 'People have died.'

'Bad people.'

'And good people.'

'Professor Doyle's father? A necessary sacrifice, I'm afraid, but the cost of human advancement has always been paid in blood. Did you know that the best anatomical drawings in the world are found in the *Pernkopf Atlas*? It's still used by surgeons today and it was written by a Nazi doctor. He dissected the corpses of executed prisoners and teams of artists created the images.'

'I don't care about any of that,' Poe said. 'It's time to go. You'll get your day in court soon enough. Although, a word of advice, Freddie; when you do, don't compare yourself to a Nazi in front of a jury – we still don't like them in this country.'

'Are you ready to start negotiating?'

'I'm not negotiating, Frederick.'

'Of course you are,' Beck said. He waggled the repurposed bug fogger to remind Poe what he was holding. 'I want a vehicle, and until I feel safe you're staying by my side.' With his spare hand he reached into his pocket and pulled out a pair of plasticuffs. The loops were already prepared. He threw them on the floor. 'Please put these on, Sergeant Poe.'

'I won't be doing that.'

'No?'

Beck put his thumb over the nozzle. Looked Poe in the eye and said, 'How about now?'

'Feel free,' Poe said.

'Excuse me?'

'You heard me.'

'Do you know what this is?'

'Your blueprints were very clear.'

'So, you know if I press the nozzle the can's contents will empty in seconds. I won't be able to stop it. This isn't a bell that can be un-rung.'

'Will you quit your yapping then and press the bloody thing,' Poe said.

Chapter 137

'What about his bug fogger?' Poe said. 'The one with the aerosolised ricin? As soon as he's cornered he'll use it to force his way out.'

'It'll be empty,' Doyle replied.

'Empty? Why would it be empty?'

'I've seen the blueprint, Poe. It's pure bluff.'

'He hasn't bluffed so far.'

'He is with this.'

'You think he's scared of dying?'

'Almost certainly, but that's not why it'll be empty. That bug fogger is jerry-built. The way he had to drill holes and reseal them. The way the single-use nozzle is being used a second time. None of that makes for a safe device. He couldn't carry it in a bag or put it in a pocket. One sharp bump and "poof", he's the next Darwin Awards winner.'

Poe laughed. Bradshaw had bought him a Darwin Awards book for his birthday. It was packed with tales of people who had died doing something stupid. His favourite was the terrorist who didn't put enough stamps on his letter bomb. It was returned to sender and the would-be bomber was so excited about receiving mail, he opened it.

'If I call his bluff and it's fully loaded, it'll be me who wins the next Darwin Award,' he said.

'Trust me. It'll be empty.'

Chapter 138

'Don't test me, Sergeant Poe!' Beck snapped. His thumb put pressure on the nozzle.

'Wait,' Poe said.

Beck smiled.

Poe pulled his phone from his pocket and held it so Beck could see. 'Hi, Estelle,' he said.

'Are you almost done, Poe?' Doyle said through the speakerphone, her voice tinny and distant.

'Nearly finished.'

'Good. Your beard's giving me a rash.'

'You've heard what Freddie had to say?'

'I did.'

'He's pretty convincing.'

'It's a bluff.'

'It is *not* a bluff!' Beck yelled, spittle forming at the side of his mouth. 'And turn that phone off!'

'One moment please, Freddie,' Poe said. 'Just how sure are you, Estelle?'

She paused, but not for long. 'Sure enough to bet the life of the man I love.'

'I'm warning you, turn that—'

'Shut up!' Poe snapped. 'This is important.' Then to Doyle, 'You do?'

'For a while now.'

'Who else knows?'

'Tilly worked it out. I think she might have told Stephanie.'

'Blimey.'

'Let's not make a big deal out of this. I'm not Kristin Scott

Thomas, you're not Hugh Grant and this isn't *Four Weddings and a Funeral*. If you don't feel the same way we'll find a way through—'

'I do,' he said.

'Do what?'

'Feel the same way.'

Other than his dad, Poe didn't think he'd ever told someone he loved them, and he wasn't about to start now, not in front of the man who had murdered her father.

'That's good then,' she said. Poe thought he heard a sigh of relief. 'We should probably talk about this.'

'Later, I promise,' he said. 'I have a man standing in front of me pretending to hold a weapon of mass destruction.'

'Don't be long.'

Poe slipped the phone back into his pocket. Left it on so she'd know he was OK.

Beck sneered.

'That was lovely,' he said. 'Really nice. Such a shame you'll never see her again.'

'That aerosol can is empty, Frederick.' Poe removed a pair of handcuffs from his pocket. Real ones, not the plastic ones Beck had thrown him. 'Please, hand it over so I can put these on you.'

'I still have my—'

'And don't say you still have the gun you used to kill Estelle's father, because we both know you haven't. People like you don't walk around with a gun. It's in a drain in Northumberland some-where.' Poe took a step forward. 'If you don't pass me that aerosol can, Freddie, I'm taking it from you and I'm warning you, I won't be gentle.'

Beck took one look and realised Poe wasn't kidding. He offered the aerosol on the palm of his hand, the same way you might offer a horse a sugar lump. Poe took it and put it on the table. He then cuffed Beck to the rear and emptied his pockets. Mathers's team would bag it all for evidence when they came in.

'Come on,' Poe said. 'Time for you to meet some of my col-leagues. It's toilet wine for you from now on, I'm afraid.'

Poe walked Beck out of the facility. Mathers met them at the door and took custody of Beck. She led him to a waiting police van. Before he could be put inside, he turned and shouted, 'I'm immortal now, Sergeant Poe.'

'Maybe, Frederick,' he replied. 'Unless, of course, we happen to discover you conducted human experiments to prepare for all this. Oh, by the way, some officers from the Japanese National Police Agency are flying over to see you. They want to discuss some dead Han Chinese. I wonder how this'll play with your adoring public?'

'Bastard!' Beck screamed before being bundled into the van.

Mathers walked over to Poe. She slapped him on the back then shook his hand. They watched Beck leave in a convoy of flashing blue.

'I can't believe that actually worked,' she said.

'You need me to make a statement?'

'It can wait, Poe. There's a lady waiting over there for you. She mentioned something about *Four Weddings and a Funeral* earlier. I didn't understand the reference, but it seems you did?'

Poe glanced across. Doyle was in the back of an unmarked car. Bradshaw was sitting beside her. Henning Stahl and Flynn were in the front. They were all looking his way. Bradshaw flashed a smile and a thumbs-up. Flynn winked. Henning Stahl was making notes. Doyle looked the same way he felt – nervous.

'You were listening?' he said.

'The server room was wired,' Mathers said. 'It was the one thing I insisted on when DI Flynn brought this to me. We didn't tell you as we wanted it to seem natural.'

'I'm glad you trusted us.'

'I thought it was insane,' Mathers said.

'Then why—?'

'Because sometimes insane is what it takes.'

They shook hands again and said their goodbyes. Poe walked over to the waiting car.

'Oh and, Poe?' Mathers called out.

He turned. 'Ma'am?'

'Don't mess this up.'

He smiled. 'I won't,' he said.

Chapter 139

Nine months later

The song penetrated Poe's dreams. It was all drums and bass and a woman singing about milkshakes. Nothing like the stuff he usually listened to. Where were the guitars, the screeching riffs, the mad lyrics?

A nudge to the ribs jerked him awake. Doyle was watching him in amusement.

'That's a wildly cheerful ringtone.'

'What?' he said, sitting up. He reached behind and pummelled the pillow. Leaned back against it.

'Your phone; it was ringing.'

'Oh, that's what that was. I thought I'd woken up in South Central LA.'

'Harlem.'

'Excuse me?'

'Kelis is from Harlem, I think, not Los Angeles.'

'Who?'

'The singer.'

'Oh,' he said. 'Tilly installed it for me. She said she was sick of hearing the default ringtone.'

'And that's what you chose?'

'No, I said she could put on whatever she wanted as long as it wasn't annoying.'

Doyle raised her eyebrows.

'I don't know how to change it,' he admitted. 'How long have I been asleep?'

'Not long.'

'What time is it?'

'Just after eleven.'

'Who the hell's ringing at this hour?'

They looked at each other.

'Tilly,' they said together.

'Are you going to call her back?' Doyle asked.

'I'm comfy,' he replied, snuggling down into the bed. It was huge, far bigger than the bed at Herdwick Croft. Everything in Highwood was huge. Like it had been built to a slightly different scale. All old stuff, but made to last. The rich stayed rich as they never had to buy anything, it seemed. He had voiced this to Doyle once and she'd reminded him that his father owned a property portfolio worth well over a million pounds.

They split their time between Highwood and Herdwick Croft. When he wasn't on a case, Poe could work anywhere, so they tended to go by Doyle's diary. If she was performing post-mortems or was working at her lab, they stayed at Highwood. If she was teaching, they preferred Herdwick Croft. They had fallen into an easy routine. When they were at Poe's they explored Cumbria and enjoyed Shap Fell. When they were in Northumberland they usually stayed in or went for a drink in Corbridge. The relationship was new and they were still feeling their way, but so far it had been everything Poe had hoped it might be.

'Call Tilly back, Poe,' Doyle said. 'You know she'll worry if you don't.'

Sure enough, his phone began ringing again. Edgar barked. Poe had no idea where he was. The spaniel, who'd grown up with only two rooms, now had a massive house to explore. He slept in a different room each night, but always slunk back into their bedroom during the early hours. He liked nestling in between them. Poe had taken to calling him a contraceptive.

He reached for his phone and pressed the accept call button.

'Hello, Poe,' Bradshaw said. 'It's Tilly.'

'I know it's you, Tilly. A photo of you appears on my screen and it says "Tilly" above it. Also, you're the only person who rings me.'

'Are you still going tomorrow night?'

'Unfortunately.'

'Don't be such a grouse. Henning Stahl is our friend and he is doing an event to promote his book. I am picking up DI Flynn at nine a.m. and we should be at Estelle's ancestral home by mid-afternoon. Henning Stahl wants to take us out for a meal after-wards. He has to go on to Edinburgh but we're staying the night.'

'You bringing sleeping bags?'

'Poe . . .' Doyle warned. 'Don't tease her. You know she'll go out and buy one.'

'Estelle says you need a tent as well.'

Bradshaw giggled. 'Unfortunately for you, buster, Estelle and I still have regular correspondence. I know you've got beds ready for us.'

'You bringing anything to eat?'

'No. DI Flynn says I am never allowed to buy food again. She says I ruined the Spring-heeled Jack stakeout.'

'*You* ruined it? I drank her breast milk.'

'Did you get the book Henning Stahl sent?'

Poe glanced at his bedside table. Stahl's book sat on it, unopened. 'I did.'

'Are you going to read it?'

'Wasn't planning to.'

'But what if he asks you about it?'

Poe looked at the book again. 'Fine,' he sighed. 'I'll skim through it tonight.'

After Bradshaw rang off, Poe picked up the book. 'What's it like?' he asked Doyle.

Stahl had sent two signed and dedicated hardbacks to Highwood. Doyle had almost finished hers.

'Surprisingly well written,' she replied. 'Bit sensationalist, and some of the science has been dumbed down. And from what you told me, he massively downplays the mess he was in when you first approached him.'

'There was a dead cat in his kitchen. Is that in?'

Poe grabbed his reading glasses and turned to Stahl's photo on the inside jacket.

'He's looking well, isn't he?' Doyle said.

'He is. Although I imagine multiple six-figure book deals, movie rights and talk of major book awards are helping him keep off the booze.'

'He still takes Antabuse.'

'You've spoken to him?'

'It's in here. Page one hundred and forty. Says he'll be on it for the rest of his life.'

Poe turned the book over. The cover was sober and understated, just a scientific drawing of a flower petal and the title.

The Nightmares You Deserve: Hunting the Botanist by Henning Stahl.

'I can't believe he used that,' Poe grumbled. 'It was just something stupid I said.'

He flicked to the index, ran his fingers down it until he got to the 'P's, hoping he'd got away with it.

Fat chance.

Poe, Washington (detective sergeant, National Crime Agency) 5–19,
    23, 45, 67, 78–83, 101, 105, 139, 145, 157–8, 198, 204, 237, 256,
    283–5, 301, 329, 385, 390–8, 402, 404, 408, 410–13
       clothes shopping 25
       death of Karen Royal-Cross 185
       erectile dysfunction 357
       evidence at trial 400
       Moroccan goat 302
       reaction to guilty verdict 414
       role in Chance's Park 234
       tabloid headlines 217
       the 'sting' 386

'Bloody hell,' he said, showing Doyle the index page. 'Have you seen this?'

'I have. Page 357 is particularly funny.'

'Are you in it?'

'I am.'

'Why aren't you cross?'

'My father's murder was handled sensitively and, at the end of the day, it's good exposure for the lab.'

'You're such a capitalist,' he said.

She winked at him.

Poe threw down the book in disgust. Perhaps it was because the pages were glossy, rather than uncoated, but it flipped open to the photograph section in the middle.

'I'll look at the pictures,' he said. 'If he asks, I'll tell him I haven't had time to read it properly.'

'I have some felt tips in my old bedroom if you want to draw a moustache on his face.'

Poe didn't answer.

'What's up?' she asked.

'You got that magnifying glass handy? The one we used when we did that jigsaw. The one where each piece was a tiny picture, but they all blended together to form the *Mona Lisa*.'

'The photomosaic? I think so. Why?'

But Poe had gone back to staring at one of the photographs. Doyle got out of bed and found the magnifying glass. She passed it to him and he took it without a word. He focused on the photograph of Frederick Beck's flat, the one with the scientific equipment.

Eventually he looked up from the book.

'I'm sorry, Estelle,' he said. 'Tonight's a work night.'

Chapter 140

Forum Books was located in a former Methodist chapel in Corbridge. A carefully renovated Grade II listed building, its character and heritage remained intact, inside and out. Poe had visited the shop many times recently, enjoying the quirky interior, the hand-painted signs on the walls, the bookshelves made from former church pews.

Henning Stahl's event was coming to an end. The bookshop owner had told Poe that author evenings followed a standard format: a reading, a curated discussion facilitated by a member of staff, then questions from the audience.

Poe, Doyle and Bradshaw were seated in the middle of an audience of around fifty. Stahl and the member of staff were on the pulpit that doubled as a reading nook and, on nights like this, a speaking platform.

'I think we have a bit of time for questions from the floor,' the staff member said. 'Is there anything I haven't covered?'

'Don't be shy,' Stahl added. 'I won't bite.'

Polite laughter rippled through the audience. Before long, Stahl was answering questions about how scared he'd been at Chance's Park, what it was like to be in with a chance of being a prize-winning author, what his future plans were.

'To have a rest,' he replied to the last one.

The member of staff checked her watch then said, 'I think that's all we have time for, so, unless there are any further questions, I think we'll wrap this up now. Henning has kindly agreed to stay behind and sign books, so if you have anything burning you want to ask him, you still have a chance.'

Poe raised his hand. 'I have a question,' he said.

'Hi, Poe,' Stahl said. 'Tilly and Estelle still keeping you on your toes, I see?'

'They're doing their best, Henning.'

'I thought Stephanie was coming?'

'She sends her apologies,' Poe said. 'Has something on that couldn't wait.'

'You have a question?'

'I do,' Poe said. 'It's about the photograph on page two hundred and sixteen.'

Stahl opened the book he had used for his reading and found the right page.

'I've got it,' he said.

'This is the photograph you took on your phone. The one taken before CSI processed the flats in north London. You were allowed to take one, then we emailed it to Tilly. Chief Superintendent Mathers then had someone delete it from your phone. Tilly emailed it back to you after the court case had finished.'

'That's right. And this demonstrates why this case was such a team effort. Everyone pulled together from day one. It's my name on the front cover, but really, this book belongs to us all.'

'You haven't asked a question, Sergeant Poe,' the staff member said.

'Haven't I?' Poe said. 'I do apologise. My question is this, Henning: why is there a dehydrator in this photograph?'

'I'm not sure I understand.'

'If you look on the table in the foreground, you can clearly see a grey dehydrator. It looks like one of those new deep fat fryers.'

Stahl frowned. 'It's what Frederick Beck used to dry out the flower petals,' he said. 'I assumed you knew that. I mention it a few pages later, I think. I thought we'd discussed why Beck had used something so high-tech when a flower press would have worked equally as well. Perhaps I'm mistaken. Maybe I mentioned it to someone else.'

'You misunderstand me, Henning,' Poe said. 'I'm not asking what it was for, I'm asking why it's in your picture.'

'I'm not following you.'

'No? Well, see if you can follow this. Before you were allowed up to take a photograph of the crime scene, Detective Chief Superintendent Mathers and I removed this dehydrator from the flat. We wanted to keep something back to weed out the cranks and we chose that. As you say, a flower press could have been guessed at, a dehydrator, not so much.'

'I'm not sure—'

'When you took your photograph, the dehydrator was in the back of a CSI van,' Poe said. 'The photograph on page two hundred and sixteen was taken before we arrived. You'd been in Beck's flats before. Probably that night you returned to Douglas Salt's house in a taxi.'

Stahl said nothing.

'And, based on this, Chief Superintendent Mathers was last night able to get a warrant to search your house.'

Stahl scrambled to his feet.

'Don't bother, Henning; it was executed this morning.'

Stahl sat down, defeated.

'And what Chief Superintendent Mathers found was very interesting,' Poe continued. 'Lots of photographs you shouldn't have had. A memory stick full of information you had no way of knowing. Drawings, plans, additional insight into Beck's victims.'

A noise at the back of the bookshop caused Poe to turn. It was Flynn, DCI Tai-young Lee and a bunch of uniformed cops. Poe winked at them then turned back to Stahl.

'Here's what I think happened, Henning,' he said. 'Beck chose you because, not only were you morally bankrupt, you'd also played a major part in his downfall.'

'I told you, I had very little to do with that story!'

'But that's not true, is it? You weren't on background research at all, you were actually the lead investigator. The only reason it wasn't your name on the story was the phone-hacking scandal had just cracked and the paper were limiting your exposure.'

'So what?' Stahl shrugged. 'I downplayed my role in the story. I was downplaying my role in everything by then.'

'You were,' Poe agreed. 'But then we come to Chance's Park.

Two things have never been explained from that day: what you and Beck discussed when his radio frequency jammer destroyed our comms, and why none of the park runners saw a man in a mask.'

'You have a theory, I take it?' Stahl said.

'Of course. I think no one saw a man in a mask because Beck wasn't wearing one. When he sat opposite you he was wearing a hat but you could see his face clearly. And you recognised him. I have no doubt you expressed surprise, but we couldn't hear it as our comms were down. I think it was then that Beck made you an offer. Report his story the way he wanted it, and get a scoop like no journalist in history. You wouldn't just be inside the police investigation, you would be inside the campaign of a serial killer as well. He told you where his flat was and what you would find there. An unfiltered crime scene for you to write about and a memory stick full of information you could use. A book for you, a legacy for him – a win–win for you both. So, you took your photograph, which included the dehydrator, not realising we would be removing it before we let you up a few days later. We thought it was the first time you had been there, but it was actually the second.'

'But it was me who found Beck's name on the lists of people who'd purchased acetone,' Stahl said.

'A cynical man might suggest you knew what you were looking for,' Poe said. 'That you needed to push the investigation along. I imagine it's what Beck wanted too.'

Stahl glowered at him.

'It'll be weeks before the true impact of your collusion is known, Henning,' Poe continued, 'but I know this: if you'd told us who Beck was the moment you got out of Chance's Park, instead of reverting to type and keeping the story to yourself, we might have been able to catch him sooner than we did.'

'You don't know that,' Stahl said.

'No, I don't. But neither do you.'

DCI Lee and a uniformed sergeant approached the pulpit. Stahl was read his rights and handcuffed. The sergeant led him through the astonished crowd.

Before they reached the exit, Poe called out, 'Oh, Henning,

Douglas Salt had a life-altering operation and he's now looking for someone to blame. I'd keep hold of all the money you got from those book deals, if I were you. He'll soon be coming for everything you have.'

Stahl struggled against the cuffs but the sergeant was big and burly and he didn't budge an inch.

Stahl spat on the floor. 'This isn't over, Poe!'

'Goodbye, Henning,' Poe replied.

After the bookshop had emptied and Poe had finished with Lee, Bradshaw said, 'What now, Poe?'

'I don't know about you, Tilly,' he said, 'but I could use a drink. There's a microbrewery opposite the bookshop and I'm buying. That sound like a plan?'

Doyle put her arm through his and mischievously pecked him on the cheek. Bradshaw and Flynn looked at each other and smiled.

'I fancy getting drunk,' Doyle said. 'We can grab something to eat before we head home. What does everyone fancy?'

No one spoke.

'Does anywhere around here do goat?' Poe said eventually.

Bradshaw blinked.

'You're disgusting, Poe,' she said.

Chapter 141

A month later

Frederick Beck plucked a dandelion from the prison lawn. He held it up to the light and admired its perfect form. The symmetry, the deep yellow, the simplicity. A design that hadn't changed in millennia. He slipped it into his pocket before someone took it from him. It was worthless, of course, but his fellow inmates didn't need an excuse to mess with him. He would press it between the pages of his book. It was nice to have a hobby.

He looked through the razor-wire-topped prison fence. The mesh apertures were only half an inch wide so it was difficult to make much out, but he was close enough to see the nearby bus stop. It was one of those with an advert pasted on the side panel. For eight days the picture had been of *The Nightmares You Deserve: Hunting the Botanist* by Henning Stahl. It was being scraped off by the billposter. Beck smiled. He knew from endless walks around the exercise ground that the adverts on that bus stop always stayed up for a fortnight.

Stahl had blown it then. Beck had known he would. Had counted on it, in fact. Knew his hunger for redemption would cloud his vision. Make him careless. He had wanted Stahl to be his first victim. His investigation, his story, had ruined his life. Made him a pariah in the scientific world. But Poe had been right – there'd been no point killing him. Not then. His alcoholism had made him suicidal; his murder would have been a release not a punishment. Beck smiled at the half-removed bill poster. But now he'd built Stahl back up, given him a life to lose.

Right on time.

As a horn signalled the return to his cell, he smiled again. Stahl would have received the parcel a fortnight ago. Beck had used yet another false name and lodged it with a solicitor in Oldham. Told him he was leaving the country and he needed a parcel posting to his friend in a year's time. The solicitor took his money without comment. It wasn't even the weirdest request he'd had that day.

He made a note in his diary and promised his new client he would post the parcel to Mr Stahl on the specified date.

Around the same time Beck had been admiring the dandelion, three hundred miles away, out on bail at last, Henning Stahl opened the door to his new house.

Damn Poe, he thought. His solicitor had told him he was going to be charged and he was advising him to plead guilty. Maybe do a short prison sentence. Stahl went straight to his fridge and pulled out a bottle of beer. He kept one in there to prove he didn't need it any more.

But, by God, he was tempted now.

'No,' he said out loud. 'I've come this far.'

Instead, he went to his bathroom cabinet and opened a new box of Antabuse. It was different to his usual brand but he figured it was just his chemist sourcing the cheapest deal.

He popped a tablet and swallowed it.

'Everything's going to be fine,' he said.

Acknowledgements

Well, what do you know, you wait your whole career to write a locked room mystery, and two come along in the same book. I had a lot of fun writing *The Botanist* and as usual I had an awful lot of help.

First off, a huge thank you to Brian Price for reading through an early draft and checking the science, and for correcting me when I'd got it spectacularly wrong. Everything the Botanist did is scientifically possible and he was using equipment and techniques that are commonly available (some of it is on Amazon). But I still managed to get things wrong and Brian was a shining beacon of knowledge in my sea of confusion. He also pointed out my misspelling of 'armour' (I'd typed 'amour') by writing 'ooh-er' in track changes. Thank you for all your help, Brian.

My friend, and Little, Brown stablemate, Roger Lytollis, gets a vote of thanks for candidly explaining how to use a penile sleeve. I don't know why he wanted this put in the Acknowledgements, but I'm an ex-soldier and used to obeying orders . . .

Superfan Karen Royle-Cross gets the nod for letting me use a version of her name for the appalling racist, KRC – probably the most unpleasant person I've ever created. The only stipulation she had was that I put in the Acknowledgements that she is in no way like her fictional counterpart. And as she's a massive fan of Tilly, I think we can safely assume that's definitely the case.

Antony Johnston helped me explain, using accessible language, how a homemade radio jammer could be constructed. Thanks, Antony; much appreciated.

Krystyna, my editor, will always get a huge thank you (as does her assistant, Christopher Sturtivant). She saw in my writing something even I hadn't known was there, and I will be forever grateful to her for giving me the career I now have. Let's do this until we're even older and grumpier, Krystyna.

Speaking of old and grumpy, I must thank my agent, David Headley. Just kidding, he's younger than me, more optimistic than me and he certainly has more energy. Thanks for everything, David. When you die, I'm getting 'Leave it to me' engraved on your gravestone (except I think you'll probably live for ever). And thanks for showing all the patience in the world when it comes to explaining things to me. In future you should probably just tell Joanne. Save everyone a few weeks . . .

The covers for the Poe series are such a strong and recognisable brand, they're now being imitated by authors and publishing houses all over the world. All down to you, Sean Garrehy. Take a bow, mate. We'll grab those beers soon.

A special thanks to Beth Wright and Brionee Fenlon in publicity and marketing respectively (I know the difference now), and everyone in sales – thank you. It's a real privilege to work with such a professional, enthusiastic and friendly team. I am in no doubt that the success of the Poe and Tilly novels is down to you guys and not me.

And while we're on the actual books, I need to thank everyone who has a hand in turning the semi-literate guff I submit into something people will spend some of their wages on. Thank you, Martin Fletcher for having an eye on the big picture, mercilessly deleting adverbs and for saying things like, 'Very nice, now get rid of it'. (I'm thinking specifically of my beautiful description of a rosebush in *Black Summer*.) Then on to Howard Watson, who gets the book next. He's the one who remembers everything from the previous books and makes sure I don't keep using the same names. He also examines every sentence to ensure: a) they make sense (they rarely do), b) a country I mention actually exists (they usually don't), and c) the timeline works (Poe joining the police when he was eleven years old, anyone? Howard caught that whopper in *The Puppet Show* when all anyone else was interested in was who was looking after Edgar). Thanks, Martin; thanks, Howard.

431

My desk editors, Rebecca Sheppard and Amanda Keats are the unsung heroes in every one of my books. It's not so much like trying to herd cats with me, it's more like trying to herd sarcastic cats who not only don't like being herded, they can't actually believe someone has the audacity to herd them in the first place.

Thank you to Joan Deitch for hunting and exterminating all those stubborn little typos. I will always be in awe at your skill and patience.

Joanne, my beautiful wife, is my first reader and easily the most brutal. The books would be worse off without her input. She's the person who tells me someone's mannerisms are too similar to Poe's, or that 'Poe would never say that in front of Tilly'. I sometimes think she has a deeper understanding of my characters than I do.

Thanks to my early readers, Roger Lytollis (him of penile sleeve fame) and Angie Morrison. Always a nervy time when the book is outside my house for the first time, but you never let me down. You find the errors and you make suggestions. The books are always better because of what you both do.

And finally, the biggest thanks goes to all the readers, bloggers, reviewers, Facebook groups (I'm looking at you, UK Crime Book Club), newsletter subscribers, Twitter stalkers, booksellers (I'm looking at you this time, Fiona Sharp) and anyone else who has enjoyed, recommended or bought a Poe and Tilly book.

Anyway, that's me. Next up, *The Mercy Chair*.

Mike.

Read on for a sneak peek at the next Poe and Tilly thriller
from M. W. Craven

The Mercy Chair

It starts with the robber-birds.

Black as gunpowder, with grievous eyes. Wild and rattling cackles as they mob what has been unearthed. Puffing out ink-stained wings, squabbling for the choicest offerings. Tearing at flesh with cruel, pickaxe beaks, voracious appetites never sated.

Crows.

Nature's clean-up crew.

Dozens of them.

Enough for a murder . . .

Chapter 1

The hospital was old. A cathedral to the sick, built when eight-year-olds crawled up chimneys and a Queen's empire was the largest the world had ever known. They called it a lunatic asylum then; now they said psychiatric hospital.

Meet the new boss, same as the old boss.

The man staring out of a high-arched, curtainless window wasn't thinking about the UK's mental health crisis though – he was thinking about the hospital's colour scheme. He was wondering if the paint on the corridor he was standing in had been chosen for its therapeutic qualities. He suspected not. It was institutional green, the type of colour not found anywhere in nature, and still smelled fresh and acrid. He thought it made the hospital seem more like a prison than a place of healing. Perhaps that was the point.

The corridor was empty and echoed like a church. The chemical stench of disinfectant soaked the still air; the linoleum floor was buffed to a shine. A fob-controlled navy double-door blocked off one entrance, a steel security door the other. The corridor had three doors and the man was waiting to be called through the middle one. None of the doors had handles.

There were no seats in this corridor, no waiting area with televisions and pot plants and magazines about idyllic lives in the Cotswolds, so the man stood. On the other side of the security door someone screamed and someone else shouted. Before long, he could hear accents from all four corners of the country. He didn't turn away from the window. Screaming and shouting and crying and alarms were the hospital's soundtrack, an aria heard all day and all night.

And he knew no one would enter this corridor.

Not until it was time.

The man watched as a crow flew into view. It wheeled overhead, then landed on the hospital lawn. Two more joined it. He watched as their strong, scrawny feet scratched at the earth, searching for bugs and beetles and worms. The man shuddered in revulsion. He had come to hate crows recently.

He turned his back on them and glanced at his watch. It was almost time. He removed his phone from his pocket to see if there were any urgent messages. There weren't. Instead, he saw his face reflected in the black mirror. His eyes seemed gritty and puffed up, like he'd slept on a plane. The hands holding the phone were heavily calloused, covered in scratches and smelled of the sea. He wondered if they would ever be clean again.

The door to the middle room opened. A shaven-headed man stepped out. He was wearing a royal blue tunic top with black trousers. He had a personal alarm clipped to his belt loop. Pulling the cord or pressing the red button would rush people to his location, like a police officer sending out an urgent assistance request.

A smaller man in a suit joined the shaven-headed man. He had the harried look all doctors seemed to have. 'Dr Lang is ready to see you now,' he said.

For such a grand building, the room's decor was dreary and flavourless. The walls were cream, not green, but still screamed institution. The carpet tiles were brown and hardwearing; the empty bookcase was cheap with sagging shelves. Thank you cards and hospital notices were taped to a red felt noticeboard. Dr Lang waited for the man behind a large desk. A beige file and a box of tissues were the only things in front of her.

She stood to greet him. She was in her early thirties and was wearing a sleeveless, quilted green dress. She wore no make-up and her long dark hair partly covered her face. The man wondered if she were shy. He then wondered if her shyness had hindered her career. Perhaps not: shy people were often the most empathetic, the easiest to talk to. People opened up to them.

They shook hands and introduced themselves.

'Do sit down,' she said.

'Thank you, Dr Lang.'

'Please, I'd very much like it if you called me Clara.'

The man was from a generation that stood to shake hands. He wasn't about to call a doctor by their first name. It wouldn't be right. 'I'll do my best,' he said, before sinking into the seat on the opposite side of the desk. It was a heavy armchair and it looked out of place in a doctor's office. Dr Lang's chair was the same.

'I'm sorry you had to drag yourself all the way here,' she said. 'I'd have preferred somewhere more suitable, but I have patients to see here today and it wasn't possible to get away.'

'It was no hardship. It's a nice drive and my boss is happy I'm finally taking the time to do this.'

'Were you waiting long?'

'Twenty minutes, but I was early.'

'And I must apologise for this office,' she said, gesturing around the room. 'It's not mine; I'm just borrowing it today. I understand it's about to be decorated, which is why it's almost empty. I'll see my other patients on the ward but, as you're not a resident here, I thought we might benefit from somewhere less pressurised. It can get a bit lively on the other side of the door.'

'I can imagine,' the man said.

'We'll find somewhere more suitable for our next session. Today's really about getting to know each other.'

'OK.'

Dr Lang smiled. 'So, like I said, my name's Clara, and although I have a PhD I'm not a medical doctor; I'm a trauma therapist. I'm experienced in CBT, somatic experiencing, sensorimotor psycho-therapy, eye movement desensitisation and reprocessing therapy, sometimes called EMDR, and all the other major disciplines. And while I don't need you to understand what all that medical gobble-degook means, I *do* need you to understand one thing.'

'What's that?'

'I know what I'm doing.'

She opened the file on the desk. The man could see handwritten and typed notes, all held together with plastic-ended treasury tags.

He saw photographs of his injuries, particularly his eye socket. He winced at the memory.

'Shall we begin?' Dr Lang asked.

The man shrugged.

She offered a sympathetic smile. 'As you know, your employer made this referral after some concerning behaviour at work—'

'I made one mistake,' he cut in. '"Concerning behaviour" is a stretch.'

'Nevertheless, they saw fit to pay for three sessions in advance. What does that tell you?'

The man didn't answer. Dr Lang removed a slim document from the file.

'This is the self-assessment form you completed,' she said. 'I would like to thank you for being so candid. Not everyone is.' She tapped the document with her fingers. Her nails were short and unvarnished. 'This is a good place to start.'

'If I'm doing this, I'm doing it right,' the man said.

'So, why don't we dive in at the deep end? I understand you're still having headaches?'

The man touched the thick, lumpy scar tissue around his eye socket. 'I am, although I don't know if that's because of my injury or because I'm not sleeping.'

'Probably a bit of both,' Dr Lang said. 'But not sleeping will exacerbate the head trauma.' She checked the file. 'It says here you've refused zopiclone.'

'I have.'

'Why is that? It's a commonly prescribed medication for patients with sleeping difficulties.'

The man didn't respond.

'Are you self-medicating? Is that why you refused it?'

'Self-medicating?'

'Excessive alcohol, depressants like benzodiazepines or barbiturates. Maybe even heroin. Someone as resourceful as you would have no problem securing something to help him sleep.'

The man smiled. 'I'm not self-medicating, Dr Lang,' he said.

'Then why won't you take zopiclone?'

A knock on the door made the man turn. The shaven-headed man entered the room. He was holding a tray. 'Got tea for you,' he said.

He put two disposable cups and a paper medicine dispenser filled with sugar lumps on the desk. He left the room and shut the door behind him. The man picked his up and took a sip. He grimaced. The tea was lukewarm. Dr Lang studied him over the rim of hers. If she'd noticed anything about the tea's temperature, she kept it to herself.

'What happens when you try to go to sleep?' she asked.

'I lie awake until morning.'

'And yet you still refuse common medications.'

'I do.'

'You don't *want* to go to sleep, do you?' Dr Lang said.

After a few moments the man shook his head.

'Because when you sleep, you see things you don't like.'

He nodded.

'Nightmares?'

He nodded again.

'What is it you see?'

He didn't answer. He put his hands in his lap and looked at them.

'What is it you see when you close your eyes?' Dr Lang urged.

The man looked up. His eyes were haunted and wet.

'I see crows,' Detective Sergeant Poe whispered. 'When I go to sleep I see crows.'